P9-DML-311

# Memoirs of a
# Dwarf

# Memoirs of a
# Dwarf

## At the Sun King's Court

PAUL WEIDNER

THE UNIVERSITY OF WISCONSIN PRESS
TERRACE BOOKS

The University of Wisconsin Press
1930 Monroe Street
Madison, Wisconsin 53711

www.wisc.edu/wisconsinpress/

Copyright © 2004
The Board of Regents of the University of Wisconsin System
All rights reserved

1   3   5   4   2

Printed in the United States of America

Library of Congress Cataloging-in-Publication Data
Weidner, Paul.
Memoirs of a dwarf : at the Sun King's court / Paul Weidner.
p. cm.
ISBN 0-299-20510-X (alk. paper)
1. Louis XIV, King of France, 1638–1715—Fiction. 2. France—History—
Louis XIV, 1643–1715—Fiction. 3. Illegitimate children of royalty—Fiction.
4. Courts and courtiers—Fiction. 5. Kings and rulers—Fiction. 6. Dwarfs—
Fiction. I. Title.
PS3623.E426M46   2004
813'.6—dc22   2004007799

Terrace Books, a division of the University of Wisconsin Press, takes its
name from the Memorial Union Terrace, located at the University of Wisconsin–
Madison. Since its inception in 1907, the Wisconsin Union has provided a venue
for students, faculty, staff, and alumni to debate art, music, politics, and the
issues of the day. It is a place where theater, music, drama, dance, outdoor
activities, and major speakers are made available to the campus and the
community. To learn more about the Union, visit www.union.wisc.edu.

# Acknowledgments

I owe many thanks to my friend Bill Stewart for being a fresh and sympathetic critic after I'd lost sight of some glaring problems; and to Melissa Stewart (his daughter) and her partner and colleague, Inmaculada Pertusa-Seva, for checking out my shaky Spanish.

Most of all I am indebted to my agent, Jodie Rhodes, who, with great energy, launched a campaign to put this book over—the moment she set out, I knew I'd fallen into terrific hands. Her enthusiasm, drive, straightforwardness, persistence, diplomacy, strategy, solid connections, and smarts have downright awed me. Let her not be an unsung hero.

# Memoirs of a
# Dwarf

# 1

WHOSOEVER READS THIS TESTAMENT:

This will be a faithful and most accurate accounting of my life, written in order that the truth be known at last, for up to now the truth has been gagged, and my entire existence, from birth to the present, predicated on falsehood; and the truth shall now be revealed for justice's sake, I vow, and by this hand; unless I die in the telling of it, for I am no longer young.

As I set out to claim your attention, reader, I will be scrupulously honest in all ways to you; I therefore confess that it took me two days to compose the opening sentence which you have just read; and already I am tempted to quit this arduous labor; I am new to writing and have not a natural wit for it. Moreover, I see that it will be as well a frightening labor, as it will force me to revisit an hundred instances of cruelty, of mockery, of slanders and hypocrisy, of injustice, betrayal, humiliation, malice, and a most vile atrocity.

But yet I am still fixed on it, to publish the truth and claim what due I may. My time is here: you shall read and judge for yourself.

Yet I would not have this account seen by any man or woman before it is published; and so I am working late at night, hidden under the eaves, with stolen pen, ink, and paper; and it is my intention to store this text down inside a hollow space inside the wall of my rookery, down where no one will come upon it until I have written on these sheets the full and complete truth. And I pray that no demon creep into that space some foul, godless night and chew my pages asunder and spit them out this way and that, and render these efforts for naught.

My Christian name is Hugues. Although the name rhymes with "fugue," yet it shares nothing with that musical form or indeed any other musical form and has not even the sound of a consonant to begin itself with. As a child, I detested my name, the mere utterance of it being so brief, its monosyllabicity bereft of any rhythmic or melodic qualities, and so muffled and snuffling a sound as to resemble the grunting noise of an animal rooting its way through a compost heap. Even other children, who could have had no aesthetic taste, shrieked when they heard it, as though recognizing that some gargantuan joke had been played upon me by whatever vicious person had labeled the defenseless lump of infancy which the world beheld at my birth. And thus it was of a great comfort to learn later in life of the existence of Hugues de St. Victor, a theologian who died in 1141; of Hugues de Cluny, the abbot of that famous monastic community from 1049 to 1109 and who achieved sainthood; and especially of Hugues Capet, whose father's name was likewise Hugues, and who was from 989 to 996 Hugues I, King of France. He was the first French-speaking king of the realm, and I esteem his preference for the vernacular.

The year of my birth, 1661, was, as it so happened, the year after His Royal Highness, Our Sovereign Majesty, Louis, the Fourteenth of that Name, took to wife Marie-Thérèse of Austria, the Infanta of Spain. I was not in fact born before that, though for many years I was uncertain and thought that it might have been 1660 as well as 1661, there being no document attesting to the event nor even no baptismal record, and the details remained murky; and it was therefore quite naturally assumed either that I had been born out of wedlock and thus was not a legitimate person and never could be; or else that I was an orphan, a situation only a jot or two more tolerable than bastardy. In either instance, no case could be made that I owned a recognized station in life, not even such as the lowly earthworm or the silent mollusk enjoys; and I might expect that very lack of station to extend beyond the grave, since there would be no opportunity legitimately to accumulate those credits and balances on this side of mortality required of one seeking salvation on the other.

It is almost certain that I was born in St. Germain-en-Laye; but I have no proof for that claim either. Yet it is reasonable to suppose at least that my birth took place somewhere in or nearby Paris; and if my own wishes could influence the matter—a fond hope, after the fact—I would place my arrival distinctly outside that city, and as far outside it as possible; for never was so vile a place on this earth as that fetid pile of buildings and humanity huddled along the banks of the river Seine.

Proceeding beyond my early history, we come upon a more fundamental matter, that of my endowments; and I state herewith bluntly and with no apology and with no misgivings, reader, that I am a dwarf. I was a dwarf at birth, though that would not then have been perceived, nor in fact until about a year after the event; I grew up a dwarf, the limited amount that a dwarf may be said to grow; and I am to this day that same dwarf and will never not be a dwarf. Now well past my prime, I am still no taller than a short hedge, and am in fact the exact proportions of the andirons which are in the François I salon at the chateau of Fontainebleau.

You will doubtless appreciate the fact, reader, that such an endowment plays a dominant role in the history of any dwarf. Thus: I live, I have always lived, in the land of crotches. Except for the odd child that wanders into my sphere, the fully grown people, male and female, whom I face, are to me, without exception, more crotch than head and shoulders or any other part. Mine is the world of below the belt; and if I should be rounding the corner of a hallway and let us presume on this occasion that I am late and therefore hurrying forward; and if at the same time there comes another person, also late, also hurrying; and if we two, at the very corner itself or thereabouts, collide, my face will plunge headlong into that region where his upper trunk diverges into two legs. I run, that is, into his crotch—his crotch or her crotch; and I have developed over time a keen habit of punctuality in order that as I round hallway corners, I may proceed slowly enough as to allow berth for others.

Now, you may have anticipated what next I state, to wit, that direct facial contact with a crotch, however sudden it may be, is not inevitably and invariably to be despised: I find in all honesty that it depends on the crotch. On the other hand, it is quite another matter for the person with whose crotch that sudden contact has been made, who will, nine times out of ten, lurch forward from about the waist up, losing whatever balance, not to say dignity, he or she may have possessed, and sprawl forward helter-skelter across the floor. At which point, I am kicked for my blunder and on occasion spat upon and cursed, not to say on rare occasions thrown down the entire length of the hallway. This was exactly the event which took place, I recollect, one morning in late April, I do not remember the year, when, having overslept and being late to chores, I happened to run into His Eminence, Emile Cardinal LeMoine, a prince of the Church and therefore a man of proportions, who was accompanied by His Excellency the Archbishop of Lisieux, of whom you are to learn more later; for the present I state only that the archbishop had even more proportions than the cardinal, various arrangements having had to be made to supply places where he might sit without doing damage to the chairs. As we made abrupt and forcible contact with one another, His Eminence pitched forward onto the floor, bringing down with him, as it happened, His Excellency, the latter then being incapacitated because of his size. But my lord the cardinal seized the day, rose from the floor, lifted me high up into the air, and with a vehement prayer (or an oath, I do not know which), hurled me headlong halfway down the passage and directly into an elaborately carved *chaise percée,* which is also known as a commode, or among the lower classes as a chamber pot, and which tipped over and spilled its unfortunate contents out onto the carpeting.

A word about furnishings. On the occasions that I am privileged to sit on a chair, that is, to hoist myself up and to sit on it, I have the sensation of perching atop a small elephant. At floor level the thick tassels that adorn the ropes holding open the tall, brocaded draperies such as you find in the north wing at St. Germain Palace are large enough, each one of them, for me to hide behind, leaving exposed to view only the lower half of my body and my stumpy feet; and this is true, reader, even allowing for the disproportionately greater size of my head, which as perhaps you know, is a feature common among dwarves, the result of minor childhood hydrocephalus, colloquially known as water on the brain.

A final note on my endowments, too long a discussion of which would be presumptuous; and it is this: I have an unusually long nose. I would not say a large nose, that word implies a certain bulk; no: but a long nose; and whatever other inferences may be drawn from that fact you may draw. There are some, I know, who do speculate upon the implications of a long nose, and I leave them freely to their liberty. I neither deny nor confirm. In the end, the question as to how much is signified by the endowment of a long nose is ultimately for the natural sciences to answer; I would add only one observation: old wives' tales are not made up entirely out of whole cloth; in each instance, some prior basis, however lost in the mists of time, gave rise to the putative myth.

Having now informed you of these basic facts about myself, I begin my narrative; and for lack of a better approach, I open with the very earliest recollection that I have: it is of sitting naked on a cold stone kitchen floor in the middle of a puddle of piss. It was not my own piss, even if at that early age I might have been forgiven for relieving myself in the middle of the kitchen floor though doubtless would not have been; nor was the piss any man or woman's neither. It had issued from the loins of a female dog, which was at the time in estrus and which was beaten and kicked outside, yapping and shrieking, for having created the stinking pool. The pool itself however was left standing for some time, and I left sitting in the middle of it, wailing in misery as the foul urine grew colder and colder under my infant buttocks; until at length, a large-bosomed, sweating battle-ax of a woman seized me by one of my arms and flung me out into the courtyard along with the disgraceful dog. I should say, along with the dogs, there being a number of them living in and around the place, all of them equally disgraceful. The creatures were constantly hungry as well, to the point that if I had had the wit to know it, I ought to have feared for my childish life (or at least for an arm or leg), being at that age still a tender chunk of meat. But the dogs, for all their villainy, were my friends, or so I fancied, certainly the closest things to friends I had there; and I was still too new to this world to know that friends can and very happily do devour one another in the twinkling of a pair of fangs.

That instance of childhood misery occurred in the place where I spent my first seven years in this world, to wit, the monastery of St. Sauveur at Louveciennes, west of Paris, where I was in the company of seven or eight other abandoned children. We were allowed the run of the kitchen floor and of the cesspool of a yard just outside, but nowhere else within the monastery or its grounds; and I do not exaggerate our wretchedness when I say that our chief nourishment was in the form of scraps tossed to the floor from various stewpots and soup basins by that same foul-smelling woman who had tossed me out among the dogs. The only positive aspect of our lives was that the kitchen, being in constant, boisterous use by the woman, was, despite the stone floor, at least a warm place to be, though insufferably hot in summer; but no matter, for in summer, in good weather and sometimes in foul, we were all tossed outside to run around with the dogs and a snuffling assortment of chickens, pigs, geese, rabbits, goats, mules, and stray cats, all of which, cats included, were unutterably and ceaselessly incontinent. I remember the livestock far better than I do the children, but for two facts: as they (the children) proceeded to grow (children will, even on a diet of grease-soaked bread crusts and scraps of suet), and as I distinctly did not, so did their cruelty to me grow, both in degree and constancy; and they managed to cripple my mental outlook far more than did the squalor created by the droppings of swine. That; and the second fact, that those children, unlike me, becoming more proper by their physical development, were, unlike me, eventually given places to sit on and to sleep in and portions of nutritious soup to eat; but that was as far as it went; for it may be safely assumed that the children were born either out of wedlock or of unsanctioned marriages (as one with a Protestant or a Jew or some other unbeliever); and as soon as any of them reached a certain size, the creature disappeared—without notice—into the shadows of some nearby workhouse and was thereby launched upon a life of unending drudgery. Eventually I saw fewer and fewer of them, wherever it was they wound up, and bad cess I say to the lot of them, and most especially to Théophile, whose particular cruelty might have been explained though certainly not excused by the fact that he was cursed with the endowment of a long, thin, scaly tail, which he kept coiled, hidden, inside his breeches: but, reader, I saw the thing one night through a hole in the privy wall, and ever after I noticed with what great care the wretch was wont to sit down; and he would never wash himself at the riverbank with the others.

Whereas for me and my lack of physical enlargement, I was considered useless to any formal work situation outside; but within the monastery kitchen there appeared to be a perverse and inverse ratio in play, and I was given an increasing number of chores; whether it was cleaning up after the dogs, or emptying excess lard into the brook, or scouring pots and vats, buckets and tubs with sheep fat and sand, or dumping whatever slops had accumulated during the day out into the vegetable field, the fact of my size seeming to have no bearing upon the strength and exertions required for my tasks; and as well, I spent untold hours hauling out ashes from four gigantic stoves and one open chimney that were in the place. These were kept roaring throughout the day, one wood stove, the others coal, the chimney wood; and so frequently shaken down for refueling that the ashes were invariably scalding hot, alive with glowing coals and flaming embers which ofttimes singed my hands or burnt them outright, the entire enterprise of ash removal acquiring over the years from my very close perspective the earmarks of a prevision of the fires of hell.

The only exception to the unremitting grind was the following: a little before five o'clock every morning, a certain Brother Dagobert, after he had started up the fires in those four stoves and the chimney, would pick me up from wherever I happened to be sleeping on the floor and place me on a table; next he would pull down my drawers and play for a while with my —— (not to be confused with my nose), an activity which seemed to afford him a certain relief if I may judge from his toothless, foul-breathed grin and certain related ministrations which he undertook upon himself, and one which in time began even to have its compensations for me.

Now I have noted this activity as an exception to the grind which constituted my life, but I believe as well that more accurately stated, that activity—and more properly, its outcome—inspired me to a higher calling: for I suddenly realized one morning in late April of 1667 that if I could serve, beyond the mere drudgery of my kitchen chores, some more special function—if I could, in this instance, afford relief to someone, even were that person no more considerable than Brother Dagobert— then such employment might enhance my standing in the world, even were that world no more considerable than the monastery of St. Sauveur; and that furthermore, given the station in life to which apparently I had been assigned, I could do much worse indeed than to pursue such an effort by whatever means I might devise or discover, and from whatever lowliest rung of the ladder it were to begin.

And I vowed then and there to my boyish self that I would quit that lowliest rung and somehow find my way up to the next; and perhaps thence even to a third; and I would keep my wits about me in this enterprise.

Thus, Brother Dagobert's innocent morning dalliance served indeed to mark me, significantly, reader, for life.

Following his ministrations, the friar would habitually toss me into a wicker hamper, close it, and lug me off to morning devotions. In the chapel, Brother Dagobert would set my basket down on the floor back under the holy water font, whereat he would join some fifty or so other unwashed, yawning, odorous, ass-scratching monks, and mumble his way through the prayers of the Mass.

This act of charity toward me—I mean lugging me off to daily Mass—might simply have been his guileless way of requiting me for my daily service to his needs; but I think in fact it was more likely to have been undertaken on the theory that as increasingly repugnant as I was becoming every day, there still existed a chance, however slim, that at some point in my assemblage I had been endowed with a soul; or at least half a soul: that is to say, that human soul there might possibly have been somewhere about me, as preposterous as that was in the face of my inelegance; and that giving it the benefit of the doubt and in the dubious interests of its eternal salvation, that soul might be allowed to hear a few prayers, unintelligible as they were, being all in Latin. And I was grateful for this early consideration of my spiritual status, as doubtful as was any benefit to me from it in the afterlife.

The hamper in which I lay was a pigeon hamper and fitted with a hinged lid, which Brother Dagobert always secured; and with small airholes along the sides. Lying in it in the darkness, able only to overhear the proceedings but not to see any of them—for the airholes were small enough that pigeons could not escape—my ears grew unavoidably disposed to the strains of the Latin *recitativo;* and very quietly I began muttering along in imitation of what I heard—with the exception of the belching, hawking, farting, and other digestive gurglings from the assembled community, to say nothing of the munching noises of bedbugs; and presently, emboldened by the splendor ringing in my head, I, too, joined my childish, piping voice to proclaiming the praises of the unseen Almighty in the rolling sounds of that sacred and majestic tongue of ancient Rome: *dignum et yustum est—sanctus sanctus sanctus—pair omnia saycula sayculorum!*

# 2

*Pair omnia saycula sayculorum.*

Those words, with which I closed my first chapter, though I do not know what they mean nor even how they ought to be written—and I have done so as best I can purely by the sounds—those words I soon came to know more and more intimately, those and indeed all the other sonorous words of the Mass; they seeped into my blood, they became part of my very bones; and over the years they have offered me solace and companionship as nothing else ever has. I can feel them in my mouth and can even smell them, for they are among the very few things I can claim as my own—along with a host of frightful, frightening memories, which are the subject of this account. And from my early youth until even now in my waning years, I have, in times of discomfort and stress, re-peated words and phrases and entire texts from the Latin Mass, whether aloud or silently; for their dear familiarity, along with their solemnity and their mystery, has always consoled me, and my very knowledge of them has conferred upon me a sense of worth, however modest.

And the fact that I came to possess them benefited me in another and even more practical way, which I shall now relate to you:

Early on the third Sunday morning of Lent in the year 1667, Brother Dagobert appeared to be in a more disgruntled humor than usual. I had noticed that disgruntlement even as he was acquitting himself of his business with my ———: there was a certain distraction in his dealing with the matter that frosty morn, a sense that he was giving decidedly short shrift to the so excellent matter that it was. Later I learned that his

11

humor was due to the arrival the previous evening at the monastery of a distinguished cleric whose visit had increased, for the sake of appearances, one of Brother Dagobert's chores, to wit, the draining of the privies; and the extra task had deprived him of sleep. Thus Brother Dagobert, that early morning, while mixing the ingredients for an illicit omelet (illicit in view of the Church's injunction to fast before the hearing of Mass, omelets in themselves being licit), by accident let fall a quantity of eggs onto the kitchen floor, which were instantly devoured by a rib-lined mongrel (it had no business to be inside at that hour, but let it pass) but which left a certain slickness across the surface of the floor, upon which, moments later, the sinful friar slid and fell, striking his head against an andiron and knocking loose—and in one instance, out—his several intermittent teeth.

Now I, being that morning of a cheerful humor, fell to laughing at the misfortune, which so enflamed Brother Dagobert's already irascible humor that after collecting the tooth, he then collected me, and roughly too, and flung me into the hamper, and kicked shut the lid. But in his great distraction and pain and rage and I know not what, he failed to secure the lid so that in fewer than five minutes, after he had abandoned the omelet and had hauled me off to my daily audience with the Divine, I was able, for the very first time, silently to push open the lid and peer out to see if I could not at last catch a glimpse of the Almighty whose praises I was singing; who was, I saw, nowhere in the vicinity of the hamper, for all that I beheld, through the billows of smoke, was a row of monkish backsides.

Reader, I was in my sixth winter—or seventh, I was not then certain; and the godly sounds which I had heard over those years now stirred my spirit; and somewhat impulsively I resolved to set out farther into the unknown territory of God's house, where I hoped at last to come upon the deity, face-to-face and eye-to-eye, and to satisfy my childish curiosity about Him; and moreover, to pursue that vow of mine to make my way in this world, whatever might come of the next.

Whereupon I took what now I realize was a first momentous step; and I emerged from the confines of the hamper and out into the chapel itself.

But Brother Dagobert, then catching sight of me, gave instant chase; and I led him up and down the aisles, in and out of side chapels, several times around the large paschal candle, and in one round directly through the rows of monks, the *dominay non sum* being recited at the time; for I was a speedy one in those days, despite my stumpish legs, and Brother Dagobert was still suffering the ill effects of his fall onto the kitchen floor. Let me not burden you with the details of that furious chase; but to conclude it: as at last I spun around a corner, I came, not face-to-face nor eye-to-eye but rather, nose—and a long one it was, shall I remind you?—nose, I say, to crotch, not indeed of the Almighty, who may or may not be endowed with a crotch, I cannot tell, but of the distinguished visiting cleric himself, the Abbé Hilaire Guibourg, S. J. That cleric, being totally blind in one eye, was not only taken aback by our encounter but indeed quite hurtled aback, and he fell, discharging first, onto the floor, an array of what looked like remarkably thin biscuits; and secondly, into the air, an assortment of foul and sewerish oaths such as my then tender ears had only dreamt of late at night under the kitchen stove.

Now you must know, reader, that I did not know at that critical moment what now I know so well: that the being which I had thrown to the floor was not in fact the Almighty of whom I had heard so unintelligibly much; to the contrary, I thought, truly this *is* the Almighty, given the infinite supply of oaths at His command. My soul (presuming its existence) trembled; yet I would not be daunted—no! not when presented with such a heaven-sent opportunity to forge some link with Him who would one day render me final judgment; and though it had turned out that despite the use of Latin at Mass, God was clearly capable of the vulgar tongue, yet it seemed that it would be more respectful for me to address Him in His own, proper language, especially in light of the delicacy of our short acquaintance; and I cried out at the top of my underdeveloped lungs the longest parts in Latin that I could think of: the part that starts out *confiteor dayi omni,* the one that starts *craydo in unum,* and a third which begins *in princhipio erat.*

At hearing my recitation, the object of my address, though still smarting from his fall, confessed some amazement; and he demanded to be told my name (Hugues), my origin (unknown), my age (seven; I chose the elder), my spiritual status (undetermined), and my current situation (humiliating and unmitigated servitude). Satisfied with my replies, Father Guibourg (for he in fact it was, I later learned, and no one with even a remote connection to God Almighty) did then and with dispatch finish up the Mass, myself not daring to move from the spot at the head of the aisle where I had landed; and he was right well pleased, I noted, that I was able to make all the remaining responses, right up through the *dayo gratsiases*, the *cum spiritus*, that one *gloria tibi* near the end, and the various *amenings*.

Father Guibourg disappeared abruptly at the end of the service (and by then I was not sorry to see him go for his breath being so vile that from up close it dispelled the sweetness of the incense, and I began to wonder if indeed the deity would ever stink so), and I was instantly snatched up by Brother Dagobert and given a sound thrashing for the trouble I had put him to, for the fact that a dwarf should know its place, and for good measure to boot.

Never could I have anticipated that my efforts to appease the wrath of God with a deluge of Latin might lead to any practical, earthly benefit; but perpend: you shall hear:

On the very next night I was snatched, this time by one of the laborers about the place, from out of my sleep; and I was bundled back into the pigeon hamper (the lid well secured this time) and taken by coach some two hours away. At which point, someone carried the hamper, with me inside, down several flights of stairs and then released me; a woman, wearing a bonnet, I recall, and black clothing, a well-built woman, rugged, vigorous, and of a no-nonsense disposition—a spleenish lad at her side addressed her as Madame La Voisin—stripped me quite bare and proceeded to examine me and all of my parts with such thoroughness that I suffered an anguish of embarrassment at that close scrutiny by a member of her sex. Despite her ill humor, I detected a particular satisfaction on La Voisin's part at the stubbiness of my fingers and toes and at the disproportionate size of my head, those clear indications—the sheer lack of height aside—of dwarvery.

Making the sign of the cross upon herself, she then clad me in a black robe that fell to the floor and indeed well past it, and a white tunic above. At which, as I held the robe gathered up about my bare ankles, Mme La Voisin hurried me through a series of halls, down yet another flight of stairs, and into a large, subterranean chapel.

She set me down on a low wooden stool and twisting my left ear, enjoined me not to budge, not indeed to budge an inch, if I valued my life one jot; whereat she disappeared. I set about to look around the place—though in doing so, not, I hasten to add, budging: for I did value my life by at least one jot. Clouds of smoke filling the room impaired visibility; nor was the place well lit to begin with, there being only four or five black waxen candles on the altar, giving off little light for all the smoke they produced; a second source of smoke, at the foot of the altar, was a large, covered metal pot, which I know now was a censer. The altar was covered with a black cloth, and the crucifix above, hanging upside down, was also draped in black. Some distance away on the floor sat a pigeon hamper; I felt an instant pang of recognition at the sight, for it had all the appearance of my own dear hamper. As well, I felt an instant curiosity as to what creature was there inside: of what sort, what size, the length of his nose and of his other parts, his spiritual endowments (had he a soul?), and the like. On second hand, thought I, might it not be a creature of quite a different stamp, one whose body was covered over with scales or whose head was small and black and with a tongue as long as its coiling tail, a creature whose teeth were razor sharp and whose claws were smeared with blood; or perhaps with a funnel inserted into its rectum, as I had once seen in a children's picture book.

Such were my boyish musings as I sat alone in the smoky shadows. But they were to be short lived, for up ahead, through the darkness, emerged three figures, the first that of the spleenish lad I had seen earlier; the second of Mme La Voisin herself—and for an instant, my previous thoughts quite running away with my imagination, I fancied I saw a tail coiling out from beneath the hem of her dark skirt, but no; and the third, to my surprise, that of none other than the being with whom I had made such memorable contact only the previous day, to wit, the Abbé Hilaire Guibourg.

The abbé and La Voisin murmured together briefly, studying me the whiles; then of a sudden he lunged toward me—I had not budged, reader! not an inch! But: "Rise!" quoth he; and with one eye on Mme La Voisin, whose order I was about to violate, and the other on the Abbé Guibourg himself, matching him, so to speak, an eye for an eye, I did as bidden. Standing quite close to me on the cold stone floor, he bent forward and began to examine me himself, prying open my mouth to peer at my teeth and tongue as one does to a horse, feeling about me, including my ——, and even lifting the rear of my vestment to study my bum. I held my breath during this ordeal, not so much from embarrassment, but because the abbé's breath was so venomous, so rank and so rancid, so reminiscent of bogs and sumps and sewers I had had traffic with, that I declined to inhale the air around him any further than necessary to maintain life. His hair was stringy and white and in all likelihood had been even whiter when last soap had been applied to it; his teeth, on the other hand, were quite black. His spine was in the shape of a convex curve, and he walked with a limp. He had lost one of his fingers, the index, from off his left hand, and his nose, bulbous and red, protruded from a face whose pockmarked skin was entirely pale. Beyond the matter of his breath was the matter of his eye: or I should say, not of his eye, which was a perfectly ordinary organ, but, on the opposite side, of his absence of eye, there being simply a whitish orb in place of it as though he had inserted a hard-boiled egg into the empty socket, the size of a duck's egg, I would say (a goose's egg would have quite distorted his appearance).

"Attend," he growled, "as you are by every appearance a dwarf, it is appropriate to our ends and to our purposes that you learn to assist at the Mass—or, that is, at the Mass as I shall recite it here; and as you have already the Latin, you are advanced toward the purpose, at least to a degree. But watch this creature's actions"—and he gestured to the spleenish lad—"and take heed, dwarf: so that as you respond verbally, you will also acquire other skills through his example—*viz,* when to hold the cup, when and where to move the book, when to ring the bells, how to swing the censer. Take warning," he continued, "for the sequence of prayer is not the same as that which you know: you must keep up as best you can, and with this knowledge: that if you apply yourself and learn, you may find some niggling warrant for your otherwise worthless existence; but if you fail, I shall have you whipped until you cry out for mercy and then I shall have you whipped some more."

With such encouragement, reader, you can imagine how wholeheartedly I resolved myself to the task, though I spoke to him not a word.

"*Aspairges may!*" Suddenly his voice cried out in the hazy darkness, and at that same instant I felt a cold shower of water dash across my face, for he was sprinkling down everything in sight, using an instrument that looked like a child's rattle which he dipped repeatedly into a bucket. "*Misereray mayi,*" he called out, and "*gloria patri,*" and so on.

"*Sicut erat in princhipio,*" I bellowed on cue, "*et nunc et semper et in saycula sayculorum amen!*"

I vowed the abbé would find in me a prompt and willing acolyte; for indeed I sensed a god-sent opportunity here to extend my services to

Mother Church and perhaps—and I say it in all true modesty, reader, pray do not misread me—to advance, as I had vowed, my station in life.

The abbé's present acolyte, the spleenish lad, who was only mumbling the responses and who reminded me of nothing so much as a frog, made lewd gestures at me on several occasions with the middle finger of his left hand, to which I replied by sticking out my tongue. But yet I did not wish to antagonize him for I was entirely dependent upon him in the conning of my future role, and I feared that out of sheer malice, he might find devious ways to mislead me.

At the conclusion of that first part, which ends *"omnes habitantes in hoc habitaculo pair christum dominum nostrum amen,"* the server speaking the final sound, the abbé flung himself into a chair off to one side, nearby to the pigeon hamper. Then immediately, through the clouds of smoke, reappeared Mme La Voisin (I had not seen her depart), this time accompanied by a second woman, clad, like madame, entirely in black but with her head, neck, and shoulders enshrouded in heavy veils; so that I could not make out her face. Next, together, the two women stepped up to the altar; whereupon with the assistance of La Voisin, the second woman, by giving herself a small hoist upwards, together with a sort of leaping motion backwards, placed herself directly upon the altar, at first seated; and thence to a prone position lengthwise across it, upon her back, so that she took up virtually the entire surface itself.

Now reader: if that strikes you as untoward, it is as nothing compared to what is yet to come: which I shall attempt to describe with all suitable modesty. La Voisin then taking hold of the hem of the prone woman's skirts and petticoats, she proceeded to fold them back some three or four times, until they came to lie athwart the woman's bosom and shoulders, exposing—and I blush to write it—to full view, the woman's parts entirely from the waist downward, for she wore no under-linens.

This is a true account of what was witnessed by the eyes of a six-year-old child. A six-year-old who had, indeed, I do not deny it, by that time already indulged a childish curiosity as to the nature of female nether parts by peering underneath the garments of certain members of that sex: for example, I remember a certain Madame Douge, Marquise d'Œu, who, bending forward one sultry July afternoon in order to retrieve a small thimble she had let fall into a fresh collection of pig droppings, was fishing about for it with a short stick or twig; whereupon the occasion presented itself for me, nearby to the droppings, to peer upward within her outer garments and observe her underpinnings, the which but whetted my appetite for more.

Yet that night at the foot of the altar, not even I was prepared for the sight which my eyes now beheld. Her legs—the veiled woman's—were long and finely shaped, the feet of modest proportions. Her hips were suitably wide for the female, and the belly sweetly rounded. But burning hot into my eager six-year-old mind and searing it forever, was the sight—indeed my very first—of the unveiled bearded triangle, that fluffy mound, that grassy nook, her —— or her pudendum, with the promise of all the mysteries which some primal, puerile itch assured me lay therein.

Now the abbé rose and approached the altar; and balanced a large goblet—a chalice, I have since learned—exactly atop the prone woman's belly. Next—and I pray you, reader, be of steady heart—he crossed to the pigeon hamper; bending over it, he threw it open and seized from within an infant; not a scaly animal with needle teeth but an infant, though a foul and most ill-shaped creature it was, with a terrible fold of skin over its eyes; which instantly set up an abominable howl, so that I covered up my ears. As it was to turn out, the creature had every reason to howl, whether it knew it or not: for its hour was at hand, its short-lived hour, sad to tell, indeed quite shocking to tell, and I confess that I am grieved to tell it. Holding the shrieking deformity in one hand, Father Guibourg withdrew from within his robes a bone-handled razor by means of which, with a practiced expertise, he slit the bawling infant's throat; and instantly he held the severed neck above a porcelain basin so that the blood streamed down into it, declaiming as he did so these words: "Astorath, Asmodus, princes of accord and of power! I hereby conjure you to accept the sacrifice which I present to you of this infant for the things I shall request of you this night." Whereupon the toadish acolyte, kneeling up ahead of me, set up his own *concerto* of wretched howling; and just as I had begun to wonder if his cries were set down in his part (soon to be mine), I saw Mme La Voisin leap from her stool and pummel the boy so viciously about the head and shoulders that I thought she must surely injure him and permanently too. But my attention shifted once again, for by this time, the infant being held aloft by Father Guibourg had drained off quite nicely into the basin, and

I watched the abbé give it a final shake or two and swiftly return it to the hamper.

"*In princhipio erat,*" I suddenly heard him cry out, and to my great astonishment: for those are the words which announce the concluding prayers of the Mass, as probably you know, they do not start the Mass, it is the *introibo ad* which starts it; and I wondered if the events I had just witnessed had not so consumed my attention that the Mass had already been spoken and I, distracted, had failed to observe one bit of the performance by the actor of my future role and was therefore liable to being whipped until I cried out for mercy and then whipped some more.

Then, reader, I heard from up ahead, "*Itay missa est.*" Quite puzzled now, I called out most vigorously in response, "*Dayo gratsias!*"; and we continued with *amen*s and *spiritu tuo* and *gloria tibi.* But just as I was beginning to despair of making any sense of the course of events, I heard, "*quod ore sumpsimus*" and the words that follow, "*. . . pura mentay . . .*" and "*. . . corpus tuum . . .*" and "*. . . qui vivis et*"; and it was only then that I made the discovery that that most excellent divine, the Abbé Guibourg, was saying the Mass—this Mass—in reverse order; or backwards; or, in all justice let me observe, he was saying it in reverse of the order which I had known hitherto, whatever order had in fact been prescribed by His Holiness the Pontiff, Bishop of Rome; and it was not to me, an illegitimate chit, to pass judgment on the matter.

And so indeed forward he charged—or rather, backward—and I rising to the challenge of keeping abreast of this new order and exercising my excellent Latin, for the toadlike knave knew almost none of it and only mumped about with it.

When at last the abbé arrived at the *simili modo,* I watched him pour the foul contents of the porcelain basin into the chalice, which stood, I remind you, upon the belly of the prone female. Whereupon and immediately after *remissionem peccatorum*—and you may imagine my amazement, reader, for recall, this was the first Mass that I had actually witnessed—I saw him raise the chalice to his lips and to the accompaniment of clanging bells, quaff down those very contents to the final dregs.

Amazement, I say. In fact, so much so that at that very moment I suffered a minor accident inside my robe.

Yet more amazement there was to come, for next I heard an interpolation into the text by the cleric, the meaning of which eluded me; and

I will only report it to you as I heard it first and without comment. He sang forth the following words:

"Alpha, Agla, Ley, Deities of Darkness! I conjure you, in the name of Solomon's collarbone and of the book which God presented to Moses, you, Alpha, and you, Agla, and you, Ley, hear me! I command you and I charge you, that you see done the following things." Suddenly I saw the flames on the black candles begin to waver and flicker as a quick draft blew through the chapel; and now Father Guibourg's voice rose even louder as he thundered forth his demands: "That Françoise may receive the present affections of himself and that they prevail in the future; that herself become sterile; that himself quit her bed in favor of Françoise, who may obtain from himself whatever she asks; that himself quit as well and no longer receive Louise; and herself, Marie, being repudiated, that she, Françoise, may then marry with himself. Hear me, ye powers, and heed my charge! Amen."

By the time he reached the end of this unfathomable petition, Father Guibourg's face was wreathed in sweat and his one good eye was fairly bulging out of its socket; he had taken to hopping about, and now I could hear his breathing, which came in frightful spurts and gasps. A sharp, chill wind whistled through the sanctuary, stirring the clouds of incense, whipping the black altar cloth, and even snuffing out several candles, which made the place that much darker.

Following that petition came the *qui pridiay quam,* which, in his excited state, the abbé shouted out shrilly, and with more clanging of bells; and then I watched with still more amaze as he plunged a knife through the center of a biscuit as small and as thin as a tiny crêpe and identical to those he had strewn across the floor the day previous; whereupon he devoured the sundered pancake. The ritual surged on, but now in great haste, and the priest began swaying back and forth and even leaping into the air as he intoned the sacred words at the top of his lungs and I in quick succession.

It was at this point that another opportunity arose for me as rare as it was golden.

Father Guibourg seized the smoking censer by a chain and proceeded to brandish it up and down, this way and that, causing the embers within to glow and the incense to spew out fresh clouds of sulfurous smoke. It next befell the toadish acolyte to do likewise, this time in the direction of the abbé himself; but the toad was so uncommonly maladroit, and moreover, by this time so fearful, his body shaking with such deep sobs, that in his hands the entire device suddenly loosened, flew apart, and sailed out in several directions at once, and red hot embers streaked across the floor and not a few upon the very altar itself. Whereupon the abbé howled an oath which I dare not repeat (Body of Christ, protect me) and landed the creature a furious blow to the back of the head, and rightly so, causing him to burst afresh into tears; at the identical moment, he also burst into flames and fled away, glowing and croaking, into the darkness.

"Hell and damnation!" exclaimed the Abbé Guibourg, and he dashed about trying to restore order and to stifle the burning embers. Now I, from my efforts in the kitchen in St. Sauveur, being well versed in the business of burning embers, did seize upon the occasion and raced up to the altar and with my fire-hardened fists began pounding out two or three small flames that had ignited the altar cloth and one that had even caught onto the veils of the prone female (though I averted my eyes as much as possible from the sight of her ——— in spite of the intense interest which I had in it); after which I scooped up what live coals remained scattered here and there and flung them into the censer, in truth burning my hands somewhat but refusing to acknowledge the fact; and in no time at all I reassembled that pot and set about to heaving it this way and that myself, as I had witnessed the Abbé Guibourg a few moments previous: and despite the shortness of my stature, I acquitted myself right well at the task, causing those present to choke and gag from the roiling billows of incense which I produced. Thus, somewhat through my offices, and I state it in all modesty, the holy service was able to reel forward to its conclusion; or rather to its beginning, for at long last I heard the intoning of the *introibo ad.*

Immediately the business was over, a firm hand, that of La Voisin, seized my ear and wrenched me down from the altar steps, through the smoke and out of the temple; but a quick glance back to the scene, which madame failed to prevent, revealed the Abbé Guibourg, his vestments hitched up high about his waist, climbing up onto the altar himself.

In the outer chamber, La Voisin restored my clothes to me; and she informed me, albeit cheerlessly, that I had done well enough in putting out the fires—which made me almost burst with pride, reader! for despite the severity of her attitude, it was, to the best of my excellent recollection, the first time that anyone had ever said anything pleasant to me.

"But take heed, Signior Hugues," she continued, "say nothing of what you have seen and performed here this night, d'you understand? For if you blab, dwarf, your own throat will be next."

She then tossed me back into the hamper, where I lay waiting upwards to an hour before someone took it in hand and bore me back to the monastery kitchen in Louveciennes, utterly exhausted, but with a rare and glowing sense of accomplishment at my service to that excellent cleric; with a joyful realization that instead of merely eavesdropping on the holy service, I had performed as an active participant; with the sunny recollection that the Abbé Guibourg had pointed out my particular value to his mission by virtue of my dwarfishness; with the happy expectation that my vow had not been in vain and that a new chapter might have just opened in the fortunes of my life; with a firm resolve never, ever, under any circumstances whatsoever, to blab, for I cared much for my throat, stumpy as it was, and the resolve was easy; and lastly, with the exultant sounds of *dominay non sum dignus,* whatever that means, still ringing in my happy ears, I fell asleep.

# 3

APPARENTLY I HAD MET WITH THE ABBÉ'S APPROVAL, for in the years that followed, I assisted him at Mass with regularity—sometimes weekly, sometimes fortnightly, though when things got slower in the summer months, monthly; and I was always transported at night by hamper and coach, unvaryingly to the exact same subterranean site (though I was unable to see where it was; I mean in what town). On the other hand, the offerings made there did vary somewhat: in addition to the wiggling, bawling, and quite lively infants presented to Astaroth and Asmodus, all of whom were boys (for the abbé had achieved an unrivaled primacy in the practice of the darker arts and would accept nothing but males), and all of whom were cursed with wretched physical deformities quite apparent even in their infancy (I mean misshapen heads, the lack of limbs or the presence of extra limbs, and the like), there was on occasion an infant at hand which appeared to be already dead and remarkably puny in size, not to say only partially formed; and it was not that that child was a dwarf, not a bit of it; it was, I was told, that he had sprung forth from his mother's loins several months before he ought to have, in which case it served the creature right to find himself in his present situation; or conversely, that he had in fact been sprung forth by others, in which case the fault could not be held to be his; for it seems that there were people about, reader, men and women, who were well practiced in the art of springing infants forth which had not yet finished their terms in the oven, as it were, but which were considered expendable for whatever reasons, including illegitimacy and other defects; and many of these arrived at Father Guibourg's altar. I was given to believe and have no reason not to, that after their deaths, many of their childish remains were buried in Mme La Voisin's vegetable garden just northwest of Paris in a town called Vouche or Souche, I forget which; and it is true that that lady conducted a thriving green grocery on the side.

In addition to the unvarying participation by the children at these Masses was the participation by the females, one of whom always lay exposed upon the altar as I have described; and it was during these endeavors that I came not only to perceive but greatly to appreciate yet another source of life's infinite variety, to wit, that which is found in the shape, coloration, length, texture, abundance, and generally pleasing (or displeasing) appearance in the crops sprouting upon the Venus mounts; now I say this in all modesty, reader, I assure you, and I will thank you to keep a modest thought in your own head.

(Those to whom the forces of Alpha, Agla, and Ley were directed were rarely identified but by their first or Christian names; and though that were appropriate to the Christian nature of the Mass, yet I wondered from a more practical standpoint how it was that Alpha, Agla, and Ley made the distinction between this Françoise and that Françoise, between one Claude and another; and I fancied that it could befall that some ignorant, slovenly whore might suddenly one day find herself advanced to the post of first lady-in-waiting to the queen or favored with some other boon of which she had never dreamt and for which she might even have had no desire; or that a babe of three months named René might be stricken by the smallpox for supposedly having had an affair with a duchess.)

Yet another feature came to be comforting for its regularity, and that was the presence of Mme Cathérine La Voisin, née Deshayes, for such was that lady's entire name. On the third or fourth occasion of my service, I made bold to ask Mme La Voisin about a certain matter, the one which had puzzled me most of all from the start, to wit, Father Guibourg's reference to my particular usefulness to him as a dwarf: for as delighted as I was that this was so, yet I could myself conceive no special merit in a liturgical assistant's having the proportions of an andiron.

"Fie," said that lady, "and you are right audacious, sir. Pray let your head not become more swelled than it already is. Suffice it for you to know thus much: it is held—and some have claimed proof of it, yet I cannot tell—but it is held that within a dwarf's low and ill-shaped proportions—such proportions, sir, as indeed render him somewhat less than human—there resides a greater quantity of the devil's essence than in proper, upstanding, and more nobler human beings. You creatures are likewise thought to have no souls; or souls that are so malformed and blackened that your links to the forces of darkness, though unwitting, are nevertheless potent. It is for these reasons that your participation in my lord Guibourg's devotions is useful, for my lord has undertaken to grapple with those forces of darkness by night even as he sings the praises of our Lord Jesus by day. But enough: ask no further about these matters, dwarf: it is not for you to question them, being of an inferior nature and incapable of these mysteries. Do as you are told and consider yourself fortunate to have been chosen."

With which, she slammed shut the lid to the hamper; and I was swept away.

I thought long and hard upon her several points, for they bore me so much relevance. I could concede that my figure was indeed low and ill-shaped (though "ill-shaped" is a harsh term); on the other hand, the presence or absence of my soul and the nature of it being still unknown to me at the time, I could take no stand upon that matter; and whether I harbored any quantity of the devil's essence (Body of Christ, protect me as I speak of it!) was likewise a matter of speculation; nor could I declare whether any links which I might have to the forces of darkness were "potent"; though I was prepared to acknowledge the well-known fact that such creatures as humpbacks and cretins, hermaphrodites, certain cripples, pygmies, lepers, and like deformities are indeed possessed of potent supernatural qualities and not of the best sort, and that thus they are both properly and profitably used in the exercise of the darker arts (Body of Christ); and I include among such deformities the anthropophagi, reader, who are beings bearing only certain of the features of man, having heads, arms and legs, hands and feet, but yet no bodies, and they are indeed most inhuman beings. Which consideration brings me to my final and most crucial remark: however I took her other points, most decidedly I could not approve—nor even entertain the notion—of Mme La Voisin's statement that I, as a dwarf, was in any way "less than human": that one declaration of hers rankled, reader, and deep within my bones; for I had always conceived of myself as being a full-fledged member of the human race, however shorter I was than my colleagues, however larger my head, indeed however longer my nose: I considered myself a human being. Yet even so, I had to concede that the anthropophagi always frightened me most of all, for they presented this doubt: if they may *appear in part* to be human and yet clearly are not, might it be possible that other creatures—like myself—similarly marked by variations on the human frame, such as disproportionately large heads, could be likewise inhuman? And thus the anthropophagi posed a niggling but grave threat to my strong conviction of my humanity. Nevertheless, I clung to that conviction, and spoke thus to myself: "Whatever my wretched station in life, I, Hugues, am, have always been, and always shall be human."

Mme La Voisin's assessment of my situation aside, there remained the comforting knowledge that I was, however unwittingly, of particular use to the Abbé Guibourg; and the sense of that new chapter opening in my life which I had experienced after my first service to His Worship remained strong. Indeed so much so that I found myself increasingly curious as to just what service it was that he—and I—were engaged in, that is to say, just what was the business of the holy sacrifice of the Mass. For, I reasoned: enriched by enlightenment on the matter, might I not have some conceivable hope of advancing one day beyond the position of a mere acolyte?—might I eventually be called upon to recite the Mass myself and to undertake those ministrations for which the abbé was so well renowned, and thus enhance my service to Mother Church? These were perhaps the idle daydreams of an impressionable youth, reader, I concede it, yet they derived from that resolve I have told you of to try to make better my condition and my fortunes, if only in some entirely unassuming fashion.

Yet the proceedings in question—I mean the Mass—were all conducted in that undecipherable, if sonorous, tongue, ancient Latin; and I saw no prospect, alas, of their ever deciphering themselves to me as for instance in some beatific vision: no, I had no such spiritual pretensions. Thus I decided that for enlightenment in the matter, I would have to seek help, and on the very next occasion that Mme La Voisin set about the changing of my clothes, I screwed up my courage and made bold a second time to address the lady. Nothing ventured, nothing gained.

"Madame," quoth I, "I should be right well obliged if you would inform me just what is afoot here. I mean, madame," I hastened to add, "to enquire of the ceremony in which I am a humble participant: can you tell me what is going on?"

She looked at me with her narrow, piercing eyes and demanded:

"What business is it of yours, sir? Do you presume to question the functions of Monsignor Hilaire Guibourg, S. J.? Or any of the business transacted here? Do you dare voice any misgivings at what matters are undertaken of which you are so thoroughly ignorant?"

She had quite misunderstood me, I felt.

"Madame, I do not: it is that very ignorance which—"

"Then sir, I suggest that you mind your own wretched business if you plan on staying in this world another while. Idle curiosity, monsieur dwarf, is the work of the devil, and let me assure you—and in no uncertain terms—that Father Hilaire Guibourg, S. J., gives no quarter to that fiendish creature, sir, but he has ways, and not a few, of dealing with him, and you will sorely regret it if Monsignor should see fit to exercise them, sir. Other dwarves there are about, sir, have no fear; and impertinent ones can be dispatched with in a trice. Do you take me?" And with that, she yanked my hair and twisted it about most painfully; and our interview came to an abrupt conclusion.

Inside the hamper once more and returning to the monastery, I could arrive at no other conclusion but that alas, the Church was not to become, however faithfully I might continue to serve the Abbé Guibourg's causes, the avenue for furthering any of my own particular causes. No: I should have to seek my fortunes elsewhere.

And yet most ironically, there occurred shortly thereafter a sudden change in my life which was in fact to open an avenue to those very fortunes which I had determined to seek. And I shall tell you of it:

That change came about either in the year 1668 or 1669. And it is a great pity for the accuracy of this account that I cannot fix exactly upon the year, so vital a part does it play in my history. But I must add that at that point in my life, I was blissfully unaware that anyone was counting the years. I saw the summers come and go, the springs and winters pass, and to me the process seemed to be agreeably in place and not likely ever to end. When at last, some while later I learned that numbers and a definite order had been assigned to those same summers and winters, I faced the news with some alarm; for it suggested a distinct finiteness to the elements of time, that we should be counting them, and as it were labeling them, checking them off as they flew by, the very notion leading me quite naturally to conceive that my own time might be finite as well and that I too might one day be checked off.

But let us continue: either 1668 or 1669 is our date; and in it, and with not a solitary word of warning, I was suddenly removed from the wretched monastery of St. Sauveur at Louveciennes and taken to live in a sumptuous house southwest of Paris, between that city and the town of Vaugirard!

Scarcely being aware at the time of where Paris was in the scheme of things, the name "Vaugirard" meant even less to me. Be that as it may, I had barely time to make my *adieux* to my former home; to the filthy curs who, by then I had decided, were hardly my friends for I had been chewed upon by not a few of them; to the pots and stoves, to Brother Dagobert and his ministrations, to my dearest pigeon hamper! and to the sweating, swearing Antichrist jade who ran the place. No, I was summarily tossed into a rustic *char-à-banc,* which set off down the road; and I believe it was the first ride in which, unhampered, I could see the trees go by and the odd farm and the people and chickens along the way; and only two hours later I arrived at that house, set in a small suburb, and was somewhat tossed, again, into the kitchen, which stood apart, to the rear of the main building. There, a Madame Amélie, a peasant woman of a certain age with a naked infant firmly attached to her right breast, made some ado about me, laughing at my proportions and most especially at the length of my nose: for by the age of eight—or was it seven?—it did appear much longer than it ought, the rest of my frame not having kept pace with it. Madame commanded me to strip; shall there be no relief from this wretched practice? thought I; but I complied, and she too made an intimate study of my person, including my ———, before she dropped me into a large pail and poured steaming water over my head; for she said that I stank, and it would not do: that I was to meet the mistress of the house and my benefactress and must not stink in the presence of that lady, who behind her back was known, Mme Amélie prattled on, as the "Indian princess," for she had spent some of her girlhood on the isle of Martinique in the French West Indies, and she was much prone to giving herself the airs of a princess: Madame Françoise Scarron, née d'Aubigné, of a solid, bourgeois family, whose husband, though crippled and twisted, had won repute as a great poet and wit about the town, and madame had gained some early station through him.

At the conclusion of my scalding bath, Mme Amélie gave me a set of clothes to put on—breeches, stockings, a cotton shirt, boots, and a neckerchief—which, though clean, were ill-fitted to my person, except for the neckerchief; but there was no help for it. She then hurried me across to the main house, through a world of awesome halls and chambers, and into a room the opulence of which I had not beheld up to that time: the floor boards were wide and of a dark hue, and a thick carpet lay upon them; and there were hanging fabrics framing the tall windows; chairs, tables, and sofas had been placed here and there; a huge brass chandelier hung from a chain high above in the center of the room; and at the opposite end was an immense fireplace. I could not recall ever having felt so intimidated by my surroundings.

Reader: seated near the chimney, fingering the beads on a large rosary in her lap, was Mme Françoise Scarron. I was not certain what to expect an Indian princess to look like, but what I saw was distinctly not it: the lady was a squarely-built woman, with no trace of anything Indian about her or of anything royal for that matter; she was endowed with ample bosoms, adorned entirely in black and with a soft black cap upon her head, and possessed of dark complexion and hair, penetrating eyes, and the undeniable promise of a double chin.

Directly upon seeing me, she appeared to become quite vexed; but she set aside her beads and nodded her head briefly; at which point, Mme Amélie ushered me, in silence, across the entire length of the vast room to within a foot of where madame sat. It was then that I perceived that the lady smelt, most unsettlingly, reader, of leeks—I know not how or why—but distinctly of leeks, and the fragrance was unmistakable.

Mme Scarron, now spoke; and in a peremptory manner; and said the following:

"Your Christian name is Hugues. I am under some constraint, dwarf, to accept you into this house and to provide you with bed and board. This unhappy circumstance sets you in no way upon an equal footing with anyone else about the premises, resident or servant, nor at all even with the child, however much younger she may be than you, nor with any other children yet to come into this household, which, as they will be of due and proper proportions and thus superior to you, dwarf, you will leave entirely alone. You will be given chores out in the kitchen and stables, and I may occasionally send for you to serve here in the drawing room when there are guests desiring a source of amusement. You will do as you are bidden; you will get a sound thrashing if you steal anything or break the cups or plates; never talk back; and if you know what's good for you, keep out of my way."

At which, she bent forward, as much as her ample frame permitted, and fixed me with a piercing and malicious stare; and then—and quite arbitrarily for I had not dared do other than stand at rigid and most respectful attention, though trembling the whiles—she seized my left ear and dealt it such a vigorous, wrenching twist that despite myself I let out a shrill yelp and struggled to free my poor member from her painful grasp. But at length she released it herself, and with a look of smug pleasure, turned back, took up her rosary once more and her meditations on the sufferings of Christ; and I was summarily hustled away from her presence by Mme Amélie and returned to the kitchen.

I resolved on the spot to keep out of the dreadful woman's way, exactly as she had bidden, for the instant aversion she had shown to me, reader, I shared, I can assure you, to her. Leeks are not my favorite legume nor is having my ear wrenched asunder my favorite pastime; and that entirely gratuitously, for I had neither done nor said anything to the lady, I had not even asked to be there in her house; such an act of willful malice I had not yet witnessed, I think, for even the children at the monastery had had some excuse for their cruelties as they vied together for preferment, and the dogs there had been downright hungry.

And I resolved as well to have no commerce with any of her offspring.

Thus I was only too hastily returned to the life of a kitchen boy and was to continue a regimen of ashes and slops, of scrubbing and scouring. Very well, thought I, I shall do it, and without complaint, for what else, pray, am I fit to do? In fact I saw that I was fortunate to have skills which could be put to use. And besides, this new kitchen was smaller and with fewer stoves; and its mistress, Mme Amélie, though many of her teeth were gone and others loose, yet she did not have a foul breath; and I saw no snarling mongrels prowling around. The daughter of the household—and the other children yet to come—superior to me though they would be, were unlikely to torment me or tease me (as my former kitchen mates had) being so much younger than myself, and their presences would likely be easily tolerated. And as long as I avoided any direct contact with them and with the head of that household, I could anticipate no vexation. So be it then.

Weighing matters all in all, this abrupt move to Vaugirard did, I quickly realized, constitute a significant improvement in my lot, and moreover, one which I had not even sought: excellent, said I to myself, if such boons are to fall into my lap from out of the blue, and with some few exertions on my own part in the right circumstances, my determination to better my prospects might not be a fond one after all: for was such betterment not already afoot? And I consoled myself somewhat for not having realized a more committed career in the Church.

Mme Amélie assigned me various chores, and I set about energetically to perform them; but the keeper of the stables scoffed at the thought of employing me unless, as he said, thinking his jest an hilarious one, it were as a footstool for mounting the steeds; for which incivility he too won my eternal enmity, though I chose not to let him know it at the time. It was true that he had already two lads who served him as grooms and no need for more; one of them, a youth a few years my senior I longed to become better acquainted with, for I admired a certain dash about him, a certain swagger, qualities which I believe were the very ones that led him to spurn my offer of friendship; though once, as I was sitting on the step, he tossed me a piece of shortbread; and right grateful I was, not only for the morsel, however stale, but for the contact, however brief.

I was given a window seat with a hinged lid to sleep in at the end of a hallway on the topmost floor of the main house; from the window above I could see several nearby estates, the surrounding countryside—a mixture of farmlands and woods—and well off into the distance the towers of a large church, which I learned later was the Cathedral of Notre Dame. Thus I had the distinct impression that my horizons were indeed widening and that here, on the highest story of the mansion, I had, as it were, somewhat risen in the world.

Some months after my arrival, and as Mme Scarron had anticipated at our short interview, a second baby, newborn, was indeed ushered into the world of Vaugirard. At the time, I was far too childish to understand the event—I mean the creation of a human being—and assumed that some bird had delivered it. My first view of the child was out in the kitchen, to which Mme Amélie carried the tiny, solemn lad one evening; and with the daughter hanging from one teat, madame summarily clapped the new arrival onto the other. Even from a distance, I could not help but note that the infant's left leg was shorter than the other and his left foot somewhat malshaped, for it was twisted inward; but what struck me most particularly was the general state of stumpiness about the foot: it was foreshortened, and the toes were decidedly stubby. My first thought was that his foot, in its stumpiness, was similar to my own two feet; and for a brief moment, I fancied the tug of some kinship with that sucking lump of flesh. But I dismissed it from my mind.

The two children were bedded in a nursery on the second floor of the main house and were regularly delivered to the head of the household for inspection by their nurse, a homely and disorderly being, almost a child herself and of a downtrodden mien; or by their wet nurse, Mme Amélie. I saw them very little myself, only in fact when Mme Amélie's duties of giving suck coincided with her function as a cook; and on more than one occasion I saw one or the other child come perilously close to falling into a boiling pot of soup. Presently the girl, whose name I never knew, appeared no more; and one day Mme Amélie told me that the child was dead and that these things happen; I knew all too well that they did. But eventually, reader, over the months, I began to grow drawn to the boy; or at least, to the idea of the boy, toward whom I had felt that initial tug; his name, I learned, was Louis-Auguste, and from some childish sense of curiosity, I resolved to keep an eye on him, albeit a distant one.

A second prediction made by Mme Scarron in our one-sided interview was also to come about: not long after my arrival, on one Tuesday evening, Mme Amélie swabbed me down again and gave me a fresh set of clothing, this one including a dark red sash with tassels and a hateful ruff to put around my throat (and I having very little throat, a common shortage among dwarves, a starched ruff around it was a grave inconvenience). I was then led to the main house and given (by a footman) a large silver tray crowded with tiny cups of flan, and I was told to serve them around to the guests who were then seated in the drawing room at sets of cards.

"Take care, Monsieur Hugues," said the leering footman, "that you trip not and fall and let spill the flan; that you walk not into the legs of the chairs or worse, into the legs of the guests; that you present the flan to the guests in the order of their rank, which you may perceive by the richness and detail of their dress as well as by the size of the chair they are sitting upon; that you gawk not at the guests' jewels nor at their whiskers; that you step not on any guest's foot and most especially not on any gouty guest's foot; that you not allow the tassels of your sash to tangle in the side buckle of any guest's breeches; that you laugh not at the fat old men or the shriveled old women nor at the fat old women or the shriveled old men; that you not hold your nose at the stench that some of them emit; that you return to the kitchen having served every guest and with an empty tray."

Taking up my burden of flan, I stole quietly along the length of the becarpeted hallway until I reached the two massive doors that led into the drawing room. On the other side I could hear chattering and laughter and the light flutter of shuffling cards. My hands were of ice, my mouth was dry, in the abyss of my stomach were ominous rumblings. Nothing that I had engaged in or beheld in all my however-many years had prepared me for the perilous moment of my entry into society.

Two lackeys swung the portals open, and I looked up into a roomful of glittering giants. There were some twenty persons in the room, all in extravagant states of finery—furs and laces, ribbons and ruffles, wigs and feathers, jewels and sashes—and illumined by the chandelier above and by banks of glowing candles; so that to me, but three feet from the floorboards and as though weighed still farther down by flan, they appeared, *en masse,* a gigantic panorama of sheer enormity. And their size seemed but to increase when, with my unexpected appearance before them bearing flan, they began to utter a series of whoops and guffaws, shrieks and roars, slapping at their knees and holding their vast sides and rocking backward and forward, such as to produce a veritable tidal wave of clamor that almost felled me on the spot; and I saw one cackling lady's teeth shoot forth the length of the room, and a gentleman's high wig went toppling into the fireplace, and the archbishop present cried out that he would bepiss himself surely, and two or perhaps three full decks of cards flew up into the air like so much confetti, and a much decorated general of His Majesty's Royal Army slid from his seat and onto the floor in an uncontrollable, quivering mass of laughter.

Silently and steadily—though within, I confess it, I was shaken by this awful challenge—I stepped into the rafter-ringing room and made my way about with the cups of flan; nor, when as happened several times, a rollicking guest dropped his flan into his lap or onto the carpet or once, in the case of one old lady, onto my head, did I veer from off my course, but did exactly as I had been bidden, making the rounds and, as seemed meet, serving last the hostess, Mme Scarron herself. That lady, unlike her

guests, was not laughing, for truly I do not believe that she was possessed
of a sense of humor, not even of a malicious order; yet as she reached to
take the final cup of flan from off my tray, there appeared on her features
a look of malignant satisfaction not only at the knowledge that she had
provided for her guests an occasion of unbridled delirium but as well at
what she must have sensed of my intense inner misery.

The following Tuesday I was enjoined to deliver another round of flan,
producing yet another round of mirth; and again, a week later; and thus
it was that I became a regular and recurring feature of madame's soirées.
But presently, as will always happen and I was right glad of it, as you may
imagine, the novelty of my performance wore thin, and I came to serve
merely as a welcome (if I may say so) but mild diversion, prized more for
the delivery of custards than for the absurdity of my appearance. I always
performed my services with extreme diligence, conscious of my newly
gained good fortune in being among that elevated society, however foolish they might have appeared to the uninitiated; and thus I made myself
a valued member of the household, even while regretting whose household in fact it was.

In some months' time, as I continued to study him, Louis-Auguste, I
noticed, began to gain more and more the appearance of an actual human
being, crawling about and making noises that roughly approximated the
sounds of speech. Yet my observations of him continued to be surreptitious, as I did not care to risk Mme Scarron's wrath by any direct commerce with the child; and the only occasions that I saw him besides his
visits to the kitchen were when my delivery of flan happened to coincide
with Louis-Auguste's appearance in the drawing room. But one such
occasion I must report to you, for it entailed a second unfortunate
encounter between my mistress and myself and other consequences of
which you are to learn.

As she had done numerous times before, the lady was in the business
that particular Tuesday evening of making much ado over Louis-Auguste,
holding him up and dandling him and parading him this way and that
before her guests, none of whom, I might note, displayed any but the
most perfunctory interest in the child, the child himself enduring her
attentions in his customarily taciturn manner.

"There's my darling baby, there's my boy," cooed Mme Scarron, tugging
at Louis's bent left foot to try to straighten it out.

Now I myself was in the business of delivering up my cups of flan with as much dispatch as possible; and in my somewhat haste, reader, and you see here again the danger of haste, I failed to notice that our two paths were on the point of collision, as indeed madame herself, in her busy attention to the child's foot, also failed to notice; so that, rounding the corner of a card table, I—along with my trayful of flan—made head-long contact with the lower half of the lady herself.

For the briefest of moments, I was quite overtaken by the fragrance of leeks; until I became all too quickly aware that Mme Scarron was lurching forward (as happens in these encounters) and that the bundle of Louis-Auguste had slipped from her grasp and gone sailing out through the air. But an alert marquis leapt up from his place and deftly caught the ever-solemn child a fraction of an instant before he went crashing into a massive bronze candelabrum; and for the swiftness of his action I am eternally grateful to that marquis, for what indeed would have been my fate otherwise? As it was, Mme Scarron administered me a second vigorous wrenching of my ear as I was struggling to retrieve the flan from all about the floor, nor did she spare me the vituperation of her tongue:

"Stumpy oaf!" cried she. "How long shall I endure your wretched clumsiness! Vile insect!" And her guests all fell about with rollicking delight. "My poor baby, my poor dearest baby!" she exclaimed as she left off battering me and flew to collect Louis-Auguste from the arms of the marquis. "Come to mother, poorest thing, let mother make it all better, my sweetest lamb!" And she went on with such-like parental outpourings as she hastened from out of the room with the infant, who, despite his brush with death, remained as taciturn as ever and quite oblivious to her solicitousness.

"Ha, ha, ha! Monsieur Hugues," laughed a certain Madame de St. Estève, as I continued gathering up the flan, "now you see, sir, do you not, the fury of a mother's wrath! Take heed, sir, ha, ha, ha, or your days amongst us are numbered!" And she chortled at my distress.

"A 'mother's' wrath," sneered a corpulent archbishop, "indeed!" And turning to the marquis: "You ought better, my dear Effiat, to have let the child strike the candelabrum; perhaps we should then be done with all of this silly charade. A 'mother's' wrath indeed!"

A flurry of applause greeted this observation.

"Charade?" cried a second lady. "Charade?" And everyone turned to face her. "Then she is not the child's true mother?"

Immediately her query was met with a round of mocking laughter.

"No more, madame," retorted the archbishop, "than she is mother to that dwarf." And the thought of a kinship between Mme Scarron and myself produced yet another round of mirth and no small discomfort to me. "She is no more than a hired governess," the archbishop continued, "a mere employee—and right fortunate to have snapped up the job, given the wretched state of her purse." And everyone concurred with the cleric's assessment of Mme Scarron's purse with hearty coos of delight.

"Then is she not of royalty?" persisted the second lady, and after a brief pause of stunned silence, the room fairly shook once more with laughter.

"Royalty! Royalty!" shrieked the marquis who had rescued Louis-Auguste. "Why, the very thought of it! Fie, and indeed she would have you to think so, madame, but she is only a silly climber—one of the wretched many one sees about these days—and using the lad to advance her own cause. Heavens, is that not as obvious as the nose on your face?" The lady's nose being somewhat bulbous, the marquis's question was met with a flurry of snickering. Turning away from the now-chastened woman and back to the archbishop: "But indeed, Your Excellency, what could I have been thinking? I vow that next time I shall not be so swift at retrieving the flying infant—and we shall be quit of her airs and pretensions—'mother' indeed!" And turning now in my direction, "Monsieur Hugues," he continued, peering down upon me, "when next might you contrive another such collision, sir? Indeed we should all be grateful!" And he roared, along with the others, at my red-faced confusion and inability to answer.

But at that moment, the second lady (it was a Madame Poulaillon) spoke up yet once again, and clearly she had not been sufficiently chastened:

"Then who, pray, *is* his mother?"

At that, reader, sighs and exclamations erupted throughout the room as the guests expressed their exasperation that one of their company should be so pathetically ignorant of the parentage of Louis-Auguste. But I confess, and without apology, that I was myself as ignorant as that lady and as keen to learn the answer to her question; but yet, alas, it never came forth that evening, for at that very instant, Mme Scarron herself swept back into the drawing room.

Pondering the news that Mme Scarron was not Louis-Auguste's mother but merely his hired governess, I found it not at all surprising; for there was no evidence of a father to Louis-Auguste anywhere about the Scarron household, which even I understood was somehow necessary to the production of a child; and Mme Scarron herself was, and no question about it, a most unlikely person to be anyone's mother. And further, it seemed to me a wonder that she persisted in playing the role of mother in the society of her guests, who, if they were not the brightest people in France at the time, were clearly shrewd enough, most of them, to know better and to resent her for it. In fact, the more I thought on it, the more irksome seemed that hypocrisy which she displayed before that knowing company and more especially, before the unknowing, helpless babe. Hypocrites, as you may know, are assigned to the innermost circle of hell.

My left ear still smarting from my second encounter with her, I lay in my window seat that night and allowed my imagination about the matter to wander, as childish imaginations will wander when set adrift—about the innocent Louis-Auguste, he whose parentage, at least to me, was, like my own, unknown; and about the deceitful Scarron, she whose bent upon assuming his parentage was so strong.

Whereupon, some sudden itch, reader—I know not whence it came, but some boyish prod from within—seized hold of that wandering imagination; and it prompted me, that itch, that prod, to rise from the window seat and to steal downstairs and out through the snow into the kitchen house; where I rummaged around in the feed bins and found a partially gnawed length of leek. A smelly thing it was, that chunk of bulb, and instantly conjuring up the mistress of the establishment. I put the leek in my pocket.

Without a sound, I made my way back to the main house, up to the second floor, and into the hallway which led to the nursery. The door to the nursery stood ajar, for the nurse was a careless creature. Cautiously, I peered inside.

A single candle next to a crib on the far side of the room cast a pallid glow, and in the crib I saw him, Louis-Auguste, propped up against a bank of pillows, staring glumly into space. It was deathly silent in the nursery, and a thick drift of snow against the windowpane seemed to hold tight the stillness within the darkened chamber.

You are as aware as I was at that frightening moment that I was about to violate one of Mme Scarron's most strict injunctions, to wit, that I should have no commerce with this child nor with any other child who might in future join him here.

Yet every youth loves mischief.

I slipped inside. Immediately, Louis-Auguste saw me, and our eyes locked. I paused; then noiselessly, step by step, I approached the crib, he remaining utterly calm and continuing to gaze at me.

As I drew near, I took the leek from out of my pocket and held it up for the child to see—and need I say it?—for him to smell. One whiff and already, I was gratified to note, a look of recognition appeared on his face.

Excellent, thought I, I have a ready subject at hand.

I slipped the leek directly under Louis-Auguste's nose, and when he had taken two or three more sniffs, I reached forward and tweaked his left ear. He looked more surprised than pained; and so I gave his ear a second and heartier tweak. Thick tears boiled up into his eyes, his face grew flushed; but yet he did not murmur.

I withdrew the leek and retreated. Still watching me carefully, Louis-Auguste at length grew pale once again; the tears seeped out and down across his cheeks, but no others followed. I waited a few moments, until presently he lost all interest in me and returned to staring out into the empty middle of the room. Whereupon I approached his crib a second time, put the leek to his nose and gave his left ear a good sharp wrench.

As the first howl pierced the deathly stillness at last, I spun on my heels and fled the room, clutching the odorous legume, just as I heard an inner door thump open and the nurse scurry in to the shrieking babe.

Moments later, back up in my window seat, my heart pounding, my breath racing, I rejoiced that I had just hit upon an unparalleled piece of childish good fortune: that with a bit of leek and a few good tweaks of an ear, I could indeed produce some mischief in that dismal household.

I went back the next night, and the next, and the next. I even dared to open the door myself when it had not been left ajar. I played variations in my boyish sport with the lad, taunting him with whiffs of leek so that at first he was not certain if he ought be fearful or not, then moving in for the final *coup,* a good snort and a solid tweak and the wails of misery that followed; then presently, setting off his howls with merely the scent of the leek itself; whilst two steps ahead of discovery by his nurse, I dashed out of the nursery and up into my window seat. I even made bold one night not to dash away at all but to hide behind a fire screen in the chimney place, from which outpost I could spy upon the nurse as she hushed the child back to his silent sleeplessness; and then, the moment she stumbled away, stole back out once again in order to inflict more torment.

And as I am being rigorously candid with you, reader (and I told you at the outset that I would be), let me further confess that the crowning achievement of my forays into that bedroom—and it did my heart enormous good to see—came on the very next Tuesday evening when the nurse brought Louis-Auguste into the drawing room and placed him into the arms of his governess and that lady began her preening and parading about with the lad before her company and kissing him on the very ear that I had so abused; for instantly Louis-Auguste, now primed by his nose for the delivery of pain, set up a loud and baleful wail such as utterly disconcerted her and thoroughly mortified her before her guests.

"Good lad, Louis," I thought to myself, "and there, madame, there's for a good twisting of my ear when first we met," as I watched her desperately trying to soothe him back to silence and as well to comfort her own afflicted breast before she was forced to flee with the bawling child from out of the room and away from the silent sneers of her company.

You will forgive me, I pray, indulgent reader, for this cruel diversion, it being the only diversion of which I ever availed myself; and I readily acknowledge it as an outright piece of childish mischief; and children, as you will surely agree, are not known for their mercy.

# 4

DEAR READER: I THINK YOU must know me and my shortcomings well enough by now—for what have we here? three chapters, some forty pages, all of which I have been storing, sheet by sheet, as I told you that I would, inside the hollow in my rookery wall—you are acquainted with me, I say, well enough by now to know that I would never pass judgment on any of my fellow human beings. Still, I pray you not to take it amiss if I state that, absurd though my appearance may have been while serving flan to madame's Tuesday guests, it did not suffer over much by comparison to that of many of those guests themselves; and secondly, in the matter of social behavior, I believe that in all modesty, I may even lay claim to relative parity with some of that distinguished company.

And now I shall tell of some of them.

Here was Madame Agnès Bèze, Comtesse de Pommeret, whose teeth having given way, had come to resemble the man in the moon as you will find pictured in a child's nursery book, her chin curling upwards as though to make contact with the downward hook of her nose, a sprout of white whiskers upon that same chin mingling with an abundance of white lace which framed a bonnet securely tied around her neck. That same bonnet caught fire one evening as the countess leaned forward—alas, too near to a candle—in her myopic study of a soft-boiled egg, for she could eat nothing but soft matter; whereupon a cleric seated next to her whisked the burning headdress from off her head; and he was rewarded for his efforts when she, unaware of having been ablaze and enraged that her entirely bald pate had been exposed to the assembled company, threw the soft-boiled egg into the cleric's face. The countess's failing vision was matched by a like failure in her hearing, a condition which a large trumpet that she brandished did little to correct, for she more often than not applied the wrong end of the instrument to her ear and thereby impaired her hearing all the more.

Here was that same cleric, His Excellency, the Archbishop of Lisieux, Monsignor Lucien de Breteuil, whom I was later (unwittingly) to topple to the floor along with His Eminence, Emile Cardinal LeMoine; I have alluded to this earlier. And I remind you that the archbishop was a man of considerable girth, such that he had destroyed upwards of fifteen sturdy chairs in Mme Scarron's drawing room, and thus he was assigned an iron fire grate to sit upon that had been in the family since the Council of Trent. The archbishop specialized in attending criminal trials and in the hearing of confessions, both activities concerned with the commission of error and both providing him therefore with excellent subject matter in his role as a gifted raconteur. He was also much given to analyzing his various digestive functions, going so far, I was told—for I never saw such a sight—as to having all the food that he ate carefully weighed and similarly all his defecations, so that he could then tally the balance and duly enter it into a pocket diary which he kept upon his voluminous person.

Antoine Coiffier, Marquis d'Effiat, that same marquis who had saved Louis-Auguste in his flight across the room, a man much feared for his caustic tongue, was tightly built and dark; and the piercing glare of his eyes, it was said, could shatter crystal, and that not of the best quality. He dressed in a flamboyant fashion, with a goodly quantity of ribbons about his linen, shoes, and wigs, and a goodly quantity of rouge upon his cheeks; and it was whispered that what appeared to be a vivid, dark mole on his left cheek was in fact applied to the spot each morning by his barber. He had, I noticed, a very handsome pair of ankles which he much favored in the manner in which he stood and, as well, an unusually long nail on the little finger of his left hand, of which he was most protective. The marquis made infrequent appearances at madame's soirées, usually in the company of several very pretty fellows, and it was a well-known fact that they were given to passing most of their extensive leisure time in the company of Philippe, Duc d'Orléans, a man known informally as "Monsieur," who was brother to His Majesty, King Louis XIV. The marquis often flew into irrational rages, and once when a clock on the mantel struck the hour for departing, I saw him seize it into his hands and dash it into the chimney place; and he had destroyed many clocks in the area west of Paris.

One of the few commoners admitted to the Tuesday soirées was Mme Marguerite de Jehan Poulaillon (it was she who had displayed such appalling ignorance about Louis-Auguste's parentage). Her husband, a Superintendent of Waterways and Forests, accompanied her every Tuesday but sat to the side and dozed while his wife ran up extravagant debts in whatever card games she found herself, which the husband, aroused from slumber at the end of the evening, would dutifully promise to pay on the following Tuesday; but being a minor bureaucrat and somewhat impoverished, he was never able to do so. Whenever she was pressed on these matters, Mme Poulaillon would begin to grumble and to mutter that everyone was biased against her and trying to take advantage of her position and that her husband was well connected in government circles and all manner of what-not, until the whole business became entirely more tiresome than it was worth. It was a wonder to me that her company was tolerated.

Since I have made no bones about my size, it will come as no surprise that I soon became more aware of what went on underneath the card tables in that drawing room than upon them; and I witnessed one warmish evening in June the servant girl of another of the guests, Mme Françoise de St. Estève, née Dumesnil, administering an enema to her mistress under the table at which the lady sat; it was clear, for I was down there and I saw it. The girl was equipped with a syringe and various lengths of hose, a basin and a glass jug; and as she went about her ministrations, at the same time she fended off three or four curs which were nosing about. When she became aware that I was witness to the operation, to say nothing of her mistress's exposed parts, she grabbed me by the —— and twisted it so painfully that I let out a small shriek and ran away. The girl never emerged that evening from her clinic, and it was not before an hour and a half later that Mme de St. Estève excused herself from the table with some dispatch and, followed by the dogs, sought out a *chaise percée*, one of which stood without in the lobby. Those dogs, I learned by the way, all belonged to St. Estève herself, for Mme Scarron would keep no animals in her house and on Tuesdays tolerated those of her guest only begrudgingly. They were so overfed by their indulgent mistress that they befouled prodigiously whatever place they found themselves in, and they made no exception for the carpets.

The hostess of Vaugirard was honored by the frequent presence of another of her guests, François-Henri de Montmorency-Bouteville de Luxembourg, not because that gentleman was a gracious, compatible, and charming companion, for indeed he was none of these; a dogmatic military officer and something of a prude, he was however prized at social gatherings in light of the fact that his penchant for looting, ravaging, and pillaging whatever foreign territories his troops overran had made him a rising star in the armed forces and thus much favored in royal circles. He was the only person, it appeared, to take open and often quite hostile exception to the St. Estève menagerie, for he seemed to be especially prone to stepping on dog turds and soiling his highly polished boots, which he would then use quite freely to kick the yelping dogs this way and that about the drawing room and even on occasion down a flight of stairs.

The Marquis de Feuquières, an amateur chemist and an excellent figure of a man with most impressive eyebrows, suffered only one drawback: he had entirely lost his left nostril in what he claimed was an explosion in his laboratory when he had been attempting to combine certain acids by heating them in an oven; but in fact it was well known that the nostril had been demolished by syphilis. He had some trouble with fleas as well. These physical drawbacks in no way dampened the gentleman's tart wit, and he quite entertained the card table where he was seated once, when his hostess set about yet again to display the infant Louis-Auguste to her assembled company; the child having been wheeled into the room by his unhappy nurse, his governess swept him up into her arms so that everyone might glimpse her tiny bundle of joy, kissing him, embracing him, and making much to do: "Say 'mama,' Louis-Auguste, come, say 'mama'; come now, show mummy a smile, my precious lamb. Now do, now do: let all our friends see his big, big grin." At which point, on cue, Louis-Auguste erupted into bedlam. "Ah, blessèd motherhood," now whispered Feuquières to his table companions, "what child shall resist the endearments of a mother? See how our dear Scarron captivates her precious little one's sunny affections!" and such-like sarcastical asides. The giggles among the marquis's company went undetected by their hostess only because she had taken to shaking Louis-Auguste in an attempt to silence him, which but increased the din.

It was whispered about that yet another guest, Mademoiselle Louise-Adélaïde Marsy, a much-faded beauty who had suffered the ravages of the pox, dabbled in the arts of the supernatural, having acquired occult powers by which she held sway over a succession of lovers, both male and female; I know nothing of this at firsthand, reader (Body of Christ, protect me). If indeed she enjoyed such powers, she had not been able to extend them to her activities at the card tables; for I saw her lose many a hand at *vingt-et-un* and *reversi,* and her temper was such that she would then stamp and shout and sometimes spit on the floor in anger and gnash her teeth. And it was during one of those very tantrums that a strange event took place, and I will describe it to you now, for as it turned out, it was an event which afforded me yet another utterly unexpected opportunity to improve my standing in that society. Therefore this partial catalogue of madame's guests has indeed come to a purpose, as I knew that it would when I set about it.

One evening, just as Mlle Louise had lost some five hundred *louis d'or,* it so happened that I was attempting to retrieve some flan for the Marquis de Feuquières that he had let slip underneath the table; at her loss, Mlle Louise threw up such a hue and cry that I froze where I stood, an unwitting decision on my part, for it left me the inadvertent target of a powerful kick which she thrust forward with her strong right leg; and her foot landing squarely on my midriff, she then peered underneath the table herself to see what it was that she had struck, thinking there may have been foul play; but she saw only me standing there with a handful of flan. And though I went on about my errand for the marquis and quite forgot the matter, she however did not: later that evening, therefore, when she happened upon me in the rear hallway, she swept me off into a neighboring passage.

"Monsieur Hugues," said she in low tones and producing a pack of cards identical to those commonly used in the drawing room, "you will oblige me by taking this deck of cards and securing it upon your person; and by slipping, unseen, as I found you earlier this very evening, beneath a card table, to wit, the third card table to the left away from the chimney place, which is where I shall play my next round of *reversi;* and by handing me when I shall signal for you to do so, below the board, any one of these four cards," and she dealt out (what I later learned were) the four aces, "and secondly, these cards," showing me the four kings. "If you refuse to do this or let it be known by anyone that you have done it or fail in any part of this enterprise, I shall invoke the powers of darkness so that you will be not only as unnaturally stunted in your growth as you presently are, but will suffer the plague of smallpox, with raging fevers and permanent disfigurement of a vile and grotesque order, and the loss of your immortal soul, if indeed you are equipped with one."

I was happy to comply with her request; and I did slip beneath the third table to the left and quite unnoticed, for by then my presence in that company was accepted and ignored—no one took notice of me down around their knees any more, or if they did they made no mind of it. And I did hand her, upon her signal, the first ace, the second, third, and fourth, and subsequently one by one the kings. Whereupon to everyone's great astonishment, given her previous history, Mlle Louise-Adélaïde swept up handful upon handful of winnings, routing her enemies, who were many, and reveling in her new-found triumph.

The following Tuesday, mademoiselle returned; and she sought me out again in private and without a word produced a second deck of cards; and once more, overwhelming victory was hers.

Now the supernatural pressures under which I served Mlle Louise-Adélaïde provided very little leeway in my dealings with her. But even so, I began to ask myself why I might not promulgate this system to some other unskillful card player with an eye toward gaining for myself some reward more positive than the avoidance of smallpox. For I was not unaware of the benefit that a little pocket money could provide me, even though the occasions for me to spend it were few. I gave great consideration to approaching the Comtesse de Pommeret, who had not yet sorted out, it seemed, the spades from the clubs; but both because she was partially deaf and therefore inaccessible except at top volume (which was contrary to the clandestine nature of my scheme) and because she was so abominably stupid in the matter of card playing to begin with, I rejected her as a candidate; and I appealed instead to the Marquis de Feuquières. I was not sure why the clever marquis failed, as he did, so repeatedly at gaming, unless it was that the syphilis which had annihilated his nostril had also affected some portion of his brain. Whatever the case, the marquis gladly subscribed to my suggestion; and we set upon a fee of half a *sou* for every game he won.

Soon the Marquis de Feuquières became another overnight success at the tables; and on occasion he remembered, even in the heat of triumph, to pay me; and between him and mademoiselle I was right well occupied; though not so much so that I did not find occasion to take on other clients, indeed some seven or eight of the most wretched of the gamesters, including Mme Poulaillon and the Archbishop of Lisieux himself (but never Mme Scarron, for although she too lost heavily at gaming, she had a prudish tone about her, and I feared she would put me out of doors at such a proposition; and at this point, I was just beginning to turn what was a proper employment and to achieve some financial reward; and to remain in that company I was dependent upon her tolerance—I was about to say "her good will," but I never saw any of that).

Having increased my attentions to my mistress's Tuesday evening guests with my now thriving delivery of cards, I found myself spending longer periods of time in her salon, under the tables; and although I do not care to say that I eavesdropped upon their conversations, yet it was unavoidable that I should hear what was spoken above board during the transaction of my business below; and I shall now recount to you one such conversation which caused much of a stir amongst the gamesters and which will furnish you some sense of that society.

Philippe, Duc d'Orléans, he whom they called Monsieur, to wit, the king of France's own brother, was married to an Englishwoman, Henrietta by name. Their marriage enjoyed but little harmony for it appeared that Monsieur was much more attentive to a group of sparkish young lads than he was to his wife—among them the Marquis d'Effiat of whom I have spoken, as well as a young Italian count and various sturdy members of His Majesty's Royal Marine barracks; but chiefest among them all was the dashing Chevalier de Lorraine. Presently, the rivalry between Henrietta and Lorraine became such that they no longer tolerated being in the same room with one another; and Henrietta grew increasingly churlish. And so it came as quite a diverting report when the Comtesse de Pommeret announced one Tuesday evening in late June of 1670, and with no small degree of relish, that that very afternoon, Henrietta, having suffered a thirst while strolling along the terrace at St. Cloud and requesting some chicory water for refreshment, had suddenly fallen into paroxysms and spasms, tremors, retchings and heavings, and within the hour was stone dead.

"Buzz, buzz," quoth the Archbishop of Lisieux upon hearing the report, "who would have thought that chicory water could have so excellent an effect?"

"Why, you are too dreadful!" replied Mme de St. Estève, laughing along with the rest of the company at the archbishop's sarcastical remark, for no one cared a jot for Henrietta.

"It depends entirely upon the quality and nature of the chicory," the Marquis de Feuquières observed, his knowledge of chemical matters now coming handily into play. "And most particularly in what region it is grown."

"Indeed," the archbishop went on, "now that you say so, I do recall hearing only the other day—and in the confessional, so that one may not doubt the veracity of the information—hearing, I say, that there is right powerful chicory grown in the area around Domrémy; there, you will recall, it was that our belovèd Jeanne heard the voices summoning her to rescue the town of Orléans and to rid us of the English menace."

Though the archbishop's remark appears utterly straightforward and even almost commonplace, it caused the entire company to bellow with so much glee that floods of tears streamed from their eyes; and fresh handkerchiefs were brought forth from the linen chest to mop up the excess water. This curious interplay served much to mystify me, I confess; but since then, the wittiness of the archbishop's observation has been explained: Domrémy—and this you will find in any child's geography—is located in the region of the Lorraine, and so the name was an allusion to the Chevalier de Lorraine, Monsieur's dashing companion and archrival to his wife; the rescue of the town of Orléans was a veiled reference to Monsieur himself, the duke of Orléans; and lastly, "the English menace," a thinly disguised double entendre signifying (one) the English forces of the fifteenth century which were driven from French soil under the leadership of Jeanne d'Arc; and (two) Henrietta herself, the chicory victim, who was, as noted, an Englishwoman. I trust, reader, that I have not robbed the archbishop's remark of the spontaneity which it originally enjoyed.

"What's that?" cried the Comtesse de Pommeret, holding her trumpet to her ear; for in her deafness, she felt unjustly excluded from the clever conversation whose topic she had herself introduced.

"An outrageous business this," announced the Duc de Luxembourg. "Preposterous."

"Monsignor," observed Mme Scarron to the archbishop, "you are quite shameless," and although she was not outwardly laughing along with her guests, she clearly took a malicious pleasure in the archbishop's several imputations.

The Marquis d'Effiat, who happened to be present on that Tuesday, did not join in the laughter either; for being of that tight fellowship encircling Monsieur, he took exception to the implication that any one of them would have supplied the poisonous chicory.

"Tush!" said he, "'tis an altogether ill-founded insinuation; why ever should the Chevalier de Lorraine set about to undo Monsieur's wife when he is so ardently devoted to Monsieur himself!"

"Ardently, ardently!" Immediately the archbishop seized upon the word. "And indeed most rarely so, as few knights *are* ardently devoted to their lords, we hear. Why, in his 'ardor' as you call it, he dances attendance to Monsieur both day"—and he paused briefly—"and night. All the more reason for that most ardent of chevaliers to clear out the henhouse, as it were." You could hear the relish in the archbishop's voice. "For they say that the cock"—and he let the word dangle a moment in the air—"crows loudest who claims mastery of the barnyard."

At which observation, Mlle Louise-Adélaïde let forth a whoop of delight, and most of the others followed suit. "That cock!" cried mademoiselle, breathing heavily. "Why, he has quite ravished the barnyard, I think!" And more laughter ensued.

"Outrageous!" shouted the Marquis d'Effiat, whose own position in Monsieur's entourage had now been challenged. "For such, I assure you, is not the case!" He leapt to his feet upon a pair of unusually high heels. "The chevalier is not the only—that is, I myself—there are many—I mean, that is to say—"

But he was unable to continue. Now quivering with rage and of a redness of face as to quite obliterate the rouge which he wore, he flung a small clock, made in part of ormolu, at the archbishop; which missed him, the marquis's aim being in want, and which very nearly struck me, for I was just then hurrying across the room to Mlle Louise's card table with her next play, the ace of clubs. The outraged marquis spun upon his heels, itself a precarious undertaking, not only for the height of the heels themselves but for the length of the shoe ribbons, and he fled the room, crying out all manner of foul and lascivious suggestions as to what the company might do with various parts of themselves; and this amid renewed gales of mirth from that company and bellowing and the smacking of lips and the eventual clamoring for yet another batch of handkerchiefs.

One singular outcome of that conversation remains to be reported: I vowed to reveal the entire truth. For whatever cause, reader—whether it were the rakishness of the conversation, the glittering array of double entendres, the bawdiness of the subject matter, d'Effiat's lewd oaths as he charged from out of the room, or another instance of which I am ignorant—yet some influence upon her had so enflamed—there is no other word for it—enflamed, I say, Mlle Louise-Adélaïde Marsy that, at the climax of the debate, as finally I hastened to her knees beneath the gaming table with the ace of clubs, she impetuously reached below, hiked up her skirts and all her petticoats, separated wide her two exposed limbs, dashed the ace quite from my grip, and, grasping my hand, placed it directly and unmistakably—my very hand, I repeat—upon the exact dimple of her bifurcation, to wit, upon the very central furrow of my lady's crotch.

Of this most unforeseen consequence of their drawing room conversation, let me say no more for the present moment.

# 5

THE RIBALDRY OF THAT CONVERSATION ASIDE, its theme impressed itself upon my mind, and I found the matter of Henrietta's death an unsettling one, involving as it did one of the darker arts and a most clandestine one at that, the art of toxicology. Most unsettling, late at night up in my window seat, in the shadows, where devils are known to lurk—more unsettling indeed than that dark art practiced by the Abbé Guibourg to which, at least tacitly, I reasoned, Holy Mother Church in her wisdom must have concurred; yet in both cases, the presence of death might easily unsettle anyone, to say nothing of a child of my then tender years. And I came to realize how unsettled indeed is the world around us, a world which, though it may outwardly appear reasonably benign, like those gamesters' causeries, is in fact fraught with the unexpected and with no small peril.

Yet there was nothing for it but to accept this new appraisal of life and to move on.

Whatever prosperous labors I had for several months now undertaken on Tuesday evenings, my daily chores about the estate did not abate; and I was usually a most diligent worker. Yet, reader, I was still an impressionable child: and I was greatly at fault in the strict commission of one of my chores one morning in the spring of 1672 (and I confess it at the outset); at that youthful age, however, I had not yet developed that habit of punctuality of which I spoke earlier (chapter one), and on the morning in question had dawdled at my task of shoveling ashes from the grate in the drawing room, my mind having filled with I know not what infantile fears and foolishness, misgivings and mischief such as a child wanting discipline may indulge in; and as a result, I was several minutes later than I ought to have been in leaving the drawing room, lugging with me a full scuttle of ashes, when I heard the unmistakable voice of Mme Scarron. An instant afterward, I saw that lady rounding the corner and entering the room. Had she not at the time been holding the shrieking bundle of Louis-Auguste in her arms and her attention given entirely over to him, she must have seen me; which she did not; and as my daily routine strictly forbade my presence in the drawing room when it was in use by others and most especially by Mme Scarron herself, I had the excellent good wit to dart to the relative safety of a window alcove, where I sought cover, with my overflowing bucket of ashes, behind a set of green damask drapery.

"Here. Set them in here," she cried above the childish racket; and she strode the length of the room to the chimney place, followed by a footman, who was carrying two wicker cradles suspended from stands, and behind him, the dismal nurse, who held in her arms a second bundle, a second child, Louis-César, who had been delivered to the household some several months previous: unlike his brother Louis-Auguste, this newcomer displayed few distinguishing characteristics—I mean no twisted ankle or stumpy clubfoot—and thus he had been of no interest to me.

When the cradles had been set up near the chimney place and the two children settled down into them, Mme Scarron withdrew some little distance away, and Louis-Auguste's weeping immediately began to subside. She dismissed the two servants; and then, thinking herself quite alone except for the two infants, she gave her black garments and along with them her undergarments, a sound rearrangement about her very solid person with a series of well-practiced tuggings and twistings, liftings and unsnarlings. After which slowly she approached the cradles once again.

"Is it my good boy then?" she said to Louis-Auguste in a whisper. "Is it my precious lambkin? And does it love its mumsy-wumsy?"

Whereupon, Louis-Auguste delivered himself of a blood-curdling howl, and Louis-César followed suit.

"Horrid beasts," said Scarron under her breath and quickly backing away. "I cannot imagine why I put up with you." Withdrawing still farther to a safer distance, Mme Scarron continued: "If either one of you gives me trouble this day, if you cry out or weep, if you so much as whimper during this interview or give forth any sign of discontent with your present situation here in this household, you will have me to answer to when the interview is done. And you will discover, gentlemen, that I know a thing or two about wrenching little boys' left ears. Do I make myself clear?"

Recovering now from their floods of tears, Louis-Auguste and Louis-César, though they were still breathing heavily, made no reply. Hearing this threat, I felt a sharp twinge in my own left ear and recalled that wrenching I myself had endured in this very same drawing room.

No sooner had these matters been done with than a loud commotion in the front hallway drew my attention there; and in that part of the lobby which I could observe from my lookout, I saw a number of madame's servants being hurriedly driven through the central hall and into the back part of the house; whereupon I heard doors slamming shut in all the rear passages. That accomplished, the chief footman, alone, took up a position facing the front entrance, and a sudden hush fell upon the place. Nor came there, in that mysteriously rarefied stillness, even the merest peep from either of the wicker cradles.

At the conclusion of those several minutes, I sensed the arrival of someone or ones in through the front door, for the footman, though ever alert, drew himself up to even fuller attention, until at length I saw three magnificently appareled gentlemen noiselessly slip into view: they stopped, observed the silence in the place and the absence of any but the footman and turned back toward the door from whence they had come; and upon waiting yet another silent half minute, of a sudden they all bowed low with great deference and reverence and condescension, joined in this act of obeisance by the correct footman.

All of this I found most impressive, not only for the elegance of the company but for the mystery of the occasion; but yet, some few seconds later, my breath was quite literally taken away when there appeared, silently through the hall and into the doorway of the drawing room—and pausing for a brief moment there, enveloped in an aura of utter calm and peace, his proud chin held high in the air—nothing less, reader, than what I must describe to you as a divine presence: radiant, mighty, gracious, serene, majestic, heroic, commanding, noble, glorious, august, sublime, most marvelous to behold, as resplendent as the sun, taller than any man that I had ever beheld and all men are giants to me, more perfectly endowed than Adonis, and with all the celestial bearing of Apollo himself. And I would myself have bowed low and with deference, reverence, and condescension before this heavenly being but that I feared betraying my own low, earth-bound, and ashen presence behind the drapery. The nimbus which wreathed round this godhead shone forth so brilliantly, reader, that I am at a loss to detail either his dress or his face upon that occasion but for one element, one feature, one particular; which was his nose; for it was a long nose and aquiline, reader, and quite unlike my own, it suited its owner as magnificently as the entire man himself suited it.

Mme Scarron bowed low as this deity, after that glimmering moment in the doorway, proceeded into the drawing room and across it to the cradles where lay the children. And he installed himself on a chair with its back to me; and alas, I completely lost the celestial sight of him.

But then, reader, there followed in his footsteps—wonder of wonders!—a second divinity, a lesser divinity but divinity no less, a most beautiful woman, excellently well shaped, the curves of her breasts echoed in the sweet curves of her jaw line, the mouth dainty, the eyes full and filled with kindness, the comeliness of her face wreathed in gentle, fair curls, a soft mantle of white lace framing her head and shoulders, her graceful progress into the room the movement of a Venus. She too approached the cradles, nodding curtly to Scarron (who continued to stand some distance away in abject terror, I daresay, that her presence might arouse the now silent babes). The moment this second divinity laid eyes upon the children, she burst into copious tears; nor was she to be consoled by the ministrations of the god but continued to weep quite openly as she lifted Louis-Auguste from out of the cradle, embraced the lad, examined his foot, and then sat down to hold him tenderly in her arms.

Reader: I cannot tell if the lady were more beautiful in calm repose or in the flood of tears which the children's presence had produced; but I can tell you that the sight of her tears in turn produced tears that coursed down both my cheeks; and I vowed then and there, foolish and childish dreamer that I was, that if ever it were in my power to rescue her from any sadness, any need or harsh distress, I would eagerly offer my very life toward that end.

Presently the lady's weeping subsided; and at length she passed Louis-Auguste over to the first divinity and lifted the second child, Louis-César, into her loving embrace. All this while, though still keeping her distance, the children's governess curtsied and smiled and nodded and simpered to the gentleman in a display of lightheartedness and effusion so uncharacteristic of her that I thought for a moment the woman had quite taken leave of her senses.

And now the beautiful lady drew forth a napkin from her bosom and proceeded, with great care and attention, to daub at Louis-César's bubbly lips.

The infant smiled.

"There's my little man," said she. "There he is indeed, indeed," she cooed to the babe in her arms, "yes, yes, indeed, my love," and such-like endearments as any mother would whisper to her child. "I am right happy to see you again, dear Louis-César," she went on, and now looking up at the other child: "And you too, my dearest Louis-Auguste, right happy indeed. And do you know," and her voice dropped to almost a whisper, "do you know who I am, little men? Do you know?" Suddenly, tears filled her eyes once more, for a note of infinite sadness had crept into her voice, and again my heart fairly burst with compassion for the heavenly woman's sorrow, understand it though I did not.

"There, there," I heard the gentleman murmur, "we must not go into it." And I saw his hand reach forth and gently touch the lady's shoulder. As for the two Louis, both gurgled and cooed as they basked in the sweetness of the loving lady's attentions.

At last (for I am only human, reader) I caught my breath: and let this be a cautionary tale to you. From the moment I had been transfixed by the radiance of the vision before me, I had completely neglected to breathe, dangerously depriving my body of air. My body being smaller than most, it requires less air and can go much longer without the intake of it; yet there does come a point, even so, when air is of the essence, and I must needs replenish my supply. And upon this occasion, as my inhalation was of a much longer duration than usual, I succeeded, with only one deep breath, in setting up a right lusty draught behind the drapery, which swept up particles of ash from out of the scuttle that flew directly into my nose; and to my misfortune this ashen intake at once provoked a series of wrenching sneezes as would have been the envy of any taker of snuff. Before I had recovered my wits, for they became as rattled as my nozzle itself, I felt a hand seize upon the collar of my shirt and I was borne swiftly from out of the room. Without seeing my captor, for my eyes were then streaming with tears, I succeeded nevertheless in sniffing her out between sneezes, and I recognized instantly the leek-like fragrance of my hostess and benefactress, Mme Françoise Scarron.

The moment we reached the outer hall: "If you cry out, sir, I shall brain you," said she; whereupon, in full view of the three gentlemen attendants and the footman, she boxed my ears some eight or nine times, setting off an array of sparks which flew about in my vision, and landing me several dark bruises about the head and shoulders which for some weeks after I had pains to conceal. But cry out I did not, reader, no, I did not, not in her presence, nor in the presence of those gentlemen, nor in that of the two smirking grooms as I limped past them, scuttle in hand, on my way to empty those same treacherous—nay, diabolical!— ashes which had been my downfall; and I felt that I understood that deprivation which Lucifer must have felt—though not his wrath nor his overweening thirst for revenge—but simply his deprivation, his un- utterable sense of loss at being cast forth from the presence of the God- head; that same deprivation in my own case in fact doubled, for I had been cast forth from the presence of two godheads, and one of them the magnificent woman whose sweet sadness I had so much pitied. And when finally I was by myself and quite out of anyone's sight, I wept into my handkerchief.

Reader: perpend. Despite what I have said above, I am not Lucifer, nor did I say that I was, no, nor nothing like. If for any reason you think that I am Lucifer, you are wrong; but you would needs close this book, for you would be reading abomination; for Lucifer is all-evil and all-cunning and would write in such a way as to make you believe that what you read was salubrious when it was not. No, no, it was in the nature of a literary conceit, my reference to the prince of darkness, reader, nothing more. For it frights me to meddle with such matters, especially when I am alone and so late at night. I should not have entered into it. Body of Christ, pro- tect my immortal soul (seven years' indulgence).

My mind was quite awhirl from that event: from the sheer magnifi- cence of the two divinities; and from the deeply held and seemingly maternal passions on the part of her whom I have called the second divin- ity. And although I had been instructed not to concern myself in any way with the babes, yet my curiosity was such that I was driven to approach

Mme Amélie that same afternoon—although very privately—and to beg her to tell me who the lady—and indeed the gentleman—were.

"Why, what a simpleton you are!" quoth she. "For that lady is right well known by everyone, and that for miles and miles around, and you do not know who she is? Fie! That lady's name, sir, is Françoise Athénaïs de Rochechouart-Mortemart, the Marquise de Montespan—she who is mistress to King Louis, yes, to that same gentleman you saw with her!" And she fell to laughing both at my ignorance and at the awe with which I received this news.

But though my ignorance may be accounted a fault, yet my awe must be accounted understandable, not to say praiseworthy, for indeed I had beheld what for most of my fellow countrymen must be no more than a distant, fantastical myth: the mistress to the king, indeed His divine mistress, for shall the divinity of a king be denied a reciprocal divinity in His choice of bedmate? I do not think it. And what was more, reader, what was even more breathtaking, I had also beheld, if all too briefly and yet with no less wonder, Him who must be esteemed the very pinnacle of divinity, Him whom I have likened to the god Apollo, indeed none other than Louis, the Fourteenth of that Name, Sovereign of the Most Royal Kingdom of France!

Louis!

Reader, even I—laboring among the steaming embers of the cookstoves, flinging out slops onto the piles behind the privy wall, shouting out indecipherable responses in a subterranean sanctuary—even I had heard of the name of Louis!

"Yes indeed, Monsieur Hugues, the king's own royal mistress," Mme Amélie chattered on, "and what, sir, do you make of that! Ha, ha, indeed you make of it whatever you will, sir. But I shall tell you, sir, what the two of them have made of it, and this is, to put it bluntly, sir, a couple of royal bastards is what they have made of it." My face must have betrayed my horror that such a rude word should be uttered in the context of those two divine beings. "Come, come, Monsieur Hugues, it is but only natural: the two of them did indeed combine, or conjoin, as you might say, to produce Louis-Auguste, and then some time later, Louis-César. And they have placed them, sir," madame babbled on, delighted to have a fresh pair of ears for her royal gossip, "they have privately placed them, I say, into the care of Scarron: for it would not do, now would it, sir, for two little bastards, royal or otherwise, to be running around at the king's own court, would you say?"

Reader, my brain was fairly reeling, as you may indeed imagine.

"Well, sir, that one," and she nodded in the direction of the main house, "and she's a right wily one, Monsieur Hugues, and make no mistake, sir— that one leapt at the chance, sir, to have them boys taken in here—they're a kind of foot in the door for her, don't you know—I mean with the muckety-mucks at court, a step or two up the ladder, so to speak, and not bad business for a widow without much to show for herself, wouldn't you say? A widow these ten years or so—and somewhat strapped for cash, too, sir, I can tell you: indeed, this traffic with the king came just in the nick, it did—so what if she don't tolerate the little ones? Never could, never had none of her own and never wanted none. No matter: if it sets her up with Himself—Monsieur Louis, I mean—to be minding His bastard pups for Him, she'll jump to it and gladly—for He's the real catch now, ain't He—Monsieur Louis Himself? And just between you, me, and the bedpost, sir, she'd as soon them pups think she's their real mum herself is what I say—getting her hooks in that much deeper, see? And what do the lads know, the innocent little buggers? Their mum! I've half a mind to tell 'em myself." And I believe she would have jabbered on the rest of the afternoon but that the stewpot suddenly boiled over and she dashed off to attend to it.

Throughout the rest of that afternoon, at my various chores, I thought long and hard about the extraordinary revelations that Mme Amélie had made to me.

Louis-Auguste—and Louis-César—now rose to a new and glorified status in my eyes, reader: for those two tiny creatures were the issue of those two divine beings, King Louis, Fourteenth of that Name, and the magnificent Marquise de Montespan!

Yet, on second thought, despite the divinity of both their parents, the two creatures were indeed their illegitimate issue, and this last was a point perversely much in their favor insofar as I personally was con-cerned, misery loving company as it does, for it meant that these two boys must endure the same unsanctioned conditions in the world as I and the same unsanctified conditions in the next; and like me, they ought not hope for otherwise. And their new status slipped downward by a notch or two.

These realizations led me to yet another: that Mme Françoise Scarron, despite the asperity of her nature and the delicacy of her situation, must have been of greater social prominence than even her Tuesday soirées betokened; for although there had been no cordiality between her and the two divine visitors, yet the lady, being charged with the care of the infants, must have had some credentials and enjoyed some station; and Mme Amélie's supposition seemed altogether reasonable that Scarron was now out to improve upon that station and by way of the infants themselves. Similarly some ranking was due, if only within the servant order, to that same Mme Amélie, whose teats, several times daily, suckled what may have been questionably royal lips, being bastard lips, but lips, even so, not altogether to be dismissed.

Ah, but reader, even so: though I did not dismiss them, let me assure you that those four boyish lips would never come—could never come—to fill my thoughts and dreams, both day and night, as indeed the two lips of their mother now began to do. Her lips, reader, and her eyes, her forehead, her hair; her carriage and bearing; her elegance, her graciousness, her radiance, her supremacy: her divinity.

But I shall get on with it.

In the light of these wondrous new revelations, it seemed to me that another, closer look at the two boys might now prove worth the effort; and thus, later that same night, I stole once more from my aerie down to the nursery. I took no leeks with me, for torment was not in my mind.

Two cribs now stood side by side in the flickering light of two candles. In the new one lay Louis-César, quite fast asleep; in the other sat Louis-Auguste, up against the pillows as usual, in his nightly sleepless vigil. A hint of recognition passed across his features when he spied me and then one of apprehension at the sight of his old tormentor; but quickly I gestured that I held no leeks in my hand, and he began to breathe more quietly.

I had never spoken to the boy and had nothing in my head to say to him at this moment; but thinking back to those many times that I had teased the creature, and sometimes unmercifully, nourishing in him that aversion to his putative mother; and aware now of his true and partially royal parentage, I felt some remorse for my cruelties, whether they were mere childish pranks or not. And I thought that if I could now somehow entertain this most solemn of lads, it might be a way of offering him some minor compensation for those cruelties.

Looking about the room I found, in a corner, a box of toys; within, there were the usual rattles and hoops, bean bags, stuffed animals, and blocks, and among them several India rubber balls. Two of these I picked out; and carefully I stuffed them up under my shirt in such a way as to resemble a woman's breasts; and these two balls being of an ample size, my two new breasts were quite impressive. Next, in the bottom of a dresser, I found a length of black cloth, I know not what it was, which I wrapped around my own clothing to simulate widow's weeds; and on top of my head I set a dark-hued bean bag to make believe a cap. With this outfit on, I quietly strode back to Louis-Auguste's crib, imitating as best I could Mme Scarron's somewhat weighty manner of walking. Back and forth I paraded before the boy a while; until I saw that rather than being amused by this impersonation of his dark and bosomy mistress, he was instead quite terrified; and he pulled the covers up to just below his ears.

Quickly I left off my pantomime and took a closer look at those ears; or rather at the left ear; and I saw, reader, how quite black and blue the poor thing was. The remorse which I had felt earlier but doubled, for I knew that I had contributed, both directly and indirectly, to that sad discoloration.

As I stood staring at the frightened child, a sudden notion struck me; and directly I set about rearranging my garments and undergarments as both the children and I had witnessed Scarron do, with tugs and twists, lifts and unsnarlings; and it was not until then, in the course of my ama-teurish performance for him, that I saw a slight smile appear upon his tiny lips. This positive reaction from my audience only spurred me onward, as it will any actor, and I began jerking, poking, prodding, thrusting, punch-ing, and jostling quite shamelessly about my person and all my clothing, until at length, the tiny smile became a grin, the grin became a giggle, that giggle a guffaw, and that guffaw a peal of laughter so loud and so un-characteristic of him that I feared it might summon the nurse.

Abruptly I left off my comic foolishness; and still striding in an imita-tion of Scarron's gait, I drew up to the boy's battered ear and whispered, in a deep, stern voice:

"Louis-Auguste, perpend: I am not your real mother."

Just as abruptly, he left off his laughter and stared up into my eyes with utter wonderment at the words he had just heard spoken; for by then, he had acquired a rudimentary comprehension of speech. I dared not believe what I had done; but done it was, that deed, and I indeed had done it; and now, seizing upon that moment of understanding between us before it should flicker away and die, I quickly cast off cap, weeds, and bosoms, snatched up a white lace runner from off the dresser, tossed it about my head and shoulders in the manner of Madame de Montespan's wrap, and approached the boy once more in what I hoped was the most feminine, delicate—dare I say "divine"?—movement that I could muster. Lightening my voice as best I could, and it was not difficult for it had not yet changed, I spoke again into his ear and said, right softly and gently:

"Dearest Louis-Auguste: it is I—*I* am your loving mother."

At first a look of amazement broke over his features; then slowly and solemnly, with an expression of utter serenity upon his face, he lifted his two arms and clapped his tiny hands together four, five, or six times. Upon which, a large tear rolled down his left cheek; and then another down his right; and then a third and a fourth, but yet with no sound from his mouth, no, not a sound of any sort. Louis-Auguste's silent tears fell, and copiously; but whether they were of joy or of infinite sorrow, I shall never know.

# 6

I REPORT THE FOLLOWING AS ABRUPTLY AS IT HAPPENED. Mme Scarron's entire household, almost overnight, moved out of the estate at Vaugirard—the mistress, the two children, the various maids, nurses, footmen, and myself—but not the surly grooms—to the royal town of St. Germain-en-Laye, where stands one of my lord Louis's most principal residences, a chateau built in 1539 by François I.

And reader, to my great wonderment, it was not only to the royal town that we moved but into that most principal—and indeed most royal—chateau itself!

And when eventually I managed to ferret out the fact—for I was informed of nothing in a straightforward manner but had always to ferret out information—the information, I say, that this same chateau was where the two divinities themselves resided and that we should all now be living under the one same roof with them, my heart fairly leapt for joy, not only at my own good fortune but at that of the two royal bastards, who would now be at least within howling distance of their own dearest mother; and I rejoiced yet again at the pleasure that such proximity would furnish her with.

Yet such are those devilish first impressions that they often turn out to be misleading, and I ought truly to have realized that Mme Scarron, as the children's official guardian, would, even in these new circumstances, allow them as little access to their parents as she could possibly contrive: for that lady, true to her ways, assumed a new degree of hauteur in this entrée to the royal court, and her possessiveness toward Louis-Auguste and Louis-César likewise assumed new heights, for was this not that further step up the social ladder which she had sought—indeed several further steps—and had those same two boys not been the very means to it? And furthermore, since the condition under which the boys lived, I mean that of bastardy, imposed a less than public acknowledgement of them by their mother, Mme Scarron held sway, and my hopes for the divinity's new happiness were dashed.

As for Mme Scarron's followers, I mean her weekly soirée set, they were now invited every Tuesday evening to her private apartment in the chateau, and it seemed not to occur to them that their excellent new fortunes were attributable directly to Scarron herself, as hers were directly to the two infants; which is to say that their fortunes were vicarious at best and likely to be tenuous. For all, even the few commoners amongst them, conducted themselves in these more sumptuous surroundings like newly beplumed peacocks, with all the same vanity and all the same cruelty which those vile beasts are wont to exhibit; and they began vying more than ever with one another with lavish displays of their feathers and with kicking sand at each other and with biting at each other's throats.

On the other hand, Louis-Auguste, Louis-César as well as Louise-Françoise, their sister, a newcomer who had arrived but lately on the scene, comported themselves in their recently enhanced living quarters with none of the arrogance of Mme Scarron and her entourage. To my great surprise, all three children, with a combined age of five, seemed even quite oblivious to the move, Louis-Auguste having now become so preoccupied with his misshapen limb and so discontent at the misappropriation of his mother as not to give two figs for where he lived, but then he was only three years old and artless; and Louis-César, at the age of two, and Louise-Françoise, an infant, quite uncomprehending of anything. There would be ample time for all of them to learn the proper ways of arrogance.

As for myself, it would be natural for you to assume that upon removal from a window seat in the topmost floor of a somewhat country house to the royal residence at St. Germain-en-Laye, famous as the birthplace of the kings of France, an eleven (or twelve)-year-old would have instantly become quite swell-headed. But by and large I did not. Yet I will not conceal from you—for truth is to be served—my awareness of my good fortune in this removal. Here again had fallen to me one of those boons, not of my own doing, but of which, even so, I might take excellent advantage; and I think you must agree with me that a dwarf employed at the royal court of France had not a little advanced beyond that same creature toiling away in a pitiful village outside Paris, even if his new assignments continued to be in kitchens, pump rooms, and chimney places; and as well, that his opportunities for advancement were much enhanced.

In all honesty, however, this report about myself must admit of one exception, an event from which I suffered a harsh lesson and learned exceeding much. And it was this:

I was most grateful that Mme Amélie continued on at St. Germain in her service to Mme Scarron and her teats in service to the Louis, for I had become right fond of the woman and she, of all the people in that set, had always treated with me fairly and honestly; and I would even dare to say that she returned some small affection for me but that I do not like to presume. Several months after our arrival at the chateau I saw one morning that madame was wearing a brand new outfit: it was dress appropriate to her servile station, both modest and sober, but yet it impressed me that she had apparently felt some compunction to acknowledge her new and more splendid surroundings and, as it were, to show respect for them in her own attire. She told me that having put aside some money, she had engaged the services of a dressmaker in the town a few weeks earlier, who had only the day previous delivered the finished dress to the chateau.

This act inspired in my own mind a sense of obligation to the new surround; and since I too had now been able to put aside some savings from my employment at the card tables, I approached the lady later that day and addressed her:

"Mme Amélie," quoth I, "I would be obliged to you if you would direct me to your tailor, whose services I wish to engage."

"Lud, sir," she replied, "and what's got into your noggin now, Monsieur Hugues? Them things you've got on is right suitable, sir, I think; and anyways, no tailor works for nothing, 'specially the ones in this town don't."

"Madame, I am aware of that; but I have now some income and am ready to meet the going rate."

Mme Amélie was quite surprised at this, for she knew nothing of my evening employment.

"So!" said she, laughing the whiles, "and pray, how much have you got there?"

"Madame, all told, it comes to one *louis d'or* and seventy *centimes*."

"Do you say so! Well, you're a right enterprising bugger, ain't you now! But sir: that's nowheres near enough for a tailor's wages. Maybe you could buy some stockings with that *louis* and a handky with them *centimes!*" She fell to laughing again at my innocence; but yet when she saw how crestfallen I was at this unhappy news, she chucked me under the chin and said, "Now, now, now; cheer up there! Tell you what, Monsieur Hugues, you go with me to market next time; I know a fellow's got some old clothes for sale—we'll see what he can do for you."

Now old clothes were not exactly what I had in mind, reader, for there was nothing old about the display of outfits which I saw all around me, and that included even what the lackeys and grooms wore thereabouts. Yet I saw no way around it, and I thanked Mme Amélie for her kindness.

A week later came market day, and we set out. Reader, it was the first time in my life that I had beheld so fine a city as St. Germain-en-Laye! Just across the road from the gates of the chateau stands an imposing church and from it there radiates a bewildering array of streets and byways—I counted as many as six—all lined with magnificent dwellings, some towering as high as four stories. Mme Amélie had to hasten me along, for I gawked unashamedly at the richness of the buildings and at the teeming traffic in all the roads, people of all descriptions coming and going, carts, wagons, sedan-chairs, and carriages, dogs, chickens, and pigs all swarming about hither and thither and crowding into the lanes. At length we arrived at the marketplace, a majestic square in the center of the metropolis lined on all four sides with tall houses—as many as seven or eight on each side—and overrun with a vast open-air market, where truly I believe you must be able to purchase every conceivable article of merchandise in all of Christendom.

Madame went about her several errands and I tagging along behind, ignoring the taunts of several dirty street urchins who I think can never have seen a dwarf before in their wretched ignorance, and staring all about me at the wonders of a city most surely in its grandeur befitting that most illustrious of its many inhabitants, I mean our Sovereign Highness, King Louis, Fourteenth of that Majestic Name!

But finally madame led me to a stall near the very center of the square, where bundles of clothing hung on hooks and lines or lay piled up in boxes and chests and some even on the bare ground. I confess, the sheer quantity of goods was overwhelming—there were doublets and shirts in stacks, heaps of breeches and vests, and stuffed in among them all, collars, shoes, stockings, and hats wherever my eyes fell.

"That fellow is an Israelite," madame informed me, pointing to a man with a long dark coat, a wide dark beard, and a flat dark hat who was in charge of the stall, "but that is no matter. Look around—it's all second-hand, and some of it ain't too dear."

Reader, I began to search about, holding various pieces of clothing up to judge of their size in relation to my own: everything seemed musty and mildewed, not to say patched, shabby, and very well worn. My heart sank: this was not what I wished to spend my hard-earned savings upon.

But as luck would have it and after a lengthy and determined if somewhat dusty search, I happened upon a woolen doublet, of a bright purple color, adorned with embroidered gold stitching down the front and along the pockets, and lined in red taffeta; the lining was shredded in places but the doublet itself did not seem overly worn, and the brightness of the colors, I thought, surely belied its age and former usage. Throwing off my own jacket, I slid my arms into the sleeves; quickly I felt the smooth lining against my back and the firm weight of the coat upon my shoulders; the colors dazzled my eyes; the embroidery felt rich as I ran my fingers over it; and even the fragrance of the material was exquisite!

"This one," I said, turning to the Israelite.

But before he could reply:

"No, no, no, Monsieur Hugues!" exclaimed Mme Amélie. "Too gaudy by half, sir! Why, you look like some kind of a carnival there! And then it's way too long—look back there where it hits your leg."

I could feel the hem against the middle of my calf, it is true; but when the Israelite hastened to point out that it was quite the fashion that season to wear one's doublet somewhat long, my mind was again resolved upon it.

Next he slipped a baldric over my head and fastened it to the right shoulder of the doublet: the sash fell across my chest and on down to my left knee. It was sumptuous, all covered in gold braid and with a fine big knot at the bottom and below, a tuft of shiny fringe.

"Lud, sir!" cried madame, speaking I knew not at first whether to me or the merchant. "Why, now you're making a downright spectacle of yourself, so you are! And no bones about it!"

But reader, I knew that the doublet and baldric were magnificent and was certain that I looked magnificent in them, and I glanced back at madame's sober dress and decided that in fact, as kindly as she was and as generous and thoughtful, the woman clearly had no taste.

I informed the proprietor that I had exactly one *louis d'or* and seventy *centimes* to spend and that I would not offer him a *sou* more; whereupon he said that the cost of the two pieces was in fact some forty *centimes* above that sum, but that because the clothes became me so perfectly and because he was eager to oblige so exceptional a lad as I, he would consent to settle at the lower figure.

"Excellent!" I exclaimed, slipping off the clothes so that he could fold them into a bundle. I would simply forego buying breeches and a shirt for the present.

Reader, when I reached into my pocket and withdrew my one *louis d'or* and my seventy *centimes* and handed them over to that most worthy gentleman and in return clasped the bundle into my own two arms, my heart leapt with the sheer joy of the purchase, and my face broke into a flush, and my head was fairly spinning! And I thought how truly estimable these Israelites can be! and what excellent good bargains the clever buyer can strike with them! and how invaluable their commerce is to our society!

That very evening, reader, as it befell, was a Tuesday, and my services were called upon as usual to distribute flan. Carefully I unfolded my new doublet, noticing as I did that there were some stains under the arms which I had overlooked in the hustle and bustle of the marketplace; but after some study I was certain that they would hardly show. I put the doublet on. I adjusted my shirt and collar. Next I attached the baldric. The fringe at the bottom, I noticed, dragged a bit along the floor; but less so if I held my right shoulder upward. I smoothed my hair down with a bit of spit and fought for a while with my cowlick. I brushed off my shoes. I set out to collect the flan.

My heart was thumping.

Gasps of surprise from the maids and butlers greeted me as I entered the kitchen building. It was only natural, thought I to myself, that these servants should be impressed by my change in appearance, to say nothing of the magnificence of my fashionably long doublet and baldric. The several giggles and the one or two guffaws that followed that first reaction came from the lower orders, I noticed, scullery maids and such, who could not be expected to have any sense of these matters. Taking up the tray of flan, I sailed away, back over into the chateau, up the stairs, and down the hallway toward the salon where Mme Scarron's guests were gathered.

I felt my heart thumping faster as I approached, my throat was dry, and once or twice I caught the end of the baldric under my left foot. Yet I pressed onward, reached the doorway, gripped the tray anew, swallowed hard, thrust my right shoulder upward, and entered the room.

Reader, to my amazement, I met, as I had met some four years earlier that first Tuesday evening in the drawing room at Vaugirard, an instant explosion of glee: the first people who saw me cross the threshold fell into gales of mirth, attracting those nearby to turn and look, whereupon they too began hooting with laughter and attracting still others, until in very short order, the entire room was shaking with hilarity, everyone pointing their fingers at me, holding their sides or slapping their hands on the tables, their eyes streaming, their wigs slipping awry, and the cards flying up from out of their hands. "Monsieur Hugues! Monsieur Hugues!" they shouted through their laughter. "What a fine doublet you have on, sir, ha ha ha! So bright and so purple! And the trim, dear God, look at the trim! And see! see how majestically the fringe simply trails along behind on the floor! Ha ha ha!" and such-like cruel and sarcastical remarks. By now the thumping of my heart had become a raucous pounding, my face was flushed as red as the shredded lining of my doublet, and I found that I could scarcely see for the stinging wall of tears that filled my eyes. In fact, I could not see, not well enough to go about my task, and having served one table with flan, as I moved to the second, I tripped on the fringe from the baldric and fell, and the cups of flan went crashing to the floor and sliding this way and that all about the room. Whereupon yet another wave of mirth erupted throughout the company.

Reader, once I had fought my way through the confusion of my tears and of the crowded salon and had recovered all the scattered cups of flan, I flew back to the kitchen and deposited the custard as quickly as I could; but not so quickly, alas, that I was not compelled to endure yet more uproarious laughter, and now from the entire kitchen staff, who saw clearly my humiliation and enjoyed freely and to the full my awful distress. Next, I raced to the brush closet where I kept my things and instantly changed back to my old clothes. And to my only clothes, I must add, for I vowed never again to don that doublet and baldric; and later that night I crept back to the brush closet, gathered up my new purchases, carried them down to the riverbank, and threw them in.

I believe, reader, that I may honestly state that not one other time have I presumed to put on airs in such a shameful fashion and that I learned a bitter lesson about the ways of seeking to better oneself in this world: for we must be aware of our proper station in society and may take measures to advance ourselves only in ways that are appropriate to that station. And in my eagerness or innocence or arrogance or I know not what youthful flaw, I had not heeded that unshakable principle of life.

Indeed, had I ever again even been tempted to assume airs that were not becoming, I was constantly reminded of my proper humility by an unavoidable aspect of life at the court of St. Germain, to wit, the presence of His Majesty's hunting dogs, being, as I was, roughly their size and operating—but less roughly than they—on their level. These creatures, which were great favorites of the king's, had the run of the palace despite an inordinate lack of house training—and they dropped great turds all about the place, which was fine and well for those who lived several more feet above grade than I. The beasts took full advantage of an ingenious system which the king had had installed, whereby hinged panels were fitted into the lower parts of all the doors, designed to align unobtrusively with the existing moldings, so that by pushing through the panels, the dogs could make their way from any room in the place to any other room. Since they tended to move about in tight packs, it was not an uncommon sight for the lower part of an imposing and stately door suddenly to burst open, as though it had flung up its skirts, and release a galloping, slobbering, yelping explosion of hounds.

Need I point out that I did not run with these hounds, reader; though more often than not I did try to run well ahead of them, but with varying results. The royal dogs were kept on the verge of starvation; as such, by sheer neglect, the godforsaken creatures at the monastery had been, those dogs which had at times tried to make a light supper of me until I learned to fend them off with smoldering coals from the grates. But the dogs of St. Germain were kept hungry by design, for they were hunters, and a somewhat edgy condition for them was desirable; and it was just that degree of edge, coupled with their natural viciousness and exacerbated by the additional irritation that they themselves were constantly being munched upon by similarly hungry fleas that provoked the animals to pursue, wherever they could, smaller game such as foxes, hares, pheasants, and, in my case, dwarves. (By contrast, I now looked upon Mme de St. Estève's overfed hounds as positively companionable.) And so, preferring not to be cornered and shredded asunder, I found that it behooved me to make use myself of their own device, to wit, the hinged door panels, which furnished me a greater freedom of movement during a chase; though clearly they too leapt through the panels as nimbly as I. But to my advantage was this fact: the irregularly shaped rooms at St. Germain (I speak now of the old chateau) and the paucity of natural light in them had led to the installation of a number of mirrors about the place. The dogs, being too stupid to understand the reflective properties of mirrors, could often be tricked into chasing a mere image of myself on one side of a room whilst I, corporeally on the opposite, stole my way to safety through a hinged panel, the dogs then setting up a howl at the mysterious disappearance of their quarry; and in frustration and revenge and I know not what other canine emotions, they would then make copious water upon whatever mirror had consumed their prey, or perform other, more hideous acts in the area.

But this ruse was not always successful and I fought for my very life with one or more of them on many an occasion, providing idlers nearby with something of an impromptu sporting event: "Twenty *écus* on the beast!" I might hear as I was wrestling with a foxhound. "On which beast?" "Why, upon the dwarf, of course!" "No, no, I raise you: thirty-five on the hound!" and so on.

That carefree gambler could not have known, I think, the pain he caused me by referring to me as a beast: all of this is by way of revealing that any elevation in status which I might have conceived for myself in the removal from the commonplace world of Vaugirard to the wealth and public animation of the chateau at St. Germain-en-Laye was well tempered by the constant humiliations which I endured, as you have now seen.

That wealth and public animation which I now discovered about me were indeed breathtaking, though I witnessed not even the half of it:

every day there were ambassadors and delegations streaming through the halls and from every imaginable land: here came Turks, giants top-heavy with bejeweled turbans, noisy, brawling, spitting, and with long hooked noses and flaring nostrils, swarthy and hairy, smelling of tallow, with droves of red monkeys in tow, leashed on silver chains, chattering and spitting as much as ever their masters did; or squinting Chinese, borne aloft on lacquered palanquins, holding silken handkerchiefs up to their yellow noses against the odors which emanated, or so they maintained, from the flesh of Europeans, whilst the towering umbrellas paraded above their heads kept crashing into the doorways; or half-naked Indians bedizened in feathers and gold, from the opposite side of the globe, from the territories of the Guyane, from Peru, and the farthest Antilles. (It is there where exist those creatures which I have mentioned earlier which are huge and have heads and arms and hands, legs and feet, all like men, but no bodies whatsoever: and they are the anthropophagi; they eat human flesh, and although that human flesh then becomes their own flesh, yet they themselves are no more human than before; and this information about them is true, for I have made a study of it.)

Here I found, of an evening, not one drawing room of gaming tables but an entire series of such rooms, some in the north galleries which formed the apartment where lived King Louis Himself with His son, a somewhat bulbous youth about a year my junior, himself a Louis, the heir apparent and known as Monseigneur the Dauphin; and in the east galleries, several more intimate rooms where the queen's apartment was located. (For, reader, there was indeed, I soon discovered, a queen of France, a childish and gluttonous middle-aged Spanish woman, Marie-Thérèse, the so-called Infanta, whose French was execrable and whose personal share in the divinity that I had come to associate with royalty was nowhere in evidence; for whether it was due to the considerable weight which she had accumulated over the years or to a certain cultural deprivation she had suffered in her youth, she was given to a great deal of noisy farting; and hawking, sneezing, and the prodigious blowing of her nose, and various other exhalations; all of which, according to the physicians, could easily have been cured with a few good bleedings; but she would have none of it; and I believe, in the end, that those respiratory and digestive activities might have been an attempt by her to have someone pay her some heed, for she was much overlooked.)

At the gaming tables, almost every evening, there assembled those members of the court who were consumed by a passion either for gambling or for being seen, which is to say absolutely everyone; and enormous sums—nay, estates, dukedoms, and entire fortunes—were lost and won with the flip of an ace or the toss of a die, the stakes here being considerably heightened above those in the drawing room at Vaugirard. Once Mme Scarron was well ensconced along with her contingent of cardsters, I was happy to learn that my offices to them beneath the tables could continue and even thrive, for indeed, with the new stakes, my list of clientele now expanded well beyond the likes of Mlle Louise-Adélaïde Marsy, Mme Poulaillon, the Archbishop of Lisieux, the Marquis de Feuquières, and others.

The Comtesse de Pommeret came to be invariably paired at cards with the queen herself, they both being unutterably stupid at anything more complex than solitaire; and people clamored to play hands opposite them, which flattered their vanities as readily as it emptied their purses. Beyond her inability at cards, rivaled only by her inability at speaking French, the queen had, which is strange, a curious predilection for dwarves; and had collected some five or six of them about her, all of them exceedingly ugly; and she cast an eye upon me, reader, I can tell you, and that more than once. Not caring to appeal for protection to my mistress, who had shown me so little partiality up to that time, and fearing that I would be swept up into her majesty's hideous entourage and subjected to attentions from her, I knew not what desperate course to take. But for the nonce I was spared; and I pray that it not appear vanity that leads me to speculate that I was simply not ugly enough to suit her wretched taste, and so was spared.

Day and night, through the halls of the royal residence, I also witnessed swarms of the general public who were, surprisingly enough, allowed to amble about, observing the comings and goings of the court. Eventually I came to avoid these creatures as much as possible, for I found that they were frequently of the lower classes, and many of them with diseases; and it was said that there were pickpockets amongst them, a consideration which meant little to me, for my pockets being situated so much lower than the artful fingers of your average thief, I felt no threat, and my pockets were empty to boot, except for my handkerchief. Here as well, and aloof from the riffraff, were bevies of princes and princesses, dukes and duchesses, counts and countesses that made up that teeming court of the divine monarch, each of them constantly jostling to be seen by all of the similarly jostling others, but most especially by my lord King Louis Himself and by the second divinity, the most glorious Marquise de Montespan, who were themselves to be seen, though quite unpredictably, about the chateau. Here were elaborate formal balls and fêtes, banquets and divertissements, attended by this restless pack; and these events went late into the night; but alas, I can report but little of them to you, reader, for I was not allowed to be present. For if there were any need of a dwarf or dwarves upon such occasions for the purpose of entertainment for the company, it was the queen's own set which was sent for, the sight of them being even more ludicrous than of myself, as I have noted.

Here I discovered as well were conducted the daily workings of the government itself, the French nation being singularly blessed to have at its head my lord King Louis XIV, to wit, God; which is why in all ways France has far exceeded other nations, none other having at its head of state God; for in this world there can be no other than one, unique God; the matter is self-evident. But many lands—Holland, Spain, the Papal States, Savoy, the Holy Roman Empire—were blind to this, it seems, and fought or sought to fight wars with France; and any blockhead would know that that was a losing proposition: God will easily prevail, and so He did. Yet even so, weighty deliberations were the order of the day in the conduct of the government, and although I never attended any of them, needless to say, yet I would glimpse various impressive officials now and then on their way to and from the Royal Cabinet Chamber, and the doors to that chamber being customarily left open during the meetings, which was an indication of the king's largesse, the public were allowed to stand off at a distance in the adjoining room and to watch the proceedings though it was almost impossible to hear them. As for myself I had not the leisure.

These men, I learned, were busying themselves with many matters, primary amongst them the annihilation of as many enemies of the king as possible, and especially of the Spanish and the Dutch; and secondary, the supervision of divers building projects which were undertaken to display to the world the grandeur of the French throne, reflecting the grandeur of God: among them, the expansion of a small hunting lodge which had been a favorite of King Louis's father, Louis XIII, in the town of Versailles some twenty miles to the south. The court made increasingly frequent visits to that lodge until at last St. Germain was abandoned (1682) in its favor; and reader, it is where I am at this present writing, at Versailles, and I am high up inside the ceiling of the chapel vestibule, and through the slits of my louver I have a partial view of the gardens below, a series of elaborate flowerbeds, fountains and groves, pathways and promenades, laid out by a certain Monsieur Le Nôtre.

But to resume: on Fridays, my lord King Louis met with His confessor in the morning and later in the day with the ecclesiastic Jacques Bénigne Bossuet, who had undertaken the education of my lord's son the dauphin; in addition to giving His Majesty spiritual counsel at these Friday meetings, Bishop Bossuet also reported to Him what progress the young man was making at his books. But it was rumored that that progress was somewhat slow, the dauphin being a reluctant scholar, even despite a daily round of sharp blows administered by the bishop.

Here I found that almost every afternoon there were noisy preparations for the hunt, the king, and those like Him who were devoted to the sport, mounting their steeds to ride off into the forest. I tried to avoid these scenes, for the dogs, anticipating the exuberance of the chase and, more to the point, of the kill, would by then have whipped themselves into a slathering frenzy, their teeth bared, their ice-cold eyes full of malice. No: I stayed away; and having no duties to perform for those preparations, it was not difficult.

Here, finally, reader, were musicians. And I recall my first impression of them, that these men appeared to be huge; indeed, much larger than the Turks I have told you of and the Indians, larger than the government officials, larger even than the Archbishop of Lisieux; but not of course larger than God. But it was perhaps my imagination and wonderment at them that fixed that impression of grandeur into my brain. Whenever His Majesty dined or whenever He called for entertainment, which was most frequent for it turned out that He was devoted to music, here came forth these giant men with their flutes, violins, violes da gamba, lutes, and oboes, with their bassoons and cellos and their harpsichords; and they would set themselves off into a thick cluster at one end of a chamber; whereupon they would begin applying themselves to their instruments, striking them, or blowing into them, or plucking at them, or sawing at them with strips of wood and gut; and they would do so all together, all at once as it were, each adhering to the speed and rhythms of all the others though himself playing a different melody; and it was frightening, reader, for the brilliant roar which they set up! and the room would grow quite full of it, some of the sounds being shrill and reedlike, but the others! the others were deep and quaking and thunderous; and as they all played simultaneously, which was the wonder of it, the pitch became magnified, and the dark, ripe vibrations resonated throughout the entire place with such beauty and splendor, with such sublimity, that I feared—nay, I was certain—that they had put devils inside their instruments, for I doubted any human beings upon this earth capable of such effects. And so I kept my distance; and indeed I am certain that upon more than one occasion, far across the room, I spied, from within the crescent-shaped sound hole of a double-bass viol, a pair of eyes looking out at me; and I would run away or hide behind some fringe or tassel, trembling.

Now you should know that these activities which I have described were often interrupted, for my lord King Louis was much given to traveling from one royal residence to another, there being four or five in the area; and whenever He went, the daily routines ceased abruptly, and the entire court went with Him; and a great deal of time was then spent packing, transporting, and unpacking the needs of the court. Athénaïs, the Marquise de Montespan, the divine, accompanied Him on these sojourns, being in constant attendance upon Him; and the queen would travel with Him as well; and occasionally even the children, Louis-Auguste, Louis-César, and the infant Louise-Françoise would be taken along as though for the ride, in which case their governess Scarron would accompany her brood.

A more delicate situation would arise when King Louis's travels took Him off to war, out to the front lines, most often in the Flanders region. It would seem a straightforward enough matter that on such excursions the king would be attended by the appropriate military personnel and such civilians as He would require at the battle area; and so it was. But as well, there developed a custom of inviting along certain ladies to join His Majesty on these expeditions. The queen Marie-Thérèse would be routinely included, even though as often as not our forces were engaged in slaughtering as many of her Spanish compatriots as they could set hands to; but it was no matter, for it was unlikely that she understood anything of what was going on outside her carriage in the first place.

Increasingly, though she had not yet achieved any official capacity at the court, Athénaïs, the divine marquise, would, again, be in attendance to my lord King Louis, though indeed her presence cannot have much pleased the queen. And as well, there was a number of other ladies, as it turned out, who, being in some favor with His Highness at one time or another, for my lord did indeed like the ladies, would or would not be enrolled on the invited list, their inclusion being an indication of the state of their favor, and similarly their exclusion, whether that favor had not yet attained full bloom or had decidedly gone to seed; and I cannot think that their presences can have much pleased either the Marquise de Montespan or the queen. (One such was a lady named Louise de la Vallière, of whom you will hear more later.) And thus there was often some controversy and squabbling surrounding the trips to the troops, which my lord, in His infinite wisdom, would invariably arbitrate with evenhanded justice, if not always to everyone's complete satisfaction.

I was privileged to witness one such adjudication by my lord from the hallway adjoining the Cabinet Chamber, where a gathering of family and dignitaries had taken place shortly before a royal excursion to the city of Ghent. It was not itself an official government meeting—as would have been routinely observable by the public from afar—but had emerged from a previous such meeting and hence, perhaps not by design, the cabinet doors had been left open. At issue on this occasion were not the ladies, for the queen, Montespan, Vallière, and a saucy young thing, a certain Mlle Le Borgne, had been assembled to make the trip; but rather the issue was the three children, all present as well in the chamber, Louis-Auguste, Louis-César, and Louise-Françoise, all crawling around in the middle of the floor to the obvious discomfort of their governess. And the wisdom of taking three babes off to the front lines was much debated, the military representatives there and Scarron all speaking strongly against it, while Montespan saw it as an agreeable outing and an educational opportunity, especially for the boys.

It was difficult from the distance at which I stood to distinguish clearly everything that was said in the chamber, and I inched forward to stand behind a large urn so that I might overhear the deliberations (I shall not say "spy upon," though you may draw what conclusions you care to); and now the powerful voice of the Duc de Luxembourg reached me easily enough:

"Our rear guard units can ensure only minimal security on or near the battle lines; Captain Oizel feels that it is less than responsible to risk the lives of the—ah—little ones"—and he did not like to state exactly whose little ones he was speaking of—"of the children, I say, in areas adjacent to the fury of the hostilities. With all respect."

"¿Por qué los niños querrían mirar una batalla tediosa?" asked the queen, but no one understood her and no one replied. Mme Scarron, however, seized upon the duke's observation.

"Sir," said she to that gentleman, "I thoroughly concur with the excellent Captain Oizel's assessment. It is altogether more fitting that the children stay here with me. Moreover, they can have no interest in battles and warfare and such-like affairs."

At which point, Louis-Auguste struck Louis-César a sharp blow to the stomach.

"And is your excellent Captain Oizel oblivious then to exposing the lives of the ladies to risk?" now spoke the divine Marquise de Montespan. "There's no earthly good in going to the front if we aren't to be close enough to enjoy the mayhem."

"Indeed, the ladies may expose themselves to risk quite freely, madame," Luxembourg replied with a curt bow in her direction, "and in full knowledge of the dangers. These children, however, can make no such judgments."

"Indeed, commander," replied the marquise, "just so: it is the duty of parents to make judgments *for* their children—one does it every day, sir."

"I should say," interjected Mme Scarron, now holding the two Louis at bay, "that it is the duty of parents to make *prudent* judgments for their children." She stared smugly at the marquise.

"Tosh! I have been to the front," retorted the divinity. "It is as safe as sitting in a drawing room with friends."

"Which is not in fact altogether a safe thing to do," snapped Scarron.

The marquise smiled: "I spoke, my dear Scarron, from my own experience."

But the governess chose rather to ignore this remark than to allow the conversation to veer thus off course. "Children of four years old—of two—will gain nothing from being carted off into battle and can indeed only be an encumbrance to any responsible military command."

"I take madame's point entirely," Luxembourg now spoke up again, seeking to end the debate. "The babes must not be exposed needlessly to danger."

And now, my lord King Louis—divine presence, radiant power, illustrious majesty, seated in the far rear of the chamber—at last, my lord spoke out, for He had up to that point engaged in none of the debate; and He said:

"Children," at which all three babes—Louise-Françoise, infant, included—left off attacking one another and gave instant ear, "you shall keep with your mother."

At that—and although at the king's command Scarron had bent forward to take the children's hands—Louis-Auguste rose on his unsteady three-year-old feet and without a moment's hesitation, hobbled his way across the length of the chamber to where the Marquise de Montespan stood; and he reached out and clutched at her skirts; and Louis-César immediately followed suit; and even Louise-Françoise began rolling forward in the same general direction.

Excellent well done, Louis-Auguste—yet again! thought I from my post behind the urn. I have taught you well, my lad. And well have you learned.

The marquise's face was wreathed in happy smiles, and yet tears filled her beautiful eyes as she lifted Louis-Auguste up into her arms and kissed him gently on his cheeks; nor was that lady unaware as she did so, of the buzz that swept through the assembly at Louis-Auguste's innocent act of honesty. In the middle of the room, for the first time that I could recall, Mme Françoise Scarron now lived up to her famous nickname, that of "Indian princess," for that lady's face, contorted into a tight scowl, became as scarlet red as any Indian's you may imagine!

And thus, reader, by a child's simple gesture, the truth—already well known to everyone there—had at last been publicly and incontrovertibly stated, and the divine marquise's love for her own dear children most movingly and openly expressed.

They accompanied their mother to Ghent and returned, in a fortnight, unscathed.

Reader: given the exalted status of the persons within that gathering— and I include the three half-regal infants crawling about on the floor— I did not think it seemly at that moment to take any pleasure, even privately within my own breast, at the thought that I, Hugues, humble servant, had played a hand, however modest, however slight, however unacknowledged, in the affairs of the royal state of France; even when that hand was for the benefit of the divine marquise and at the expense of the conniving Scarron. Nor to this day do I think it seemly to take any such pleasure; and thus I shall make no further comment upon it.

# 7

AMIDST ALL THE MANY CHANGES in my life at this time—my new and unfamiliar surroundings, my daily battles with the canine population, the longer hours demanded by my expanded clientele—I found that at least one thing remained as constant as before, which was the offering of the holy sacrifice of the Mass by Father Hilaire Guibourg, S. J.: for those nighttime devotions in that chapel continued, reader, with my assistance, and the very singular order of the liturgy which he spoke and the strange exhortations to the various deities of darkness. Likewise, Mme La Voisin was ever steadfast in attending to my proper attire for the ritual and in escorting me into the chapel itself, where, as always, I would be engulfed in billows of dark smoke; as always, behold the extinction of a tiny, wailing victim; and I would rejoice, as always, in Father Guibourg's reverberant calls of *aspairges may* and *hoc est enim corpus mayum* and in the thick waves of incense, in the jangling sounds of the bells, and in my own hearty cries of *kyriay aylayison* and *dayo gratsias!*

And so, that part of my life was unchanged and unchanging; and I was grateful that Father Guibourg continued to employ me in pursuing his services to the lord at that familiar location. Imagine then, my surprise when I discovered that that same excellent cleric was also pursuing various services at the chateau of St. Germain, a fact which bespoke his prominence not only in ecclesiastical but in royal society. And I shall tell you of an encounter with him at the chateau which served, by virtue of my constancy (in turn) to him, to have not a little significance for my own degree of prominence there.

I begin that account by noting that whenever His Majesty and His guests were off on a sojourn, whether to some other royal residence or away to the front lines, the absence of the two radiant divinities left the old chateau at St. Germain-en-Laye a silent and gloomy place. Gone was the celestial glow of His solar majesty and of those mortals nearest in orbit about Him; and lesser members of the court, those of the outer circles, were left behind to wander the abandoned hallways or huddle together in chilly corners awaiting the return of the sun.

Now one of those of the outer circles was another cleric you have already met, I mean the Archbishop of Lisieux; the archbishop's droll wit and his expertise at gaming (with my assistance) assured the continuance of his position in Mme Scarron's coterie at St. Germain, and his was a daily presence, doubtless at the expense of religious consolations sought by the citizens of Lisieux. But no matter: there was an excellent criminal court in the town of St. Germain, where he made arrangements to be seated in the afternoon hours; and he undertook the hearing of confessions at the nearby Church of St. Louis, greatly relieving the pastor there of work and sharpening his own skills in administering that sacrament; and thus he was able to continue to tap both sources, wherein sin and crime are the order of the day, for dazzling anecdotal rewards.

The Abbé Guibourg, it turned out, and the archbishop were well acquainted with each other, most certainly in some prosecution by them of spiritual excellence, for Father Guibourg was on occasion at the chateau in the archbishop's more private company, and their association was acknowledged to be well established, whatever it was they were up to.

Yet a third ecclesiastic seen at St. Germain was the Reverend Jean Ferrier, S. J., a recently acquired client of mine whose family holdings in the Lorraine I had rescued more than once; and he was none other than the king's private confessor. Now very briefly I digress, for that brings me to a matter: I think that he could have had very little to do, the king's confessor, for what sins would the king confess? What sins does a God commit? I believe that God *could* commit sins should He see fit to: if, as we are told, one of the attributes of God is omnipotence, then He is capable of doing anything He puts His mind to, which must include the commission of evil; but others maintain that evil is perforce contrary to the perfection epitomized by God and therefore contrary to God's very nature; but, I insist, if He is all-powerful, why may not God make some adjustments in that nature? It is a dilemma, and it puzzled me greatly, and I had given some thought to addressing the matter to those three clerics at St. Germain, if the occasion were ever to present itself (though Father Ferrier likely had more firsthand experience in the area of godly sin than either of the others; each, however, in his own way, being well acquainted with ungodly doings); and I resolved the very next time I ran into them to make bold and to do it.

I arrive now at that encounter which I would detail for you: for I did run into them one day; but not as I would have wished, for I ran most directly into them in one of those hasty, harrowing, corner-turning situations—I was late that morning, no matter for what reason, I no longer recall—literally running into one of them, or more accurately into the crotch of one of them, I do not know which but believe it to be His Excellency's of Lisieux, who took down the other two with him. It was not, then, the occasion to propose a debate on the matter of God's capacities for evil, none of them being of a mind for it; and most especially not the archbishop, who unleashed a volley of oaths and curses as all four of us lay sprawled across the floor.

It was not difficult for me to right myself, nor for the Reverend Ferrier; but the Abbé Guibourg, eyeless—though only on one side—and lame and extensively curved along the spine, required some assistance; which (since I had been the agent of his downfall) I felt myself obliged to offer, despite the horror of being in the path of his breath. At length, with Father Ferrier's help, I succeeded in rocking him back and forth on the floor a number of times along his spinal column until we gained enough momentum in that action to vault him upward to a standing position. But all three of us failed entirely to raise the beached archbishop, and we would have called upon footmen, but that they—and the entire court—had all taken off for the weekend to the Tuileries.

"Not again! I shall have that beastly dwarf executed this time!" shouted the archbishop. "I shall have it done!"

But Father Guibourg and the royal confessor remonstrated with him and begged him to be calm.

"Calm!" quoth the Lisieuxian, looking up from the floor. "I shall not be calm, and I shall have the creature put to death, and I shall travel myself to the Tuileries this day and advise the king that it is to be done, under threat of excommunication!"

At this, Fathers Guibourg and Ferrier exchanged quick glances, Father Guibourg's being twice as quick for he had only one eye to satisfy.

"Not so," said Father Guibourg to the archbishop, "this dwarf ought not be put to death, that were to do a great wrong." Reader, now you have it: for that good cleric's defense of my very life I believe in all modesty that I may cite my years of loyal service to him; and again I was most grateful for that service and for his remuneration of it.

"Indeed not!" Father Ferrier exclaimed, joining in the defense. "Nor sent away neither, for whatever mischief he may get up to." For without my services he feared for the family estate in Metz; and yet both of them, being beneath the rank of archbishop, could not override their superior's demands.

"Not put to death? Not sent away?" bellowed the archbishop.

"No, no!" chimed the other two clerics, but I sensed they were somewhat cowed.

"Why, I vow that he shall be," said the archbishop, "for in falling I have bes———t myself, yes, I confess it, bes———t myself; and since I cannot now have the matter properly weighed, my gastrointestinal tallies and calculations, my reckonings and computations for this entire week will be all for naught. Away with him!" And turning to me: "Damn your soul, sir, I say!"

(In truth, I found some comfort in that oath, for the archbishop seemed to presume that I was endowed with a soul, capable—indeed, worthy— of being damned; and I reasoned that as a cleric of some prominence, he must surely have known.)

"Indeed," allowed Father Guibourg, "the creature should be punished." And I believe he spoke less from moral conviction than from a need to concede somewhat in the debate for appearance's sake.

"Dwarf!" continued the archbishop, looking up straight into my eyes. "This is the second time, monsieur dwarf, that you have been my downfall, sir! I warn you, sir: the next time I vow you will not be spared! For I shall myself pull out all your hair, twist your arms, thrash you senseless, and kick you down the stairs!"

"Nor shall he be spared this time," rejoined Father Ferrier, seizing upon the archbishop's less rigorous threat, "for he will suffer for this and right swiftly, too."

Now I do not know if the archbishop's preoccupation with the issue of his bowels, the weight of the matter, and so on, served in any way to inspire the good Confessor Ferrier, or if it were a question of some extraordinary coincidence; but the punishment devised for me—and I do not care to shock you, gentle reader—my punishment, I say, was that I was charged with emptying out and scrubbing twice a day the vessel which formed the lower part of His Majesty King Louis's royal *chaise percée.*

I confess it would never for an instant have occurred to me that King Louis XIV, Sun King, Apollo—nay, God—would ever make use of such a thing as a *chaise percée.* And if someone had told me that that was indeed the case, I should have argued most earnestly with him; and if he were not to be dissuaded, I might have conceded then that upon scrutiny of the royal *chaise percée* one might possibly find inside its vessel a quantity of rose petals or of goose down or butterfly wings or some other such beautiful matter. But I should have been wrong, reader, and proven so; and I was, for it seems that my lord King Louis XIV did make use, and prodigious use, of the royal *chaise percée,* which required somewhat extraordinary emptying out; and from that fateful moment on, I was assigned to the task, which I took up directly upon the return of the court at the close of that weekend.

Irony, oh irony! It is the very height of irony: for Father Jean Ferrier, S. J., had conceived of this task as a punishment for me in order to placate the archbishop, and one that should even exceed his threat to pull out all my hair, twist my arms, thrash me senseless, and kick me down the stairs.

But yet I state categorically and with no niggling reservations that the punishment devised for me that gloomy morn was a signal and sun-filled honor!

I note that that same punishment—that so great an honor—did not bring me any closer to His Majesty's person, closer though it brought me to the issue of His person; for the vessel to be emptied was removed each morning and evening from the royal bedchamber by Monsieur Henri Montreuil, Marquis de Lamballe, who had purchased that office the previous July with the assistance of the Marquise de Montespan herself; and having paid twenty thousand *écus* (for which he had sold one of the most excellent stables of stud horses in Brittany), he was in no humor to relinquish the privilege; but he agreed, under pressure from Father Ferrier, to a system whereby he would carry the vessel from the royal bedchamber out to the door of the antechamber, where I should be ready to receive it, take it away, empty it, clean it, and return it to him forthwith. In fact, the Marquis de Lamballe being of a somewhat fastidious nature, I believe that he was secretly relieved to have less commerce with the matter, for to him, to a man of his rank and position and of some aesthetic accomplishment, all the benefit of the office ended abruptly at the bedchamber door, that is, once beyond the royal presence; whereas for me, lacking in any official station, to be seen bundling through the antechamber, where there was always a throng of onlookers, and into the hallway beyond, then down the side stairs and out into the courtyard where the row of privies stood, and bearing the very vessel, or as you may say, the very tureen upon which my lord King Louis had lately sat and into which he had lately s——t, was a distinction which, six months previous, I could scarce have dreamt of. And I myself was not of so fastidious a nature as my perfumed and powdered lord of Lamballe, that, after a brief initial disappointment at not finding rose petals, goose down, or butterfly wings inside the vessel, I could not actually relish my assignment, first, purely for its own sake, for we are speaking here of a royal issue, which is to say of a divine one; secondly, for the pride to be taken in cleaning the vessel with great diligence and care; and lastly, for the heightened position the assignment furnished me in backstairs circles: and I pray this may not seem self-serving, nor even vindictive in light of that humiliation which I had suffered earlier in those same circles on the occasion of serving flan.

And further: it was to grant me somewhat more freedom—and much welcomed freedom—from the clutches of Mme Scarron, for I now had duties and responsibilities in a realm quite removed from hers and even in ways superior to hers (I do not believe that I am presumptuous to say that). Thus, at this same time, I sought out my own place to sleep, which I chose convenient to my early morning duty, a space up under the roof above the hall leading directly to the royal apartment; which enjoyed no view such as I have at present and only scant headroom, but was relatively warm and only occasionally overrun by vermin (that same ceiling nest at St. Germain was doubtless where I acquired my taste for living in eaves or attics, or up inside cornices and pediments—in rookeries). And presently—wonder of wonders!—I began even to be taken along on those trips which the court made to the other royal residences, so indispensable did I make myself to the outer circle of service to my lord

King Louis, for no one had so thoroughly cleansed the royal vessel up to that point as I (I used a combination of wood ashes, salt, sand, tallow and lye soaps, scalding hot water, rosin, and pumice stone; and the vessel, which had curious blue floral patterns both within and without, shone like new whenever I returned it into the marquis's hands).

A final note on this matter before we must move on to a question of the state. I was directed to empty the divine vessel into any one of the privies which stood against the north wall of the lower courtyard; and in foul weather I did so. But when the day was fair, I would venture somewhat farther afield, bearing my load out into a nearby meadow, where I emptied it, thinking to put to better use, as fertilizer, the godly waste; and my plan was right well rewarded, reader, for there sprang up of its own accord in that same meadow, exactly in the middle of January, a miraculous profusion of golden sunflowers; and members of the court, who saw them as they went out later, that crisp afternoon, to the hunt, much remarked upon them; but I never revealed their origin.

Thus, reader, as a result of that violent encounter with the Abbé Guibourg and his two colleagues, and of the abbé's resolve to preserve my life for his purposes, I had at last achieved an acknowledged position in the royal court, and indeed, if it is not presumptuous to say it, in life. What more might an uneducated, illegitimate, spiritually dubious dwarf ever wish for?

With the return of the court to St. Germain, I became aware of a new and right lively debate now afoot in the upper political and social circles—for such debates trickled down throughout all levels of court society—and it was concerning a rumor then circulating that the divine Marquise de Montespan had presented a highly confidential petition to His Divine Majesty and Monarch of the Realm, Louis, that He now make legitimate the three fruits of their mutual loins, to wit, Louis-Auguste, Louis-César, and Louise-Françoise, and thereby recognize publicly and officially that parentage which was already common knowledge.

I confess that when I first heard of the proposal, I wondered greatly at the prospect of so extraordinary an event; and I concluded that were such an alteration in a child's status possible, as the marquise's proposal presumed, it must perforce partake of some nearly miraculous, not to say mystical, element that would override the lamentable fact that the child's parents had not, upon the point of its conception, been blessed by the sacrament of marriage; and that therefore only a person who was possessed of divine attributes might perform that miraculous alteration with the effect of truly making it stick; and thus to conclude, that the petition by the divine marquise to my divine lord, whose position as the head of state would also endow such an act with full legal force, made perfect and incontrovertible sense.

Little did a group of the old Vaugirard gamesters realize that beneath the very card tables at which they sat and quarreled about the issue, and even sorting out cards below for them to play above during their debate, was I, who had hardly stood altogether aloof from the controversy (although, and I say it in all modesty, reader, I had dared meddle, as you know, only with the tiny creatures around whom the controversy swirled and only with the eldest one of them at that and only quite late at night).

"I say this whole legitimization proposal is outrageous," announced General Montmorency-Bouteville de Luxembourg, and despite his obvious emotion, he was speaking in a very subdued voice.

"Legitimization? Is there some proposal for legitimization?" asked the Marquis de Feuquières ironically. "Why, whatever can you mean?"

"Tosh, man, the wretched matter has leaked out," Luxembourg replied in a hushed tone. "Pray do not make light of it. And it is outrageous! And I shall say it again, outrageous!"

"But not exactly without precedent," the Marquis de Feuquières continued with some relish. "Bastards have always been able to get themselves cleaned up—if they have the right connections."

"Outrageous!" repeated Luxembourg. "Where is the proper order of things nowadays, I ask you!"

"About where it was five years ago—or was it six?" replied the Marquis d'Effiat, "when the Longueville brood got sorted out." And he giggled into his handkerchief. "I reckon if those two little brats can make it—" But he did not finish his remark in the flurry of laughter that greeted it.

"Outrageous—it was outrageous then and it is outrageous now," the general doggedly persisted, trying to quell the hilarity.

"I understand, by the by, that our mistress the queen is completely baffled by the idea of legitimizing the children," the Archbishop of Lisieux said in something of an aside. "She somehow has got the very peculiar notion in her head that those dreadful creatures are perfectly legal and actually belong to Mme Scarron."

At which, the company, with the exception of Luxembourg, Mme Poulaillon, and the Comtesse de Pommeret, all chortled and smacked their lips at the queen's unforgivable stupidity.

"Ha, ha!" laughed d'Effiat. "I think Scarron cannot be much taken with the idea—it would put her quite out of business." And he launched into a high-pitched imitation of the children's governess: "Oh my precious little angel! Oh my sweety little mummy's boy! Now please: now wait, now please, no, no, precious lamb, don't throw up on mummy, sweetheart, don't you do it, no, no, now, don't you do it! Ah, curse you, devil! Vile bastard! Pig-faced sod!" And by now, peering from beneath the table, I could make him out sprinting about the room as though looking for a place to set down a retching infant, to the catcalls and applause of his audience.

"What is he up to?" shouted the Comtesse de Pommeret, clearly disapproving of whatever it was the gentleman was up to, and I heard her strike her ear trumpet against the table.

"He is up to making silly mock of the entire grave situation," replied General Luxembourg when calm had once again been restored. "But it is nevertheless—however much fun you may choose to make of it—it is an outrageous turn of events. If these children are legitimized, the king's shameful liaison with the Montespan woman will become fully known—"

"But it is fully known already!" protested d'Effiat.

"Keep your voice down!" the general ordered; and then he continued in almost a whisper: "Fully known, I say; and what's more, the illicit parentage of the three babes will also become fully known—"

"Already fully known as well!" retorted d'Effiat, not keeping his voice down.

And now the Marquis de Feuquières joined in: "Why, even the four-year-old babe knows what his illicit parentage is!"

"And the babe's two-year-old brother and his one-year-old sister," cried d'Effiat enthusiastically and clapping his hands.

"The walls have ears!" Luxembourg pleaded.

"*And* his two-year-old brother *and* his one-year-old sister," reaffirmed Feuquières, nodding to d'Effiat with a laugh.

"And indeed!" insisted the Duc de Luxembourg. "The entire shocking affair will become fully known, I say, and even, messieurs and mesdames, and even—quite scandalously—embraced by the throne before all the world, and it will make the entire nation a laughingstock. And furthermore!" he went on, sensing some new rising impatience from his listeners, "it is an affront to the Church: how His Eminence—or how His Holiness the Pope, for that matter—can tolerate such—"

"I cannot vouch for His Holiness the Pope," said the archbishop, feeling some professional need to address this latest wrinkle, "but His Eminence the Archbishop of Paris has four illegitimate offspring of his own: I venture he may put in a bid for the regularization of his own affairs."

"Mark my words!" the general said, ignoring this unfortunate ecclesiastical information. "It is a danger to the sovereign state, an imminent danger, I say, to raise those three children to the peerage. Why, clearly, they will only start making more and more demands—"

"The children haven't asked for a damned thing," the Marquis de Feuquières slipped in.

"—until before you know it—" and despite his efforts, the general's voice was beginning to rise, "—on the basis of royal parentage, they'll be trying to push the dauphin aside! Which has happened before, and you all know it!"

"And which is not such a bad idea," said the archbishop. "A right dull fellow it is, the dauphin, and I have it from his tutor. I for one do not relish the prospects of succession."

"Outrageous!" Luxembourg shouted, now throwing caution to the winds; and he leapt up from the table. "Blasphemy!" he shouted and began pacing around the room.

"Well, *I* say," said the Marquis d'Effiat now speaking intimately to his tablemates but yet clearly for all the room to hear, "*I* say there's plenty more to come where the first three came from, and I say pish! legitimize the pack of 'em, why not?"

"And just so!" Luxembourg rejoined, trying once again to lower his voice, "'the pack of 'em'! A pack of dogs! How many more of the wretched bastards shall we have to put up with? No, no, they are bastards, I say it and it's so—bastards, and all of the rest to come will be bastards, too—and I say let them all be put out to work farms and not dare to sully this sovereign court! Outrageous!"

"Oh, la, la, la, enough is enough! Honestly, why are you so pigheaded!" Clearly the Marquis d'Effiat was at the end of his patience. "They are

here, those three, in this world, at this court. What ridiculous hypocrisy, my dear general, outright hypocrisy to pretend that they don't exist
or that their parents aren't who they are—or to go on about it like
this, covering up what every sensible person (which does not include
the queen, I'll allow) already knows for a fact. Hypocrisy! Sheer royal
hypocrisy!"

"I see," replied Montmorency-Bouteville de Luxembourg, now grown
strangely calm and in full possession of himself. "The hypocrisy, my dear
Marquis d'Effiat, is what you find so intolerable, is it? Very well, sir. And
shall we, sir, then proceed to clear up one or two other royal hypocrisies
which we have all come to live with? Shall we, sir, readdress the matter
of our beloved Philippe, our monarch's own dear royal brother, and of
the hearty company he keeps? And, sir, of how he goes about entertaining
that hearty company? Shall we revisit that outrageous bit of hypocrisy,
my excellently well-enlightened Effiat?"

Reader, at this scathing reference to Philippe and his infamous entourage—Effiat being, as you will recall, a ranking member thereof—I
could sense the entire company, now holding its collective breath, slowly
turning to stare at the unfortunate marquis; who rose—I saw his be-
ribboned legs withdraw from beneath the table—to his full high-heeled
height; and I knew that his face must indeed have been ablaze, his shoulders shaking, his wig a-tremble, for I had seen him in rage before; and
his throat was so utterly constricted that all he could manage to blurt out
before he stormed from the room was a single word:

"Outrageous!"

A low hum or I know not what sound of infinite satisfaction echoed
throughout the room at his defeat, even at the hands of the pompous,
self-righteous, and priggish Luxembourg; for as you know, reader, any
humiliating rout is better than none.

"Outrageous," now repeated the general, "outrageous." And he would
surely have pursued his tirade against Louis-Auguste, Louis-César, Louise-
Françoise, and their cause but that another player in the game and a most
pivotal one now entered the room.

"And what is so outrageous, pray?" I heard the voice of Mme Scarron
as she crossed to her place at the head of the center table.

General Luxembourg sputtered for a moment, not daring to engage
Scarron herself in so delicate a debate, and then replied:

"Why, this hand of cards I have been dealt, madame; it is quite out-rageous!" And I heard a handful of cards being flung down upon Mme Scarron's table and the martial retreat of the general away from the company.

A silence followed.

"Why, so it is," Scarron said quietly, "outrageous. Quite so. I do not blame the general one whit. Shall we, even so, play on?"

And the several games of cards took up again.

Now I have thought it fitting to inform you of this very private debate; and it will hardly surprise you to learn that I favored the position taken by the Marquis d'Effiat in support of legitimization and by all the others of his view, despite their occasional derisions and irreverences. And deep in my being I wished that I could have had some opportunity to report these expressions of support to the divine marquise, so sympathetic did I feel not only to her cause but as well to that most beautiful and rare lady herself; yet I knew there was no way for me to do this and that I might only pray earnestly in my heart for the eventual success of its outcome.

I have not done with these chattering, squabbling, sneering gossips—though I have for the moment with that particular delicate issue; but I am now come to an even more delicate issue; and it is not my desire to put you out or embarrass you or give offense in any way; but it being an integral part of my account, it must be related and in full.

I need not remind you, I believe, of my enterprise beneath the gaming tables with the less capable card players, Mlle Louise-Adélaïde Marsy, the Marquis de Feuquières, Mme Poulaillon, and the Archbishop of Lisieux, among others. (Though the archbishop rejected my services after our encounter in the hallway, but then was obliged to resubscribe; for he was on the verge of having to sell off a number of profitable Christian convents in the Auge region to meet his gaming debts; yet it cost him in his pride to re-engage me. "But," quoth he philosophically, citing those staggering debts, "you cannot take it out of my flesh like the Jew in the English play." This was a literary allusion well beyond my scope; but if some Jew in an English play had devised a means to take debt from out of the flesh of the debtor, he would have much obliged the archbishop with the informa-tion, for the gentleman was greatly supplied with that currency.)

You must already be aware that life as observed at crotch-level beneath an assortment of tabletops presents a vastly different aspect from that of above board, where despite any number of noxious breaths, yellowing teeth, the ravages of syphilis, hearts aching for vengeance, minds throbbing with malice, and wills unalterably set upon mayhem and the destruction of others, the appearance of at least a modicum of civility can be mustered up; but below! below, take heed: for here are to be found the least admirable pursuits of humanity; to wit, the passing of wind; the covert loosening of various articles of clothing, depending upon the heat of the evening and matters of girth; the scratching of bums, of ——s, of ——s, of groins, of feet, of ——s, of knees; the pursuit of fleas and other parasites in the lower hypogastric region; the occasional administration of enemas as I have already reported took place at the house at Vaugirard but which, it turned out, was not peculiar to that establishment; manual stimulations of divers parts (I blush to write it); and lusts of various orders, all of them lower, much lower, and most of them manifestly apparent to one who was privy to the nether regions as I had indisputably become.

I am obliged to refresh your memory of an incident which I have reported upon briefly and in only one paragraph, which appears on page 49; and this was the incident wherein Mlle Louise-Adélaïde Marsy, having become enflamed by the prurient nature of a drawing room conversation regarding the uses of chicory, reached beneath the gaming table at which she sat (and allow me to quote my own words), "hiked up her skirts and all her petticoats, separated wide her two exposed limbs, dashed the ace quite from my grip, and, grasping my hand, placed it directly and unmistakably—my very hand, I repeat—upon the exact dimple of her bifurcation, to wit, upon the very central furrow of my lady's crotch."

Now this action taken by Mlle Louise had apparently afforded her some comfort; for I had had the wit, reader, to undertake several digital manipulations within mademoiselle's bifurcation, recalling instinctively at that crucial moment the daily manipulations of parts of my own bifurcation by the good Brother Dagobert at the monastery of St. Sauveur, and the sense of well-being afforded us both; and I perceived that such was what Mlle Louise then desired of me, despite the difference in the anatomy; and I supplied her it. When she was quite done, she put my hand away and lowered her skirts; whereupon I retrieved the ace of clubs and slipped it to her. But the next Tuesday, as I was deliberating whether she should next play the king of hearts or the ace of diamonds, up went the skirts again and I was put to performing the business once more. This time I took note of Mlle Louise's fluffy crop—and you will recall that this was not unknown territory to me, for I believe I have intimated my interest in the female parts as a function of my service to the Church; Mlle Louise's meadow being of a reddish hue interspersed with touches of gray or silver, for mademoiselle's beauty had somewhat faded. A short while later, I had produced, a second time, the desired effect, for my hand was again thrust aside. Thus began an ancillary service required of me by that lady each Tuesday evening; and her commerce with the supernatural left me but little choice in these matters; moreover, she began actually to pay me for it. I came to believe that this service was of an even greater value to her than the cards I supplied her with; for she hiked up her garments immediately upon the very first round of *vingt-et-un,* and with a degree of urgency so that I must set about it forthwith.

But further (be not of faint heart, gentle reader): to my astonishment, upon the third or fourth encounter, she even devised an elaboration on that service, whereby she seized me vigorously by both my ears and made bold to clap—and I believe that word will serve, clap, certainly as well as clasp or cleave or clamp, clap will do it quite well—clap then, she made bold to clap my two lips to her own.

Now the quality of my service to Mlle Louise's grasslands having, it seems, so vastly improved with this innovation, there was no chance I should not continue with it and to the full. But what is more, I found that apparently mademoiselle was indiscreet and passed on to another word of my unusual skill: for why else, quite suddenly one warm June evening, should a lady named Marie Mancini, an intimate to mademoiselle, have seized me under the table by the ears and clapped—it continues to be the word—and clapped me to her own abundant underbrush during a simple round of *lansquenet?* And I having no opportunity then to present her the king of spades? (Her particular Van Dyke, by the way, reader, was the first I discovered to have about it an aroma of fish, in her case a flounder.)

Now you must understand, that it was a singular honor for me to be approached by Marie Mancini, for in addition to being an intimate of mademoiselle's, Mancini had at one time been an intimate of my lord King Louis; in fact, it was she who had initiated my (then youthful) lord Louis to the charms of the bedchamber and had made a right excellent job of it to judge by subsequent activity. Indeed the king, quite smitten, had even fashioned a nickname for her derived from her maiden name of Mancini, and she was affectionately known by Him and by all about the court as "the Mancinette." (His enforced surrender of her to marry the Spanish princess had been quite tearful; and she, I think, over the years, never forgot their dalliance.) Thus, by my enrolling the Mancinette into my roster of female clients, there was achieved a certain affinity between my activities below the tables and those (in earlier and doubtless more accommodating surroundings) of my divine lord. Think of it! And I welcomed the Mancinette right heartily among my clientele.

This sudden doubling of my enterprise showed promise of supplementing my income quite nicely, and I decided to seize the day and to actively seek, on my own, other ladies for whom my services would offer some reward, as indeed those same ladies would offer me in return. This was, indeed, a delicate matter. And it was one which I did not like to speak of openly, not even to any lady whose business I sought, lest there be any embarrassment for her; and thus I was obliged to broach the offer of my new service to the uninitiated by slipping my hand—and later even more of myself—though uninvited and quite unexpected, in amongst her skirts and petticoats and thence upward, in order to introduce to her what I proposed to supply on a regular basis. I suffered occasional bruises from these unsuspecting ladies and once a bloodied nose; but it became quickly apparent as to who amongst them were the straightlaced prudes who must not be tampered with again, and who the more open, as it were, whose business, once solicited, might then be taken on.

A diverse clientele it turned out to be, reader, including for a while even the commoner Mme Poulaillon, whom, since in fact she rarely paid for the service, I soon summarily struck from the list. But I shall burden the reader with but one more name for the moment, Mme de St. Estève, a lady whom you know somewhat already who had risen in rank to become a lady-in-waiting to the Marquise de Montespan herself, the divine; this did not appreciably interfere, it seems, with her card playing nor likewise with her enemas, the latter of which she continued to undergo with aplomb; and yet I perceived a kind of warlike reaction to my particular services, for she uttered various whooping noises at the appropriate moment, which were interpreted (by the ill-informed) as a hearty, if not undue response to whatever hand of cards had been dealt her.

The passions of the netherworld are strong, compelling, and, I might say, all-consuming: and the gaming fortunes of those voracious ladies plummeted in direct proportion to the rising frequency of my service to their meadows, for in the midst of their abandon, they would indiscriminately fling out onto the table any number of cards and invariably lose the round. But I confess that my reputation in court now rose (though it could not be officially acknowledged) and there was no small gratification in that. And I became right expert in the business. The only risk involved was the occasional appearance into the drawing rooms of the royal hounds; for were I to be about my task with some lady and a foxhound come nosing in under the table and start nipping away in turn at me, the sudden intrusion could provoke some jarring on my part of the lady's delicate region; the whole affair dissolving into perturbation and the eruption of shrieks on the part of the lady, who might very well toss away a whole fistful of face cards. But there are risks in every undertaking.

I trust, modest reader, that the details which I have just outlined concerning my new employment have not upset the delicacy of your sensibilities; or indeed, if they have, then I must crave your indulgence once again in the simple name of truth.

# 8

AT ABOUT THIS TIME, A FUNCTIONARY was appointed to transport
me from the chateau at St. Germain whenever I was needed by the Abbé
Guibourg; and I was right grateful, for the new arrangement seemed to
betoken a degree of permanence in my ecclesiastical service. This functionary was a deacon named Emil Vergeyck (a man of Dutch ancestry, as
I understand, and he was from the area near Antwerp). Now the chateau
of St. Germain being a vast place and Vergeyck being new to the task, he
could not always find me promptly, and he would fly into a rage; he
was rough-hewn and low, and he was obliged to wait in the kitchen until
some errand sent me thither; whereupon he would seize me and twist
both my ears until I was certain they must snap off in his peasant hands;
and with no regard for my duties to the cardsters, he would toss me into
a muslin sack and strap it onto the back of his horse; which he would ride
at a furious gallop to our destination.

I do not know if it is a habit among the Dutch, but Emil Vergeyck was
much given to talking to himself, in a constant obbligato of mumblings
and mutterings, complaints and curses, all under his somewhat rank
breath but loud enough for me to catch a phrase now and then. And on
more than one occasion he chose to comment upon the towns through
which we were speeding. I recall once, after leaving the town of St.
Germain, that he let off a volley of oaths upon the town of Louveciennes;
and somewhat later, on the town of Vaugirard; so that I felt that I were
in a manner revisiting my past life, the bulk of it spent in distinctly lesser
circumstances. At length, according to Vergeyck's diatribe, we reached

the western entrance to the city of Paris itself, where his wrath knew few bounds; and it was at that moment that I discovered a hole in the muslin sack; there being a full moon that night and a clear sky, I was able to see, though upside down as I was slung upside down upon the horse, where we were going; or rather, where we had been, for I was hanging from the rear of the animal, upon its rump. Presently I saw, on the other side of the fetid river, a long, dark building at the back end of which was a somber, square fortress; and this, I realized, must be the chateau of the Louvre. The air, I recall, was warm and thick and smelt of mud. Finally, as though from up out of the wretched bankside bogginess, there rose a huge stone pile of a building with two square towers framing an imposing doorway. Years earlier I had seen this same building across the plains from my window seat at Vaugirard: the Cathedral of Notre Dame. Along all the side of the cathedral was a row of flying buttresses, which looked, from my particular vantage point that night—that is to say, from upside down—like taut cables gleaming in the moonlight from which the bulk of the cathedral was mystically dangling beneath the canopy of the earth. It was a miraculous vision.

And it was into this suspended cathedral that we went, and that in fact I had been going now for years, I realized: where I found, as usual, La Voisin and, below, the excellent Guibourg. And I recall on that particular occasion that all the familiar liturgical practices, both comforting and frightening, in that smoke-filled chapel took on a new and more wondrous dimension as I perceived the magnificence all around me and above me of the ancient, moonlit cathedral to which I had just been transported.

That same perception led me, moreover, later the next day, to take stock of where my various fortunes had now brought me—and without seeking to be immodest, where my own efforts had led; and I observed that bit by bit I had come to achieve a seemingly permanent position not only in the principal seat of religious observances within the nation of France but, as well, just slightly off center in the wealthiest, mightiest, most celestial court in all of Europe. Yet despite that privilege, my life was hardly one of indolence, and I did not deceive myself: it was by virtue of my various services that I enjoyed the privilege and not, as would have been so much more natural, by birth. That life of service, however, I readily embraced. Realizing that my chiefest assignment, that to my lord's vessel, must take precedence over all others, for it involved the Godhead itself, yet I felt a certain conflict therein with my assignment to Mother Church, which involved Godhead as well (though of quite a darker sort), and which had bearing on the health of my immortal soul (for despite the common wisdom, I had decided by then and did believe that I was possessed of a soul, whatever its size, and one which by now had been well nourished by healthy applications of Latin and incense; but one which, of course, could be damned to everlasting perdition and hell-fire by a vengeful cleric in less time than it would take him to say so).

My obligations to my clients (including now the very prestigious Mancinette)—I mean supplying them with playing cards and other nether sport—while it smacked of no divinity, yet it yielded some return, economics being economics, and I had certain costs. One must buy hose and oysters, as the poet says, and I might add, fresh straw from time to time, a bit of suet, needle and thread to keep my jacket in repair, and various philters useful in warding off the smallpox, sores and rashes, diarrhea and dysentery, piles, scrofula, toothache, constipation, fistulas and stones, and baneful supernatural influences. Nor were my daily chores to the fireplaces of St. Germain of slight account, for if a fireplace is not properly swept clean of its ashes every day, the quality of subsequent fires in it is adversely affected, even so far as to threaten danger from the flames to the furnishings in the room, and thence to the room itself, thence to the wing in which it is located and to the entire royal residence of St. Germain-en-Laye, and finally to the members of the royal court in residence, including most especially the divine marquise and the Divine Louis Himself. Thus I bore a moral obligation to the French nation to perform the ash removal in a proper and timely manner, and like any responsible Frenchman, I gladly embraced that obligation.

Now all my other duties, I concede, were less demanding, those various tasks in the plumbing system for which my size rendered me apt, cleaning up after the dogs, lard removal, bailing work in the cellars during heavy rains (for the sump pumps were notoriously ineffective), and the like. But I was blessed by the regularity of the daily schedule; and could perform my duties to the Marquis de Lamballe every morning at seven thirty and every evening around eight; those to my clients in the later evening hours; those to the grates, cellars, sewers, and so on during the day; those to the Church at night.

Adding to these responsibilities were those duties which arose on a more ad hoc basis; and the time has come to tell you, I am pleased to say, of one such instance wherein I lent my services to a particular event that was a joyous one for a number of persons concerned and a downright triumphant one for the dear Marquise de Montespan: for I shall now relate the matter of the formal legitimization of her three children and the open acknowledgment of their true parentage.

I have indicated a joyous note for many; but it was not so for Mme Scarron, who sent for me one crisp morning in December of 1673 and, ill concealing a quite bitter state of mind, addressed me thus:

"Sir, you are to be employed to perform a chore tomorrow in the chapel. You will accompany my footman there and be guided by him throughout; you are to carry the infant Louise-Françoise into the chapel; your path will be indicated to you. If you drop the infant on her head or trip and fall with her yourself, or if you disrupt the proceedings in any manner, or if you gawk like a fool at the company there, or if you tremble from fright at the splendor about you, or if you make any error whatsoever in the conduct of your mission, you were best not show your face hereabouts again, for you will be thrashed into oblivion and flung down into the moat outside. And furthermore, Monsieur Hugues," she continued, "pray heed me, sir: if any of the crowd assembled there should find your presence untoward or should laugh at you or jeer at you or make fun in any way of your appearance there, you are to ignore every bit of it and go about your business as you are accustomed to doing in my drawing room when you are charged with serving flan." And leaning down toward me so that the aroma of leeks became almost unbearable, she added, "You have my drift, dwarf?"

"Madame," I acknowledged with a deep and most respectful bow, "I have."

"Look to it." And she turned and strode out of the room, slamming the door behind her with such force that all the windows rattled.

I was somewhat mystified by her injunction for I did not know then what ecclesiastical event was planned for the following day, and she had not informed me; and although I knew very little of Louise-Françoise, that child being an infant and quite removed from any of my comings and goings, I hoped that the babe was not on the point of being offered up to Astorath and Asmodus. Yet despite whatever apprehensions I felt about bearing the little girl into the chapel, at the same time I trusted that the aplomb that I had so often practiced in bearing flan throughout madame's drawing room would not desert me on this more public and perhaps more harrowing occasion.

Therefore, the next morning—and a sunny, nippy morning it was—I washed my face twice, once out at the privies and again in a basin in the kitchen, and put on a blue velvet suit with a fine collar and sash which Mme Amélie had brought to me for the occasion—a modest enough ensemble, reader—and combed my hair and brushed my shoes and then combed my hair again and my cowlick. As the footman hurried me along toward the entrance to the chapel, I quickly stole a glance at my reflection in a hall mirror, and reader, in all humility I tell you that I scarcely recognized the splendid figure which I cut; and I could hardly conceive of the fact that a dozen years previous, the infant that then I was had sat naked on a stone floor in the middle of a puddle of dog piss.

At the chapel entrance (which is through a side door from the inner courtyard of the chateau), we were met by a flurry of nursemaids who had in tow not only Louise-Françoise (in one of the women's arms) but as well Louis-Auguste, on his unsteady feet, and Louis-César, in a lace-and-ribbon-strewn carriage. The moment he caught my eye, Louis-Auguste, recognizing in me the agency of many a tormented, tear-filled night in his nursery, fell to trembling and cowering and seeking to hide his face. But quickly the footman brought him up short and seized the boy's hand and instructed him to stop fidgeting and to stand next to the carriage, which had now been lined up facing the doorway; and the little boy did as he was told. With some misgivings, the woman carrying Louise-Françoise placed that child on a satin pillow into my arms, as directed by the footman, and I took up my post behind him, Louis-César in the carriage and Louis-Auguste on foot. What, I wondered, were we up to?

When at length our cue was given, the five of us advanced into the chapel and turned left to face the altar up ahead. It is a right handsome chapel, with high and light-filled windows and elaborate tracery across the ceiling; I recommend you a visit; and on this day it was adorned with flowers and banners and awash with the glorious sounds of a brass ensemble and redolent with the sweet aroma of incense, a fragrance already well known to me though under somewhat different ecclesiastical circumstances. Proceeding at a stately and dignified gait, we made our way through a crowd of richly bedecked and ogling spectators and on, up to the railing in front of the altar. Reader, I scarcely dared look anywhere but straight ahead, so concentrated was I on my task of not dropping Louise-Françoise on her head, or falling with her myself, or disrupting anything, or gawking like a fool, or trembling, or making any error whatsoever; yet I was gratified that the reaction of the spectators to my appearance seemed, if I judged it correctly, more one of utter astonishment than of derision.

Despite the intensity of my concentration, I shall confess that once we stood before the altar, I did glance—the merest of glances, but I glanced—one brief moment to my left; and there I saw, seated upon a throne near the altar, the magnificent, serene, illustrious, all-powerful, glorious—nay, divine!—figure of His Majesty the King, Fourteenth of the Noble Name of Louis; and standing a distance off to the side, the beautiful divinity which was the mother of His offspring, the radiant Marquise de Montespan.

Did I, in that most fleeting of glances, detect an expression—though only the slightest, I would assure you, reader, a mere soupçon of an expression, but an expression of some humor on the face of my divine lord at the sight of me, a dwarf—a well-turned out dwarf on that occasion, I'll allow, but lowly dwarf no less—bearing the youngest of His progeny to this ecclesiastical event? Did I detect that, reader?

An acolyte shot me a wicked leer and then opened the altar gate; a priest led Louis-Auguste into the sanctuary, a second priest picked up Louis-César from out of the carriage, and a third took Louise-Françoise from my arms; at which point, a fourth priest, a bishop with miter and crosier, now intoned in Latin a lengthy prayer, one which I had never heard before (but the sounds were nonetheless reassuring to me on that awesome occasion); bells rang out and puffs of fresh incense swirled around the three children's heads; and the musicians played a stirring fanfare. Then silence fell.

"*Legitimus sit Ludovicus-Augustus,*" intoned the bishop, who was now kneeling before the altar.

"Let it be so," intoned my lord King Louis, still seated on the throne.

"*Legitimus sit Ludovicus-Caesar,*" the bishop continued.

"Let it be so," my lord responded again.

"*Legitima sit Ludovica-Francesca.*"

"Let it be so."

Whereat the priest bearing Louise-Françoise walked over to where the divine marquise was standing and passed the child into her arms; and similarly, Louis-César; the third priest prompted Louis-Auguste to cross to his mother and to stand next to her.

A second fanfare roared forth, and a choir in the rear of the chapel burst into the *Tay Dayum*.

Reader, I stood there transfixed by the solemn majesty of the occasion; by the sight of my lord and of the marquise standing proudly with her children before all the world; and by the sounds of *Tay dayum laudamus tay dominum confitaymur* ringing through the air; and I confess that at the same time, I was not a little relieved that I had managed not to drop Louise-Françoise on her then—but no longer to be!—illegitimate head.

And next, reader, to my great surprise (and to the surprise of every-one there) and as well, to my deep mortification, Louis-Auguste, still standing respectfully at his mother's side, and in his newly elevated con-dition, caught my eye once again; this time, what appeared to be a smile began to spread across his face; but before it reached completion, it shifted into a leer of disdain; at which, the boy shook his fist at me and stuck his tongue out as far as he could stick it and waggled it. All startled eyes spun downward in my direction, including those, most unmistak-ably now, of His Divine Majesty and of the divine goddess. Suddenly, my heart pounded, I felt a crimson flush suffuse my face, my knees turned weak. All that I could think to do at that horrifying moment was to offer a bow of most humble reverence to the figures before me; the which I began; but it was interrupted—nay, summarily aborted—by a quick, tight clasp of fingers on my shoulder, the footman bidding me turn and retreat with him out through a side door; and as he hastened me along, I dared take another glance and glimpsed yet another principal in the mighty drama of it all: Mme Françoise Scarron, watching from well off in the wings, with a look on her face of wretched defeat.

Once retired to the kitchen, I flew to shed my unwonted costume and to restore my own clothing and to resume my chores and to return as quickly as I might and as unobtrusively to my accustomed anonymity.

But let not my own embarrassment becloud that day's momentous events, reader: for I subsequently learned that later that very afternoon, in legal testament of the divine act which had been performed in the chapel, His Majesty signed three letters patent, which were then duly and publicly registered in the Parlement in Paris on the twentieth of the month, and which confirmed the status of all three infants to be thenceforth completely, thoroughly, and unquestionably legitimate, both in this world and in all matters related to the next; whereby Louis-Auguste became the Duc du Maine, Louis-César the Comte de Vexin, and Louise-Françoise the Comtesse de Nantes, with all the position, favor, soundness, and privilege of any noble child born to man and woman united in holy wedlock!

And although my short-lived and unspoken bastardly affinity to those children was now demolished and any vestiges of it quite swept away by Louis-Auguste's grimace at the altar, yet from a broader outlook, I was obliged—and quite elated—to celebrate that act of legitimization, whereby the children were accorded fully recognized status as complete and utter human beings, an act which was a true and manifest miracle, as befits the motions of the divine: for the marquise being endowed with all the virtues and might of the divine, and His Divine Majesty being in celestial harmony with her, she had indeed prevailed in her wishes for her children, as was meet; and so great was that metaphysical accomplishment and so full of awesome wonder that holy deed, that in order that they might be properly and fully appreciated, I now close this chapter upon them, however much shorter it is than most.

# 9

STILL REVELING, IF THE WORD IS NOT TOO STRONG, in the aura of that event, I will tell you now of yet another spiritual event, saintly reader, which affected the fortunes of many of us about the court, but in quite a different manner.

A certain well-known Jesuit preacher, Father Louis Bourdaloue (born at Bourges, 1632), having been recommended, as I overheard, to my lord King Louis by none other than Mme Scarron herself, was requested by His Majesty to preach the Lenten sermons at court for the year 1675; and by the extraordinary force of his message and of his oratorical skills, Father Bourdaloue created, in the spring of that year, a crisis of major proportions.

"I know you!" he thundered to the congregation in the Holy Chapel at St. Germain the third Sunday morning in Lent. (I was now allowed to attend Mass in the chapel; this, by the way, I took to be an official acknowledgment that my spiritual life was worth attention. I was warned not to call out the Latin responses, for such was not the practice there, they being the sole province of the acolyte and the choir; those in attendance at the holy liturgy were to hold their tongues and not meddle in the business.) "I know you!" thundered Father Bourdaloue (a giant of a man with huge, raw hands), "I know you!" to one and all, and even to Athénaïs, Marquise de Montespan, and even, what is more of a wonder to tell, to my lord King Louis Himself; but not, I think, reader, to Mme Françoise Scarron, for it was through the offices of that lady that the cleric now stood before that royal assemblage, and he would hardly have directed his scathing castigations to his benefactress. "I know you! And here are your lusts, yes; and here are your vices; here your abject failures and here your utter baseness!" And he went on in that manner to expose our lusts, our vices, our failures, and our baseness, most of them having to do, in that year 1675, with the fact that certain of us, it seemed, and my lord King Louis the Godhead chiefest amongst us, had made no plans for, nor had any intentions of performing our Easter duty, as all Christians are enjoined to do by Holy Mother Church; that is to say, to partake of Holy Communion some time between Ash Wednesday and Trinity Sunday, which is the Sunday following the Feast of Pentecost. And Father Bourdaloue placed great emphasis upon the matter insofar as 1675 was a special Jubilee Year for the Church, proclaiming that all Christians—and implying the king Himself as the world's most Christian monarch—must surely perform their Easter duty in that year of all years.

But—and this I learned later that evening in the gaming salon, where rumors swarmed and fed and fattened like flies on a soft and vaporous pile of dung—my lord King Louis XIV, Divinity, could not, without committing considerable blasphemy, have taken communion unless He were first to confess his adulterous liaison with Athénaïs and put her aside from out of His bedchamber; for according to Father Bourdaloue, who I think must have known something about it, our other Lord, Lord Jesus, was quite determined that Lord Louis should be content to spend His nights exclusively in the bedchamber of the middle-aged, shapeless Spaniard whom He had married fifteen years previous, the Infanta, Marie-Thérèse, who was queen of France.

Speculation flew about in all circles of the court society as to how my lord would address the predicament presented by the stern cleric, the overwhelming consensus being that He would never suffer the loss of the magnificent Montespan and that life was likely to proceed fairly much as it then was, whatever the spiritual consequences. I myself felt certain that my lord, being divine and hence omnipotent, would have at His command the means to satisfy both parties, I mean the marquise and Lord Jesus, with perfect and godly equanimity. Yet a few there were who insisted, in their prudish outlook, that this dilemma, after all these years, indeed spelled the downfall of Mme de Montespan.

"Tosh!" said Mlle Mancini one evening to one such prudish count not long after I had finished up my exertions in her grasslands and she then feeling most refreshed. "And do you believe then, sir, that at the behest of Scarron—think of it!—and of her agent, this Bourdaloue fellow, His Majesty will sacrifice the marquise for some trifling 'Jubilee Year' rubbish?"

"He will indeed, madame," replied the count. "I know Him for the Christian king which He is. He will confess the sin and virtue will triumph!"

"Five *louis d'or* says rotten eggs!" cried the Archbishop of Lisieux from across the room. "I am an expert at shriving, and I say He'll never do it!" And laughter rang out.

"Ten!" countered the count. "He will do it, I say!"

"Fifteen!" cried another voice whose owner I could not distinguish. "I raise it to fifteen!"

"Twenty!" cried the count.

"Thirty!" shouted a third voice and "Thirty-five!" the count, now desperate but obstinate; and "Fifty!" yet another voice and "Seventy-five!" the count; and in this manner the bidding flew back and forth about the room.

Now as shocking as all this may seem to you, reader—and it would certainly have shocked Mme Scarron had she been of the company that evening, but she had abandoned cards for Lent—I pray you, take no offense; for I truly believe that it was all quite in jest; and being thoroughly beyond the earshot of both divinities, for they were entertaining guests in the northeast drawing room as usual—being, as you may say, behind their backs, it was but the product of innocent, harmless high spirits.

On the other hand, as the bidding reached well above four hundred *louis d'or* (for such was the obstinacy of the prudish count that he topped every bet), it was somewhat of an indication of how great an issue the matter had become.

As it transpired, my lord King Louis took it quite seriously Himself. For in a mere two weeks' time, it was announced that, prompted by His spiritual mentor, Bishop Bossuet of Condom, He had indeed been right well shriven by His confessor; and He then did indeed make His Easter duty in that Jubilee Year; whereupon, to everyone's complete astonishment, He then summarily sent packing Athénaïs, Marquise de Montespan, second divinity, from out of His bed, from out of her apartment, from out of the royal residence at St. Germain, and off to the former Scarron house at Vaugirard!

I confess that I was as astonished as anyone there.

Now this did not much displease Mme Scarron, I can assure you, who, in her pious manner, herself took Holy Communion at the same Mass as my lord King Louis, thus performing her own Easter duty for all to see; and who, I have it from a good source, watched the Marquise de Montespan's carriage as it swept from the grounds of the royal palace; and she did so from an east window on the first floor, which as it happened, was a window in what had been the marquise's apartment, vacated only moments before. Nor could the irony of her rival's exile to the house at Vaugirard have much distressed Mme Scarron; nor the fact that the marquise was once again separated from her brood, who remained with their governess; and she was reported to have celebrated her own private jubilee that Easter season.

(With his newfound wealth, I was told, the prudish but victorious count retired from the shameless court which he reviled and opened a home for wayward youths in a suburb of Chaumont; such was the reward for his unwavering faith in King Louis; but the home fell later upon hard times, and it was closed down by the Ministry of Finances, and all the land and various holdings confiscated by the ministry, and all the youths conscripted into the army, which is exactly where they should have been in the first place.)

Now that gloom which, as I have reported to you, descended upon the palace whenever my lord King Louis and the divine marquise left St. Germain descended once again; though by any logical calculation it should have been only half as pervasive a gloom, there being only one of the two divinities now absent; yet I vow, it seemed to me considerably more than half, which is either (a) a true and factual tally or (b) the impression of one much smitten by that absent half; but yet I ask, who could have failed to be as smitten as I by such an one? And therefore I conclude that that gloom did indeed reach proportions well over the halfway mark and for everyone there, with only the exception of one, Mme Scarron, for whom, it is a certainty, the gloom was transformed into quite positive delight.

But, reader, whatever these reckonings, I myself was disconsolate, for although I had not moved within her circle nor enjoyed any but the most fleeting and distant contact with her, yet the mere knowledge of the divine Marquise de Montespan's presence in my general vicinity could warm my heart and bolster my spirits during the long and ofttimes tedious hours of my labors. And now that she was no longer at hand, now that she had been cast away and sent as it were into exile, I began, in all my youthful foolishness, to dream of how I might myself hasten to her side, storm her prison, rescue the lady, and restore her to her wonted glory—for had I not so vowed when first I had beheld the lady weeping over her two little boys? Or if such a gallant rescue were not possible, why then how I might offer her some smaller succor—some kind remark, a friendly gesture, that would brighten but a moment of her exile; or at the very least, send word of my compassion through a gallant messenger, a blushing female confidante, a letter. But alas, reader, I knew no messengers nor no confidantes neither and in my wretched ignorance of the arts of reading and writing could fashion no letter, even might I summon up the courage to the task.

Therefore you will understand the unparalleled amazement and the infinite joy which I experienced when the following took place a mere week after the marquise's departure:

Early one crisp spring evening, as I was finishing up my duties to His Majesty's vessel—and I was out in a secluded area just to the north of the stables, between them and the latrines commonly used by the grooms and gamekeepers—I was approached by a young woman shrouded in a dark cape and shawl who very quietly identified herself to me as Mademoiselle Claude des Œillets, a waiting woman in the employment of herself, the Marquise de Montespan.

My heart leapt at the sound of that lady's name, of that divinity who had been but a week ago in the bosom of the definitive divinity, mother of three of His offspring, radiant goddess herself.

Quickly, des Œillets ushered me behind the stables, where we could speak even more privately in the twilight shadows.

"Monsieur Hugues," said she, "it seems that my mistress has been aware of you for some time, sir, indeed ever since your arrival at St. Germain with Mme Scarron and the children; and most especially since your participation in their rite of legitimization." Reader, I felt a deep blush flooding across my face. "And sir," mademoiselle went on, "well before her departure hence, she had begun some enquiry about you, sir—I mean, where you are quartered, the matter of your employment, and such-like information whereby any person's circumstances are known. And sir, she has learned, by chance, still more about you, Monsieur Hugues," mademoiselle continued, now touching a dainty handkerchief to her forehead and lowering her voice though there was no one about, "I mean, more than those mere dry facts. For she has learned, sir, of your particular service to certain of the ladies here at St. Germain—" and reader, I blushed even more profusely at those words, discreetly though mademoiselle had framed them "—and she herself has become most curious about that service, sir; and in the poor lady's unfortunate banishment from the presence of our lord the king, sir, she desires me to inform you that your attentions are requested and this very evening, sir, to the service of her own—how may I delicately express it, sir?—of her own particular meadowland."

I was—and I am still—quite unable to find words to express the boundless elation which I felt at hearing that petition. Here was that blushing female confidante—that very one!—of whom I had dreamt, now standing most materially before me! and with a request that defied belief!

Thus it was arranged that as soon as I had returned the royal vessel to the Marquis de Lamballe, I should rejoin Mlle des Œillets in a carriage awaiting me in the Rue de Pontoise a little distance from the palace grounds; the which I promptly did and swiftly; and the two of us, at breakneck speed, flew through the towns of St. Cloud and Boulogne all the way back to Vaugirard; whereupon in a trice, I was trundled into the house and privately escorted back into that drawing room I knew so well and where in fact I had first beheld so many of those who figure prominently in this account, not the least of whom were my lord King Louis XIV Himself and the divine Athénaïs, Marquise de Montespan, herself.

My head was fairly reeling!

Now, reader, when I say that I was privately escorted into the drawing room, let me explain; in the outer passage I quickly concealed myself beneath the skirts and between the limbs of Mlle des Œillets, who then proceeded forward into the inner chamber in what must have been a somewhat awkward fashion. For who shall stride gracefully astride a dwarf? Yet, however she did it, proceed she did; though first she made a scratching sound against the door to announce her arrival, whereupon, without waiting for leave to enter, she entered; and the two of us, as one, made our four-legged way to the appropriate card table; and the upper one of us, mademoiselle, then served the goddess with a bowl of warm flan (the irony!) whilst the lower, myself, slipped beneath the table unseen to serve her with other warm undertakings.

Whereupon, I perceived immediately that I was surrounded by four sets of legs, eight limbs, two pairs of the male order and so clad, two of the female and clad in the female mode by skirts, petticoats, and other trappings beneath; but in one instance, as the skirts and several undergarments had been gathered upward, there was revealed—and it is probable that you will needs steady yourself at this point—there was revealed, I say, the unmistakable presence of the celestial muff.

Divinity of the divinity!

Having been directed directly to it in person, reader, I can do no more at present than to direct your mere attention to it: to the golden fairness of its down, to its luxuriance, to the subtly curling patterns which it formed within the chaste borders, to the gentle roll of the hillock upon which it grew, to the ivory beauty of the adjacent moors. I shall not for the moment delve more deeply, though at that moment, delve I did; but I shall add two points: that above and to the left of that sacred garden, just beyond its outer limits, lay a small, dark mole. I refer not to the tiny shrewlike creature which burrows into the earth, reader, but to a point of pigmentation, a mole such as may appear upon the skin of any man or woman and in no way to that mortal's discredit; and certainly in this present case, in no way to the discredit even of the divinity; for in its small, brown way, the mole actually enhanced the prospect of the excellent landscape which I beheld. And my second point is an olfactory one, reader; for the scent of halibut drifted quickly to my excellent nose: fresh-caught, fresh-bought halibut, filleted with a good sharp, serrated knife, and ready to be lightly sautéed.

At this point I shall be discreet.

Now when I had quite done with my cultivation of that Elysian field, I was grateful that no thought whatsoever had been given to my escort from beneath the gaming table; for the efforts I had undertaken had transported me, and I was fortunate to enjoy some leisure to return to a lower plane, though in her presence it was not possible to be entirely earthbound; and so I stayed there. Privately I gave thanks to those babbling gossips among my female clients who must have informed the marquise of my enterprise. (Could it have been, I wondered, Marie Mancini—the Mancinette—who had so advised her?) And rather than fret that my clientele were robbed of my services this evening, I amused myself to think, ironically, how frantic they must now be at my absence; as well as the gentlemen, who would be grasping at the empty air beneath the tables in search of my handout of cards. Next I gave thanks—and thanks again!—to that sweetest of confidantes, Mlle Claude des Œillets, whose embassy I felt that I had somehow miraculously summoned by the very power of my dreams and boyish fancies. And I listened to the voices from up above and made some sport for myself in trying to distinguish who were in the divine woman's company that evening; and I recognized what was possibly the voice of Philippe, my lord's own brother, and was gratified to think, if my guess were correct, that at least one member of the royal family had continued to be faithful to the marquise. But at length—for the gambling hours droned on—I drifted off into a deep slumber, lying at her dainty and exceedingly divine feet, reliving the rapture of my encounter with her in my dreams.

When, much later, I awoke, I found that I was alone; and I crept out from beneath the table and into the room. Pale moonlight streamed in through the row of windows along the eastern front; on the opposite side, from the remains of a fire in the grate, there rose wisps of dark smoke, some of which drifted out into the chamber itself. Without thinking, I clamored up the leg of one of the chairs which stood at the table: cards lay strewn across the tablecloth and here and there thick, caked droplets of wax. Directly above, as though floating high in the air, I saw the heavy brass chandelier, its tapers blackened with soot. Suddenly I realized that I was standing on the same spot where she herself had sat, upon the very altar where her flowering meadow had been offered—and taken—in a distinctly private holy communion celebrated solely by the two of us (was ever such an Easter duty done?). Trembling, I lowered myself partway down from the chair and paused; and I dared to lean forward and implant a chaste kiss on that very spot before I slid on downward to the floor and hurried away to my old window seat upstairs; with a quick glance out across the moonlit plains and over to the towers of Notre Dame Cathedral, I burrowed deep into my snuggery to ward off the chill night air; yet within, I felt warmed by the divine sacrament at which I myself had officiated that evening.

The following morning, I set out in search of Mlle des Œillets, for I was now in something of a quandary: all my duties at St. Germain, and most especially that duty to the royal vessel, were being neglected, and I must needs find some means to return to the residence. Yet I moved cautiously through the familiar house, for I knew neither who the housekeeper was any more nor the servants and feared they would take me for an intruder. As I reached the lower hallway, I saw, at the other end of it and coming toward me, a party of females. Immediately I withdrew up against the wall, removed my cap, and bowed quite low and with much deference and respect, hoping thus to escape undue notice.

The company stopped in front of me.

"Ah—this is he, is it not?" And the voice which spoke, reader, was golden and godly; and I felt my heart begin to thump within my breast and my knees begin to tremble.

"Yes ma'am," I heard Mlle des Œillets reply.

"And you say that he is addressed as Monsieur—?" the godly voice enquired.

"As Monsieur Hugues, ma'am."

"Monsieur Hugues." Reader, I did not know if that repetition of my name were merely that or a summons to leave off my bow and to present myself; and so, fearing to give any offense, I looked up.

There, standing before me, was she: Athénaïs, the goddess, the Marquise de Montespan; and I caught my breath in awe at being so soon again in her presence. Accompanying her was Mlle des Œillets, along with Mme de St. Estève, Madame Marie-Céleste Vivonne, the marquise's sister-in-law, and two or three other of her women, but they appeared as mere shadows in the radiance of her sweet presence.

The Marquise de Montespan, Athénaïs, goddess, did then approach me, reader; and she did bend down toward me and she took my chin in her hand and she did fall to studying my face, which had turned beet red, I can assure you, beet red, I was quite—, I had not—, I wished—, nothing which—, no, I could not—, no, no, quite beet red, I can assure you, beet. And after a brief moment of her study of my features,

"Be so kind," she whispered to me, and only to me, "as to unfurl your tongue, Monsieur Hugues."

Trembling, I did as bidden.

"It is a long tongue, Monsieur Hugues," said she, still in a whisper, "indeed a long one for so short an animal as possesses it."

She smiled at me.

Beet red, beet red.

She smiled at me.

Yes: bending closely over me, she smiled at me. The other women stood a distance behind her, I have no witness to it. But she did smile at me.

She straightened up and I withdrew my tongue. "And it is an excellent long nose there upon Monsieur Hugues," said she aloud to the company of females, most of whom then tittered and giggled at the innuendo. The marquise smiled once more, winked at Mlle des Œillets and set out again down the passage; yet des Œillets lingered; and though I scarcely heard her directives to me, yet I followed them; and found myself in the carriage once again, to return to St. Germain. But I saw only a blur of trees and houses and riverbank along the way, so high in the clouds was my recollection that the only creature in the world—save only my lord King Louis XIV Himself—whose regard—nay, whose mere glance—was for me a prize of towering and infinite worth, had smiled on me.

Now continuing: for, wonder of wonders, reader, I have not yet done with these matters:

Some two days later, I was grappling with a beagle in the west gallery, two gentlemen nearby having placed bets on the match, one a client of mine, Monsieur Hector Champville, Marquis de Villacerf, the other a Monsieur LeMouël from the neighborhood of Rennes, when suddenly Mlle des Œillets approached the brawl; and seizing a pair of tongs from the chimney where I had been shoveling ashes, she gave the hound a fierce blow to its muzzle; and the vile beast fled through one of the hinged panels, littering the way with blood and shards of broken teeth. He had quite badly ripped the sleeve of my jacket and I fell to studying the damage, but mademoiselle swept me down to the other end of the vast gallery away from the crowd which had begun to gather and spoke thus:

"Monsieur Hugues," quoth she in a low voice, smiling at me and smoothing down the cowlick in my hair, "it seems that my lady was right well pleased by your visitation to her the other evening; and she desires me to tell you the following: that now that she is living elsewhere, her purpose is to send for your services upon occasion, with myself acting as her private emissary in the matter; and she would have you place yourself then at my disposal and to stand ready for my summons; and this employment is to be attended with the greatest discretion and concealment."

At those words you may imagine how close my heart came to bursting apart and how my brain spun with a kind of ferocious delirium! I quite forgot the rip in my sleeve. Think of it! To be entering into the service of her whom I had come to worship, however furtive that service was to be; nor did I deceive myself, I believe, in thinking that that very furtiveness in fact but increased the honor given me, for I was hers, all hers, and right secretly hers, precious to her innermost, intimate self! Reader, I was drunk! drunk with joy; and I believe—nay, know!—that I exulted more at that moment even than I had upon being appointed to bear the royal —— to the privies, and I hope that that may not appear heretical; and only the fact that the tidal wave of uncontainable exhilaration which I experienced caused me to suffer a slight accident in my breeches succeeded in restoring me to a more properer sense of reality.

I quite put aside any concern about my clients at St. Germain now, including even the Mancinette, for I felt, perhaps recklessly, that as long as I could continue to honor those duties of mine to the royal household, and most especially to the royal vessel, and those others to Holy Mother Church, I would gladly sacrifice the economic benefits of my evening activities whenever I should be sent for by my lady. Thus do we begin to establish priorities for ourselves in this world.

And when I was informed in private, again by Mlle des Œillets, that the marquise herself—the divine one—had told her the following:

"If I am to forego His Majesty's favors, why then, so be it: but I shall have my dwarf about me—a somewhat less majestic comfort, to be sure, but comfort nonetheless."

—when I was so told, reader, I felt that truly my labors in that most divine of gardens had quite transcended all earthly enterprise; and that in short, I had attained paradise.

But now I return to solid ground in order to continue:

Restless in her exile, the marquise traveled occasionally back to the town of Versailles, where construction for her of a small chateau—the chateau of Clagny—had begun the year previous; it was a stone's throw from His Majesty's hunting lodge, but in a state of some disarray, the final stages of its construction being still under way, and there were workmen about and plaster dust, scaffolding and the milling of lumber; but I believe that it was that short distance to the aura of His Majesty much more than some plaster dust that made the place irksome to its mistress, and we would return in a day or so to Vaugirard, even with its tedious quiet.

More and more frequently, after rendering my services, I persuaded des Œillets to let me stay overnight in the upstairs window seat, as I had on that first wondrous evening; and thus I even devised with the Marquis de Lamballe, as distasteful as it was to that delicate gentleman, to undertake my duties to the royal vessel on those occasions when I should be away. I confess that I was much torn by these conflicting interests since on the one hand my service to the marquise afforded me an intimate position in her private household while on the other, my service to my lord King Louis was the very basis of my position in the royal household. Thus I was most heartened when, once again, His military obligations summoned my lord Louis off to the wars in Flanders, suspending for the time being disposal of the royal load at St. Germain; and thus, at least temporarily, I, Hugues, benefited from the unholy machinations of the enemies of France, and I blush to say it.

It was gratifying to see that the arrogant stableboy whose friendship I had so coveted in my earlier residence at Vaugirard was still consigned to shoveling horse manure: nor did I offer to lend him a hand, let me assure you. Presently less and less attention was paid to concealing my visits there (though their ultimate aim was always quite discreetly fulfilled, I promise you), and I became an accepted member of the household, staying there over longer and longer periods and even most willingly assuming various other duties in the service of madame and her guests, and thus artfully abetting my new position in her entourage.

Now and then the marquise held entertainments at Vaugirard, although when any prominent member of the court dared to call upon her ladyship, the gathering was perforce of a most private order. She even was bold on several occasions to receive Philippe, Monsieur, Duc d'Orléans, the king's own brother, along with the Marquis d'Effiat, the Chevalier de Lorraine, and other waggish, wit-snapping young bucks as were so much favored by Monsieur. And the fact that those occasions were entirely clandestine did not dampen the high spirits of those gallants; and at one point their boisterous conversation came, to my great embarrassment, to center upon me.

"Size, madame?" quoth Monsieur in his high-pitched tones, peering down at me, his face quite close to me for he was myopic. "Size? Why, I think there must be little of it to recommend hereabouts; for all here of this tiny creature is in miniature; and we should need to seek other like miniature parts to fit together with Monsieur Hugues's plumbing, madame, in order to match his size!"

At which, Mme de St. Estève burst into laughter: "Fie, fie, my lord! You are quite brazen!" As a woman now in service to the marquise, she felt entitled to make comments occasionally.

"Ah, but observe, sir," said the Chevalier de Lorraine, who was an acknowledged connoisseur in such matters, "when it comes to the fellow's nose, that is no miniature feature; no, it is a most excellent long nose!" And he looked across at Monsieur with what I can only describe as a lascivious leer.

"Is it so now?" said Monsieur; and with that, he reached downward with his hand and boldly seized my ———; the which, though modestly clad within my breeches, nevertheless responded to his attentions; for I was at the time full fifteen years old; and I had, you will recall, received some early training in that area at the hand of Brother Dagobert. "Why yes, indeed, I find I can report to you, and firsthand," continued Monsieur and chuckling the whiles, "a most excellent lengthy nozzle!" And the company fell to laughing vigorously and stroking the lengths of each other's noses, the Marquis d'Effiat scampering from one gentleman to another, the Chevalier de Lorraine even making bold to stroke the royal nose, I mean Monsieur's. Mme de St. Estève, giggling with the others, fanned heartily at her blushing face with a handkerchief.

"Leave off, leave off!" cried the marquise, herself not a little amused by their amiable sport. "Sir, you are too forward with my dwarf!" And she thrust away the prince's hand from my ——— and said, "You shall not tamper with him, no, you shall not!" And laughing merrily, she nudged me lightly away from the circle of admirers.

"But madame, I protest!" cried Monsieur. "It is not my fault if your dwarf has a prodigiously lengthy tool, ha ha ha!" And everyone roared at his choice of the word. "Gentlemen, what say you?" But the gentlemen were laughing too lustily to reply. "And madame," then continued Monsieur, casting a meaningful eye at the marquise as if to signal some devilment afoot, "Monsieur Hugues's nozzle is nearly as long as my very own brother's: would you not say so?"

At that, there fell a deathly silence upon the room; and everyone sensed the cruelty, under the present circumstances, of any reference to my lord King Louis, to say nothing of the length of His nose.

In the stillness, the marquise rose slowly from her chair and faced the duke with an icy stare.

"The length of any gentleman's nose is a matter of indifference to me, sir—"

"Ohhh," Monsieur interrupted her, "say you so, madame?"

"—of indifference, sir, I say, as may indeed be attested by noting the snouts here present among my gentlemen guests."

It now befell to those gentlemen to suffer some mortification; and they could think of nothing more to do than to look about at each other's snouts and, as though to save face, snicker.

"I shall bid you good evening, messieurs," announced the marquise, and she turned and withdrew from the room; and she took me with her despite their cries of "No, leave us the dwarf! Madame! Take pity, I say! Monsieur Hugues! A tape, a tape—we shall measure his snout!" and such-like foolishness as hearty fellows will indulge themselves in.

Alas, reader: the marquise's sudden shift in humor that afternoon, though understandable, was not uncommon: for I began to see that there were days when, in spite of the occasional guests and in spite of my own ministrations, I am sorry to admit the fact, there were days, I say, reader, when the marquise suffered great bouts of despondency; and it was not difficult to tell that her exile from my lord King Louis was taking its toll upon her spirits. She would grow languid; and silent; and then quite out of sorts; and no wit could divert nor any sport distract her from her melancholy.

This present chapter I close on this most piteous note.

# 10

I SHOULD ADD AS A FOOTNOTE TO CHAPTER NINE that coincidental to my lord King Louis's campaign at the northern front that spring, Father Guibourg greatly increased his nocturnal devotions, making it an ill time for the infant male population of the Paris region, both newly born and not yet born. Ironically, a number of the Masses at this time were offered for the relief of some "unhappy creature deprived of the light of the sun"; I say "ironically," for we who were at Vaugirard were deprived ourselves, in a manner of speaking, removed from the radiance of my lord the Sun King; but I took the reference to be a less poetic one denoting in fact some member of the military or of the civilian entourage who was engaged in the campaign; for the front lines were then in Flanders, which is quite far north and sunless.

This increase in my ecclesiastical activity made me right grateful to be spending more time back at Vaugirard, where the itinerary was much lighter than at St. Germain: there were fewer grates to shovel out, fewer dogs to clean up after, a simpler sewer system, and overall more efficient sump pumps. That lighter work load, coupled with the decline in my business activity (I was now separated from most of my clientele), made it possible to find some extra hours of sleep; for my regular hours of sleep were severely curtailed by Father Guibourg's calls upon me. I do not know how Emil Vergeyck and La Voisin bore up under the increased strain, to say nothing of the good cleric himself; but he was a robust man despite his physical peculiarities.

Nevertheless, I was pleased to note that at about the same time of the king's return from the front, the number of nocturnal Masses declined sharply, the "outcasts" having now returned to the sunny Paris region. But I would not give you the impression that I begrudged my service to the abbé; for indeed I did not; and I continued to be comforted by the sounds of the Latin: even when my eyelids were heavy for want of sleep, a rousing *dominus vobiscum* or a *kyriay aylayison* or an *oratay fratres ut mayum ac vestrum sacrifichium accheptabilay fiat apud dayum patrem omnipotentem* would quickly goad them from their lethargy.

The occasion of my lord King Louis's return from Flanders very much affected Athénaïs, the divine marquise, and all those of us about her. In a benevolent act of Christian charity and at the king's own behest, expressed in an official statement the gravity of which accorded with His reconciliation at Easter with our Lord Jesus, the Marquise de Montespan was permitted to end her exile at Vaugirard and to return to the royal residence; and the apartment which she had previously occupied there was, as a gesture of largesse, restored to her. The occasion being a right solemn one in the life of the court, my most Christian lord, King Louis, graciously consented to appear briefly at it Himself in order to formally receive the marquise once again at the palace.

In acknowledgement of the king's zealous obedience to Mother Church, the company waiting upon the marquise that morning was composed of many pious females, not the least of whom was Mme Scarron, who had had, you will recall, a hand in His conversion, herself recently returned from a journey in the Midi whither she had taken Louis-Auguste, Duc du Maine, to the waters in the hope of curing his lame leg and club foot; though from the way the duke continued to limp, I believe the waters may have only served to erode whatever healthy bones there were in his leg in the first place; and the hobbled child of six years would not leave off an incessant blubbering that morning, no matter how many times he was vigorously taken up and shaken. Madame herself was quite out of sorts upon this occasion and made little effort to conceal it, and it was not so much due to du Maine's sniveling as to the occasion itself; for she would have been right well pleased for the marquise to stay on at Vaugirard indefinitely and would have felt the cause of piety much better served.

Yet chiefest amongst the females, at least in rank if not in piety, was the queen herself, Marie-Thérèse, emitting her various exhalations and accompanied by a most hideous Portuguese dwarf, who, on the way to the occasion, had been attacked, I was pleased to observe, by a greyhound: the foolish creature—the dwarf, I mean—had not yet perceived the system of hinged door panels whereby he might have escaped his tormentor; and so he had been severely mauled, which in fact did not greatly mar his appearance. (During one or two moments before the arrival of His Majesty to the reception, I had the distinct and uncomfortable impression that the queen was casting an eye upon me, as though the notion that I might serve to increase her retinue of dwarves had slowly begun to dawn on her thick mental powers; and I contrived as best I could to edge out of her eyeshot.) Also attending her was the Comtesse de Pommeret, though admittedly not there for her piety either but simply because at the card tables she had wheedled her way into the queen's good graces, not a difficult task, there being no one else seeking to try. The countess's eyesight had failed over the years along with her hearing, and quite frequently she stuck her wig on backwards, for she had not the money anymore to engage a woman to assist in her toilette.

Doña Elvira María Inez Jesús Juanita e Isabel Mecklembourg Barca de la Cruz, Baronesa de Valdepeñas, a widow and, like the queen, a Spanish woman, was another member of the formal party; she had been in deep mourning for two-and-twenty years and wore seven or eight rosaries about her neck; and had for some good while, along with Mme Scarron, also been most outspoken in her criticism of the Marquise de Montespan's previous liaison with my lord King Louis.

Filling out the assemblage were Mme Françoise de St. Estève, attendant to the marquise and looking sterner than usual; Mme de Vivonne, the marquise's sister-in-law; Gabrielle de Rochechouart, the marquise's sister, who was an abbess at Fontevrault and heavily veiled; and two Ursuline nuns from a convent near Médan.

And being counted now as virtually a member of the marquise's entourage, it was deemed fit that I should be included that day in the company as well.

This pious grouping, along with the divine marquise herself, who had returned from Vaugirard only that morning, was gathered in a stately room adjacent to her bedchamber in the southeast section of the palace where the reception was to take place. We remained standing, including the queen, near a large mantel to the rear of the room and were quite silent. At exactly the appointed hour, we heard from afar, in some distant room or hallway to the north of where we were, the voice of an usher: "Gentlemen! The King!" followed by the sound of three pairs of footsteps and one walking stick; and "Gentlemen! The King!" cried out a second usher, closer this time as the footsteps grew more distinct; and "Gentlemen! The King!" a third. A wave of anticipation swept through the waiting party; or perhaps for some it was a wave of mounting apprehension as for others a kind of awe, which grew, as the footsteps approached, almost into a sense of terror.

Louis-Auguste, the Duc du Maine, stopped crying.

"Gentlemen! The King!"

Suddenly the double doors burst open, and into the room advanced my lord King Louis, Fourteenth of the Name.

He was dressed with great sobriety, in dark-hued breeches and doublet; His shoes were barren of ribbons or of any ornamentation save the buckles, which were more functional than decorative, though they shone; He wore a subdued, twin-peaked wig and carried His hat, there being no feathers or other adornment upon it, under His left arm. In His right hand He held a stout walking stick.

Accompanying Him were Bishop Bossuet, who had urged my lord's act of piety at Easter past, and, behind him, Father Louis Bourdaloue, S. J., whose sermons had prodded Him to it. Like the bishop, Father Boudaloue was robed in a black cassock; and in his giant red hands he carried a thick Bible.

The king stopped; and to the deep curtsies into which the women had all fallen, He made a most elegant bow, full of respect and condescension, His hat, now in His hand, lightly grazing the floor as it swept downward and back. My own bow being as deep as I could make it—but you understand, there are limitations upon the depth of a dwarf's bow—I could see no more than the tip of my lord's shoe which was the more forward of the two. But when at length we had all recovered from these acts of obsequiousness, I was able, though my head was still lowered, to make out my lord's godlike features: the high, noble brow, the commanding eyes, the firm jaw and chin, the heroic lips, the perfect and quite excellent nose.

"Mesdames," announced my lord Louis in a reverberant voice that sounded much like the hum of a cello.

"Your Gracious Majesty," murmured the females, quite like a cluster of flutes.

Whereupon, herself, Athénaïs, the divine one, she to whom I had yielded up my heart whilst she to me her garden—stepped forward and once again offered the king a most respectful curtsey.

"Madame," said my lord, "I am right well pleased to see that you are in good health."

"Your Highness," quoth she in response, "indeed my health has much improved within this past moment; and I thank Your Highness for it."

Whereupon there was a light buzz of approval from the assembly at the pretty speech which with such deep respect she had offered; although the buzz produced by Mme Scarron might more nearly be described as a low snort. And just as the marquise was about to turn her head in madame's direction with a smile of the greatest serenity, Father Bourdaloue stepped in closer to the group, the Bible clutched to his breast, and raised his right hand in benediction.

"*Benedicat vos,*" he began, whereupon everyone dropped to one knee but for the two nuns who dropped to four, "*omnipotens dayus patair et filius et spiritus sanctus.*"

"*Amen,*" everyone replied and rose.

Then with a most delicate, most graceful, most elegant gesture whereby He lightly touched two of the fingers of His right hand—the middle finger and the ring—to the marquise's left elbow, my lord King Louis indicated that she should withdraw privately with Him across the room into the alcove of a window; the which she did, herself matching His delicacy, grace, and elegance with her own. And we watched as the two of them spoke together in low tones about what I know not, for I could not hear nor did not think it meet to strain to catch their words, however great my curiosity; but the Comtesse de Pommeret clapped her trumpet to her ear and leaned forward, though clearly to no avail.

Presently, we witnessed the marquise apply a fine handkerchief to her upper cheeks and then directly to her moist eyes; and in moments, the king followed suit, for they were both weeping quite openly.

"Yes, clearly God is well pleased. It is an excellent and most reverent conclusion," said Bishop Bossuet, speaking in a low tone to the females so as not to dispel the piety of the moment. "May Christ reward their penitence and bless their newfound holiness."

"Christ bless them," said Father Bourdaloue, S. J.

"Christ bless them," said the Ursulines, blessing themselves the whiles.

"Christ bless our gracious sovereign," added Mme Scarron.

"Christ bless Him," said the Ursulines, blessing themselves once more.

"Amen," said other members of the company, blessing themselves as well, so that by that time everyone in the room was right well blessed.

"And may Christ also bless our belovèd pastors who have wrought such a miracle," said Scarron, to which devout sentiment both priests nodded in deep gratitude; and blessed themselves again.

And then, reader, believe the following or not, but it is in all the history books, you may confirm it for yourself: my lord King Louis, at that moment, again touching the divine woman's elbow to guide her gently forward, the two of them moved slowly across the room to a door opposite, turned and made their reverences to the females, to Bishop Bossuet, to Father Boudaloue, S. J., and even to myself; at which, my lord King Louis opened the door and led the divine Athénaïs into her bedchamber; and He closed the door behind them.

And He locked it.

There was a long and horrified silence among the party left standing in the outer room, and even Mme Scarron was rendered quite speechless. But presently Marie-Thérèse the queen spoke up:

"*¡Esa puta cabrona será mi muerte!*" said she, a remark which, translated from the Spanish, means "That rotten whore will be the death of me!" Whereupon she let fly a tremendously noisy and redolent fart and sailed—as much as a fat, middle-aged glutton is capable of sailing—from out of the room and away.

"What did she say?" asked the Comtesse de Pommeret, but no one took the trouble to repeat the statement as the group broke apart and began drifting off.

In the shock of this resounding spiritual reversal, which was not unlike the setback she had suffered upon the legitimizing of Montespan's children, Mme Scarron could think of nothing else to do but to give the one of those children present, the Duc du Maine, a sound drubbing and to drag him from out of the room, though for once in her company, he had been utterly well behaved.

Only Doña Elvira María Inez Jesús Juanita e Isabel Mecklembourg Barca de la Cruz, Baronesa de Valepeñas, lingered alone in the reception room; and after I had closed the doors, the last to leave, I stooped down, quietly lifted one of the hinged dog panels, and peered back inside. The most devout baroness had fallen to her knees; but not in an act of piety, reader, no, not a bit of it: for I saw that she too knew panels and their uses though she was neither a dog nor a dwarf (being a rather large-boned woman, in fact) and had lifted one of the panels on the bedchamber door and was straining to hear what was going on inside.

That same evening, the Marquis de Lamballe rejoiced with a loud shout of "Huzzah!" when he found me waiting once again, at eight o'clock, outside the royal bedchamber to receive the royal vessel, for he knew that now I would again be regularly at my post; and my clients at the gaming tables rejoiced as well, though their reaction was perforce more restrained, each of them believing—if it were possible after all this time!—that he or she was singularly favored with my services. And here they all were again, all of them, their fingers down between their legs, grasping at aces and kings and sometimes at queens and even at jacks, gnarled fingers, pudgy fingers, bony fingers, flabby fingers, stubby fingers, or fingers so lined with rings that they could maneuver only as a kind of grim metallic paw, fingers with dirty nails or cracked nails, hairy fingers, greasy fingers, leathery fingers, clammy fingers, sweaty, stinking fingers, fingers dark with liver spots, and sometimes even missing fingers, all of them clutching and snatching at the thin slices of cardboard as though their very lives depended upon them, as more often than not they did; and here again were other parts of the female clientele, all of them likewise—but hold: I shall not continue; for my Lady Modesty steps in and draws shut the curtain that no offense be given, no impropriety nor mortification endured.

(Here I stop and report a delay suffered in continuing this account. I found, directly upon waking this morning, that at some time during the night a chunk of the ceiling beneath my aerie had given way, that is to say, a section of plaster had fallen down into the chapel vestibule below and shattered into a thousand scraps; and I believe truly that it was due to the ongoing reconstruction in a drawing room adjoining the vestibule and that it reflects the shoddy workmanship of the present age; although it is equally possible that a length of freshly laid plaster had failed to dry properly, what with the wretched dampness of this place, and had simply given way. Whatever its cause, the event opened up a gaping hole in the

floor of my rookery; and I have spent the better part of the morning moving my belongings—meager as they are—northward within the eaves to
the next air louver over. You may imagine my horror when, for a brief
while, I thought that a large part of my manuscript had, like the plastering, fallen away, and although it would not have been shattered, it
might very well have been scattered, so that my text might have been
discovered by an enquiring public well before the moment appropriate
to its publication, and to boot, in an utterly disjointed order. But—and
I have thanked St. Anthony of Padua for his help—the fact is that the
manuscript had merely slid three or four feet farther down into the lath-
ing, from which I was able at length to retrieve it; yet in doing so, I let slip
one page of chapter three from my grasp, and it flew through the dreadful
hole and sailed down into the dusty vestibule below; and when I hastened
down to collect it, I found that it had been pissed upon: not, I am quite
sure, however shoddy their work, by any of the construction laborers,
but more likely by one of the royal dogs. The page, number 30, contains
a reference to the holy rosary and ought not to have been pissed on; I have
hung it up to air. For these reasons, however, reader, I have lost nearly an
entire day's worth of writing. The matter is regrettable; even so, I believe
that my new situation, now somewhat farther north and more removed
from the hubbub of the work site, will be beneficial to these efforts.)

From my standpoint, the only vexatious matter resulting from the
reuniting of the two divinities was that my services to the female half
were less frequently required; and yet it was not the moment for despair,
for I had still the memory of that Eden, and unlike our first most sinful
parents, the faint hope of a return to it under some future circumstance.
And I believe—no, I am quite certain—that the marquise quite well
understood the rigor of my banishment and was sympathetic to me for
she did often smile upon me when we met and did me many a small
kindness: yet can any kindness offered by a goddess truly be considered
small? For her every gesture toward me, every glance in my direction,
her merely passing through a room in which I was, each bounty to me
was conceived in the majestical, and each could uproot mountains as
easily as make a dwarf begin to blush and stammer. I shall relate you such
a kindness; and you will understand.

It occurred on the occasion of Louis-Auguste, the Duc du Maine's,
seventh birthday—an anniversary considered of great moment to a child

by the Fathers of the Church, who instruct that once arrived at our seventh birthday, we have attained the age of reason; so that from the seventh birthday onward, whenever we elect to sin, we do so fully possessed of the knowledge of our sinning and of our sinfulness: we sin, so to speak, with our eyes wide open and our colors nailed to the mast, we sin with all our heart and soul; and therefore we are to be quite properly rewarded with eternal hellfire by God—or by those same Fathers of the Church, who may withhold the absolution of our sin if they suspect the repentance which we proclaim or if they have simply taken a disliking to us.

As the Duc du Maine arrived at this momentous occasion, a formal observance of it was arranged for the unhappy child—for who would not be unhappy to abandon the state of childish irresponsibility in which you might do absolutely anything you chose, to face a long life of intentional, reckonable sin? The day being a fair one, in May, the event was held in the English garden; for my lord King Louis is fond of the open air; but Mme Scarron, governess, protested that the delicate child should not go outdoors for fear of contracting the ague; but she was overruled. Many notables were present: my lord Himself, King Louis (Louis-Auguste's father); Athénaïs herself, the Marquise de Montespan (his mother); Her Majesty the Queen Marie-Thérèse (of no relation to him and of no interest); Mme Scarron (his governess); Louis the Dauphin, then sixteen years old and already quite overweight (his half brother); Monsieur (Philippe), the Duc d'Orléans, himself recently home from Flanders (his uncle); Louis-César, Louise-Françoise, Louise-Marie (his brother and two sisters, the last-named newly hatched); Françoise-Marie (his third sister, who though present was as yet unseen, for she still had some months left to cook); Jacques Bénigne Bossuet, Bishop of Condom (Louis-Auguste's brother in Christ but otherwise quite unrelated); the Chevalier de Lorraine and the Marquis d'Effiat, companions to Monsieur (unrelated); the Comtesse de Pommeret, companion to the queen (unrelated); and others numbering some thirty to forty persons, including the Mancinette, herself in excellent array.

Louis-Auguste, who quite hated all gatherings of more than two people including himself, wished more than anything that day to hobble off alone and catch insects and pull their legs and wings off; but suddenly realizing that such a sport was very likely a sin against God's creatures and that he would no longer be able to enjoy it on a debt-free basis, he determined to endure as best he could the first day of the age of reason; but he could not, even so, put a halt to any number of large tears which welled up in his eyes and rolled solemnly down both his cheeks.

After some feasting and the performance of several musical passages from *La Princesse d'Elide,* a ballet by Monsieur Lully, there were gifts offered to the young duke: three excellent books, Bishop Bossuet's *Exposition of the Catholic Faith,* a *Dictionary of Ancient Greek,* and the Duc de Luxembourg's study of the *Siege of Gravelines,* which the author had been obliging enough to inscribe; a selection of some fine linen handkerchiefs, which Mme Scarron advised the child to make immediate use of; and a felt cap. It was at this point that a role for me in the festivities, as graciously assigned me by the Marquise de Montespan, came into play: for the final gift to the young duke was to be a metal rack for his faulty leg, a new one and larger than what he had been wearing since the age of four, a device which, by the employment of screws, turn-bolts, and an iron collar secured around his ankle, was designed to stretch the entire limb (though not to correct the club foot) in order to render it the same length as his other leg. (Over the years, the device proved, by the way, to be highly effective, for it did indeed lengthen the afflicted limb, and even some several inches beyond the length of the healthy one.) But it was the marquise's pretty conceit that it should be I who presented this gift to the duke, for, as she told Mlle des Œillets privately and with a twinkle in her eye, I was right well experienced in matters of the lower limbs; and moreover my own size would serve as a foil, to heighten the impression made by the new leg lengthener; and such-like pleasant ironies which she delighted in, and which did me great honor, reader, and truly it was a signal honor to be designated such a role by her in that exalted gathering: so that I blushed, as you may imagine, when, upon my cue, I stepped forth from the adjacent crowd, bearing the gift, to approach the six royal figures who were seated in chairs upon the grass (for you must understand that no one but the royal family, however notable, was permitted to sit in the presence of His Majesty; and we were all standing in a loosely formed semicircle some distance away); and I did first an obeisance to my lord King Louis XIV and a second to the queen, who peered down at me from above her several chins, a third to Monsieur, a fourth to the dauphin, a fifth to Louis-Auguste (he sat upon a footstool), and a sixth to the divine marquise herself, which were well received with a light round of applause; and I blushed yet more deeply. My heart was thumping in my breast, my breath came in spurts, my cheeks were aflame as I proceeded to Louis-Auguste's stool, which stood nearby to a hedge about my own size; and I placed the gift into his hands. Whereupon Louis-Auguste stared at the device, then let loose a maniacal howl, for he knew right well what that gift was, such a thing as he had already endured some three most agonizing years; and it brought to mind those other torments I had visited upon the lad some years since in the privacy of his bedchamber, which struck a pang of remorse in my breast; and I believe that Louis-Auguste would have run away but that he was restrained by his governess, who then approached the family circle and curtsied to my lord King Louis:

"Your Highness," quoth she, "the child indeed has the ague, it is quite certain; and the evening air cannot be but harmful to his condition." And turning to the Marquise de Montespan: "As his guardian, I can detect the signs of the child's broken health."

"As his mother," the marquise replied with a gentle smile, "I can detect the signs of his broken heart."

"¡Ridículo!" replied the queen, reverting to her native tongue. "That is a most willful niño—wrap the handkerchiefs around the throat, this will ameliorate." And she ordered another service of sugared prune tarts from a footman.

But his divine mother took up Louis-Auguste, Duc du Maine, onto her lap and comforted the little boy with many there-there's and now-now's and tush-tush's; and "We shall leave off the hateful brace, shall we not? Yes, my little man, at least until after the summer heat, yes, we shall, yes, yes," said she.

Whereupon Scarron retreated with an ill-concealed snort to where she was standing in the outer ring.

"Monsieur Hugues," continued the marquise in a quiet voice, "pray set aside the brace, leave it there behind the hedge." And when I had done so, "Well done, Monsieur Hugues; and well presented too," she cried, and laughing, "and then well set aside!" And she let fall upon me a radiant, most loving smile, at which I blushed once more and to which I bowed once more. And at that moment I would most gladly have exchanged places with the Duc du Maine—club foot, short leg, rack, snotty nose, governess, and all—if I could have sat there upon her lap, been held in her arms and caressed by her lips; but I knew that I must be grateful for what kindnesses she did bestow upon me; and so I truly was. Moreover I knew that the Duc du Maine might quite justly and openly claim those attentions which he received from her by virtue of having been purged of bastardy; and although as you have seen, the process had in no way favored his outward person, his leg continuing to be disproportionately short and his nose continuing most objectionably to run, yet the favors which he enjoyed publicly from the marquise were an indication of the profound efficacy of that purge.

"You may stand down, monsieur," the marquise said quietly to me, nodding her head in approval; and I turned to rejoin the crowd.

And then:

"Madame." Suddenly behind me, I heard the majestic and sonorous voice of my lord King Louis; and reader, I stopped in my tracks, as though caught in some wondrous spell. "Has the boy then," I heard my lord continue, "become your personal dwarf?" Reader: He was speaking of me, for there was no other dwarf in that assembly—the queen had not her pets about her—my lord was actually speaking of me! Without thinking, and as though still swept up in the sudden spell He had cast, I turned; and I bowed to His Majesty; and when I stood up again, I lowered my gaze out of great respect to His divinity, and I felt the eyes of all the rest of that august company shift (downward) toward myself.

And now I heard the second divinity speak:

"Why, yes, Your Majesty," said the marquise, almost as though surprised by the notion, "it seems indeed that he has; for he serves me many a useful purpose, my lord; it is a right handy dwarf to have about." She glanced quickly over to where Mlle des Œillets was standing and smiled. And at her words of praise, I blushed deeply yet again.

But Mme Scarron blew her nose with a certain vehemence.

"Beg pardon?" I heard the Comtesse de Pommeret enquire, for she was standing not far from Scarron in the outer ring. And so Scarron blew her nose once more.

"It is not an ill-looking youth," said His Majesty, appraising me up and down, "not at all, as dwarves go. Would you not say, Philippe?"

"An excellent creature," Monsieur agreed, "and one I recently inspected myself, did I not?" And he glanced out to the crowd in search of the Chevalier de Lorraine.

"Why, truly," said the chevalier and making bold to venture a few steps toward Monsieur and bowing somewhat, "indeed it is certainly a more presentable creature than what d'ye call him? Alonso? or Alberto or Alfonso or what d'ye call him—?"

"Alfonso," said the queen.

"—and surely more so than Diego." And he fell to laughing and clapping his hands. (His references were to two of the shorter members of the queen's entourage.)

Her Majesty sniffed.

"Diego! Diego!" hooted Monsieur, joining in the laughter. "No, you have passed the limits! No, no; but on the other hand, Monsieur Hugues is not so handsome as Jean-Yves Laval, would you say?" And he turned to the Marquis d'Effiat, who stood not far away. "Didi?"

"No, no!" replied the marquis, hurrying forward as swiftly as his shoe ribbons allowed and bowing several times. "But I would add as well that neither is he as pretty as the young viscount."

"Tosh, the viscount!" said the chevalier. "Why, the viscount uses paint!"

"Never!" exclaimed the marquis, and his face began to grow quite red. "Never say so!"

"Oh yes, I have seen the smudges," replied the chevalier. "Yes, yes, yes, I have," he continued above the marquis's protests, "do not contradict me, I know it. Though even so, I grant you, I grant you, the viscount is in fact a pretty lad."

"Yes," said the marquis, his dignity somewhat restored by this concession. "Yes, he is. And the stableboy, too."

"Oh yes, the stableboy, oh God! yes! His ankles!" the chevalier readily agreed.

"Yes, yes, his ankles, indeed, the stableboy," Monsieur corroborated. And the three of them fell to smirking and grinning. And the two courtiers began sporting about with each other at the distance where they stood.

"¡Qué porquería!" said the queen. "Such wickeds: you must be ashamed of youself—all three of you does!" And she threw a prune (which she had picked from out of her tart) at her brother-in-law which landed directly into his wig; immediately Monsieur shrieked, leapt up, and called for his valet, who was in attendance a distance away, and together the two retired behind some boxwood in order to repair the damage. And we could hear Monsieur's cries of indignation, for apparently the prune had become lodged quite deeply into the intricacies of the wig. For her part, the queen emitted loud guffaws at every shriek from behind the hedge and cried, "¡Qué puntería!"

"Indeed," said Mme Scarron, "indeed," in agreement with the queen's censorious opinion, and she eyed my lord King Louis most directly, who ignored her; but she did not feel free in that company to level, verbally, her own censure of the gentlemen's idle prattle.

"Come here, boy."

Instinctively I looked up: for when the conversation had devolved upon me and my merits relative to other lads'—I shall not say "beauty" relative to theirs, reader—I had bent forward and as though quite shrunken into myself: which, as now I think upon it, must have produced a most minuscule package in the midst of so grand a gathering.

"Come here, boy."

And yes: it was in fact the cello voice of my lord King Louis XIV; and it was in fact, dear reader, directed to me. I felt my knees begin to tremble.

"Hugues! Do as you are instructed," Scarron called out. "Do you idle? Do you hesitate?"

Whereupon, my heart once again thumping in my breast, I stepped forward and approached my lord. He: regal, proud, mighty, of a most majestic bearing; nearby to Him, the marquise: serene, radiant with maternal love, and of a truly celestial beauty; and the queen: thick, dowdy, and most evenly distributed across the entire surface of her chair.

King Louis, Fourteenth of the Name, then studied my person intently.

"No, no," said He, though I think I could scarcely hear Him for the pounding in my chest and the ringing in my head and the clanging in my ears; and His Majesty was now speaking in a low tone and quite privately to the two women. "No, no, the boy is a proper enough boy. Yes?"

"As you say," said the queen, now eyeing me fixedly, "it is."

The divine marquise smiled.

"How old are you now, boy?" my lord asked quietly.

Not being at the time entirely certain of the answer to that question, I may be forgiven, I hope, for choosing a more advanced age.

"Your Majesty, Sire: I am seventeen years old."

"More young," retorted the queen and quite peremptorily. "These infante he does make exaggerates."

Now I was at first somewhat surprised that the queen should hold an opinion of the matter; but then I recalled that since she kept a bevy of dwarves about her, she very likely considered herself an expert on their qualities, whether in fact she was bright enough to do so or not.

My lord King Louis scowled at her.

Monsieur now sauntered back into the family circle as though nothing had happened to his wig. "What is it?" he enquired.

"Indeed," said the Marquise de Montespan, ignoring the interruption, "is it of any great concern, Sire? What if he be younger by a year or so than he claims; it is surely a common foible among children."

My lord turned back to me. "Quite so," He said, "and I think that the sudden loss of a year or two has not diminished to any degree the growth of Monsieur Hugues's nose; for mark, see what right excellent an organ he has there in the middle of his face."

To which the Marquise de Montespan replied once again: "My lord," said she, "Monsieur Hugues is a good and worthy subject: you see how readily he has embraced Your Majesty not only for his master but for his model as well." At which pretty compliment, the queen relieved herself with a prodigious belching effort, to which the Comtesse de Pommeret, from across the lawn, responded in kind; but my lord inclined His head toward the author of the gracious remark.

"And I vow," said Monsieur, tugging somewhat at his wig and now speaking aloud to the full gathering so that his two friends might hear, "there has been growth elsewhere about Monsieur Hugues's person." He paused and rolled his eyes at the queen. "Why madame!" he continued, in a mocking, simpering tone. "I mean upon the lad's chin—pray, what else could I possibly have meant?" a remark which caused the Marquis d'Effiat to giggle uproariously into his handkerchief. "See, madame, there is some excellent growth sprouting upon his chin, as it is only proper for a lad of—what is it? eighteen years?"

"No matter," said the king.

"More young, more young, I say," replied the queen with a snort at her brother-in-law.

"Ah, fifteen, is it then? Sixteen?" he replied. "Why then, it is a right manly creature! Well done, Monsieur Hugues!" And he clapped me soundly on the back.

"So it is," said the divine marquise, now studying the two or three random tendrils that stood upon my chin. "But still, he is not grown so manly that he does not blush—for see, he has turned quite as scarlet red as a late summer beet!"

"My father," said the queen, smacking her lips at my discomfort, "he was also like a beet."

"What did she say?" cried the Comtesse de Pommeret from the crowd; but no one obliged her.

"It is grown quite damp," said my lord King Louis, and He stood up; and the rest of the party, the five who were seated, also stood up—the queen aided by a sturdy waiting woman, the marquise with Louis-Auguste still in her arms, the dauphin, and Monsieur; the company standing beyond all bowed and curtsied deeply and then retreated as though to make way for the royal family though there was ample room for its passage; and when they had done so, my lord quit the gathering, followed by the other five; whereupon the rest of the company then began to disperse through the dewy, darkening grass, back toward the chateau; and we who brought up the rear of the company could hear from up ahead a quiet weeping as the Duc du Maine was turned over once again to the charge of his governess.

I was only grateful that as the year of my birth had become a topic of discussion, the matter of my stature had not, or at least no more than the unavoidable reference here and there; but the stumpishness of my legs and feet, the pudginess of my fists, the proportions of my head and body—those details had not been remarked upon. And that was to me a boon, especially in that company where Monsieur and his waggish companions would doubtless have made great sport at my expense. But yet I would have gladly endured any of that sport had it been the price to pay for the attention bestowed upon me that evening by my lord King Louis; for I experienced—during those brief moments, reader—the joy which an abandoned child must feel when, after years of loneliness, he is at last restored to a kind and loving father. And for a fleeting moment I let myself imagine what it would be indeed to have a father, yes, and a mother too as long as we are allowing ourselves to indulge in a fancy, and what it would be to be a proper and whole offspring like those I saw all about me. And like Louis-Auguste, Duc du Maine, I wept; but my tears of longing for what I was not to have were mixed with tears of gratitude for the royal munificence which had blessed me that evening.

The following morning—and here is the instance of the marquise's kindness which I promised to relate to you—just as I had returned from the meadow to the privy area and was about to begin washing out the royal vessel, Mlle des Œillets approached me; and she handed me an object wrapped in a napkin.

"Monsieur Hugues, my lady the marquise sends you this," said she. "And has instructed me to say that it is small wonder that there is confusion as to what age you are, for no one has ever taken note of your birthday; this then is a birthday present for your sixteenth year—or seventeenth, or whatever is the case."

Reader! At that I became quite giddy in the knees, and I stood there like a gawking fool, and suddenly I felt a burning sensation in my eyes as the tears surged up into them, and I said nothing.

"Why, open it then, Monsieur Hugues!" said mademoiselle. "See what it is the gift she has made you!"

And so, slowly and carefully I undid the napkin; and within lay a razor, its handle made of bone, the blade of which could be folded back down inside the handle when not in use.

"See? It is a fine razor which my lady sends you," Mlle des Œillets whispered to me. "And she said that you are to make good and proper use of it; and that you are to take care," and here entered a note of merriment into her voice, "that you not cut your throat with it nor your nose or your tongue, ha ha! or any other part about you except the whiskers on your chin." And she laughed prettily, ruffled my hair, and hurried away.

But I found that I could scarcely see the beautiful razor, for the tears in my eyes began brimming over and went coursing down my cheeks; and so I closed the razor and hugged it to me and sat upon the ground for a short while until I could recover myself; and thence returned to the washing of my lord's vessel.

But that very evening, reader, I applied some tallow soap to my chin and then the razor and made my chin quite smooth; and so I did every day thereafter; and I was right proud of my fine smooth chin, and I never grew a beard, nor a mustache, nor a goatee, nor sideburns neither.

# 11

IF YOU WOULD TRAVEL FROM St. Germain-en-Laye to the town of Versailles, you must pass through Marly, then nearby to Louveciennes and through Le Chesnay on the St. Germain Road; and eventually you reach Versailles and thence the chateau, which is your destination. Indeed there can be no other reasonable destination in Versailles: the town is ill situated in a low-lying, marshy area; and as your open coach hurdles forward along the road and the wind strikes against your face, you perceive more and more the odors of stinking water, of fetidness, of old and lingering swamps. Subsequently the views which you have of the town itself do little to dispel this pervasive miasma; for Versailles is quite a foul place, with rude shacks for houses, piles of slops and pools of stagnant water in all the roadways, and with pigs and goats running loose through the sewerage. The inhabitants contribute no better impression, for they are beggars and peasants, thieves, the diseased and infirm, cripples, whores, Jews, pimps and pickpockets, vagrants, coxcombs, and all manner of squalid and reeky humanity, if humanity they may indeed be called.

And yet you do come at last upon the chateau; it has changed considerably over the years and I daresay will change more in the years to come, for it is constantly in a state of renovation and enlargement; but when first I saw it rising nobly above the construction yards and indeed above the rank boggery in which it stands, it was apparent to me how zealously every effort was being expended to raise a structure befitting the First Divinity of all—befitting Apollo—befitting indeed the Sun King Himself, the Fourteenth Majesty of the Name of Louis.

Indeed, in its vastness and grandeur, the chateau is an entire royal city unto itself and as large, but utterly different from the vile one through which one must pass to reach it.

The structure stretches wide on either side of a central, recessed court; and it soars to a height of three stories but is twice as high as so many stories normally are. These dimensions I came to perceive in full as the coaches which bore me and all the court made their bumpy way through the teeming activity of the workmen and approached the building itself. For if, as is customary with me, I feel somewhat daunted by the proportions of ordinary, everyday things about me—chairs, hedges, men, women, hunting dogs, and the like—I felt, as we drew near to the Palace of Versailles that day, quite overwhelmed at being flung into an extraordinary world of titans: and so indeed I had, it is a most apt figure of speech.

Even once past the splendor of the chateau itself and shunted off onto a side street, where I was left standing before a structure called the Grand Commun (which serves in part as kitchen for the chateau), even standing, I say, before that lesser but still royal building, I felt its door towering above me; and indeed I was obliged to wait until someone chanced by and opened it, for I could not reach the handle myself; and the journey across the threshold into a vast central hall required, it seemed, though my memory may exaggerate, almost a minute's traveling time.

This being my first trip to the new palace—we were to stay there several months—it was allowed me to arrange my things—my clothes, my brush, my picture book, and my razor—on a ledge in the kitchen broom closet; and a straw mattress was set behind one of the washtubs where I should sleep; it was only some weeks later that I began my exploration of the upper story of the palace building itself and into the attic and garrets, in search of more suitable roosting, which in time I found: it is in the western side of the north wing, quite near the central section, and looking down, through a louver, onto the gardens' north parterre; louvers like my own have been found to be most useful throughout the entire structure to allow the circulation of air within the eaves and above the interior ceilings, where dampness is a problem, given the extreme humidity of the area.

I had been brought hither (for I am at Versailles as I write this) by the Marquise de Montespan, herself traveling with the court, to spend some

several months; and it was a new recognition—or so it seemed to me—
of my position in court circles (though I assure you, in the outermost
ring) that I was not left behind as before, alone in the drafty, empty halls
of St. Germain. It is true that I was still assigned chores to perform,
superior and inferior, in these brilliant new surroundings; but the palace
being so much vaster than the chateau at St. Germain, there was a much
larger staff to provide services and upkeep: footmen and chambermaids,
cooks and butlers, ushers and housekeepers, all ranging in a well-defined,
closed, and thoroughly inflexible hierarchy; and thus, despite my tasks,
it was some time before my own position in the ranks could be clearly
determined.

Here as well, reader, among the staff were the blue boys; these formed
a corps of pages, sons of the nobility, aged twelve to eighteen, who lived
together in a barracks up in the garret of the Grand Commun, and who
fulfilled many functions about the place: the serving of occasional food
and beverage, the running of errands, delivering private letters, fetching
footstools and cushions—generally lighter and more privileged tasks
than ash-shoveling, sewer tank repair, and the disposal of slops; but not
in any way more privileged, I should add, than those very delicate enterprises of mine beneath the tables. In the afternoons the blue boys were
given instruction in riding and dancing and other arts, in Greek, Latin,
orthography, oratory and rhetoric, ethics and maths; and their uniforms
were of a most magnificent blue woolen material with splendid embroidery and with white hose, and thus it was that they were called the blue
boys; and the camaraderie amongst them was most boisterous—and so I
have heard was the buggery. They did their own battles with the royal
hounds and frequently conspired to visit various forms of torment on
those devils. Some certain of the boys had begun, like myself, to require
the use of a razor every morning (or every other morning), I observed,
for I studied them as closely as I could, albeit from a distance, and especially those boys nearest my own age; and I could see signs that some
of the shavers had been careless and not mown the chin crop evenly nor
reaped as smoothly as I, or had on occasion even nicked their chins and
applied plasters to the cuts. Even so, I thought them excellent, excellent
lads! and right handsome in their uniforms! and full of such jovial humor
and mischief and high spirits, like fine young beagles! But yet I was careful to steer out of their way; for I was not so naïve as to think that the

blue boys would ever befriend me or that they would not delight in making sport of my size and shape; which on occasion they did, three of them
stuffing me once into the drawer of a small cupboard and closing it shut;
where I was obliged to stay some two hours and a half, for I could not
budge the drawer, having no leverage, and it was pitch dark within; until
a housekeeper happened to open the drawer in search of some bolster
cases; and she kicked me smartly for sloughing off my chores that afternoon, though she had no idea what they were; and so I avoided the blue
boys; but I continued to look at them from afar.

Aside from the major constructions on the exterior of the Versailles
Palace, a great interior project had been undertaken that year within the
northern flank, which was the rebuilding of the extensive state apartments. This included, which is a thing I noted immediately, the execution
of ceiling adornments throughout those apartments, vast paintings, alle-
gories depicting various deities streaking across the heavens in several
states of *déshabille* and accompanied by unidentified members of the
heavenly host; the effect of these decorations was most impressive, if not
a little trying on the neck as one gazed aloft at all that bustling celestial
activity. Below, in all the bustling restructuring of rooms and hallways in
that wing, some of the work had been finished by the time of our arrival,
but much remained to be done, chiefly the plastering, which had proven
difficult in the pervasive dampness; and soggy chunks of plaster would
drop down without warning from above and it was wise to attend to
where you were going. In addition, the plasterers had set up barriers here
and there and huge scaffoldings, which increased the sense of confusion
about the place, for the palace is complex. Adding to that confusion was
work being done on most of the doors throughout the entire building, whereby the same system of swinging panels was being installed to
accommodate His Majesty's dogs as was at St. Germain; and wrangling
broke out frequently between the workmen and members of the court
whose privacy was disrupted by the persistent opening and closing of
doors and sawing and hammering and nailing upon them during their
reconstruction.

Reader, I shall not linger more on this description of the palace; you
may go to see it for yourself, you know, it is open to the public; but
you must arrive early in the morning, the crowds are quite numerous;
and you may stroll at your leisure into many of the interior rooms and

may even observe my lord King Louis XIV take lunch, as long as you stay in the queue formed for that purpose and move on through the room when so directed by the officers, doing nothing to interfere with the service and maintaining a respectful and silent courtesy. You may likewise watch the Royal Council meetings from the outer room, standing away from the portal as at St. Germain, although members of the court will have preference of place in that area. Pray wear a hat, it is only decent; and if you have not a hat, then you may rent one at the gate outside for fifty *centimes* a day, which is not dear when you consider the dignity of the place; you must take your hat off if addressed by a high-ranking person, civilian or military. In wintertime, it is advisable to keep your coat on indoors, for the Versailles Palace is immense, and the fires in the chimneys do little to ward off the cold. But be advised to dress soberly, not ostentatiously; I have observed many a vain and presumptuous visitor to array himself in gaudy, immoderate finery and to present some vulgar show, as though he himself were a member not of the general public but of the court itself; and he puts on not only this garish dress but haughty airs too, and thus he holds his nose aloft and pretends to a grandeur which he possesses not. On the other hand, pray do not appear naïve; nor gawk foolishly at the many richnesses which will delight your eyes nor exclaim loudly at the height of the ceilings or at the paintings adorning them nor at the massiveness of the moldings, like some bumpkin. Do not feed the dogs; do not taunt or call to any of them, do not throw things at them or stand in their pathway; do not block any doorway panel in use by the dogs. None of the *chaises percées* is for use by the public, nor none of the chairs, stools, or footstools nor none of any of the furnishings whatsoever. Do not impede the flow of traffic, as for instance by lingering to stare at some wondrous sight or (as I have actually seen) stopping to pick at your scalp or at your companion's scalp: this is not the place, you had best do that elsewhere. You are also advised, though it is not expressly forbidden, not to enter the corridor known as the Rue de Noailles, which leads to the Noailleses' apartments, it being more often than not congested enough as it is; the family is large and with many enterprises. Sedan chairs requiring considerable room, you will be obliged to stand back when any pass by; likewise kindly stand apart for cows: for they are not there on some whim but are being led to the quarters of the princes of the blood in order to provide fresh milk, and to delay them is intolerable (there are those foolish visitors who laugh and sport to see a cow walking about indoors; but the beasts are not to be upset, lest the quality of the milk be adversely affected). Do not spit; and even though you will see many courtiers disobey this rule and commit other acts of uncleanness, that does not give you license to do likewise. If you should be outside the chateau and you come upon a company of servants bearing His Majesty's lunch or dinner toward the building, you are required to remove your hat, bow and enquire respectfully, "Is this the king's meal?" But do not expect a reply. If you follow these instructions, reader, you may pass an edifying day amidst the splendors of this remarkable structure.

In keeping with the overall grandeur, I discovered, immediately after I had begun my evening rounds in the gaming salons (for many of my clients having become established at the court at St. Germain, they traveled with us to Versailles), that even such everyday furnishings as the tables and chairs here, all of which were made of silver, think of it! were larger—and higher—than their counterparts at St. Germain. This overall increase in proportions very much benefited me, reader, providing just those several inches more of headroom and making circulation that much easier. On the other hand, there are certain tables both at St. Germain and at Versailles with infernal devices called stretchers; a stretcher is a horizontal member about six inches from the floor which stretches between all four legs and joins them together; and they are a constant bane to anyone employed below board, and I have suffered rips in my hose and breeches and bruises and lacerations to my shins in my unending struggles with the wretched devices.

As the ceilings were more lofty at the Palace of Versailles and the doorways wider, as the gardens spread across a broader acreage and even the card tables stood taller, as the household staff were more numerous, the rooms more immense, and the proportions of everything more colossal, so too, reader, were the expenses; I mean the myriad costs incurred by every member of the palace society, both to maintain their positions at court and when possible to better them. Lodgings were rented in the palace itself to over six hundred households, whose heads, their relatives, and servants numbered about ten thousand, though many of those households were consigned to attics or garrets, and it was rumored that one impoverished count lived in a cupboard; and the competition for even the most squalid closet was fierce and costly. An intricate sliding scale

determined the price of this lodging, based on the amount of space provided; location; proximity to the royal apartments; number of doors,
windows, and fireplaces (if any); rank of occupant; number of mistresses,
servants, and dogs; quantity of furnishings; and the like. Likewise the
price of offices at Versailles was high, considerably more so than at St.
Germain; so that if you wished to buy, say, the privilege of winding the
palace clocks every day or of sharpening the palace pen nibs or of oiling
the palace hinges, you must needs find your way (for a fee) through a
series of middlemen to secure the requisite letters (for a fee) which
would authorize the necessary licensing (for a fee) by the Department of
the Superintendent of the Royal Buildings.

Competition for these amenities amongst the courtiers and, as well,
the hangers-on, was fierce; and a rat race, the likes of which I had only
glimpsed at St. Germain, took up, and the rats were vicious: everyone's
financial situation became a cause of avid speculation, particularly when
they involved irregularities or questionable practices; and balance sheets
began to circulate that had been drawn up on pure conjecture and that
were then intensely studied, compared with others, and at times shrilly
fought over, the only person with any reliable knowledge on the matter,
the actual holder of the assets, being omitted from consultation. Even the
finances of people whose incomes would appear to be quite steady and
above reproach were now subject to appraisal, as for example the bishops;
for many a poor box was overturned daily to keep the primates afloat
at *vingt-et-un,* which was all well and good for the wealthier dioceses,
but it became a matter of much concern to bishops from impoverished
parishes beset with smallpox and a suddenly dwindling congregation or
with famine or other such pestilence; in which case, that bishop's days
at Versailles might well be numbered. Careful note now was taken of the
number of servants attending upon each inhabitant of the palace, for
the dismissal by Lord So-and-So of a footman or of a lady's maid might
presage the beginning of the end, to everyone's delight; whereas, by contrast, the addition of a footman or maid would indicate improvement
in the financial picture and be cause of understandable resentment and
rancor. Even the appearance on Madame Whoever's face of an inferior
grade of powder, and of corn starch in the more advanced cases, now gave
rise to elaborate fiscal calculation as to how long it would be before she
were bankrupt and of no further use to anyone. One such unfortunate

and impoverished noblewoman was so bent upon wearing powder of nothing but the finest quality that she offered herself up for sale in the street, or so the report went; but as she had no powder on at the time and was thus quite frightful to look at, for she was not graced with natural beauty, she was set upon by thieves and vagabonds, who thrashed her soundly and left her for dead; but it was rumored that in parting they flung a handful of coin into the ditch where she lay, for, they said, it was heartily satisfying to beat the woman senseless and indeed far more so than bedding her down would have been.

The financial situation of my lord King Louis was the only one above any speculation, as of course it was totally above question; though I understand that from time to time many of His financial advisors began to make efforts to curtail my lord's expenditures; yet that was foolish indeed, for does not my lord dispose of all property in France? And do not all monies in the kingdom belong in the end to Him? And all the wealth of whatever kind? Yes, indeed, I believe it is so. So that if my lord has need of funding, say, for the conduct of a war or for the building of some worthy edifice or for some sumptuous entertainment of ballets, concerts, and play going with the accompanying feasting and celebration, why, He has but to call in the funding from the nation for His purposes, and there can be no dispute about it.

One of His Majesty's less financially secure subjects was driven, in the interests of position at court, to most desperate means; for Mme Poulaillon, a somewhat benighted lady whom you have met briefly amongst my clients, was now, as more and more time was being spent at Versailles, finally expelled from the company, on the grounds that she was a commoner and no longer qualified to be of the group in their new and exalted surroundings; but it was in fact that she had run up unredeemable debts to most of them. Mme Poulaillon, now enraged at being ostracized, sought out the sponsorship, it seems, of a certain nobleman, the Marquis de la Rivière, a handsome fellow, the son of the Abbé de la Rivière; and she determined to rid herself of her husband Hector in order to be free to marry the marquis and become a member of the noble order; and for these purposes she had enlisted the services of a professional toxicologist. That expert had prescribed a regimen of arsenic, to be administered in the following manner: the victim's shirt was to be soaked in the arsenic solution, which would then produce severe inflammations upon his skin resembling the ravages of syphilis; such a regimen having two benefits: 1) arsenic is not easily detected, even in a cadaver; and 2) the syphilitic victim's reputation would be damaged, to say nothing of the victim himself, resulting, at least theoretically, in outward sympathy for the wife, who could then, after a perfunctory period of mourning, join forces with the marquis.

(Body of Christ, protect me. The subject of toxicology is not one to be taken lightly, reader, so that now as we enter upon it, you would do well to have about you some holy water or a crucifix.)

Fearing to take any chances in the business, Mme Poulaillon also purchased a Mass to be said for her diabolical intentions, and thus it was that I came personally to know of her endeavors. For one chilly night in December, as I was attendant upon the Abbé Guibourg (and using my handkerchief less to administer to my winter-cold-afflicted and runny nose than to smother out the reek of that cleric's breath), I heard his graveled voice thunder out the following invocation:

"Hear me! Alpha, Ley, Agla!" cried he at the top of his lungs. "Atoum, Sekhmet, Khnoum!" (For there had been added over the years the names of certain Egyptian divinities.) "By the bones of Judas and by the tree of Jesse, by the blood of this infant and by the blood of the Infant Jesus, I conjure you! And I do command you! That you see done the following: that Hector fall ill and that Hector succumb, and right swiftly, to the potions prescribed, and that Hector do so within forty days and forty nights of their administration to him. Hear me, Satan and the Powers of Darkness! I command it!"

By the end of this supplication, his voice had grown hoarse; and the chill wind that whipped through the sanctuary just at that moment could not have helped it, any more than it did a bit of good for my head cold; and as usual, the blast extinguished several candles. Reader, as I stole up to the icy altar to rekindle those flames, I could not but spy upon her who lay on the altar that night and upon her meadowgrass; and I recognized that meadowgrass, reader, and it was the meadowgrass of one of my former clients—no matter now briefly a client, I spotted the lawn—and that client was Mme Poulaillon herself! If, up to now, you have not fully appreciated madame's resolution in this matter, you will surely do so now; for she herself, upon the altar, was serving the abbé and his efforts in her own behalf; and although I had never before witnessed the sponsor as an actual participant in these devotions, this was, as it turned out, not to be the last time that I would do so.

Now it developed a day later that Mme Poulaillon's maid became alarmed when directed by her mistress to launder Monsieur Hector Poulaillon's shirts in arsenic, and she refused to do as bidden; and it is perhaps a sign of the times that a member of the servant class should decline to obey orders quite upon her own whim, and I sincerely hope that Mme Poulaillon dealt harshly with the creature. But in the event, the influence of Alpha, Ley, and Agla, to say nothing of the Egyptians, did not prevail over Hector Poulaillon, who, having discovered the entire business (might it have been the maid who informed on her mistress? and is such a state of affairs tolerable?), promptly and swiftly dispatched madame off to a convent, thus depriving her of her designs upon the Marquis de la Rivière and a return to the royal residence.

Now Monsieur Poulaillon's action deprived the Paris Police Force as well: that is, of making an arrest. Yet I think that deprivation will have been slight; for Mme Poulaillon was only a commoner as I have said, and by this time, the police force had begun to find its hands quite full of similar cases of nefarious doings and involving people of much finer standing than the wife of a petty functionary, the race for position at Versailles having now become quite reckless; and the police force did its job right diligently, being a vigilant band and led by the command of the excellent Lieutenant General Gabriel-Nicolas de la Reynie, who considered that his responsibilities went well beyond the regulation of "muck, street lights, and whores," as the popular saying spoke of police work; and he much inspired his officers and men.

The police were aided in their vigilance by people willing to blab, like that servant girl, for maids and valets will always know more than you wish them to, it is advisable to be cautious in their presence; but as well, and more significantly, by an increasing number of even less reliable members of society, I mean such people as supplied the arsenic to Mme Poulaillon and her like, that is, I mean ironically enough, the toxicologists themselves. For a number of them, when faced with arrest or having fallen under it, began to turn coat and to name the names of still others of their profession, hoping (vainly) thereby to escape punishment; and the more that were named and arrested, the more there were available and eager to add yet other names to the lengthening list.

Beyond the servants and the toxicologists, there was yet a third source of intelligence that came to blossom at that time, and this was the father confessors, especially those assigned to the parish of Notre Dame; at first they reported to the police merely that a number of penitents had been seeking absolution from the sin of murder by poisoning, the secrecy of the confessional not being violated by these revelations as long as no penitent's name were divulged; this restriction, however, could be circumvented for a reasonable price; and it was; for the Paris Police Force, along with its vigilance, was well supplied with funding, and it paid right handsomely; and thus General de la Reynie's men began rounding up people from all walks of life who had sought absolution from the divine of their sins and in some cases been given it, but who had, even so, not yet answered to earthly society for their designs; and they in turn named their confederates, and thus were also rounded up yet more workers of iniquity and indeed entire cabals of them, whether they were poison mongers, fortune-tellers, grave robbers, sorcerers, or abortionists, or merely the clients of these creatures, who themselves all named yet more names; and so the entire affair began to grow by leaps and bounds, as did the extraordinary number of arrests; and as it gathered greater and greater momentum, it created more and more of a furor throughout the city of Paris and all the surround, to say nothing of the town of Versailles and of the palace itself, including its innermost chambers.

Now I think I have done with this nerve-wracking subject for the moment.

But of a related subject, I must tell you that not all the machinations in court society involved such extreme measures as poisoning and murder; for people advanced their causes, whether it were of a professional nature or political, financial or titular, social or amatory, and some chose to do so by groveling and bootlicking to gain their purposes, by toadying and the like activity; and which, reader, in all candor, is the baser: slipping an honest dose of arsenic to someone or humiliating oneself and crawling about on the floor to achieve some niggling advantage? I shall leave it to you to judge.

Louise de la Vallière had been one of the king's earliest mistresses—though not before the Mancinette—but had fallen from favor and now was merely tolerated about the court; and she found herself in that latter category, I mean of the grovelers; but yet that had not caused her to cease making demands even after her sun had quite indisputably set. And one matter on which she based certain claims was the legitimization of the offspring of my lord King Louis and the Marquise de Montespan. La Vallière took stock of these doings and compared them together with the fact that she herself and my lord had also produced an array of bastards, five all told; three of whom had died relatively young and not having been legitimized, I presume they suffer for it to this day in hell, which is meet. But La Vallière now began a campaign that their two surviving children, like Louis's other offspring, should also be made whole and most especially the male child, whose name was Louis.

She was, alas, in no position to press her claims (though that did not deter her), for she had long since been abandoned by my lord except in one instance: my lord's nocturnal journeys to Montespan's apartment led directly through La Vallière's apartment, an arrangement originally established in order that His Majesty's shift in preference to the marquise might not be perceived at the time by the public; and the arrangement had been maintained over the years, even after the word was quite out and the marquise triumphant. And it is said that once, as He made His way through La Vallière's lodging, and she ever eager to plead her son's cause and with weeping and beseeching and the rending of her handkerchief, my lord tossed her the gift of a little dog in the hopes that she would leave off her wretched groveling; for no one except her was desirous that her child be made legitimate and most especially not the victorious Marquise de Montespan, who would brook no rivals to her own brood.

Yet eventually, reader, the persistent La Vallière succeeded in wearing my lord down, for He was always loyal to people even well after the fact; and thus, to many an objection, voiced by the brave and whispered by the craven, my lord saw fit finally to grant legitimacy to that same child Louis, and He granted it. La Vallière's delight, however, will be seen to have been quite short lived, for as the price of that royal favor she was summarily shipped out to a convent; and at last she encumbered the court no longer.

Yet the effect of La Vallière's campaign and of my lord's eventual acquiescence served to revive all the old arguments as to the wisdom of ever legitimizing the illegitimate; and many of the debates expanded beyond their original political nature and entered into a broader, more philosophical realm.

It was duly noted that although, as in the case of the Duc du Maine, there are no physical changes attributable to legitimization, that is, no betterment of limbs, yet the overall benefits are prodigious nonetheless; common belief holds that legitimated blood is thicker and redder than illicit blood and that the other humors are similarly enriched; and it is a demonstrable fact that any newly established person may own property, enjoy inheritance, and enter upon commerce, his name now having achieved a distinct value; and we have noted the spiritual benefit. And thirdly, the person may present himself to society no longer fearing that he will be shunned or ridiculed but with every proper expectation of a cordial reception; and his choice of a mate is thence extended to females not burdened themselves by the condition of bastardy; and thus his entire condition as an upright human being is much enhanced amid general appreciation and approbation. And he finds within himself a sense of self-esteem and confidence in the fullness of his enhanced membership in the race of mankind; and now he makes his way about this world with much assurance and aplomb. And he may set about legitimately—it is the apt word—to acquire such credits which will offer him a fighting chance in the next.

I point out that in other climes, this same code, alas, does not prevail; for only a channel's distance away, on the island of Britain, as preposterous as it may seem, already now there have actually reigned two monarchs who were illegitimate offspring: Athelstan, b. 894, "not improbably" a natural son of Edward the Elder; and secondly, Harold Harefoot, b. 1017, "baseborn Harold," who by most historians is deemed heathen and brutish. And it is indeed a reflection upon the inhabitants of that brumous, unhappy island and upon their utter lack of self-respect that they should tolerate such baseborn rulers, and it signals their own brutishness and the generally degraded level of their civilization.

How much more excellent then is our own sun-filled, enlightened civilization wherein my lord may create bastards at will, yet may as readily set aside their wretched status and render them full-fledged human beings whenever He sees fit to do so. And it was with much longing—I shall not say outright "envy" for that is one of the deadly sins, and I had no slight concern for my immortal soul—but with much longing that I looked upon those various legitimated children and upon their most rare great good fortunes. And again I fell to musing, as youths will do, if it were not possible that I too, though low of station—for I was surely not within the ranks of royal progeny nor even halfway there nor even half the way to that—but that I too, I say, might not conceive my own legitimacy—nay, the more I thought upon it, might not demand it as my due. And likewise, others like myself, quite out of wedlock flung into the world, might not we all stand up one day as members of the human race, to claim our whole estate!

Ah, reader! Young men will dream, they cannot help themselves, and grow ambitious plans, set free their minds, inventing visions of illustrious future lives; and even when they know that these are dreams, mere dreams, they dream; they cannot help themselves.

And likewise, reader, I assure you for a fact: young dwarves will dream; and know they dream; and neither can we help ourselves, but dream we will, believe it.

# 12

THERE OCCURRED AT ABOUT THIS TIME an incident which served most vividly to remind me how many circumstances there were in the course of my life over which I had absolutely no control: I received word one morning that Marie-Thérèse, queen of France, had sent for me.

It was a summons which I had come to dread, most especially following some contact between the two of us, however fleeting, on several recent occasions; and you have read of them. But yet I had no choice in the matter: for if the queen of France, whatever her personal qualities such as those less than pleasing ones which I have described to you, if she shall send for a dwarf to appear before her at any hour of the day or night, that dwarf will answer that command.

Even so, it was with no little trepidation that I presented myself, after no small search for her quarters in our new surround, within the hour as bidden, to that lady.

I found Her Majesty seated in a large wooden chair, fitted at its four feet with wheels; and her left leg was propped up under a blanket on an extension built out from the chair; and as she herself was surrounded within the chair by five or six quite fat cushions, so was the chair itself surrounded without by five or six quite fat dwarves, who glared at me with their piggish eyes as I bowed most courteously and most obsequiously to the entire company.

"Señor Hugues," the queen said, and she actually smiled down to me at this point, an action which served to markedly broaden her several chins, "you see hereabouts me my exthellent boys, like sons these is to me: these is Felipe, Juan, Diego, Juan Menor, Alfonso, *y* Esteban." At the sound of his name, each dwarf thumbed his nose or stuck out his tongue or made some lewd gesture in my direction. "*¡Niños, niños! ¡Comportaos!*" the queen commanded, at which the vile creatures fell into a bout of hilarity, doubling over or striking one another or engaging in other sport. "These," the queen continued to me over the noise, "is you brothers, no?"

The word struck terror into my heart, reader, for any association with the likes of these particular dwarves was anathema to me, and most especially as I saw now on closer inspection how dirty their hands and faces were, how greasy and matted their hair. But further: if somehow these creatures were to become my putative brothers, would she then, in the order of things, become my putative mother? The prospect was unbearable.

"*Sí,* you fine brothers," the queen insisted after a pause, for the notion had struck me dumb and I had made no reply, "with these you shoulds habitate now, Señor Hugues: for these is the very amiable wish of you highness queen." My jaw fell open in unabashed astonishment and horror. "With these and with me, too," she announced and with a note of happy triumph in her voice. "Come habitate with alls of us!"

I felt my heart begin to thump and a light sweat break out upon my forehead; but I knew I should not have been surprised at her proposal, given her curious interest in the collecting of dwarves. Having issued that proposal, she settled back even deeper into the mass of cushions and waited: it was, alas, my cue to speak.

"Your Most Excellent Royal Highness," I began, and the Spanish dwarves now all stared at me in wonder, for they understood not a word of what I spoke and moreover could not believe that one of their kind should be endowed with the official language of the royal household. "Alas, I am not free to choose, madame. I am presently in service to others and have not the will to come and go as I please."

I believe at that point the queen must have farted; it is certain that the dwarves fell to snickering and fanning at their noses.

"Thervith?" she asked somewhat guardedly.

And so I enumerated some of the various services which I performed, ash-shoveling, vessel-cleaning, turd-collecting, and my chores in the plumbing and sewer systems.

"Thus Your Majesty will readily appreciate the fact that I am not at liberty to be, as it were, my own man."

There was a brief pause.

"You ith troubling me!" the queen next replied, and a dark scowl descended over her features. "You troubling me, Señor Hugues, I do no like." The dwarves picked up the abrupt shift in her manner and began jeering at me. *"¡Silencio!"* she shouted, and she struck at the large head nearest her. "You troubling me," she announced again to me.

My thoughts sprinted forward.

"But Your Highness must understand that these duties are in the service, madame, not of any ordinary master but of my lord His Majesty the King, Louis, Fourteenth of that Name, and to my lord's extensive royal residence. As well as those duties which I rightfully owe to—others. Although," I quickly thought it wise to add, "I am deeply honored by Your Majesty's cordial invitation."

"Ith no invitation," announced the queen. "Ith order." I felt a horrid chill race up my spine. "You do duties to royal rethidenth in the days, but come habitates after here." It was not an altogether unreasonable suggestion. "Why you don't desire to habitates here?" she said next, and her tone changed again, shifting from command to pathetic entreaty. "With me. I am kind lady. *Simpática.* These boys is good boys, sir, being friends to you." She gestured to her entourage, one of whom grabbed at his ——— and leered at me.

"Madame, there is no doubt of what you say, none whatsoever." Then I began to stammer, for I could see no clear way past her apparent determination and a certain logic to her argument. "Yet, madame, I—that is to say—" Suddenly, reader, there came to my panicky brains an idea, which was, moreover, little more than the obvious truth. "I feel most certain, Your Highness, that madame the marquise would never consent to release me from her household."

There was a long silence. The dwarves began peering up at their mistress, sensing that what I had just spoken had taken some toll, though they knew not how. My words settled slowly into her comprehension.

"Marquise, marquise," the queen began to growl and then, "Marquise, marquise!" she suddenly erupted in full voice. *"¡No oigo nada más que* marquise! Marquise!" And "Marquise, marquise!" now shouted Felipe, Juan, Diego, Juan Menor, Alfonso, and Esteban all together, shaking their pudgy fists and laughing and spitting and scowling; until at length the queen called out above the din:

*"¡Llevadme de este cuarto! ¡Llevadme!"* And she struck another large head nearby. At which, three of her company began pushing the heavy chair forward across the room and rolled it into the adjacent apartment. But Felipe, Juan Menor, and Esteban remained where they were; and now the three of them approached me. Felipe struck me in the face, Juan Menor kicked at my shins, and Esteban spat on my jacket. And so I struck back and kicked back and spat back too, and there ensued a lively, snarling fray, and I, outnumbered, getting the worst of it, including a bloody nose, but yet giving back as best I could; and I was gratified to hear them cry out several times from the pain which I inflicted. At length I was able to break free from the furious tangle which the four of us had become; and I dashed to escape headlong through a door panel but encountered instead only solid wood crashing against my crown, at which my tormentors fell about in great glee, slapping at one another and rolling around on the floor; and I opened the door and fled. Instantly they gave chase; but I rounded a corner up ahead and shot through a door panel that actually existed. As I stopped to catch my breath and mop my nose I heard them, on the other side of the door, clearly dumbfounded that I had disappeared so immediately, the foolish creatures not having discovered, it seemed, the handy device of the panels, their mistress's apartment not being fitted with them (very likely in order to protect her flock from the ravages of her husband's dogs).

And I was right grateful and much relieved, reader, that at that fearful interview it had dawned upon me to call to my use the matter of rank, though not of course of my own rank, which was nothing, but of that of my protectress the marquise; and thus I arrived at a second realization relevant to that incident, to wit, that just as it was for me, there were many circumstances in the course of her life over which Marie-Thérèse, royal queen, had absolutely no control; and for an instant, there appeared in my breast an outrageous sense of kinship with the overweight creature.

On the other hand: upon reflection, the sight of those wretched dwarves—those pets, those mere toys—served to remind me of that resolve which I, dwarf, had made ten years ago in the monastery of St. Sauveur, being at the time at Brother Dagobert's beck and call, to wit, that I would seek by whatever means I could to advance my status in this world. And so I had done, reader, for had I not some few accomplishments to name? No! I would not now lower myself to become, like those dwarves, a toy! nor some ignorant pet, some minion, harnessed, en-slaved, and little better than a parasite! And in fact, the mere prospect of such a diminution in my status served but to whet my appetite yet more sharply for that one endowment which I lacked within, and for which I yearned: to be, by proclamation divine, a whole man.

Yet before I could devise any means toward the satisfaction of that appetite, there erupted at the court several quite tumultuous events which form part of this account, as you will perceive, and which even-tually prompted me, in a most direct manner, to pursue my aim.

Anne de Rohan-Chabot, Princesse de Soubise, was a great beauty at the court; and she had turned many an eye by her comeliness: or many a pair of eyes, it is more accurate to say, for one would hardly turn but a single eye upon the princess, not upon such rare beauty as hers—unless one's other eye were blind, as in the case, for example, of the Abbé Guibourg, who would have no choice but to turn but one eye upon her; unless he deliberately elected to turn a blind eye upon her, that one of his which contained the hard-boiled egg, in which case he would not see her at all; yet I think that not even he would likely do so; unless it might be that he wished not to be distracted at the moment from some pious meditation.

For her beauty was indeed distracting; and most especially the prin-cess's captivating smile, which could soften the hardest of hearts and rejoice the most dejected of spirits; and her smile was well known not only throughout the cities of Paris and Versailles, but throughout the entire region of the Ile-de-France and even as far away as the valley of the river Loire. But such distances were of minor significance, for quite close at hand not the least of the eyes which were turned by the princess's smile, in fact the mightiest, the most noble, most glorious and majestic pair of eyes, indeed, the most divine of orbs which were turned by the princess upon herself and upon her smile were those of my lord King Louis XIV.

And as my lord's eyes roved in that direction, so too there came a point when all the rest of Him roved in it as well; and presently, whenever the lady's husband, Monsieur le Prince de Soubise was called away to La Rochelle upon business, Madame la Princesse de Soubise would don a fine pair of emerald earrings, by which most discreet signal my lord King Louis would know that the beauty was disposed. But it was not difficult for the rest of the court also to take note of emerald earrings, emerald earrings are easily noted; and soon it was much commented on in the gaming circles that such and such an occasion was an "emerald" occasion, when madame was not encumbered, or sometimes a "verdant" occasion or more simply a "green" occasion; and green peas, which were a popular vegetable at the court, my lord King Louis being fond of them, became indeed most highly fashionable, and dinner guests wishing to make sport devised the means to lob green peas at one another from off the tips of the cutlery (when there was cutlery) or otherwise flick them with thumb and forefinger from a furtive position just above the level of the table; so that the target of the striking pea must needs guess from whence it had been launched; and these games could be played in an amatory manner.

And green, green, I fear me, most vividly green was the passion of that second divinity, I mean of the divine Athénaïs, as the emerald occasions not only continued but increased in frequency.

"Slut, slut, slut!" cried she as her coach rattled over to the new house at Clagny on one particular green occasion; and those of us within the coach cowered, for the divine rage had attained unearthly proportions; and indeed I had rarely seen her anger, and it was most frightening. "Harlot!" And we cringed yet lower. But her wrath extended even to my lord King Louis Himself, for "Cradle snatcher!" she cried next, the Princesse de Soubise being her junior by a full seven years; and we none of us dared utter a word and were only glad that the journey in that crowded carriage was a short one.

That very night my services were sent for; and I must say that once again in the presence of the divine meadowland, so gloriously fertile, so delicately accented by the light brown mole that hung like a star above and to the left, so velvet to the touch, serving as so modest a veil for the central ha-ha that lay hidden beneath it and enhanced, moreover, by the subtle aroma of fresh halibut, I could not imagine that my lord King Louis might have preferred any other field, whether it were the Princesse de Soubise's or another, in which to run, in which to frolic and gambol, in which at length to lie; I do not presume to call into question the royal judgment, reader, but I render to you only my own brief judgment; but one, you will concede, based not upon inexperience.

And when the business was concluded:

"Hugues, Hugues," said the divine marquise and with a touch of melancholy in her voice, "only you are faithful to me, dwarf; only you are true." And she let fall a pitiful sigh. "And, poor creature, you have no choice, have you, poorest of creatures: I send for you; and you come." And a tear cascaded down upon her white breast.

"Truly so, my lady," said I quietly and with deep respect. "But indeed, were I to be transported some great distance away, out to the farthest antipodes; were I to be shipwrecked there, adrift, cast forth upon some tropic isle, boatless and lost in solitude; and were I then to learn that you were sad or in any want, my lady, I should instantly rush to be at your side."

"Hah!" said she, and she smiled. "Prettily spoken, dwarf, prettily done; but you could never do so; for how were it possible, and you adrift upon some tropic isle?"

"Why, madame," quoth I, "I should return with whoever it was had borne me the word of you."

Whereupon she laughed, lightly, at my quick rejoinder, which truly rejoiced me, reader; and then she told me to be off. But as, having scratched upon the door for Mlle des Œillets to unlock it (for she always stood guard outside), I turned to bow to the marquise, as it was my custom to do, I saw that she had once more fallen into a despondency, much as I remembered during that earlier exile at Vaugirard. And truly my heart went out to her; and a tear came to my eye at the piteous sight of her who was wont to be so cheerful and gay and who was, even so, as beautiful in her despair as in her joy.

We returned to the chateau at Versailles in a fortnight, the marquise having satisfied herself upon certain recent constructions at Clagny in the gardens, for that was her ostensible purpose in going there; and arrived, just as misfortune would have it, directly in the midst of a bright green occasion.

And only a day later, after a hearty supper of garden peas, some several exertions in the card salons, and then a light nap, I was borne away by Emil Vergeyck through Paris, bouncing around in a muslin sack, and once again to the Cathedral of Notre Dame, where once again I was to serve at the Abbé Guibourg's devotions. Mme La Voisin attended to me, as was her wont, and I, in turn, attended to the abbé. On this particular night, I inundated the subterranean space in plenteous waves of incense, for it was summer, reader, and most close in that space, and in all honesty the Abbé Guibourg's breath had achieved something of an apotheosis of stench; and thus visibility in the chapel was at a minimum.

We had done with the *simili modo* through to *remissionem peccatorum,* and the quaffing; whereupon:

"Hearken unto me! Alpha, Ley, Agla!" cried out the vicar. "Atoum, Sekhmet, and Khnoum! Hear me! By the femur of Isaiah, I summon you; yea, and by the serpent and by the horsemen, by the cup and by the Ghost I order you to attend me, dark ones! And by her immaculate hiatus, I do now command you, that you see done the following: that Anne suffer some hideous and disfiguring physical deformity so that she no longer please. Infernal deities! Let it come to pass, amen. *Qui pridiay quam pateretur . . .*"

The strong, biting wind that tore through the clouds of incense snuffed out several candles on the altar as usual and blew the smoke rising from the dead wicks out in all directions. Now sighing and weaving about, his hair standing out from his head on every side and the sweat coursing down his cheeks, the Abbé Guibourg alternately mumbled and shouted his way through the rest of the Mass as usual, and at length, gasping for breath, concluded it.

I did not much wonder who this Anne might be whose deformity was sought; and my presumption was but confirmed on the exact next evening after that Mass. I was standing patiently beneath a table occupied by the Archbishop of Lisieux, the Marquis de Feuquières, and Mlle Louise-Adélaïde Marsy, the three of them awaiting a fourth, Mme de St. Estève, for a round of *reversi,* when suddenly hurrying in from the hall-way came St. Estève, quite out of breath from excitement, followed by four or five dogs, some royal, others her own.

"Did you see it? Did you see it? Did you see it?" she squealed as she dashed to take her place at the table. "Oh, I shall not contain myself!" Which squealing, the archbishop and the marquis both joined with a deep, rolling sort of gurgling roistering; which quite angered Mlle Louise-Adélaïde, who, having returned to court from her fortune-teller's only late that afternoon, was thoroughly uninformed upon the latest news.

"What *is* it!" quoth Mlle Louise. "What, what, what? Tell me, what?" And she began rapping her knuckles upon the table.

"Oh no, no, it is too rich! Too rich by far, by far, for these ancient bones of mine!" Mme de St. Estève squealed once again, to the continuing thoroughbass of masculine chuckling. "I shall collapse, and directly upon the spot!"

"No, no, but tell! Tell! Oh, you are cruel, you are too cruel, I shall strike you! Leave off and tell me!"

At length, after a final burst of merriment from the three who knew of the matter, Mme de St. Estève blew her nose and spoke:

"It is the Princesse de Soubise," quoth she to Mlle Louise. "The lady appeared as usual at lunch today, but clearly under the greatest of duress, her face quite as long as a mule's; and she sat as silent as a clam and did not open her mouth once to take a bite nor once even to address the company. But then—" and suddenly madame began a series of rollicking, whooping cries, which were again ably underscored by the two gentlemen and now joined by boisterous yelping from the hounds.

"Vile, vile, vile not to say on! You are vile, all of you, vile!" shouted mademoiselle; and she began stamping upon the floor; and she even spat once or twice—I saw it hit the carpet—for her temper was quick and vehement. And the dogs began growling and snarling in accompaniment. "Vile, vile, vile!"

"Wait, I will tell it, I will tell it!" shouted Mme de St. Estève, attempting to calm both herself and the infuriated lady opposite her. "Hold, I will tell! As I was saying then: the princess was at last obliged to open her mouth when she was addressed by the Montespan—for we returned yesterday from Clagny, you should know, mademoiselle—who with great sarcasm enquired thus after her—the princess's—health: 'My ladyship, I trust, has fared well in my absence?'" At this irony, the marquis guffawed loudly. "No!" continued Mme de St. Estève, "but hold, I am not done; and you know it, wretched man! Said the marquise, 'My ladyship has fared well in my absence?' To which the princess replied, 'Right well, madame.' But it was not her reply which so enthralled, no, not a bit of it, but that at last she had been obliged to open her mouth in order to make the reply; and there, in the middle of her mouth, for all the world to see—and much of the world was there at the time, I can tell you, and witnessed—was a great, empty, gaping crevice where her front tooth had been wont to hang! She has entirely lost her front tooth! It has dropped out or has been pulled out or knocked out or whatever befell it I know not, so that, ha ha ha!, her smile, her smile! ha ha!, it will be yet more famous than ever it was before!" And she nearly rolled off her chair as a tidal wave of gut-wrenching laughter overtook her once again. To which not only the gentlemen added again their *continuo* (which is an Italian term), but Mlle Louise now struck out for herself in her own quivering, spasming counterpoint of glee; and the dogs took up again with a lively chorus of barking, and so loudly that the marquis, setting upon them with his stick, gave them a rude thrashing and at last drove them away, Mme de St. Estève vigorously protesting his harshness to them and insisting that they were well-bred; and when at length the room had again grown somewhat more quiet:

"But how?" enquired Mlle Louise. "How, pray, did it happen that Soubise lost her front tooth?" And the mere question threw them all once more into paroxysms of mirth.

"Ah yes," said the archbishop; and I heard his breathing quicken slightly in the way that it did whenever some especially clever conceit had struck him. "Just so, just so, mademoiselle. An excellent question. Now: there are some about the court who are saying that my ladyship walked—inadvertently—into a bedroom door."

"Oh?" said the Marquis de Feuquières, taking up his part and exactly on cue. "And into whose bedroom door might it be that she walked, I wonder?"

But before the two ladies could attack his quick innuendo with their shrill laughter, the archbishop continued:

"*And,*" quoth he, "*and* there are others who say that she broke her tooth whilst falling—inadvertently—out of bed."

"Oh ho!" said the marquis. "Oh ho: and out of whose bed was it, I dare to wonder, that her ladyship fell?"

"But yet!" cried the archbishop, still commanding his audience's rapt attention before they could erupt into laughter, "but yet there are still others about," and he paused slightly, and I heard the eager panting of the three members of his audience, "there are still others, I say, who claim that she broke her tooth—inadvertently or not, I cannot say—upon some hard bone."

There was the briefest of silences.

"Ah ha!" said the marquis. "And upon whose—?"

But he made no effort to complete his question, and indeed would not have been able to; for at that point there was no controlling any of that company, which hooted and roared and even began yelping and barking so that from beneath the table I was not certain that the wretched hounds had not returned; and I was fearful that had they, given the degree of hysteria within the room, they would also be raised to an hysteric frame of mind; but they had not returned; yet it was some minutes before peace was restored to the place as the company of four fought to recapture their breaths.

"And is there, pray, knowledge of the present whereabouts of the missing member?" enquired the archbishop.

"Member?" rejoined the marquis. "And is the member missing as well?"

"No, no, I mean her ladyship's tooth," replied His Excellency.

"Why, what might she have done with a broken-off tooth but throw it into the slops?" replied Mme de St. Estève. "Indeed I should certainly have done so."

"Unless she swallowed the thing," said Mlle Louise.

"Swallowed it?" the archbishop asked.

"Her tooth! In the shock of the moment, I mean, she may have unwittingly—"

"—inadvertently—" the marquis slipped in.

"—inadvertently—" mademoiselle allowed, "she may very well, in the shock of the moment, have inadvertently swallowed her tooth."

"In which case," rejoined madame, "it must simply wait for a day or two to arrive at the slops."

"Tush, 'tis no great matter," said the archbishop. "I thought only that at the demise of her ladyship's tooth, it might have been fitting to administer extreme unction to it, which was my sole purpose in enquiring."

And they all roared at this new witticism and even at themselves for having taken his question seriously to begin with.

The next day, reader, when I chanced to spy her, out and about in Monsieur Le Nôtre's garden, the Princesse de Soubise was indeed a most sorry sight: you have seen portraits, I am certain, on which some mischievous brat has blacked out a tooth and rendered the subject of the portrait most foolish looking. Such was the plight of the Princesse de Soubise; and it was quite as well that the Prince de Soubise himself soon returned from his business journey and that they both retreated, neither one of them smiling, to their estate in Paris. And my lord took no further interest in her, for upon her sudden fall from grace He had returned quite happily to His rightful place in the bed of the Marquise de Montespan. (The Princesse de Soubise died many years later of a cold.)

The which restored the divine marquise's spirits once more; and me to my own happiness, reader, for I so much loved to see her smiling and laughing and full of pretty wit and charm, that I gladly endured my own exile from her private favors at the jubilant return to them of my lord the king; and I rejoiced to see her life resplendent once again in the radiance of the royal sun.

Hark, reader: the sun is monstrous large. I have read that it is several times larger than the earth, and some astronomers maintain that it is hundreds of times larger; but that appears to be exaggeration; yet the sun is certainly larger than the earth, it appears smaller because of its distance away. And it is brighter than earth: for if you will stand outside on a summer's day at noontime and look about you, your eyes will be dazzled by the brightness of a meadow or of the tops of trees or of the surface of a lake; yet if you try to look upward at the sun, you cannot do so, you are blinded by its greater brilliance. And the sun is hotter than earth, a thing which is evident: turn away from the sun and the shade falling across your face will be cooler than the rays across your back. And I have also read, somewhere—it escapes me where, though it may have been in Monsieur Huyghen's *Astronomical Discoveries* or in some related work, for the sciences are thriving these days—I have read, I say, that moonlight is nothing more than reflected sunlight; which would seem indeed to double the apparent power of the sun: for here now are two celestial bodies, the largest two in the heavens, both of the same size, which give light entirely from the rays of only one of them; and that signifies the greatness of the sun.

Now to achieve and maintain that greatness, the sun, which is a mass of fire, must daily consume a prodigious amount of fuel, though from whence it comes cannot be stated, nor whether it be coal or wood, or peat, charcoal or tinder, oil or some sulphurous matter, which is brimstone, or yet some other fuel unknown to us and unknowable; and it is this consumption which allows the sun unstintingly to give forth such enormous quantities of brilliance and heat; and so it commands all the heavens, for clearly it is the mightiest object in them, the stars being mere pinpricks, the moon a cold, parasitical oyster, yet the sun a flaming orange.

Reader: how illustrious then is that monarch who would proclaim Himself a Sun King! Who clothes Himself in the glory and grandeur of the sun and resides in the solar majesty of His kingship. Indeed, the latter endowment, that of His kingship, requires no claim by Him; it derives naturally from no less than God Almighty, by whose leave my lord holds sway within His realms and takes precedence in those realms over all other men, and even over the Vicar of Christ.

And being also, by the authority and weight of historical tradition, a mortal partaking of the divinity of the Almighty, and being, secondly, by His own divine assertion, a king as mighty as the sun itself, He must, in order to burn the more hotly and thus shine the more brightly, also be endowed with an appetite as great as that of the sun or of any godhead, Christian, foreign, or pagan.

And so King Louis was. He had a most hearty appetite at table, for He consumed soup and meats, poultry and fish, vegetables and fruit in prodigious amounts, the chamber of His stomach being larger than that of an average mortal; but He was moderate in drink. And He exhibited a similar appetite in administering the complex affairs of state, holding lengthy sessions with all His ministers, and maintaining as great a knowledge as any of them about the conditions of His subjects, the economy and finances, diplomacy, law, and governance. Likewise His capacity for military pursuits was unbounded, and His enemies the world over feared Him. The zeal with which He conceived new building projects, whether at the royal residence or even in Paris, kept many architects and financiers scrambling to meet His expansive demands. And in like fashion, in the pursuit of pleasure, whether it were at the boisterous gaming tables; or at a concert or upon the stage Himself, dancing with exquisite grace and strength; or ahorse and hunting out across the open moors and through the darkest woodlands, His panting, yelping pack of dogs racing at His side; or at night, in those more private sports which every man craves but few attain, my lord displayed a keenness and enthusiasm, in short, an appetite, which far surpassed those of the mortals left behind in His wake and which was, in degree and size, in intensity and vigor, no less than Olympian.

The man was God; the God was man.

Mademoiselle Marie-Angélique de Scorailles de Roussille was possessed of the most ravishing pair of young breasts in the territory of the

French nation and was just sixteen when she entered into the service of Monsieur's second wife, and therefore into the royal circle; her blond curls, some willful few of which—do what she might!—dangled waywardly across her forehead and along the nape of her neck; and her lips, which seemed fairly to skip from glittering smile to girlish pout; and those two breasts which thrust upward, pressing against the taut fabric of her chemisette their sweet, pink buds; and the movement of her petticoats, which, most especially as you watched her frolicking away from where you stood, danced and switched about in a most becoming fashion; and her eyes, which spoke greater volumes than her mouth would ever do and which said "no" one moment and "yes" the next and then both of them together; and her merry, child-like laughter, which scattered through the solemn drawing rooms and off along the garden paths and out across the surface of the river; these several attributes of Mademoiselle de Scorailles, I say, caught the attention of that divine and royal appetite which I have just described to you; though it were likely more accurate to say that they enflamed that divine and royal appetite; nor, reader, did mademoiselle's attributes require at all as much time to accomplish their task as I have taken in the telling of it; for the deed is quickly done—within the passage of a moment, it is quickly, quickly done, were that moment but the most fleeting:

The thrill—the catch of breath—the sudden, burning glow
Across the face; the instant leap within the beating
Heart; the fever racing up from down below.

Here is how it first happened:
Upon the Duc du Maine's eighth birthday, that child having survived an entire year of cognitive sinfulness, or having accomplished it, I know not which, but upon his eighth birthday, the royal family had traveled to Versailles for a picnic out on the Grand Canal, which lies at the far end of the gardens; and at the end of the late May afternoon, the company had set off to return to the palace; and we were halfway there along the lengthy stretch of the Royal Avenue, when there came, as though from nowhere, one of those sudden spring rains, an immediate and drenching downpour, what the English call (I have been told) "raining cats and dogs" (which is an extraordinary image for people so much devoted

to metaphor; but let that pass, for I have made no more study of the
English tongue than I have of the ancient tongues, and it was a gentleman, much advanced in years, who had spent considerable time among
the inhabitants of that rain-swept island, who told me of their tumbling
pets). All of the large company being much inconvenienced by this
freakish whim of nature, umbrellas were summoned from the valets and
blue boys, but they had brought none; the queen was much too heavy to
move with any swiftness in search of shelter, even with the assistance
of her wretched dwarves; and I must acknowledge that even the divine
marquise had lost some of that quick mobility with which she had
been graced some seasons previous; Monsieur and his gentlemen were
plagued by the fashion of their footwear (for the gardens of Versailles
having been built upon marshy ground, the soil instantly reverted to true
and soggy form under such a furious deluge), and the gentlemen kept
pitching backward as their extremely high heels mired down into the
mud, and in several cases they sprawled backward quite into the mud
themselves; the Duc du Maine, fearing that the metal rack which he wore
on his leg would become rusted in the rain, began to add to the moisture
of the occasion a quantity of his own and indeed sat down into the mud
to do so, much to the irritation of Mme Scarron, who, attempting to pull
the boy back up to a standing position, herself slipped down and joined
him in his soupy quagmire; and my lord King Louis was obliged to wait
in the rain, though partially sheltered by a quick-thinking butler who
pitched some picnic remains from off a large silver tray, raced forward
and held the tray above my lord's head, while the blue boys, those who
were charged with the royal sedan chair and who had fallen behind far
to the rear of the party, attempted to sprint forward through the crowd
toward the king, yet slipping this way and that along the slow and slimy
path; so that the entire assemblage drew to a halt under its various en-
cumbrances, grounded like some giant elephant which has fallen upside
down upon its back and can find no purchase for its thick, helpless, fluttering legs.

Yet all at once, out from the water-logged mass, there emerged, and
with youthful, buoyant agility, a radiant nymph: Mlle Marie-Angélique
de Scorailles de Roussille; and this occasion was the first that mademoiselle had been part of the royal entourage, this her moist debut into the
royal purview. And she promptly kicked off her shoes, reader, hoisted

high her wet petticoats, and upon her dainty, naked feet, tripped forward up and well ahead of the band, the rear of her skirts switching this way and that in the way that they did; and when she was a distance up the path, Mlle de Scorailles turned back to see the elephant that lay flattened behind her; and it was witnessed that the rain had much soaked her blond curls so that they lay in damp ringlets clinging to her face and neck; and it was further witnessed, reader, and right clearly too, that the rain had so much soaked the front of mademoiselle's chemisette that the thin fabric clung tightly to her two exquisite breasts, revealing the shape not only of each firm mound but of its tender peak; and yet as drenching as the rain had been, it had not swept away in its torrent the girlish pout that played upon her dewy lips nor the capricious glitter of her eyes as they beheld the Sun King (whose less than sunny state began perceptibly to brighten at that very moment), nor, as she fell to outright laughter at the sprawling elephant, the spirit of a child who was to be child for but a short time more.

And only four months later, that child, no longer child, made no attempt to hide the fact that she herself was now *with* child; and speculation as to the identity of Him who had indeed got mademoiselle with child was hardly speculation; and yet it was further speculated that the yet-to-be child, I mean the one still in the warming pan, would enjoy instant legitimization at its birth, given the degree of infatuation now borne by my lord for its mother; for she had the run of the place, as you may say, and quite brazenly wore a dress about the court made of the same material as my lord King Louis's coat; and she took to kneeling at Mass directly opposite to where the divine marquise was wont to kneel (that lady this time adamantly declining to oblige my lord by exiling herself away from His palace, suffer exile though she did from His grace); and soon the girl was made a duchess, that of Fontanges; and when, during the hunt, for she was a sporting thing, her horse rode somewhat too near to a low tree branch, which swept her hat off and caused her hair to fall down about her shoulders, she quickly tied her curls back up upon her head with a simple, loose ribbon in a fashion so becoming and so much favored by my lord that all the ladies of the court were obliged to rush about for lengths of ribbon with which to tie their hair, and the ribbon vendors both of Versailles and of St. Germain-en-Laye, and even of Paris itself and the outlying regions, suddenly throve; and licenses to sell ribbon were most hotly contested, five duels about the matter being fought within a single fortnight.

The divine marquise, on the other hand, had all the ribbons forthwith removed from her wardrobe and ordered her women not to wear them neither, which edict produced great vexation amongst them, who were thereby consigned to appear the least in fashion of all the females at the court; and I know for a fact, for Mlle des Œillets told me, that most of those same women quickly supplied themselves with detachable sets of ribbons which they could hastily pin to their hair whenever the marquise was not about. Yet on more than one occasion, the marquise caught some in their deception, one of whom she struck, a second of whom she kicked down a flight of stairs, and a third she dismissed from service, sending the weeping girl back to her family, who lived northeast of Lille and who were, ironically enough, ribbon manufacturers. For the divine marquise was not at all in an obliging state of mind, nor need I tell you this, reader, as you have been witness already to those increasingly stressful exiles which she endured when another's star was in the ascendancy.

No good can fairly be ascribed to this wretched state of affairs, none whatsoever, none; for no good can come of the unjust suffering of so excellent and deserving a goddess, or of the suffering which that suffering inflicted upon others: the tears, the rages, the hours of melancholy, the hatreds and jealousies, the deepening lines upon the face; the gnawing ache to tear, with sharpened fingernails, at ribbons, bodice, hair, that tiny waist, those two pink-budded breasts, that youthful, youthful face. No, no: no good can come of it, dear reader, none.

And yet.

And yet: think me not selfish or of so mean a spirit as to place myself before another's interests, and assuredly not before another of so rare a virtue as that which the marquise possessed; but as she had now fallen again from grace, I was now risen again to it; and my services to that most estimable pastureland, with its gentle, grassy hillock, its secret trenchwork, and its subtle bouquet—that blessèd meadow that was hers and that now again was mine (or so I boldly imagined during our moments of intimate contact)—my services, I say, in this her third exile from my lord were summoned once again, the summons answered, and my world, my quite small world, become once more a boundless universe.

"Hugues. Ever constant Hugues," quoth the marquise one evening as I approached her, in yet another passing expression of her gratitude to me; and she ran the tip of her divine finger along the short length of my jaw and across my chin; and I held my breath; I held my breath; and I was right glad that I had shaved my face anew that evening so that it was fine and smooth to her touch with no bristle or curl to be seen thereabouts, for I kept my razor excellently well sharpened, a simple effort now excellently well rewarded. And later that same evening, when Mlle des Œillets had unlocked the door and I was on the point of leaving madame's apartment to return up into my eaves, where I should spend the night, a kind of angel, I, guarding her slumbers from above (or so I fancied), suddenly she rose from her chair; and I watched in some awe as she crossed the room toward me; and when she had drawn near, she reached out her hand and she tousled my hair, saying, "Good dwarf, good dwarf"; and right glad I was that I had given my hair a vigorous wash not two weeks prior and had picked my scalp, so that it was neither full of greasiness or dust nor stank nor were there many fleas on it. Then, reader, she leaned down toward me, and cupping my head in her divine hands, she fell to studying my face with such an intensity that it quite startled me; yet the instant she smiled into my eyes, sheer rapture overwhelmed all other emotions in my breast, my face grew warm, tears shot up into my eyes, my heart began thumping, my breath bursting in spurts. And when at length she stood upright and turned away with a kind of sadness in her gait, I reached for the door to steady myself before I proceeded quietly from the room.

Consumed by the recollection of her touch, of her eyes, and of her smile, I did not sleep that night, reader; and as I kept my silent vigil in the eaves above her, there began to take shape in my mind, inspired by the warmth of affection that had passed between us, and with a sudden clarity, a notion which had been forming over the course of several months, if not in fact of several years, if not in actual fact of the greater part of all my eighteen seasons, or at least of twelve or thirteen of the latest of them: for no child of four or five has yet the wit to conceive of such a matter as now quite arrested my thoughts and commanded my sleepless attention; and I determined forthwith that I ought—nay, must—address that matter and that not another day might elapse without my doing so: nor was this merely an impetuous whim, but in truth an instance wherein, in our shifting tides upon this earth, several hopes—in this case, mine—and several circumstances—the principal one for me my growing closeness to her who had the power to advance those hopes—may chance to converge, whether by divine design or by mere human happenstance: and one senses, in that instant of ringing clarity—indeed one knows—that he must strike for good and all, the iron being hot, or lose the God-sent moment then forever more; and in fact die with—and perhaps indeed from—the tearful regret of it.

And you shall learn what this matter was; nor will you, I believe, be in any way surprised at what I had conceived but will clearly appreciate it and will as well endorse the thing. And so, attend:

At the end of the following day, after I had performed my duties with respect to the royal vessel, ash deposits (which in May were few), dog droppings (which knew no season), lard and drippings, sump pumps, sewerage tanks, and conduits (much in use that spring what with the heavy rains)—and I made haste at these tasks—I made yet greater haste on the way back up to the eaves, to the rookery, and to my box of clothes, where with great care I put on another, finer shirt, neckerchief, and breeches, all recent acquisitions from the Versailles livery closets; after which, again with great care, I shaved my whiskers and brushed my hair, moistening with spittle the cowlick to make it lie flat; and carefully, so that it would not bleed, picked a large scab from off my left hand, reducing the blemish to a pinkish splotch (it was from an old dog bite); and put fresh tallow upon my shoes and rubbed them; and brushed and wet my hair again.

It being by that time nearly nine thirty, I was certain that I would find the divine marquise alone in her apartment or with only one or two women about her, at repose before the evening meal, which on Tuesdays began at ten; and so I did. The sight of her whom I had so much loved the night before and who, I believed, in her own way had loved me in return, quite took away my breath. But I summoned my courage and approached her. It was difficult to gain her attention at first, for she was somewhat distracted, which made me suddenly wonder if this were indeed the most opportune moment to present myself; and yet I knew that for the length of her exile she was like to remain distracted or, worse, to grow peevish or greatly saddened or even hostile and angry; and that if I waited for the exile to come to an end (which might be months away) and her spirits to lift once more, she would no longer be partner to the bond with me which her unhappy state had now produced. Indeed I had weighed these several considerations many times that day, reader, whilst about my chores, and I quickly weighed them once again now that I stood in her presence; and I decided therewith to pursue and to present my petition; for it was a right reasonable petition, as you shall presently see, and would not be difficult, I thought, and still do think, for her to grant me; and so I did present it; and thusly and in these words; or thus to the best of my recollection, which for weighty matters is somewhat excellent, though I should not say so; and so; thus:

"Madame," quoth I, and I confess that I was trembling then even as my hand now trembles in recording these words, "Madame, I should be singularly obliged to you, upon a matter of personal honor, if you would be so gracious as to present this, a petition of mine own, to my lord King Louis XIV, Sovereign Ruler of France, upon whatever particular occasion your own best judgment may deem propitious, requesting in all good faith that—although my origin is quite unknown, my parentage most dubious, my unhappy status in this world that of bastardy—it not be seen, I pray, to be presumptuous on my part if I assert that were my lord King Louis, He whose glory and puissance makes all Europe tremble but whose bounty toward the least of His creatures stirs gladness even in the hardest of hearts, were He, I say, in His magnanimity to see fit to extend that bounty and to grant to me my own legitimacy and a fair and upright name amongst my fellow human beings in place of that of bastard (as indeed He has most openly and munificently done for Louis-Auguste, Louis-César, Louise-Françoise, and Louise-Marie, and others, and as He yet may likely do for Louis-Alexandre and Françoise-Marie, and others), an act which indeed His Majesty may prefer to execute in this instance privately and without announcement: my gratitude to Him would be as boundless as are my present loyalty, devotion, and admiration, as similarly, madame, for your gracious intercession in this on my behalf which I now humbly request, I would be no less indebted to Your Ladyship than I am presently faithful and constant both in your service and in your worship."

If for any reason you are surprised by that request, reader, I pray you consider the following: now that I had been inspired, foolishly, I am sure, by that heightened intimacy with her divinity which had been my good fortune the night previous, I had come at last to believe myself eligible to take that one step further up the ladder, in search of that interior— nay, spiritual—betterment of my person, which was legitimacy.

And yet, in all honesty, as compelling as that conviction was, yet I add here another compulsion which moved me, reader, and which at the moment indeed crowned all other considerations: for let us have none of it, let us have the truth: for let it be known that I was in love, reader! I was fallen deeply in love with her! And you have seen it for yourself, confess it. And the truth was more, and it was this: that I yearned for her now to see me in a different light—as I had her own children afresh in their new legitimacy—to see me not as the useful dwarf whose hair you may affectionately tousle and whom you may address as "constant Hugues," "good dwarf," and other such-like charitable expressions, and to whom you kneel as to a child—or to a pet—and fondle in a moment of affection—no! but to see me rather as a legitimate and full-fledged human being, reader, for her to see me now as a most complete and proper man!

At the conclusion of my speech, I held my breath as I watched the divine marquise turn slowly at last to look at me; for she had been gazing out of the window all the whiles.

"What?" she queried.

There followed then a deathly silence.

I knew not how to respond to that "what" of hers; "what," though it be short and to the point, may yet express some dubious nuance and ambiguity; what of that "what" indeed!

But, "Madame," at length I replied in the only straightforward manner in which I could think to, and choosing to take that "what" as a mere request for me to repeat what I had just spoken, "I should be singularly obliged to you, upon a matter of personal honor, if you would be so gracious as to present this, a petition of mine own, to my lord King Louis XIV, Sovereign Ruler of France, upon whatever particular occasion your own best judgment may deem propitious, requesting in all good faith that—although my origin is quite unknown, my parentage most dubious, my unhappy status in this world that of bastardy—it not be seen, I pray, to be presumptuous on my part if I assert that were my lord King Louis, He whose glory and puissance makes all Europe tremble but whose bounty toward the least of His creatures stirs gladness even in the hardest of hearts, were He, I say, in His magnanimity to see fit to extend that bounty and to grant to me my own legitimacy and a fair and upright name amongst my fellow human beings in place of that of bastard (as indeed He has most openly and munificently done for Louis-Auguste, Louis-César, Louise-Françoise, and Louise-Marie, and others, and as He yet may likely do for Louis-Alexandre and Françoise-Marie, and others), an act which indeed His Majesty may prefer to execute in this instance privately and without announcement: my gratitude to Him would be as boundless as are my present loyalty, devotion, and admiration, as similarly, madame, for your gracious intercession in this on my behalf which I now humbly request, I would be no less indebted to Your Ladyship than I am presently faithful and constant both in your service and in your worship."

I watched her carefully, reader, during the repetition of my speech, and I saw a look of great surprise sweep across her features at the words "grant me my own legitimacy"; and I believe she scarcely heard the remainder of my request, so lost was she in that wonderment. At the conclusion of my words, I continued to watch her, silently begging my knees not to crumple beneath me nor the pounding of my heart be heard beyond the din which it produced within my own ears; and as I stood before her, roughly at eye level with her most divine and intimate part, whose several component parts I knew so excellently well, I held my face turned upwards to look into her eyes, those gentle eyes whose kindness and generosity I had seen bestowed upon so many beings for all these many years and even upon myself. And she appeared at first to be quite speechless, a phenomenon which I had never before witnessed, she being normally so expressive and endowed with so ready a wit.

But then at length she spoke, leaning slightly forward in her chair in order to study me more closely; but only one word did she utter; and it was this:

"Legitimate?"

Reader: the sound sliced through the still air; and the tight, sharp consonants spat out like so many clattering, rotten teeth upon the floor. All at once I felt the hair fly up on the back of my neck; a sudden chill shook my frame; and then I heard a shriek of laughter hurl out across the room; and now I saw her shoulders start to shake with laughter and then her breasts; and the laughter grew, catching for breath whenever it could;

and now she opened wide her mouth and fairly spewed the laughter forth, which in turn then overtook her; and tears went coursing down her cheeks, and still she laughed, and now with rolls of laughter, with roars of laughter, nay, with very hoots of helpless laughter; until at length she threw back her head and let loose a kind of braying sound indeed devoid of laughter, a dry, harsh bray, a hee-haw bray, a mirthless, steady, stubborn bray—and deadly.

I bolted from the room! And "hee-haw!" shrieking in my ears, I raced away, waddling frantically from side to side, out through the hallway and down the flights of stairs, I raced! upon my stumping, stumpy legs I raced away from out the place and out, outside, into the moistening darkness, away from her I had adored, divinity transformed to brutish mule, away and out, far out—onto a sudden, moonless heath of shame and loss.

# 13

MY FACE WAS BLAZING HOT as I bolted across the dark grass, running I knew not where but only away; and the tears that flooded from my eyes flew back on either side of my face in streaks that dried across my skin, until those streaks were washed away by a second flooding and that flooding by a third; and my very long nose ran, wetting down my fresh-cropped cheeks and jaw; and the sobs that wracked me forced me now and then to stop until I recovered my breath: for the sobs quite took it away; whereat I was able to continue my aimless flight.

Oh, reader! If you could but know how she had broken my heart! Oh, reader!

But wait, let me not be swept away again all these many years later by the force of that passion, nor tangled once more in the thicket of that grief. But let me rather master that passion which, alas! seems at this writing as fresh as ever it was out on that friendless plain; and let me attempt calmly to explain, and rationally. My grief came not so much from the loss (by her rejection) of any practical benefits of legitimization: I had held no expectations for enrichment of my blood or of the other fluid humors, no, I was content with those internal matters as they stood; nor did I hold any material expectations, not for the purchase of any property, for I had nothing with which to purchase more than a cake of soap and the occasional fresh straw; nor for any inheritance neither, there being no one from whom I might anticipate such bounty; nor for commerce, for I have not the wit for such affairs, I think. Nor, given my condition, and I speak now of my dwarfdom, had I set my sights upon any elevated rank in courtly society nor even sought the opportunity to mate with any female of whatever station; for what self-respecting woman would give her hand to a dwarf, whether he were legitimate or not? Similarly, yet less materially, the status of my soul in the afterlife was not my first concern; I harbored no pretensions that, did my soul exist, it would be one of any magnitude, and thus had come to believe that any afterlife of hellfire and damnation would be little more than a minor irritant. No: but reader, it had been my sole and singular hope to achieve a simply and merely proper name, no longer besmirched by the ill muckings-about of my parents, whoever those vicious, wretched, unwed creatures were. And I felt, keenly, in my awful journey in the darkness of that night, how utterly Mme de Montespan's sweeping dismissal of that hope, her swift refusal to give it any thought, nay, even a token nod, had not only destroyed what shred of dignity I had but indeed had doubled that inner lack of esteem for myself which my request had sought to rectify.

Nay, but I suffered yet another loss and heavier yet it was: the loss of a love which—foolishly, I confess it, pridefully perhaps—I had conceived then to be mine, that love that I had felt so deeply for her which I had thought returned in some small part to me. For clearly now she scorned me, and clearly now she did not love me; for you may not love that which you scorn. Scorned I was, reader: nay, held in mocking contempt; that ferocious annihilator which humiliates us and robs us, as much as any lack of legal recognition, nay, more! which robs us, I say, of our portion of mankind and levels us to the ranks of the less-than-human being.

And so, headlong I dashed across the inky fields, blindly and foolishly, as though I could escape that loss; until reeling, I tripped and stumbled, pitched forward and fell; and sank into the darkness all around me.

I woke many hours later.

My mouth was filled with earth; damp grit ground against my chin, pellets of dirt were caked among the bristles of my lashes and brows and in my knotted cowlick; for I had fallen into the darkness of a ditch; and had snouted down beneath a thick layer of leaves; old, old leaves they were and wet, in places they stuck to me, slimy and pitch rotten, and they stank of bog and of the black flesh of the earth below. From my own warmth some of the leaves had dried, and now they formed a kind of scratchy blanket across me, like a layer of coarse wool. But it was the darkness that lay beneath the leaves and down inside the earth embankment which comforted me; it was absence that I craved: oblivion; to be nuzzled into the silted darkness, down among the sightless, scaly moles, where I could see neither woods nor fields nor sky; nor towers in the distance nor dull star, dangling in the heavens above the sunless landscape; nor my own stumpy hand in front of me; but could only breathe the fetid air; smell my own flesh, the clotted leaves, the dirt, the sodden ditch; and taste the bitter, muddy misery in my mouth.

Reader: I did not know it at the time, but yet it was most true: Harold Harefoot, detestable monarch of the British isle, detestable for his bastardy, and yet still more for his arrogance in ruling for even three short years in such a vile state, Harold Harefoot, I say, did not however give way to any grief or desolation when faced with his wretched condition and did not suffer his losses willingly; indeed, Harold did set about to prevail; and although his example was not before me that cold dawn, for I learned of Harold only many years later, yet that same resolve of his in the face of ill fortune began to steal upon me, that purpose and determination; and thus, at the first pink glow of morning, I crawled back up out of the ditch, scraping bits of dirt and leaves from off my person as best I might; and I set out to return to the palace and to my daily round of chores: back to the royal vessel, to the sewerage tanks and pumps, back to my babbling, thick-skulled, witless clientele—and back again to the service, when commanded, of the disdainful marquise herself; but now with a newfound resolve in my heart, to pursue, I knew not how nor when nor what the outcome, but to pursue, relentlessly and with neither cease nor let up, what was no longer my mere desire but my entirely righteous cause for wholeness and legitimacy; and in that pursuit to prevail.

An entirely unexpected and surprising occurrence now took place: along with that sense of resolve, I suddenly began to experience yet other new sensations: welling up within me I felt the stirrings of a most vicious hatred for the marquise, whether she were divine or not, and of a most intense malice toward her; and accompanying these, a strong sense of vengefulness; all of which emotions much affected my heart: for I recognized these new-felt passions as clear and most reassuring evidence of my true and full participation in humanity.

# 14

THAT SAME DAY, I TURNED MY THOUGHTS to what means I could employ to put my newfound resolve into motion; and the study of that problem quite preoccupied my brains even as I went about my chores that afternoon and all the following day. Taking into consideration that the several acts of legitimization which my lord had already performed—as mystical as they were—had, on a more mundane level, been executed through governmental agencies and by governmental mechanisms—the issuance of letters patent by the lawyers, the formal registration of them by the Parlement, and the legal acknowledgment of their validity by the judges of the realm—considering, I say, these very official functionings by His Majesty's government, I hit upon the idea that in pursuing my own legitimization, I could do worse than to inform myself as thoroughly as possible about the actual workings of that government. Indeed, it was one of the few practical steps I could think of taking (there being no feasible way I could imagine of addressing the mystical aspects of the legalization process), and one which I hoped might open up, I knew not how or from what quarter, some other avenue toward calling my lord's attention to my petition; for the avenue I had previously thought available to me was now quite barred.

Over time, I had become aware of the regular meetings of the various governmental councils: I remind you that their deliberations took place apart from the public but quite visible to it, the doors being left open in order that onlookers might watch from the rear of the adjacent lobby. And now, thought I, might it not behoove me to join that observant

public and try to learn from those deliberations myself; and I devised
thenceforth to hasten through all my chores in order to find a few extra
moments each day toward that end. This meant that I adopted a highly
ordered and disciplined regimen and admitted of no distractions or
diversions whatsoever. Not that my life theretofore had been all carefree
folly, although like any boy—like any yearning adolescent—I was always
drawn to whatever playful pastimes might present themselves, however
infrequently, in the course of the daily grind. And while we are at this
subject: that attraction to a sense of play is not altogether to be despised,
I think, for a sense of play, though it seem outwardly the province of simple, happy childhood, in fact displays a mature and well-developed aspect
of the human condition and is concomitant with what we call humor,
or drollery, which, it is said, distinguishes the human creature from the
lower orders; at the same time, in our perverse tendency toward error—
for to be human is also to err—we ofttimes distort that humor, with
the purpose of inflicting harm upon our fellow man, which is malicious;
and it is said that often at the very core of humor is the intentional act of
setting a distance between ourselves and the object of our ridicule, thus
barring him from our company, exiling him in effect from us and from
those who snicker with us and chortle and giggle at his unhappy rejection; similarly, language, though it appear outwardly a beneficent form of
communication between people, can, like humor, serve to exclude: for
if you and I shall be speaking together in any public place, perhaps in an
open field somewhere or in some byway, and conversing in the French
tongue, and there should come along one who speaks only in English,
for example, or in Spanish, then we—you and I—may exclude him from
our society, continuing to use our common speech to render him sepa-
rate from us; and this is the basis for tribes; and that Spaniard will be cut
off from human contact until he undertakes to learn the French tongue.
As indeed in any case he would do right well to do, for all nations celebrate French as the universal tongue, that of commerce, of diplomacy,
of science and the arts, of war, and indeed of every other useful human
endeavor save that of religion, which some hold to be useless and others
inhuman; and therein your Latin is the appropriate means of communication, because few understand it; for God moves, it is said, in mysterious
ways, and it is not yours or mine to fathom His. We are but human, reader,
furnished with the characteristics of humanity, which include thumbs, a

proclivity to err, and an appreciation of the humorous. Observe: unlike man, God has no sense of humor, I trust that I am quite correct in stating that; or if He is possessed of any at all, it must be of a diabolical nature, given what one sees in the world these days, and shall we entertain such a paradox? No, we let that pass. Likewise, God cannot err; and I shall not speculate upon the existence of His thumbs, though I know He has a very long white beard, I have seen it in pictures; but I shall leave the matter of His thumbs to the ecclesiastics, whose province it is and who will deal with it—or may have already for aught I know—and entirely in Latin, as is meet. But I cannot give you full assurance on all of these theological issues: as I have said already, I am only human.

(I do not apologize for this philosophic excursion: these are thoughts that have been lately in my head and deserving of an airing.)

I resume: by fairly sprinting from one labor to the next throughout the day, I managed to carve out some fifteen minutes or so in the middle of the mornings when I could position myself in the lobby outside the royal apartment to gape, along with everybody else, at the proceedings within. Indeed, the sight which I now beheld was most impressive, with the array of ministers and cabinet officers, generals, lawyers, secretaries, bishops, judges and magistrates, messengers, footmen, and blue boys all milling about the distant figure of my lord in the conduct of the business of His illustrious state. But alas, though we could watch to our hearts' content, we could scarcely hear, standing as we were so far away, and thus it was almost impossible to follow anything that was going on; and besides, the public was constantly murmuring and fidgeting; and moreover, what few scraps I did manage to pick up were of such a highly legalistic complexity that I was hard put to understand them; and soon I despaired of my mission; and I returned, discouraged, to my wonted routine.

Yet eventually that attention to matters governmental did come to bear fruit and in the following manner: it was but two weeks after my interview with the marquise that early one morning I was in my rightful place, waiting on schedule outside the royal apartment for delivery of the royal vessel by the Marquis de Lamballe, armed with a poker against a bloodhound which had trailed me up from the scullery; and I witnessed the following: joining the crowds who were already milling about the place an hour or so before the council meeting—a mixture of noble persons and general riffraff (many of them putting on the airs of noble persons themselves)—joining these crowds, I say, and invading the space and in fact summarily forcing those crowds over to the sides and back of the room, was a large and impressive delegation. I shall not burden you with the names of the entire cast of characters but to note the powerful presence of Monsieur Jean-Baptiste Colbert, Second Secretary of State; and another gentleman, who although he was not chiefest among the illustrious delegation, yet he appeared to be by virtue of his imposing bearing and of an entourage of most excellent-looking officers, the distinguished Gabriel-Nicolas de la Reynie, the Lieutenant General (which is to say, the Commandant) of the Police Force of the City of Paris.

It was then only seven thirty in the morning.

No sooner had these figures taken their places in the chamber, where it was apparent that they were awaiting the pleasure of my lord King Louis and indeed with some visible impatience despite their unscheduled appearance, than the door was flung open and the Marquis de Lamballe passed the royal vessel out to me. I made my customary obeisance, turned and left; and I heard the royal door close, as usual, behind me. By then the crowd was so numerous that indeed I was obliged to somewhat fight my way through it toward the guardroom exit while protecting the royal vessel and its contents with my very life.

But on reaching the guardroom, I paused. And I set the royal vessel down upon the floor—a most unusual state of affairs, reader, that I should interrupt my service to the royal vessel—but I did set the vessel down; and I struck the persistent bloodhound a sharp blow on its rear shanks with the poker, which sent it wailing out through a panel; and I turned and peered back into the antechamber. For it was a most curious thing indeed that this delegation, and so large and so impressive a delegation, should have gathered at such an early hour in the day to meet with my lord. And as well that it should include the Commandant of the Paris Police Force and his corps of officers.

"Be busy," a voice within me now whispered. "Stockings up. Feelers out: there is something here afoot."

As I stood there peering through the crack in the doorway at the bustling mob, I saw the royal apartment doors swing open once again; and I heard several shouts ring out though I could not make out any words above the general din; whereupon—and recall, it was only minutes after the act of royal defecation, which indicates the gravity of the circumstance—the Chief of Police was hastily admitted into the royal apartment itself, followed by his officers and the entire band of government worthies.

And they closed the doors behind them.

Silence fell. At once, the noble persons and the general public surged back across the room, though now holding their breaths and fairly tiptoeing (and with care for their long shoe ribbons) as they hastened up to the door in order to hear what was going on on the other side.

Something was distinctly afoot.

Walking now on my own tiptoes, I set out to make my way back through the mob of eavesdroppers—for so we had now just become: no longer a gathering of mildly curious onlookers standing respectfully at a distance and aloof, but, with the closing of the doors, a veritable swarm of eavesdroppers, spies, hungry for secrets of the royal state.

Now either because they were right well accustomed to my presence bustling about below them (the nobles) or because they were so ostentatiously turned out in laces and ribbons and feathers and various states of tawdriness on the occasion of their day at court (the general public) that they literally did not see me as I fought through the maze of frippery; or they were all of them together so preoccupied by their eagerness to hear what it was that was afoot; or they thought, as I nuzzled through among their lower limbs, that I was merely one of the dogs in that place—whatever the case, reader, I was able at length to work my way, in that lower zone where I travel customarily, all the way back to the royal door itself. Whereupon, my heart pounding in my chest and my knees aquiver, I seized upon the example of that most pious of women, Doña Elvira María Inez Jesús Juanita e Isabel Mecklembourg Barca de la Cruz, Baronesa de Valdepeñas; and very carefully, so as to reveal my ploy neither to the crowds on my side of the portal nor to the august delegation on the other, I pushed forward one of the hinged dog panels by the merest inch and thrust my ear into the narrow opening.

At first I could make out only the sound of clamor, for many people were talking all at once, it seemed; even so, in their voices I could detect a degree of emergency and of crisis; and it quite startled me to perceive so swiftly that sense of alarm, and I became fearful.

But at length there was heard a strident knocking and cries of "Gentlemen! My lords!" and several more knocks and cries until at last the room grew silent; and the silence, I believe, as charged as it was, was every bit as frightening as the clamor had been; and I prayed that the pounding of my heart might not be noticed amid so deathly a silence, on either side of my open panel.

"Sir." I now recognized the thunderous voice of Monsieur Jean-Baptiste Colbert, Secretary of State. "Sir," he said, "in light of his character and of the services to the nation rendered by the marshal, His Majesty finds the accusation not only to be audacious but scarcely to be tolerated; we dismiss hearsay and innuendo out of hand; which being the case, you are nevertheless instructed to submit in writing to His Majesty and the Council the exact and specific charges brought against the marshal."

"My lord," replied a second voice, and it was that of Monsieur de la Reynie, Commandant of the Police Force, and a most firm and resolute voice it was: "I have prepared it, you have it before you, sir." And there was some rattling of paper.

"We shall address this matter directly," said Monsieur Colbert. "Proceeding!"

"Proceeding, my lord," countered Monsieur de la Reynie.

Above and behind me I heard murmurs and whispers of "What did he say?" and "Fie, it is impossible to make it out!" and "Has His Majesty spoken?" and such-like confusions; for they were all too tall and too high above the ground and their noses held too much upwards for them to overhear the proceedings as I could do and easily, down at the level of your average sniveling cur.

But to return: "In the third instance," Monsieur de la Reynie was continuing, "in the third instance, my lords: the prisoner has charged her ladyship the Duchesse de Vivonne, Marie-Céleste, with attempting to purchase and with purchasing over an eight-month period a number of quantities of nitric acid and of arsenic trisulfide from the aforementioned cleric Lesage."

At that statement, there were several audible gasps here and there within the chamber; then complete silence.

"His Majesty would understand you aright, sir," announced Monsieur Colbert. "You are now asserting, as I have heard you to say, that the prisoner has accused the Duchesse de Vivonne; and with trafficking in toxicological elements: is that indeed your actual statement, sir?"

There followed a pause of some length.

"My lord," replied Monsieur de la Reynie, "it is."

At which the room erupted once again in a most terrible din; and indeed on my side of the portal there now arose a second din as the eavesdroppers, failing miserably in their efforts to overhear, began again to complain and loudly: "'Sblood! Why must they all speak at once?" and "Curse 'em, they will not speak up enough!" and "Noise! Noise! Noise! Be silent, you fools!"

Whereupon suddenly there were loud footsteps approaching the door from within; but alas! I found that my ear had become stuck in the crevice of the panel and I could not escape it before the door was abruptly flung wide open, and I was swept back some 180 degrees and banged up against the marble plinth behind the door, striking my forehead; where I lay, my head throbbing, my ear bleeding, for it had been wrenched right sharply; and I heard an officer shout, "Stand back! Stand clear! Confidential proceedings!" Whereat the crowds fled away in a crush to the far side of the antechamber once again, and many began fighting to get out through the guardroom or down the stairs at the opposite end; some dogs set up an earsplitting howl (and I assure you that my ear being already split, it needed no more of it); and then the royal apartment door slammed shut, sweeping me back to my original placement.

At length, extricating my bleeding ear—and this, thought I, must be proper enough reward for an eavesdropper that his ear should be nearly ripped asunder—I pushed my way past the officer now stationed on our side of the door and through the few straggling spectators who were left in the antechamber, and I quit the place; and took up the vessel again and went about my business, a much-chastened spy.

But, reader, as bruised as I was by the episode—my head aching and my ear in need of a plaster—yet I could not entirely put from my mind what I had heard: I made nothing of the charges brought against the marshal, whichever marshal it was and whatever he had been up to; yet I did quite clearly understand that a charge had been brought against the Duchesse de Vivonne, an accusation of criminal activity in the purchase of nitric acid and arsenic trisulfide, and the Duchesse de Vivonne, I remind you, was the divine marquise's own sister-in-law.

Here—I suddenly realized—was no incomprehensible scrap of legalistic mumbo jumbo caught on the wing from afar, but rather an actual piece of intelligence, now dropped down upon my plate, of which some practical use might be made. For this business of eavesdropping, not entirely new to me, may indeed serve merely to satisfy our curiosities; but may it not also, I reasoned to myself as I emptied out the vessel that morning, produce some benefit of a more purposeful value, to wit in this instance: if, in some discourse with the marquise herself, I could allude to this bit of intelligence—but only partially—might the marquise, in her eagerness to hear the entire truth about her sister-in-law, not consent to make some payment for that truth?—if not with funds (for I would never be so gauche as to ask her for money nor would that have satisfied my purpose) then with a degree of yielding in the direction of my purpose, that is, with some willingness to entertain the cause for which I had petitioned her help but two weeks previous.

Might she not indeed!

And so it was that I conceived the notion, reader, that information, which had always come so easily to me in my rounds amongst the gossiping card players and which until now I had taken entirely for granted, might indeed be a powerful tool in the pursuit of my new resolve.

And busy I would be about it that very day.

Now, before I proceed with the business, you should know this: I have put off reporting it because it is an unpleasant and painful subject for me, but the time has come. This: that despite her scorn of my petition, I was still enjoined to provide the marquise my usual ministrations beneath the table. Her current exile continued: Mlle de Scorailles had only recently been made the Duchesse de Fontanges, which was a significant mark of my lord's favor towards the young woman. Yet the prospect of coming face-to-face with the marquise and on such delicate occasions, reader, given my resolve to retaliate against her cruelty one day, had now become so abhorrent to me, that I had persuaded Mlle des Œillets to summon me betimes so that I could take up my place under the table *before* the marquise entered the chamber and might thus avoid, I shall not say "contact" with her, but contact of any more than a purely physical nature.

And as perchance I was summoned that very evening to her bidding, I resolved to seize the opportunity, after I should have finished my exertions and she be in a more receptive frame of mind, to broach the issue of my intelligence concerning her sister-in-law, which I would offer to divulge for a consideration. (I regretted that the plaster on my split ear rendered me a somewhat less prepossessing sight than usual, but there was nothing for it, the timing was all.)

Thus it was that, escorted by des Œillets, I had taken up my place under her table—it was a vile one, somewhat lower than the Versailles tables, for we had repaired, yet again, briefly, to St. Germain; and it was equipped with a stretcher, and as usual, I had had to maneuver somewhat to slip under the surrounding tablecloth and find footings in that crowded area—when the marquise entered and sat down at her customary place. As I waited, however unwillingly, for the skirt to be lifted and the petticoats unfurled, I heard, to my surprise, another person enter the room.

"Your Ladyship," a gentleman said.

"Monsieur," was the marquise's curt reply. And then: "Leave us, des Œillets. Be seated, Monsieur Pussort."

"Madame," I heard Mlle des Œillets reply, "I pray you forgive me; but I should remind Your Ladyship that—"

"Leave us, I say. Did you not hear?"

"But, madame, I must—"

"Are you grown deaf, girl?" quoth the marquise, her voice rising. "Out, I said." And she rapped her knuckles on the table. Whereupon Mlle des Œillets withdrew and I heard the door shut behind her. "Now, Monsieur Pussort," the marquise continued, and her voice dropped to a most intimate level, "sit down here and let us have done with it."

Whereat two angular male legs, in breeches and hose, were thrust into the close space under the table, and I heard the lower half of Monsieur Pussort settle into the seat next to the marquise. I dared not breathe, reader, as I believe you can imagine.

Here was a curious thing: Monsieur Henri Pussort had actually been part of the morning's delegation to my lord King Louis! I had seen him there! (He was a member of the government, a legislator.)

"The prisoner is talking much more freely now," said that gentleman. "And there is some danger; if she is to be believed—"

"Why? What is she saying?"

Monsieur Pussort lowered his voice yet more.

"She has accused Mme de Vivonne."

"No! Marie-Céleste?" The marquise's tone denoted no particular surprise that Mme de Vivonne, her own sister-in-law, had been accused, but rather a sense of vexation. "What a devil the creature is!"

(Nor was I surprised either, reader, as you know; but I was most greatly and thoroughly vexed: for with his revelation, Monsieur Pussort had quite let the cat out of my bag and utterly undone all of my careful strategy! Fie, thought I, so much for this business of espionage—if every knave is to be busy at it and then jumping to the head of the line!)

"Madame's sister-in-law a devil?" replied Monsieur Pussort. "Your Ladyship is most harsh."

"No, no, I mean the prisoner—a devil if ever there was one."

"Ah," rejoined the gentleman, "the prisoner, quite so. But devil that she may be, she has nevertheless named Mme de Vivonne, along with Mme de la Mothe."

"Tosh," said the marquise, "I care nothing for that twit. And of what is Marie-Céleste accused?"

At that I thought I heard the beginnings of a chuckle from the gentleman, but it was squelched.

Now you may credit this next matter or not, but it is true: out from between Monsieur Pussort's legs, from under his jerkin, there suddenly appeared a small, glistening, reptilian head, which looked about beneath the table and at me and then spat at me and withdrew; and it did not appear again, though in mortal terror I kept my eyes riveted to Monsieur Pussort's crotch while continuing to listen to the following conversation:

"May we not be candid, my dear marquise? We have all been keenly aware of the decline in your dear brother's health these past few months—and not from his habitual afflictions. It has been rumored for some while that Mme de Vivonne has had commerce with a certain Abbé Lesage, a toxicologist of note; and now, quite simply, the matter has been stated and publicly—though after a bit of persuasion, I grant—by our very own La Voisin."

At the mention of that name, I started, and so much so as to almost betray my presence to them: had he named Mme La Voisin herself, she who was attendant to the Abbé Guibourg? she who had on many an occasion berobed me and then disrobed various supplicants upon his altar? Was it she who had now leveled charges against her ladyship's sister-in-law? I could scarcely believe my ears! And my astonishment almost replaced my vexation at having lost out to Monsieur Pussort.

"Persuasion?" enquired the marquise. "What do you mean, persuasion?"

"Routine, routine, Your Ladyship; pray, may we keep to the issues."

There was a pause.

"How long has the interrogation been going on?" the marquise demanded.

"Some three weeks or four," Monsieur Pussort replied. "But what may be more to the point is how long it is likely to continue: Monsieur de la Reynie contends that La Voisin has only begun to speak; for you should know, there is a degree of bargaining afoot: the longer La Voisin continues to name names, the longer she stays free of the gallows."

The gallows! Then La Voisin herself had been up to some considerable mischief! The gallows! La Voisin!

"Add to that the fact," monsieur continued, "that hers is not the only trial in session: for as it happens, that same Lesage whom she named, the toxicologist, I mean, is now likewise undergoing interrogation—a fellow it is of some devices, madame, for he is known in certain circles as a cleric and yet in others as the layman Adam Cœuret; in others as a Monsieur Dubuisson and likewise—"

"Yes, yes, get on with it."

"This Lesage, then, has countered La Voisin's charges with his own against her (for we have begun something of a contest here between the two informants); to wit, that La Voisin has supplied powders, potions, and I know not what to the Marquis de Feuquières—"

"That would not surprise me in the least. He is devoted to the sciences."

"—and moreover," Monsieur Pussort continued, slowing his delivery for effect, "that La Voisin has been the source of various incantations solicited by the Maréchal de Luxembourg."

Even beneath the table and the heavy tablecloth I could hear a gasp from the marquise. "Why, that is so preposterous, surely no one could credit it."

"Ours is a fitful age, Your Ladyship," replied Monsieur Pussort. "One charge leads to another and that to a third; and credibility, I fear—" and he paused to find the words "—credibility, Your Ladyship, being elastic, stretches."

"But Luxembourg! That priggish—"

"Just so: Luxembourg. His Majesty's most renowned commander, it is truly a wonder. Charged with using various spells and a horoscope and powders in order to entice the Princesse de Tingry—how shall I speak delicately, Your Ladyship? Or need I indeed do so at all? And similarly, other spells to rid himself of his wife, and yet others for victory on the front lines."

There was another pause.

"Marie-Céleste," said the marquise, returning to the matter of her sister-in-law, "is an ignorant slut: I would not put any such chicanery past her. What is the situation?"

"An arrest warrant is being drawn up tonight by Monsieur de la Reynie: it will be delivered with all due haste."

"Fie!" said the marquise. "How could she be so careless! Indeed she deserves to be carted off for being such a fool! But yet, no, there is no question, it will not do, no, not for the family. I shall direct you, then, Monsieur Pussort: the Vivonnes are presently in Chalon, but I do not doubt that Monsieur de la Reynie is aware of that, too; yet I direct you to send word to her immediately—tonight, I mean, it will take two full days to reach them—that she is to go directly to Switzerland and stay there; Louis-Victor is to return immediately to Paris, indeed it will give the man a bit of respite. Marie will stay on in Lausanne till this crisis runs its course." She snorted. "And good riddance, too," she said. "What else?"

"Only details, madame, details."

"It is therein that the devil lurks, Monsieur Pussort," the marquise said sharply. "I shall thank you not to spare me them."

"As Your Ladyship pleases," replied Monsieur Pussort. "His Majesty was most displeased by this intelligence—which he received only this morning."

"I should hardly call His Majesty's displeasure a detail—does His displeasure seem a detail to you, Monsieur Pussort?"

"I shall accede to Your Ladyship's superior judgment," Monsieur Pussort replied after a moment's pause. "Over and above the charges against one of the nation's most outstanding commanders, His Majesty seemed quite upset that such—ah—vexation should have come to touch upon Your Ladyship's family." If my ears did not deceive me (and I grant, one of them was covered with a plaster), I heard a light hint of satisfaction in Monsieur Pussort's tone. And I confess, though it may make me seem less worthy in your eyes, reader, I shared it with him.

"That is my affair, Monsieur Pussort," said the marquise. "You will oblige me not to meddle in the matter."

"Madame."

There followed another pause.

"Well? Is that the business? Those are your 'details,' are they, sir?"

"But one other item, Your Ladyship," Monsieur Pussort said. "Messieurs Colbert and de la Reynie are not convinced that this Abbé Lesage may not have more to tell. And so we must keep a close eye upon the man."

"Tosh, tosh, it is a minor player, this filthy priest," said the marquise peremptorily. "I dismiss him: foolishness. No, it is not he who bears the scrutiny; but rather La Voisin. She——" The marquise paused.

"I have your drift, madame," Monsieur Pussort said in an even tone.

"Then see that you keep it," snapped her ladyship.

"This is my present intention," Monsieur Pussort replied with great care, and placing the very slightest emphasis upon the word "present," a subtlety not lost on the marquise.

"Pray you, cry mercy!" she suddenly exclaimed, her voice now instantly reverting to that of old, full of charm and warmth and persuasiveness. "Alas, I have been churlish: it is as you say, monsieur, ours is a fitful age. I am much obliged to you, sir, much obliged, and you shall know it."

"Madame," replied the gentleman, "I am moved by your gratitude." And he stood up. "With madame's permission, I shall take my leave."

"Pray then, make haste, monsieur," said the marquise. "Time flies; Monsieur de la Reynie is wretchedly efficient, and Marie-Céleste is not the swiftest."

"Madame." And I heard him withdraw from the room. The marquise sat several moments, drumming her fingers upon the table; I made no motion that would have given away my presence; yet standing stock-still beneath the table, I could not but detect a light whiff of halibut, which recalled most unpleasantly my ostensible purpose in her chamber; yet I did not move. And so preoccupied must the marquise have been by Monsieur Pussort's report that presently she stood and withdrew, and my services that evening were abandoned.

Alas! abandoned as well my careful designs upon her ladyship, my act of espionage of no avail, my intelligence now quite spent. And I gave the table under which I had been standing a solid kick before I left the room myself. But as discouraging as this outcome was, I recovered from it and vowed to double my resolve and the speed with which I must make use of the next morsel that would come my way. For morsel there would come, I doubted not.

It is distinctly worth noting, in these details, that when next I was taken by Emil Vergeyck to serve the Abbé Guibourg at Mass, for the first time—for the very first time—Mme La Voisin was not on hand, and this is confirmation of what you and I have both just learned, that she was in the custody of the Paris police. This disruption upset me for I had grown accustomed to her attentions to myself, however peremptory, and to the female who served as altar cloth. Instead, however, it was her daughter, the buxom Mlle Marie-Marguerite La Voisin, who, it seems, had assumed her mother's duties, a girl of about twelve who nevertheless examined my person as closely as madame had on that first occasion. Yet being curious about the elder La Voisin's well-being, at length I asked the daughter how her mother was.

"In gaol," she replied curtly. "How do you think she is?" And then she advised me to mind my own business if I did not want my ears boxed; to which I made no reply and was given a boxing for my pains even so. And so I might as well have pursued the matter further with no less inconvenience; but in either case, mademoiselle did not appear to be of a talkative bent at the time.

In less than four days' time I stationed myself once again in the antechamber to the royal apartment, up against the royal door, and once again concealed beneath a plethora of fringes, frills, and such-like frippery worn by the crowd, with my ear held close up to—but not this time within—the slightly opened panel; for into the council chamber, only moments before and quite early in the day, had swept once again a delegation of worthy officials led by the estimable Monsieur de la Reynie. And once again the doors had been shut behind them.

"—did indeed make it known to the prisoner Lesage (and this was the day before yesterday, my lords, at Vincennes Prison)—or rather, let me say that I did indeed lead the prisoner Lesage to believe that he might hope for some extraordinary leniency from His Majesty and release from prison, if he were to produce whatever revelations were necessary in order that justice might be done in this wretched business of the poisonings; whereupon he, Lesage, did agree to provide such informations in return for leniency, expressing at the time some surprise that I should be the bearer of the proposal, for he had thought me so intimate with the Maréchal de Luxembourg and with the Marquis de Feuquières that I should have rather persecuted him for having spoken out against them than proffered him any clemency. Such, alas, is the present state of the nation's morals that I should be suspected of Machiavellian designs. And I shall be heartily gratified on the day that this foul creature is sent to the gallows, which, as we all know, must take place within a fortnight or so—his evidence will soon run dry."

I would gladly have told you before that it was the voice of General de la Reynie which I was overhearing, but I did not like to interrupt so eminent a gentleman.

Following the general's address, there was a moment, I do not say of conversation, but of a kind of murmuring about the room, the sound of which had a positive tone to it; whilst on my side of the door there was murmuring of a very negative order, for once again the eavesdroppers were having pains to hear what was going on. Presently, the murmuring within subsided and next I heard what appeared to be a very private colloquy, and now I could make out nothing; which upset me, for I could not hear the drift of it, and I feared I would be as unsuccessful as my fellow spies huddled above me.

"His Majesty is right well pleased," at length spoke Monsieur Colbert aloud, "for it is His intention, as you know already, that the interrogations be conducted in a scrupulously correct and strict manner; that leniency not be applied *in fact* but offered only as another ready means of persuasion, as is clearly your intent, sir; that likewise, all physical coercion be administered liberally, by the most effective and established principles and sparing no expense; that whatever persons are named and found guilty, of whatever rank or station, possessing of whatever connections or relationships, in short, whosoever they may be, they are to be fully and impartially prosecuted and to the utmost letter of the law."

Again there were murmurs, this time clearly of approval. Once more, Monsieur de la Reynie, commandant, spoke:

"I respectfully thank His Majesty for His most evenhanded clarification of a delicate issue," said he, "particularly in light of certain further developments. It is no secret to His Majesty, nor to you, my lords, that internal security at Vincennes Prison is much in want—do what he may, the governor there is understaffed, most especially in recent months; so much so that he has impressed his own children into service. Security, I say, being in want, it was within a matter of hours that my confidential proposal of leniency to the prisoner Lesage reached the ears of the prisoner La Voisin. That lady, much incensed that no similar suggestion had been proffered her, began to rant and rave and to tear at her hair and to spit from the window of her cell at passersby below and to throw things about, crying aloud that she herself could name many more notables than any Lesage could cite and that she would right gladly do so; whereupon, being invited to do so, she did do so; and did accuse yet another woman and one—ah—indeed of some station." In the brief pause that followed, there were murmurs on both sides of the door.

I now decided to stop up my other, unused ear with my thumb in order to try and shut out the grumblings of the public behind me; and my thumb being as thick and stumpy as it is, it served as a right excellent plug and thus I was able to put all of those unhappy people on my side of the door quite from my mind.

"Proceeding," commanded Monsieur Colbert. "She has named another woman?"

"Proceeding, my lords," replied Monsieur de la Reynie. He paused once again and caught his breath, using which he then pronounced the name "Marie Mancini."

You may imagine, I believe, what an unequivocal murmuring flew about the chamber at the naming of that lady: she, the Mancinette, who was indeed, as Monsieur de la Reynie had pointed out, a person of some station, not the least of which derived from the favor shown her when she was younger by my lord Himself and indeed the favors which she, in return, had shown Him; even I, on the opposite side of the heavy portal, was acutely aware of the effect which that lady's name had on that august company.

"And of what does La Voisin accuse the lady?" Monsieur Colbert enquired, his voice maintaining its steadiness.

"Of attempting, some years ago," said Monsieur de la Reynie, and now his voice dropped to a lower tone, "unsuccessfully, as will be apparent, with poison and with religious incantations, to end the life of Mlle de la Vallière in order to—how shall I express myself?—in order to reopen a former path, so to speak, which she—Mancini—had been wont to use."

(To refresh your memory, Louise de la Vallière had also been one of my lord King Louis's earliest companions and had borne Him children.)

This time, an icy silence filled the room, for the charge made against Mlle Mancini was indeed a grave one and approached the very throne itself. There followed what I took to be a second private consultation, after which the voice of Monsieur Colbert announced most solemnly:

"Let Mancini be sent for," he said, "in order that she may be directed to leave town." He paused. "His Majesty would not have that particular lady compromised by such slander."

A clamor of assent and approbation went up instantly about the room; and next I heard the footsteps of one approaching the door; and this time I was most wise to have my wits about me, and I hastily pushed away from the door despite the forest of legs, lace, and ribbons surrounding me and indeed fought my way through that forest and in a timely fashion shortly before the doors swung open, producing something of a tidal wave within the layers of eavesdroppers. Not wishing to be discovered amongst that company, I fled the spot forthwith, seized up the royal vessel from where I had stowed it, and hastened from the antechamber; but as I raced around the corner which led to the landing above the king's staircase (not one I commonly used but at the moment the closest to foot), I once again—alas!—suffered an encounter with a crotch, my face plunging quite headlong into it; and it was the crotch of Mlle Marie-Angélique de Scorailles de Roussille, the Duchesse de Fontanges, a crotch somewhat overshadowed that autumn morn by her six-month-old royal pregnancy; and the youthful duchess, already in a manner out of balance until she might be delivered of the royal burden, was thrown yet a great deal further out by the sudden impact and flew sprawling across the parquet. For my part, not wishing the royal vessel to go crashing to the floor as I myself was then doing, I held it aloft with all my willpower; though, alas, not steadily enough to prevent its tipping backward and spewing its royal contents down upon my head and shoulders as I landed on the floor not far from the duchess.

"Vile dwarf! Vile, vile dwarf!" cried out her ladies and they would have struck me with their parasols but that they did not wish to soil them. But presently, the duchess, having recovered her unsteady footing and finding herself still intact and in no imminent danger of a premature delivery, she made various adjustments about her person, being particularly attentive that her two most excellent features were again well positioned within her décolletage; and I watched as she swept on forward across the antechamber, through the milling public, who scurried and fell about to make way for her, and directly into the king's private apartment through the royal doorway, which, mere moments before, had been thrown open by the blue boy dispatched in urgent search of the Mancinette.

# 15

ALL DAY LONG AFTER THAT second private council meeting—an overcast and blustery day as I recall, during which I went about my usual chores—I pondered what profitable use I might make of that morning's intelligence; but could find nothing: His Majesty's policies on the treatment of prisoners, La Voisin's unmannered behavior, and even the charges against the Mancinette could serve me no purpose; and alas, to my vexation, the Mancinette had even been a client and would now be leaving town. You might easily assume that with such stillborn results from my investigations, my curiosity would have begun to grow jaded; but that is not consonant with the perversity of human nature; for we find that the more we consume of others' vexations and distresses, the hungrier we become; and indeed, the more such feeding is done upon the miseries of persons whom we know, and especially persons of preeminence, still greater is our appetite for the heavier sweets and richer foodstuffs listed upon that menu. To my surprise, I discovered that even the loss of a client (Mlle Mancini) was now as almost nothing to the delight I took in satisfying that hunger. "There is something about the misfortunes of our dearest friends which does not altogether displease us," La Rochefoucauld wrote in 1665 in a somewhat gentler rendering of the sentiment. And now that we have come to this honest understanding of our all-too-human natures, it will not surprise you, I think, to learn that on that Thursday evening, I had placed myself once again in the Marquise de Montespan's drawing room in pursuit of yet more delicacies. I had no summons to attend upon the marquise that evening, for she was distracted; and so, absent that summons, I stowed myself in the chimney place behind a firescreen; and it was a chimney I knew well. For I had reasoned that, if it were Monsieur Pussort's habit to report to the marquise about the confidential conferences with His Majesty, I might learn what had transpired in the second half of that morning's conference which perforce I had missed and the succulent information therein.

Moreover, I had resolved to countenance no unturned stone.

Shortly after the marquise had entered into the drawing room, I heard Monsieur Pussort himself fairly burst in through the doors, which he then closed; and he approached the marquise.

"Your Ladyship," he murmured, "I fear that matters have not gone at all as we might have wished; you will be displeased with what I have to report to you, I do not doubt."

"What is it!" the marquise demanded abruptly.

"We did not succeed, alas, in reaching your sister-in-law in Chalon, madame, not, that is, before a party of police officers did. And she has been brought back in their custody to Paris, Your Ladyship, and was sent this day to Bastille Prison; and she is there at present, and I fear will remain there until——"

"Bastille!" exclaimed the marquise. "Bastille! And not Vincennes? Why was she sent to the Bastille? And how is it that she is being thus wretchedly discriminated against? This is outrageous! The Bastille! The Bastille is for whores and pickpockets: why was she not sent to Vincennes?"

"Your Ladyship," Monsieur Pussort replied, and once again I thought that I detected a slight hint of satisfaction in the gentleman's voice, "alas, the matter is not in my hands."

"Fie! What a nuisance the woman is!" she cried. "The Bastille! Why, it is preposterous!" And she rapped her knuckles against the back of a chair. "It is an insult! And not to be tolerated!"

"Your Ladyship," Monsieur Pussort concurred.

"A Mortemart in the Bastille? Why, I assure you, His Majesty will be——" But she did not finish her thought. "Bother, then, bother! There is nothing for it." She crossed the room and sat down at a writing desk not far from where I stood but out of my view. "Here, sir, I shall request that you deliver a note to Monsieur de la Reynie which I shall write directly; and I pray you, be as discreet as you are swift, there is no——"

"Your Ladyship," Monsieur Pussort interrupted and quite smoothly. "I have taken the liberty of anticipating Your Ladyship's desires in the matter." He paused.

"Yes? What?"

"Madame, I have requested Monsieur de la Reynie to accompany me here this evening. He awaits without." Once again he paused. "I trust, madame, that I have not been—ah—presumptuous."

There was a silence.

"Why, sir," the marquise said at length, "I see that I have somewhat misjudged you, sir; and that moreover, I vow, I am, as always, quite in your debt."

"Madame," murmured the gentleman.

"Pray, sir, I bid you, desire Monsieur de la Reynie to step into the room."

Monsieur Pussort retired; whereupon I next heard a key being fitted into a lock and turned, a drawer opened, something removed from it (or so I might presume), and the drawer closed and locked once more.

"Your Ladyship," came now the robust voice of Monsieur de la Reynie, Lieutenant General of the Paris Police Force, followed by his impressive figure and the sound of the drawing room door being shut and locked.

"Monsieur de la Reynie," announced the marquise, rising and crossing back into view. "It is an outright scandal, sir! An outrage! And I shall not tolerate it, sir! That Mme Marie-Céleste Mortemart, Duchesse de Vivonne, has been incarcerated in the prison of the Bastille! The place is a hellhole! It is an insult not only to the duchess herself, but to the entire Mortemart family, sir, and I protest it most vigorously, most vigorously I do, sir!"

"Your Ladyship—" began Monsieur de la Reynie.

"Sir, I shall entertain no explanation nor any excuse; for indeed the matter is both inexplicable and inexcusable. But I shall insist, sir, that Mme de Vivonne be removed from that vile place this night and more-over, for the most offensive insult done her, that she be restored to her residence in Paris; and that the warrant for her arrest be delivered into this gentleman's hands forthwith"—she nodded toward Monsieur Pussort—"and that the entire scurrilous matter be dismissed. It will not do, sir! No, not a word! It will not do for these frivolous issues to become exaggerated and drawn quite out of proportion." She paused a moment; and her tone then became somewhat less harsh. "It is all well and good, Monsieur de la Reynie, that the guilty be apprehended; and I applaud your most excellent work, sir; but the Mortemart family, sir, and I believe that you must agree with me, is quite beyond reproach; and its responsibilities to the court, sir, are not to be taken lightly." And now her voice grew gentle and full of warmth, as of old. "I know that you, General de la Reynie, are a gentleman most sensitive to such issues and most respectful of the law and of all people of good birth and of the higher social order; and therefore I pray you, sir, that in the munificence which doubtless you will extend to my belovèd sister-in-law, you may be so generous as well as to accept this token from me for the considerable pains—and without question the expense, indeed the expense most assuredly—to which you have been put by this unfortunate and most irregular incident." She paused again briefly. "We know, sir," she continued, and reader, her "we" had about it the merest hint of a royal one, "we know, sir, I say, that the Paris Police Force and its most distinguished commander in chief can be relied upon to stand in service to all that is moral, righteous, and virtuous throughout the realm in these troubled times."

There followed a brief silence.

"Madame," said Monsieur de la Reynie, Lieutenant General of the Paris Police Force, "I am entirely at Your Ladyship's service."

"Indeed, monsieur," said her ladyship, "I have never doubted that gallantry for which you are so justly renowned; and I am right well gratified that now in our present discomfort, I may count even myself as rescued by its generosity. I thank you most heartily, *monsieur mon général,*" she continued, "I shall not soon forget your valor, sir, nor call upon any more of your valuable time this night. And I bid you an excellent good evening."

Whereupon the door was unlocked, and the commander withdrew from out of the room, closing the door gently behind him.

"There now," the marquise said almost as though to herself, "enough of all that." And then to Monsieur Pussort: "Pray be seated, sir, and deliver me the rest of your report."

"Madame," that gentleman replied.

They both sat at the table. And then I listened as monsieur recounted to her the matters of Lesage, La Voisin, Mancini, and Vallière, and I detected that madame's mood quite changed for the better: in fact, she laughed outright at the report of the Mancinette, for she quite loathed her and was wont herself to entertain at suppers and other diversions on Thursday evenings with the express purpose of wrecking that lady's Thursday salons, she quite outranking her; yet Mancini was never fazed by these machinations, or at least never appeared to be, which irked the marquise all the more. And so she was glad at Monsieur Pussort's information.

"I vow, monsieur," the marquise said, "the day has been a rich one in the matters you report: I congratulate you! and most heartily, sir."

Monsieur Pussort cleared his throat. "Your Ladyship may find the rest of my report somewhat less, shall I say, deserving of congratulations."

"Oh?"

"It involves the final charge by La Voisin made yesterday, accusing one of your own women of skullduggery, madame; to wit, Françoise de St. Estève."

Since entering Mme de Montespan's service, St. Estève had come to enjoy some station at court and had even been of a company of ladies who had visited the front lines in Flanders the year previous; still, I had never cared for her personally, what with her incessant enemas, her partiality to dogs, and her overly vigorous reaction to my attentions. Moreover, her eyes were set much too far apart; hence a charge against her was not at all unwelcome.

"St. Estève?" retorted the marquise. "And what has the creature been up to?"

"It is alleged, madame," and Monsieur Pussort was speaking so intimately that I was tempted to put my head out from behind the screen, but I did not, "it is alleged by the woman La Voisin that that lady actually purchased from her several philters of arsenic trisulfide which were destined for Your Ladyship's afternoon tea."

By which revelation, it appeared that the marquise had been struck dumb, for I heard no reply for some while.

"Sluttish hag!" she cried at length. "What a vicious whore she is! I'd have her raped by a band of black heathens and hung out naked on a rusted pike."

"Your Ladyship," Monsieur Pussort acceded with much politesse.

"Tea? My afternoon tea? Arsenic trisulfide in my afternoon tea?" the marquise continued. "Why, I do not even *take* tea in the afternoon!"

"Ah, then there you have it," said the gentleman. "Your Ladyship has doubtless spared herself some considerable inconvenience."

"Ever since that scabrous jade went to Flanders she has given herself airs, thinking she would replace me in my lord's affections. And now this! This bald-faced scheme!"

"It is most intolerable."

"And His Majesty?" the marquise demanded. "What was His Majesty's pleasure upon the hearing of this monstrousness?"

"Madame," replied Monsieur Pussort, "His Majesty's ire was unmitigated."

"And—? And—? 'Unmitigated'? Is that all you have to tell me? Did His Majesty not immediately order the villain's arrest?"

"Madame, Monsieur Colbert indeed gave orders for her arrest half an hour or so later. But I am quite convinced that His Majesty would certainly have done so Himself, there can be no question, but that the Duchesse de Fontanges having arrived some minutes prior, began to grumble loudly to all present that she was right bored by such 'dull doings' (as she put it, madame) and was impatient to be getting along to the morning hunt, however rainy the day was; so that His Majesty found it needful to entrust certain unfinished matters to the competence of His advisors."

The next thing that I heard was an earsplitting crash as the marquise, suddenly possessed of a titanic strength, flung the heavy chair which she had been sitting in up against the wall opposite—I could see it as it struck the plastering, burst into pieces, and thundered back down to the floor.

"Fiend!" cried the marquise; upon which, I could hear her striding across the drawing room and the deafening slam of the door behind her as she left.

In the silence which followed I dared not breathe; presently I heard a low, extended chortling coming from the direction of Monsieur Pussort.

Several minutes went by, and still that gentleman kept his seat. Then I heard, very gently, the handle of the drawing room door being turned, and the door was opened and closed.

There was another lengthy silence.

"Yes?" Monsieur Pussort enquired of the newcomer in a low tone.

"Two hundred *louis d'or.*" It was General de la Reynie, who had returned.

"Ahhh!" Monsieur Pussort's voice expressed both surprise and pleasure. He rose. "As much as that! Her ladyship is generous indeed."

"A most agreeable figure," the general concurred.

"Well, I should say that that was deftly done, commander, exceeding so, and I commend you once again."

"And I you, sir."

"I think neither of us will cavil at a hundred *louis d'or,* and for so brisk an operation. Yes, commander?"

"Quite so," the general answered. "The Bastille does indeed have its purposes, monsieur."

"A most worthy institution," said Monsieur Pussort, "a most reliable one." He paused briefly. "Do we know what madame's other relatives have been up to lately?"

There was no reply to that question from the police commander; but when next he spoke, his voice betrayed a note of keen amusement.

"I bid you an excellent good evening, monsieur."

"I am ever at your service, Monsieur de la Reynie."

At which both of them left the room together; and they closed the door very quietly behind them.

That same night, and despite a driving rainstorm, the marquise gave orders that her carriage be readied; and she repaired forthwith to her estate at Clagny and so precipitously that she left behind most of her women as well as myself. Given that her humor could be expected to be quite foul for some time to come, I was well out of it.

Now as furious as everyone at the court presumed my lord King Louis to be at these recent revelations—His mistress's sister-in-law named in a murderous scheme, a former royal mistress similarly named, attempts made quite directly upon the lives of two royal mistresses, both former and present—still, the vexation to His Majesty, it appears, did not entirely turn His attention from other matters of weight and urgency; thus, shortly thereafter, the court packed up once again and hastened back to the Palace of Versailles, where certain engineering questions had arisen demanding the king's immediate consideration before cold weather should set in. So that in no time, reader, I found myself back in my niche in the north wing of that vast palace; but to my surprise, many revisions in the building having been completed in the interim and swiftly too, my particular nook, though stationary, was newly situated directly above a recently devised chamber, one designated as a private reception room for none other than His Majesty Himself. It was, I believe, an act of fate, this shuffling of the rooms below my rookery, affording me a singular opportunity. For so recently had that new chamber been completed, I found, that some of the plaster had not quite set—let me remind you of the perpetual dampness about the place, which was truly a bane—so that with painstaking efforts, I was able to lift out small chunks of sodden plaster, thimbleful by thimbleful, from a concave segment which formed part of the ceiling cornice along the east side of the room, effecting a small hole, not perceptible from the distance of the floor below but through which, by dangling from my knees along a wooden rafter above the ceiling and lowering my head toward the rear of the cornice itself, I found that I could actually peer down into the chamber beneath me.

You are doubtless aware of the depth to which my scruples had sunk when I should go so far as to carve out a hole in the cornice of a ceiling and hang upside down in order to continue my espionage activity. And this requiring no small effort, it committed me yet further to the life of a spy, and now not only from the lower regions—beneath gaming tables, from within fireplaces, and through panels in the bottoms of doors—but as well from aloft in the eaves themselves; and it occurred to me that what I sought to do from up there had a curious relevance to the very term "eavesdrop" itself; yet I prayed that an altogether literal interpretation of the term might not come into play, whereby the entire cornice, having suffered that damage at my hands, however slight, would one day cave in and plunge down into the reception room below and myself along with it, producing indeed a genuine instance of eavesdropping. Yet I remind you, reader, and I protest that I was driven to these new heights of espionage by that continuing resolve of mine to secure for myself a proper name in this world and, to a lesser extent, by an altogether natural nosiness; I pray you judge me harshly on neither score, especially on the nosiness, what with my natural endowment. And you will grant me, at least, a certain resourcefulness in taking advantage of the rearrangement of the palace rooms and of the particular climatic conditions which prevail at Versailles, those which conveniently delayed the setting of the plaster. I am quite aware that such boons fell into my lap as though from the gods, and yet I hold that initiative on my own part was called for as well; and it was duly supplied.

I had no time during the average day to spend in spying upon activities in the king's private chamber; though it were a curious sight indeed to see, from above, men coming and going and only to perceive the tops of their heads, their shoulders, and their feet darting about fore and aft (unless they were of such rotundity that their girth were likewise visible); and it afforded me great amusement; yet I had my chores to perform, and you understand that.

But yet one gusty morning in November, in the beginning of the following week, while going about my business, I happened to hear a great clamor; and presently there hurried around a corner yet another delegation of all the ministers of state, who were gathering once again in the lobby, accompanied, again, by Monsieur de la Reynie, and that gentleman in a state of perturbation such as his habitual reserve seldom betrayed. I fairly flew up to my rookery, although rounding the three corners along my way with care that I not collide with anyone and lose precious time, I flew, I say, up to my rookery (where I could hear the wind as it blew against the high-pitched roof above my head), swung myself down from the rafter, affixed my right eye as closely to the opening as possible, and peered below into the chamber.

To the bewigged head, shoulders, and lap of my lord King Louis, who was seated near a table, and to the bewigged heads and shoulders of His inner cabinet, who stood nearby, there approached, I estimate, some twenty heads and forty shoulders, the former likewise bewigged, the latter varying in proportion and shape, all of which, once arrived, bent forward together in great obeisance to His Majesty, affording me a brief view of a score of backsides, for what that was worth. Whereupon, newly risen, the bewigged head of Monsieur Colbert (Secretary of State) in a short address presented to His Majesty the bewigged head of Monsieur de la Reynie, who advanced to a position directly before the king.

"With deepest respect," began Monsieur de la Reynie, and his voice had not its usual steadiness, for he was clearly in some agitation, "I crave permission to issue to His Majesty the following additional report: the female prisoner La Voisin has spoken out yet again, this time with information which—ah—" and Monsieur de la Reynie paused "—I do not like to be indelicate in the presence of His Majesty."

"Get on with it, man," said Monsieur Colbert, and somewhat gruffly. "His Majesty is not so easily offended."

There was a silence.

"Sir," said Monsieur de la Reynie to Monsieur Colbert with a nod of his head. "Then I proceed. Information, I say," he continued, now lowering his voice, "which touches upon—or shall I suggest at least approaches—the person of His Majesty Himself."

At that statement, you may imagine the low murmur which circulated about the chamber.

"Yes?" With which single word Monsieur Colbert's voice stifled all sound.

"With respect," said Monsieur de la Reynie, plunging ahead. "It is La Voisin's contention that a certain Romani, a man who is the brother of a priest in service at the Church of St. Sauveur, has been engaged—though the woman adamantly refused to reveal by whom, but I pray you, my lords, and with His Majesty's gracious permission, I shall address that vital issue presently—this Romani has been engaged, I say, to present himself as a merchant of fabrics to a young lady well known about the court, which is to say, with all due respect to His Majesty, one Marie-Angélique de Scorailles de Roussille, the Duchesse de Fontanges." (A second murmur rose from amongst the company.) "And that," Monsieur de la Reynie continued, and a most stalwart man he was proving to be, I did wonder at his fortitude, "Romani is to display to that young lady a selection of fabrics for her consideration; and that these same fabrics are to be—how shall I express it?—impregnated—" and reader, in the circumstances, the word hung somewhat heavily in the air, it was an ill-chosen word, for all of Monsieur de la Reynie's customary diplomacy, an indelicate word for him to have spoken—"impregnated," he repeated nonetheless, "with divers noxious solutions primarily of the hydrocarbonic family such as would cause a most virulent, extrusive illness to any woman making use of those same fabrics for clothing, and thus endanger—" Monsieur de la Reynie paused and cleared his throat. "With all respect, my lords: and thus most seriously endanger, I say, the term of any such woman should she happen at the time to be with child."

At that, every bewigged head turned toward that of my lord King Louis, who nevertheless remained stationary.

The winds outside came to a standstill.

"And that," Monsieur de la Reynie continued, and all the heads spun back to his, "and that should the duchess not choose any of those same fabrics for purchase, Monsieur Romani is to be in possession of a pair of gloves, a pair of similarly toxic gloves, which have been sent to him from Grenoble and which it is felt no stylish young lady could possibly fail but to admire."

Monsieur de la Reynie paused a moment.

"And where is this Romani at present?" enquired Monsieur Colbert, his voice echoing the tension in the room, a most palpable tension, reader, perceptible even to me up in the rafters.

"Sir: our officers and men have opened an extensive city-wide search for the culprit Romani; and I doubt not that we shall apprehend the man forthwith."

There was a second pause.

"And pray, upon what day, lieutenant?" Monsieur Colbert enquired. "Or in what month or year, sir?" But before Monsieur de la Reynie could reply: "This information is unsatisfactory, sir!" the minister continued. "The threat is grave and imminent. That you have not—"

"Sir! I beseech you, if I may," said Monsieur de la Reynie, daring to interrupt him, "the matter is well in hand, sir, I wish to assure His Majesty; and indeed I assure you, my lords, as well; and yet my report is not complete, sir: and I shall be much obliged, sir, if I may proceed."

There was a pause. Outside the wind picked up.

"Proceeding."

"Proceeding, sir." Monsieur de la Reynie drew a deep breath, and then I saw his head turn back to the Godhead who was seated silently at the table. "With all respect," he began anew, "continuing our investigations of the Romani case, we have as well interrogated La Voisin's daughter, His Majesty should know, one Mlle Marie-Marguerite La Voisin, a child, sir, of twelve years; and the child has confirmed her mother's accusations; and—and I pray you, with the deepest respect to you, my lords, and to our most Sovereign Majesty, my lords—" and a most evident constriction in his voice betrayed the state of his nerves "—the girl says— that is, the girl—the child—claims, sir, it is her entirely unsubstantiated charge, sir, that Romani has been engaged at the instance of the Marquise de Montespan."

At which moment, reader, a ferocious gust of wind rattled all the window panes in that chamber and I doubt not all the window panes throughout the palace as well and possibly all the window panes within a radius of ten miles if not throughout the kingdom; and so fiercely that I thought indeed they must all shatter and break; and in fact one window did fly open, crashing furiously against its frame; and several officers hastened to close it but with great effort.

"Has the creature—the girl—been arrested?" Monsieur Colbert enquired when at last silence had been restored to the room.

"Sir, the child is twelve years old," replied Monsieur de la Reynie.

"Is she under arrest?"

"No, my lord, not at the present time."

"Arrest her."

There was a pause.

"It is a simple matter, Monsieur de la Reynie."

"Sir." The police commander acceded.

"Monsieur de la Reynie," continued Monsieur Colbert, "your report is most unsatisfactory, sir; you bring us information of heinous doings, monsieur—I believe that I do not exaggerate," (and there was a buzz of approbation about the chamber) "and I shall not mince my words to you, sir—of most heinous doings which bear closely upon many personal interests of His Majesty's. And yet firstly, from La Voisin's testimony— the primary testimony, sir—you omit what is most relevant, sir, that is, an indication by her as to who it is has perpetrated such doings with the agent Romani; while secondly, in addressing that same issue, you announce to us from the child's testimony such preposterous and slanderous lies, such dismissible calumny, that I marvel you even dare approach the court and bearing such detestation. Clearly this is some smokescreen which the two females have concocted in order to protect the guilty party or parties. Moreover: this La Voisin creature, the mother I mean, has been under scrutiny a number of months now, if I am not mistaken; how is it that you have taken thus long with her? And thus long, sir, to have produced such thoroughly unreliable, such unacceptable results? Nay, we shall scorn to entertain any further charges from either of these bawds when to do so is to entertain pure lies and outright fabrication. The mother appears to be quite treacherous; but the child! the child must consort with the devil himself." Monsieur Colbert paused, and I doubt not that he fixed Monsieur de la Reynie with his cold stare. "Altogether," he growled, "your investigations are become, sir, incompetent." And he quite spat out the word.

"My lord, with all respect, sir, I beg to protest!" replied Monsieur de la Reynie. "Sir, the woman La Voisin claims to know only of the machinations of the agent Romani; if she knows nothing of his employer in the business, that is not the fault of our investigations, sir. And as for the child, sir, why, sir, I am obliged in my duty to His Majesty to report whatsoever information I receive: whether it be from a child or not, and however scurrilous or calumnious it is. Sir: I bring no charge myself, sir; I report to His Majesty and to yourself, sir, and to the court, the results of our interrogations, sir, however base and false they may unquestionably be."

"Monsieur de la Reynie, you would do well, sir," Monsieur Colbert replied, "not to discharge your duties to His Majesty in quite so rigorous a fashion, when to do so is thus to scandalize this most royal and eminent court."

Once more a hush fell throughout the room, during which Monsieur Colbert's wig inclined toward His Majesty's as the two spoke privately together.

"It is His Majesty's conviction," Monsieur Colbert announced, "as I have anticipated, that the child's accusation being entirely without merit, it is to be stricken from the recordings of this interview." Another murmur of approval swept through the room. "On the other hand," he continued, "it is His Majesty's express intention that mother and child both be put to the rack: the child in order to be punished for outright perjury; the mother in order that she divulge, once and for all, whoever it is she is protecting. His Majesty wishes to know; indeed, it is His avowed intention to know."

All wigs turned again to Monsieur de la Reynie; and that gentleman, now speechless, made a deep and most reverent obeisance to the king. Whereupon all twenty-five gentlemen made deep and reverent obeisances; for they all, even to the highest minister amongst them, were, as much as Monsieur de la Reynie, in great fear of His Majesty's righteous anger.

"It is our intention to know." Now spoke for the first time His Royal Majesty, King of the French, the Divine Louis, Fourteenth of that Name; and it was not a shout that He uttered, but yet the words thundered out from deep within His mighty frame; and they filled the entire space within that royal chamber, making ring the rafters from which I hung, so that for a moment even my own ears hummed with the godly force of them: a mere six words each one of which did seem a very volume; and their lingering echo joined forces with the winds outside and flew away in many directions; upon the which, my lord King Louis rose from His seat and stepped forth, and the field of already lowered wigs drew back on either side before Him; and my lord King Louis strode majestically through the caesura thus created in the room and left the chamber.

His Majesty's wrath being consummate, categorical, and transcendent in its totality, nothing more dare be said within this chapter.

# 16

ON THE VERY NEXT DAY, READER, the court of France, its royal center ablaze with the cosmic fury of a midday August sun, packed up once again, quit the Palace of Versailles, and, in the midst of a thick snowfall, stormed into the city of Paris. This was done in order that certain high-ranking members of His Majesty's government could be closer at hand to the police interrogations which had just taken such a critical turn, and where the trials for divers murders, both foiled and successful, were set to begin in a week.

The wretched place to which the court now repaired, the Palace of the Louvre, is a grim fortress set above the banks of the Seine, itself a squalid creek which winds through the city; inside, the palace was dark and cold that November, and moreover quite filthy, not to say rat-infested, for none of the servants there had expected our appearance and they had been leading quite indolent lives ever since the court had abandoned the place many years before; none of the flues had been swept out for some while, and the fires sputtered and smoked and filled the vast rooms with soot; here and there were broken panes in the windows, and drifts of snow blew in across the dirty, cracking floors; and where the windows were securely closed, the air was stale and thick. Except in the westernmost wing, there was very little furniture—a chair here, a table there—producing an even stronger sense of drafty isolation. And thus you will not be surprised to learn, reader, that once everyone had arrived, they fell into the most foul humor; tempers flew out of control, ladies struck their servants and spat upon the rugs, and gentlemen, out of pure spite and resentment at having, as it were, to be imprisoned in the Louvre, relieved themselves on the tapestries and carpeting, those furnishings already so rank that no one noticed a thing. None of the doors in the ancient building being equipped with swinging panels, the royal dogs kept crashing into solid wood, then howling and blubbering and weaving away with snarls of fury.

But canine fury is as nothing to royal fury, reader; and my lord King Louis struck, more sharply than any dog his head against the door, great terror into the hearts of all who beheld Him striding back and forth throughout the frigid, reeky hallways; for He could not sit still, such being the height of His wrath that He stalked darkly about the palace from room to shabby room, His valets and gentlemen dashing about to keep pace with His robust divinity. But yet the following afternoon, the sum total of anger at the palace was vastly increased when there arrived, out from her voluntary exile at Clagny, the Marquise de Montespan, herself even more enraged than she had been at the conclusion of her interview with Monsieur Pussort a fortnight previous, for the news of the La Voisin child's accusations had most assuredly reached her ears; and I would not wonder that the marquise sensed, for she had excellent perception about such matters, that any continued removal by her from the court could lend an air of credence to the wretched child's assertions. Thus she returned to the court; but in no way did she appear abashed or apologetic about her circumstances, but right boldly she made her return, and with Marie-Céleste Vivonne once more quite conspicuously among her female entourage; and she was not a bit reticent to let the full extent of her wrath be known and felt.

One person indeed there was quite untouched by the prevailing humor of irascibility, though quite central to it, which was Marie-Angélique de Scorailles de Rousille, Duchesse de Fontanges, she being, to put the matter quite bluntly, simply too stupid to know what was going on; and she waddled about the dark and filthy rooms and hallways in her state of rampant pregnancy, not able nor even trying to keep up with anything.

I was not personally glad that Mme de Montespan had rejoined the court, even though that lady was the target of my somewhat thwarted operations; and I think you will understand these inner conflicts and contradictions, for I did not care a whit any longer for rendering her my customary service. Thus, I found myself avoiding her, or more accurately, avoiding Mlle des Œillets, who was her emissary. But one brisk morning as I was by myself out at the privies (which at the Louvre are located on the south side not far from the river embankment, which is convenient), attending to the royal vessel, I saw des Œillets approaching. I had glimpsed her while en route that morning through the moldy hallways, she remaining some distance behind me but taking the same path as mine. She was bundled up in a wrap against the cold; and though we had not seen each other in some while, she greeted me right warmly; whereupon she proceeded in the following curious fashion:

Reaching inside her clothing, she drew forth a razor: it was similar in manufacture to the one which she had presented me as a birthday gift from the marquise several years previous, but not, it seemed at first glance, as finely wrought in its design nor as well crafted in construction.

"Monsieur Hugues," said she, "I am right certain that your old razor must have grown quite dull over this much time; and see? I have found you another one! And I vow, as pretty an instrument as the one you have."

I did not like to differ with the lady in matters of taste, for I held to the principle, and still do, that there is no use discussing them. But on the other matter, the condition of my own razor, I felt it needful to set her aright, for the daily reaping of my chin was, and is, an important issue to me.

"Mademoiselle," I replied, "I am most grateful for your thoughtfulness," (and indeed I was, reader, no false politesse that: for I was but rarely the object in those days of any act of generosity, nor have been since) "but I assure you that I strop my excellent blade each morning, and I would stake my life upon it that it is as sharp as any in the kingdom!"

"Yet see," she persisted, and holding the razor out for my inspection, "see, this one can be nicely closed when it is not in use!" This was exactly the construction of my own razor, the one she herself had delivered me, but I did not care to dispute it. "And now look how I can unfold it to form a handle with the sheath." Whereupon she opened it out; but at that very moment, her hand slipped and the sharp blade sliced downward and directly across the back of my own hand; and it cut a deep gash into my flesh, and the blood began to flow quite freely.

"Alas! Monsieur Hugues!" cried she. "How clumsy I have been!" And forthwith, she drew a napkin—a prettily scalloped one—from her bosom and applying it firmly to the wound, sopped up the bright red flow. At length, the bleeding slowed and stopped; and mademoiselle bound my hand with another pretty napkin which she had about her person; and she apologized to me, and most profusely, and left me. She left as well the razor, where it had fallen to the ground; and I picked it up and examined it. Seeing that, although somewhat simpler than my own, it was a perfectly adequate tool and quite up to the task for which it had been made, I resolved on the spot to keep it and thenceforth to use it daily instead of the one which had been the gift of the marquise; for that gift had now quite lost its luster in my eyes, as had indeed its giver; and I had continued to use it only from sheer necessity, having no other. And with my new razor securely in place on my rookery ledge, it gave me enormous pleasure the very next morning to take the marquise's razor, which formerly I had so greatly prized, and to pitch it far out into the filthy river Seine, where I hoped it would soon rust and then crumble into pieces.

I continued to keep at a remove from the marquise and her lady; this was not difficult to do, for although the Louvre is not as immense as the Palace of Versailles, yet it is vastly more complex, having been constructed in many stages over many centuries and by many different hands; and I found that with care and attention, I could go about my daily chores without seeing very much of anyone of note, whilst my business in the evenings, that is, serving my dwindling clientele, was restricted to one of the lesser areas of the chateau where Montespan never appeared.

The preoccupation that season amongst that clientele was with the arrests of a number of notables—some already accused, still others unannounced—including, after costly and now quite futile delays, the Maréchal de Luxembourg, Mme de St. Estève, the Marquis de Feuquières (all former clients of mine, as you know), and numerous others; even the toxicologist Romani was finally apprehended. This turn of events, as I heard it told, very much rattled every level of Parisian society, but most especially the uppermost, wherein my clientele counted themselves, whether rightly or not; so that the depositions and trials of all these notables, having turned into clamorous public affairs, were as well most hotly debated during private rounds of *reversi*. The judicial proceedings were conducted in various courtrooms about the center of Paris, and thus there was a constant flurry of people hurrying from one hearing to another in an effort to keep abreast; getting about Paris was not at all easy that winter, the weather adding considerably to the normal obstacles of crowded, narrow, rubbish-strewn, and barely passable roads; and ofttimes several trials were being conducted simultaneously, which fact necessitated either rushing from one site to another to pick up scraps of testimony or exchanging information with other observers—and sometimes buying it from them—and earnestly comparing impressions and assessments.

The Archbishop of Lisieux being a most reliable follower of court procedures, hastened about to attend as many as his obesity would allow and had been witnessing both Mme La Voisin and the Abbé Lesage on the stand as they fought to outdo one another. And he was always present when the actual questioning of Lesage was taken up: fellow cleric though he was, however, I do not think that he was present at the abbé's ordeal in any ecclesiastical capacity: for he took a kind of mirthful glee whenever he recounted Lesage's claims such as would have been inappropriate to one charged with the integrity of the clergy; and yet I cannot tell: the archbishop's sense of humor being as acute as it was, he may very well have been given to laughing out loud while administering the sacrament of confession for all I know.

"Lesage continues his charges, and now directly at the lady," observed the archbishop one evening, "which is most damaging; for he accused La Voisin of burying in her vegetable garden upwards of twenty-five hundred aborted children." From beneath the table I could only imagine how his copious sides must have shaken. "How resourceful the man is! It is truly a pleasure to behold!"

"Twenty-five hundred! An excellent thrust!" exclaimed the Marquis d'Effiat, giggling. "The man is indeed ingenious!" And the entire room of gamesters joined in the mirth.

Now reader, I would not myself have named so great a figure; but had they asked me, I could easily have revealed to Monsieur de la Reynie and his staff the use that La Voisin had made of her vegetable garden; it was no secret to me, who had witnessed the steady parade of tiny victims at the Abbé Guibourg's devotions; still, I would certainly not have thought twenty-five hundred, it is excessive.

Yet as avidly as the trials were attended, perhaps an even stronger interest manifested itself in the public executions which followed many of them: for it truly did one's heart good, as I have heard it expressed by more than one witness to a hanging or a burning, to see a murderer or an occultist, a toxicologist or a peddler of poisons, an abortionist, a sorcerer or an Antichrist meet his just and agonizing reward; and lest you charge me with dealing in mere secondhand instances of such satisfaction, I myself can attest to this fact by my own witness and shall do so; for I had the enormous good fortune to behold, and with my own two eyes, such a public execution; and you will be quite surprised, I do not doubt it, to learn not only whose painful end it was that I saw but that I was right well satisfied by it: for it was Mme Cathérine La Voisin's herself.

Now you may cry out that I am unfeeling and cruel to derive any satisfaction from the death of one with whom I had—you may not say "enjoyed"—but experienced so long a contact over the years; and yet as the reports of her lurid testimony continued to multiply that winter, I could not but come to agree with those who held that the woman, even though seeking to best her rival Lesage, had reported such excesses that she must surely have gone mad; for by the end of her prison days, she had accused one cleric of having performed upwards of ten thousand abortions, a figure which must be a gross exaggeration, requiring over (let us say) a five-year period the gutting of some five and a half fetuses a day; she charged that Archbishop Champvallon was holding midnight satanic orgies every second Tuesday atop the royal tombs at St. Denis, whereat the participants indulged themselves in Spanish fly and other aphrodisiacs, in opium, morphia, and even on occasion hemlock; another person, a marquise, she accused of the destruction of the entire population of Rungin, a farming town in the southwest, whose water pump the marquise had presumably polluted with steady doses of corrosive sublimate and various sulfurous compounds; no one at the hearing could dispute the charge; and when the town of Rungin itself did in fact dispute it in a written deposition signed by the mayor and a number of its notables, who clearly had not been destroyed, at least not at the signing, the charge was summarily dismissed and the accuser discredited. Notoriety had gone to La Voisin's head: so that even the Paris Police Department, ever vigilant as it was for new evidence of mischief, grew suspicious of her and began to discount everything the woman spoke; moreover, her several days on the rack spent at my lord King Louis's behest produced no credible new revelations; and most especially nothing whatsoever as to who it actually was with malevolent designs on the

Duchesse de Fontanges; and thus, having at length no further use for her, the police were right well justified in pressing for her execution, and she was appointed to be publicly bound to a stake and burned alive on the following Sunday afternoon. And a good decision it was, say I, reader: let us have moderation in all things.

That Sunday was a clear, cold day. I had just finished tossing out a scuttleful of ashes (for some parts of life are constant) on the south side of the palace near the privies, when I was much surprised to see the figure of Emil Vergeyck lumbering down the embankment toward me: for I never saw the man except quite late at night, as you will recall, when he would fetch me to serve at Mass.

"Come, Monsieur Hugues," said he, "we'll see the baggage off."

Now, reader: I did not know at the time of La Voisin's death warrant; yet so clear was it that the man presumed I understood his purpose that I did not like to enquire what it was; besides, Vergeyck was a fellow not given to conversation except with himself and that in so dire a manner that I had never dared to respond. Yet I could not simply abandon my task and fly off with him, for my scuttle was to be returned to the scullery; and so I pulled myself up to my full height, which was but a third of his, and addressed him thus:

"M. Vergeyck, and you will allow me to return my scuttle to its rightful place, sir, I will be with you presently and will most gladly accompany you to see the baggage off."

"Make haste, then, Monsieur Hugues," said Emil Vergeyck, "for it is like to be right crowded in the square."

Whereupon I took the scuttle back inside and downstairs to the storeroom, running all the way and going over in my mind the whiles what chores I should be neglecting in the interests of seeing the baggage off; but matters in the Louvre being still in such a state of general disarray, I doubted not that my absence would be overlooked. I did, however, take the time to scramble up into my lodging, which was behind a cornice in the newly built Colonnade, where I examined my chin for any undue growth; but it was quite smooth; and I combed my cowlick and spread some spittle on it to keep it down; and I put a muffler around my neck.

When I rejoined Emil Vergeyck, he, not caring to be seen with a dwarf for he was a man sensitive to the taunts and jeers of others, placed me as usual in a cloth sack and flung me over his powerful shoulder; and the two of us set out. Through the weave of the sack I caught glimpses of the Colonnade itself, a right handsome façade, then of a church, and then of the warren of streets through which we passed until some ten minutes later we reached the Place de Grève; that is the square bounded by the Hôtel de Ville on the east and which on the south slopes down to the river Seine, and the place where executions of criminals were held every afternoon, which made it one of the most popular and lively spots in the city.

Emil Vergeyck did not remove me from the sack nor would I have expected it; but he did place the sack upon his right shoulder and held it there as though it were a sack of potatoes so that I might have a view, through the mesh weave, of the proceedings. And now I peered out at a raucous and festive mob of people, milling about nearby to a wooden stake and a pile of straw, with the bulk of the Hôtel in the distance, all under a bright, clear sky.

Presently, up from the riverbank there rolled a cart with horse and driver, which began to make its rattling way across the square; whereupon the crowd let out a mighty roar, for seated in the back was the object of their entertainment: a hag, reader, I can describe the creature only as such, a hag: her hair was entirely disheveled and flying about in all directions and even her eyebrows were shaggy and wild; her face was gaunt and quite filthy; she wore a thin, cotton, shift-like garment and hugged herself against the biting cold; and a rope hung about her thin neck like a leash upon an animal. But it was not until the cart drew up near to the stake—and we were quite close to it ourselves, for Emil Vergeyck being the somewhat giant that he was, he was able to claim an excellent location—that I recognized who indeed the hag was: so this was the baggage we had come to see off! Herself: Mme Cathérine La Voisin, née Deshayes.

As soon as the cart stopped, there appeared a burly fellow I had not seen before, who, grabbing hold of the rope and tugging it quite violently, forced La Voisin to clamor down as swiftly as she could from out of the cart lest she be throttled on the spot; though a case might well be made that a good throttling would have been a more merciful death than the one that now she faced. Next, the executioner began pushing her up onto the pile of straw; yet she began to resist his efforts and to scuffle with him despite his considerable brawn, striking at him and crying out, and although he quickly prevailed and succeeded in binding her securely to the stake, yet great batches of straw had been flung about in the struggle. The crowd was quite beside itself with the spectacle, laughing, catcalling, and shouting out many rude epithets at the wretch and even throwing things at her; whereupon Mme La Voisin began answering them back:

"Fools! Fools!" she shouted to the mob. "I know still more criminals I can name—all of them murderers! abortionists! poisoners! Why will you kill me before I tell you their names! Hear me! Listen! Listen for the love of Jesus!" And she began an entire catalogue of names, shrieking them out at the top of her lungs into the cold winter air: "Mme Hautefort! The Marquis de Vexin! Coligny! Ursins! The brothers Blémy! Claude Gicquel! The Princesse de Vaudémort!" And as she saw the executioner now set fire to an oily torch he held, she grew increasingly passionate and indeed quite reckless, reader, for now she cried out, "And others higher up! Much higher! Françoise de Mortemart is guilty! The king! The king is guilty of abomination!"

At that, I quite lost all patience with the woman; for although I had much revised my opinion of Françoise de Mortemart, the Marquise de Montespan, and no longer in my view the divine marquise, yet it was reprehensible, nay, downright blasphemous for La Voisin, however desperate she was, to name my lord King Louis guilty of abomination, and she so close to her reckoning before our dear Lord Jesus; blasphemous, I say, for we know that divinity being what it is, does not commit sin, nay, that it cannot commit sin. And I am as well aware as you, reader, of that dilemma which I cited some pages previous which states that divinity being divinity can do whatever it likes. And yet all in all, I come down on the side of a sinless divinity: for if a divinity, however omnipotent, can change its nature and go around committing foulness and evil at the drop of a hat, then surely, reader, chaos reigns. Such too was my thinking that crisp afternoon in February of 1680 on the Place de Grève; and thus my outrage at La Voisin's sacrilegious charge.

And thus as well, I was right well pleased, every bit as much as the boisterous crowd itself—though not wishing to embarrass Emil Vergeyck, I held my tongue—when the fire was at last applied to the straw which was piled up around the godless La Voisin's feet; and I lifted my heart, if not my voice, in praise of so just an execution even as the flames themselves lifted upward toward the stake; we watched enthralled as one tongue of it leapt up ahead of all the others and caught the woman's eyebrows on fire, arousing the crowd yet more; and when her wisps of hair began to smolder and then to burn, we could not contain ourselves.

"Jesus! Maria!" she cried out, at which the bonfire engulfed her cotton shift and she disappeared in an explosive burst of flame; the final sight of any part of her being that of a long, thin, and hairless tail which writhed for a mere instant out from the swirling inferno and then burnt to a crisp, and I swear that I saw it, reader, as I believe many others did as well; and presently a light scent of cooking flesh wafted out over the hysterical, jubilant mob.

Now the fact that at the last moment she had cried out, "Jesus! Maria!"—an incontestable fact, I was present and I heard it myself—was a sign later among the pious that the woman was in fact a blessèd saint; but among those more down-to-earth, it was evidence that to the bitter end she had remained a true hypocrite, and they marveled greatly at her constancy; and thus she was much admired by both factions, though indeed somewhat after the fact. But I knew her, reader, for the wily churl that she had always been, and hence I sided with those celebrating her fraud.

I have elected to recount La Voisin's execution, since from time to time she has figured prominently in my account and I thought it meet. Moreover, it has served me as an opportunity to do honor to that exalted institution, the public execution of criminals; for these acts not only serve our society as deterrents to malfeasance and mischief but provide as well healthy outdoor diversion to people of all ages. And it was most heartening to witness the number of dear little children present that February afternoon, for how better might our future generation learn of the gravity of misdeeds and of their consequences than to observe at firsthand a burning at the stake, a hanging, or a beheading? The matter requires no advocacy on my part.

(I will take the liberty here of adding a point about one of the splendors of the Palace of Versailles, to wit, the chapel. Its construction required many years of effort, but last week on the fifth of June, 1710, it was finally declared ready for dedication, and it was duly dedicated, and it is a most magnificent temple and among the crowning glories of Versailles. Now an interesting detail in that chapel, though "detail" may seem a small word for so mighty a subject, is the portrait of God the

Father which adorns the very center of the immense ceiling fresco: for it seems that God the Father does indeed have thumbs: it is evident there in His outstretched right hand—though obscure in His left, but no matter; and I assume that those gentlemen who executed the fresco knew what they were about, for they have most accurately portrayed God's long white beard. Thus I encourage your visit to the chapel not only for its beauty but for your own religious edification.)

Now: to return to my text, taking up from the execution of Mme La Voisin. As fate would have it—and it is indeed a fateful event which we now approach—for a second time that same day, though late at night, Emil Vergeyck came to fetch me, to take me to serve at Mass for the Abbé Guibourg, that cleric continuing his devotions, even amidst the tumult of those days, in a steadfast manner. The abbé was quite steadfast as well, it seemed, in another custom, that of rigorously declining to cleanse in any way whatever fragments of his teeth there yet hung in his head; so that as soon as Vergeyck delivered me up, I was nearly felled by the stench emanating from His Worship's mouth; and moreover, although I had served him at Mass only a matter of weeks previous, I had the distinct impression that February night that Father Guibourg's spinal curvature had become more pronounced, for he could scarcely command a view of what was up ahead of himself and kept bumping into the walls; unless it were of course that his cyclopean eyesight had deteriorated since last I saw him. However it may be, it was necessary for me this night to conduct the priest down into the catacombs myself, an office which before had been performed by one or the other of the La Voisins; but no one had taken their place, and I looked upon Father Guibourg's present shorthandedness as an unhappy sign of the times and a sad comment on the current state of worship in the land.

Arriving in the chapel, I quickly observed that the female designated to serve as altar dressing that night was already stretched out, her clothing folded neatly up over her head, as was meet; but what with having to guide the Abbé Guibourg here and there about the place and to assist him with the babe being offered that night to Alpha, Ley, Agla, Atoum, Sekhmet, Khnoum, Astaroth, and Asmodus, in addition to my customary tasks of lighting candles and filling the chapel with incense, I had not the opportunity to observe more than cursorily the female parts on the altar. But I assure my reader that it was not for want of curiosity on my part: no, I was twenty years old, and I had not grown so blasé over the short course of those years that my lady's private parts held no further delights for me, no, no; even despite the extensive experience I had gained in matters of their outward appearances and their ofttimes distinctive aromas, to say nothing of those deeper mysteries of which they rightly boast; no, not a bit of it.

We proceeded into the sacred rite, the good abbé and I, in a romping course through the *itay missa est,* the *quod oray sumpsimus,* and thence to the *simili modo.* Whereupon as usual, His Worship emptied that night's bloody contents of the basin into the chalice; then, reader, I observed, and with no small astonishment, the following: the abbé withdrew, from a small bundle which I had not noticed before upon the altar, he withdrew, I say, none other than Mlle des Œillets's blood-soaked napkin; I swear I knew it, for it had prettily scalloped edges, as you yourself will recall. The blood upon it had dried and was flaking in places; and the cleric held the cloth above the open chalice and twisted it this way and that so that particles of dried blood—my blood, reader, my own dried blood, the miracle of it!—should drop off and mingle with the fresh, warm, and still liquid blood of the sacrificed child.

I could scarcely credit my own two eyes!

*"Simili modo."* As the abbé launched that prayer, I fell to wondering upon this curiosity but had time to reach only the following hasty conclusion: that because as a dwarf I brought some innate value in my service of the Mass to him (for that, you will recall, was the incentive for training me as an acolyte in the first place), so too then might my dwarfish blood have been of special merit to his purposes, being considered (though inaccurately) to possess "less than human" qualities. But I left off that musing, reader, for it was at this point that the particular intention of the Mass was set forth, the celebrant quaffing down the contents of the chalice and crying out the following startling petition:

"Alpha, Ley, Agla; Beelzebub, Ahriman, Abaddon, and Belial; Infernal Potentates, I command you! By the belly of John and by the very organ of the most Holy Savior, hear me! I summon you; and by the penetralia of our first mother Eve, again I exhort you; and by the blood of Satan Himself, by this babe's blood, and by that of the House of France, again I do command you! that you cause the fetus now carried by the female

Marie to shrink! and thenceforth to expire! and thenceforth to be cast off from out her entrails! And further: I exhort you in this my second exhortation, that that same woman Marie de Fontanges herself suffer a prodigious loss of blood! And that she herself eventually perish therefrom and die! And may these things come to pass with dispatch even before the next midnight has elapsed. Hear me, dark potentates! Amen. *Qui pridiay quam pateraytur . . .*"

Now reader, let me quickly remind you that you have read of earlier efforts made for a miscarriage to afflict that same Marie, she who was the Duchesse de Fontanges, for such was the toxicologist Romani's undertaking to have been, had his dark designs not been revealed in time, he apprehended, and the miscarriage thwarted. And so I was startled to hear that such a fate was still being sought for the young duchess; and most specifically by name—not simply for "Marie" but for "that same woman Marie de Fontanges herself"; and I was moreover quite alarmed to hear that the deities were now being petitioned, not only for a loss of blood on her part, such as would be normal in a miscarriage, but even for her death.

For her death, reader! We had come once again to murderous doings!

And yes, I was alarmed to hear this, I can tell you, and I was much shaken; and as I felt the chill of a wind sweeping in from the icy plains of some hideous frozen hell and as I inhaled an acrid, sulphurous exhalation blown up from God-alone-knew-where unless the devil himself did too, my heart suddenly leapt in fear—rank fear, reader; I felt the hairs start up on the back of my neck and my heart pounded and my eyes began darting about, seeking I knew not what refuge from the bloodthirsty terror that now filled that sooty sanctuary; until they chanced at last to light upon that which they had not thus far seen, and little refuge it was from fear when now they beheld the female pubescence which had lain exposed before me on the altar all this while.

I shall describe with care that particular pubescence: it was a gently rolling hillock, covered with a fair and quite luxuriant down, with subtly curling patterns throughout its expanse; the adjacent moors were ivory white, with but one exception: above the field and to the left and just beyond its outer limits, reader, there was a mole: a mole, reader, a small, dark mole such as I had seen—nay, the very same which I had seen on many a prior occasion; and as I stood there, rapt in wonder at the sight, there wafted, even through the suffocating stench of the incense and sulfur, there wafted up to my nose—and I need not remind you of the capacities of that particular tool—there wafted, I say, at that most crucial moment, the delicate aroma of fresh-caught halibut.

# 17

THE MOMENT WAS TERRIFYING.

And terrifying all the moments after as the Mass swept forward, on to the *introibo ad* and thence to its conclusion; terrifying the moonless journey back to the Louvre; terrifying the tossing, sleepless night, terrifying, terrifying the dawn. To have heard, with my own two ears, that exhortation to the powers of darkness for the duchess's demise—but to have actually seen, with my own two eyes, the very author of that plea: the Marquise de Montespan, surely now divinity no more if ever she had been! For how else explain the presence of that particular meadowland which I saw exposed atop the sacred altar? No: to know—even with my nose—that which my lord did crave to know, believe it though He had refused to do, incense Him though it would.

To know what now I knew!

And was this not precisely that most profitable information I had sought for all this while? Yes! I had it! And all remaining now for me to do was put the thing to use, was that not so? But yet I trembled, reader, standing with it on the brink of what it promised, I trembled. For this was not about a tinkering with the law, a bribe, a scheme to get your sister out of town, a flirting with the regulations; this was no childish mischief-making among the mighty; nay, this was a thing of murderousness, of vengeful murderousness; and in the very heart of the most splendid, most illustrious, and most royal circle of them all.

So crowded was my mind that winter morn, so teeming my brain, that I was floored by an event the which in fact should not have come as any surprise to me at all.

The Duchesse de Fontanges had a miscarriage.

Whether it were Alpha, Ley, Agla, Beelzebub, Ahriman, Abaddon, and Belial who, by the belly of John, had prevailed; or some purely medical or physiological, not to say embryological, coincidence I cannot state; but I know that it happened and that very same morning, for I ran into an entire phalanx of surgeons and physicians (though I steered clear of their crotches) not in this instance because I was running but rather because all of them were, and they were running and in great haste to the duchess's apartment; and despite my state of mental distraction, yet intuitively I turned about and began to run with them; and we arrived at the door of her apartment, whereupon the gentlemen withdrew within; but out of curiosity and a well-developed habit of keeping my ear to the ground, I lingered in the lobby outside and listened as a slatternly midwife regaled a handful of charwomen about the momentous event.

"Christ! Why them fools is in such a rush stretches all my powers of comprehension: the sty's broke open and the pig's fled and that's it. And it's her own damned fault too, it is, all that horseback riding—and with a bun in the oven? Such a blockhead the girl is; and it was just last month she fell down from off the horse, and so I chops up a piece of silk ribbon and made her eat it then and there with three fresh eggs, which done it, she kept the damned thing in. So then what does she do but go out again—again!—the less than half-wit, and gallops off to hunting again! So's I don't much wonder the scrawny thing fell out. Six months' worth it were. And a stinking bloody mess it made too all over the sheets and floor. Her piss was pink last night, she ought to have knowed. Won't listen to a soul, though, the tart, thinks she knows it all, so it serves her damned right, I says. A boy the thing was—or would have been. A hairy little bugger with a right proper-looking tool started, for his years. Or months, I should say." At which bons mots, the charwomen laughed and began sporting about with one another in a most suggestive manner. "Good riddance," continued the midwife, "I flung him in the cookstove, don't you mind the stink, ladies." Which prompted a second round of hilarity. "And I reckon His High and Mighty Bloody Lordship will be right put out. Though who knows? With all the bastards that old goat's set loose in the world, He probably don't care one bright green pea." And they fell to laughing yet again, this time at the reference to green peas, which even those depraved old crones knew were objects of great attention at the court.

You may imagine my outrage that the divine Louis should be called a goat; but she was an ignorant slut that said it, and very likely from Paris, which teems with commoners of the most vulgar order. Still: I hope her teeth fall out.

Presently the door to the duchess's apartment burst open, and the charwomen flew off in all directions; but the midwife remained where she was, imagining, I presume, some kinship to the members of the medical profession who now thronged out into the lobby, although for all the heed they paid her she might as well have gone on about her business. These gentlemen consulted together for some while as to what ought to be prescribed for the duchess's condition; but there was great disagreement amongst that medical community, centering in sum on whether matter should now be drawn from out of the young woman by means of bleedings, purgatives, and enemas in order to reduce any residual septicity in her system or whether, given the fact that her system had already discharged a fair quantity of matter, various elements ought now to be introduced into it, *viz*, doses of sulfur and quinine and a diet of eggs, red meat, oils, and other products including the testicles of a sheep. And thus two great schools of medicine locked horns.

Reader, though I understood little of such weighty scientific matters, I doubted not that with such an excellent array of medical regimens available to the Duchesse de Fontanges, the pretty creature would quickly regain her wonted vigor and health, yet much to the vexation, I dared to conjecture, of Alpha, Ley, Agla, Beelzebub, Ahriman, Abaddon, and Belial; for you remember, of course, that those deities had been requested to bring about not only the demise of her unborn child (which task they had now discharged) but that of the duchess herself, and even before the passage of another midnight. But yet these matters are delicate and not easily categorized; and on second thought, it may well have been the opinion of Alpha, Ley, Agla, Beelzebub, Ahriman, Abaddon, and Belial that one murder was enough for the time being; or even that the Duchesse de Fontanges, as utterly charming an object as she was to behold, was not, from any other conceivable standpoint, worth the bother.

What was most certainly not recommended by the distinguished medical faculty attending upon the duchess was that she be moved that same day, with great haste and at some distance away, in freezing and most inclement weather and over roads which were normally hazardous and rendered yet more so at the time by the abnormally severe winter; and yet that is precisely the prescription dispensed to her and in fact to everyone at court, without reference to their reproductive situations: for my lord King Louis ordained that the Louvre be abandoned anew and Versailles once again occupied and with all dispatch; for He deemed the dangers afoot in Paris as exemplified by the duchess's brush with death akin to those dangers which, during the period of political turmoil in His youth, had inspired His original abandonment of the unruly city. And so return to Versailles we did and were arrived there by early afternoon, I spending the length of the journey deep, deep in thought: until I resolved that with events breaking as swiftly as now they were, I must make my move.

I found that my aerie at Versailles was still situated above the king's new reception chamber, there having been no rearrangements down below; although a great quantity of scaffolding was still to be found throughout the palace, as there would be for years to come. The opening in the cornice which I had carved out only a month earlier had been covered over with a fresh layer of plastering; but it was of no matter to me, reader, for I was sure that my days of eavesdropping were now quite done with.

As soon then as I had unpacked my clothes and returned my brush, my handkerchief, my picture book, and my new razor to the wooden beam which served as a shelf in my rookery, it being about nine thirty in the evening, I went in search of Mlle des Œillets. It was relatively easy to find her now that we were back at Versailles; and I did find her; and I requested that she admit me, if possible, to the marquise's drawing room and to her ladyship's presence before supper.

"Ah, then, Monsieur Hugues, you desire to see her again, do you?" And she smoothed down my cowlick and adjusted my neckerchief in the sweet manner in which women do such things. "We had thought you no longer cared for us, sir! But you will find madame in remarkably good spirits for a change; and I believe, monsieur, we both of us know why." And laughing merrily at her quick reference to Fontanges's miscarriage, mademoiselle led me to the drawing room; she scratched lightly at the door, listened with one ear against it, then opened it and stepped inside; presently she admitted me into the room, closing the door behind her as she left and as usual, for privacy's sake, she locked it.

Madame's private drawing room was small and intimate; and I was quite puzzled to observe now, that piled everywhere were mountains of furniture—tables, chairs, screens, commodes, even pictures and rolled up carpeting leaning against the wall—such as I had never seen there before and which created a most palpable confusion, much beyond the confusion associated with a routine move from one palace to another. I later learned that during our sojourn at the Louvre, the marquise's apartment at Versailles had been restructured and reduced by several rooms, those rooms then being incorporated into an adjacent apartment being fitted for use by the Duchesse de Fontanges; and the young duchess had maintained that the furnishings in her newly acquired rooms were used and shabby and that she required newer ones as more properly befitted her youth and recently gained position; thus, all the older furnishings had been temporarily moved into the marquise's drawing room until they could be redeployed. Only two areas stood relatively clear of clutter: the chimney place, where in fact a fire now burned, and the opposite side of the room, where a table stood in front of a window at which the marquise was seated having a cup of tea.

I paused a moment to study her features from afar, for I had not been in her presence for some while; and I noted that despite the disorder of the room, the expression on her face was remarkably tranquil, and was reminiscent of her divine serenity of old; yet change had taken place: for her cheeks had developed a certain fullness, a jowlishness which had not been quite so pronounced before; her chin now hinted somewhat of doubling itself; and her elegant breasts were on the way to becoming bosoms.

When she saw me, a sterner look came over her face.

"So: it is you, is it?" said she. "Where, pray, have you kept yourself? Do you think to go about at your own pleasure? It will not do, sir, no, this giving yourself airs, indeed! Look to it."

Reader, this greeting did not presage the fruitful interview which I had come for; and so I was somewhat relieved to hear her continue:

"Well, but even so: now that you are returned, dwarf, you know your business: pray be about it."

I was somewhat relieved, I say, for I felt it advantageous to my purposes, however much I cared not to perform the business, that she and I should be restored to more familiar ground. And even though she had not sent for me on this occasion, yet here was now an opening which I could use to my benefit.

"Madame."

I crossed the room and slipped beneath the table.

Modesty now steps forth, and once more draws the curtain closed before the scene. Yet I take the liberty of noting that the marquise's thighs, it seemed to me, had attained a certain girth since last we visited; otherwise all else was as before: her floculent triangulation, as before; the mole, the ever-constant mole above and to the left was as before; and as before, the lingering scent of *hippoglossus hippoglossus*, a term from the Latin, reader, which I found recently in a dictionary of scientific names in order to accurately identify that creature which our fishwives commonly call the halibut. All was then as before: and was indeed as I had observed it, I remind you, only the night previous under startlingly different circumstances.

Now when the business was concluded, reader, and the marquise then in an even more comforted humor than when I had first entered the room, I withdrew from beneath the table and pursuant to my plan, stationed myself before her, and at not too great a distance either, for my message was for her ears alone, and walls are known to listen.

"Madame," I began, "with your leave: I make bold to recall to Your Ladyship that petition which I presented to Your Ladyship some two months previous in which I did request most earnestly and indeed most respectfully Your Ladyship's intercession on my behalf with my lord King Louis the Fourteenth, in the sincere hope of securing from His Gracious and Most Sovereign Majesty the legitimization of my person and the establishment for myself of a fair and upright name amongst my fellow creatures."

I paused. I had played only my opening hand; yet I hoped for some sign of a response.

Silently the marquise studied my face for moment or two.

"Is it to be that nonsense all over again?" she asked with impatience. "Are we to unearth Monsieur Hugues's desire for legitimization once more? Pray be off with you."

"Madame," quoth I, pressing my suit, "that is indeed my most deferential request."

"And why, pray, dwarf, might you believe that my response would now be favorable? Do you presume to think me so fickle that I would now, for some whim, embrace that frivolity of yours? That I would find deserving what merely a month or so ago I scorned?"

I did not bend before her withering assault, I did not!

"Madame," I replied quietly, "I believe indeed that now you may."

There played about her eyes a glimmer of a frown, for somehow, she gleaned that this time she could not so easily toy with me or dismiss me quite so casually as before; and it was a thing which she sensed but did not understand, a thing which, I fancied, made her somewhat unsettled.

"And wherefore might I now, Monsieur Hugues?"

I swallowed hard. What next I said I said in a hushed tone and pronouncing the words quite slowly and evenly:

"Madame: my eyes have witnessed," quoth I, "that which you would wish that they had not; and my ears have heard, madame, what you would not have had them hear. I have nosed about. Madame," I concluded, "I know a thing."

(To say that I had "nosed about" was not, I think, boastful on my part, however prominent a feature my nose was. I believe it was a simple, honest statement.)

At that, reader, the marquise paled slightly, and the lines upon her forehead tightened; but she did not let down her guard.

"Come, Monsieur Hugues," she said with great care, "games are for children, sir. Kindly state your position, up front and like a man. Though you are," she added, "but half of one; and I am being liberal at that."

Vile, ungenerous woman! Thus to impugn my manliness! Nay, reader, now there would be no turning back! But yet my manly heart, I confess it, was thumping.

"Madame," I said, and I took a deep breath, "last night, in the catacombs of Notre Dame Cathedral in the city of Paris, a Mass was said. It was a Mass somewhat out of the ordinary though most certainly not unique, and it was said for the avowed intention of inflicting harm upon Marie-Angélique de Scorailles de Roussille, the Duchesse de Fontanges, that she should suffer a miscarriage, a goal which has been readily achieved; and furthermore, that she herself should perish from prodigious loss of blood. Madame: I was in attendance at that Mass." At which point I paused a beat. "Madame: and so were you."

Thus to insert the knife with but four short words—"and so were you"—though it were a fearsome, fearsome thing to do, yet it so fed the maw of vengeance in my breast that I felt a quick rush of elation, being a complete and entire member of the human race.

I watched as her bejeweled fingers now quickly gripped both arms of the chair. Upward from her heaving bosoms there swept a hot flush of redness, which spread across her neck, her chins, and thence her face; but it was not a blush of modesty, reader, as I think you may have guessed: nay, it was the quick rubescense of rage.

"You lie," she hissed, "you lie, dwarf."

"Nay, madame," I tendered quietly, "I do not lie; and you know that I do not. I am in private service to His Worship the Abbé Hilaire Guibourg, madame; I serve him as his acolyte, madame, and have done so now for years. At his Masses I have heard divers petitions, petitions for this and petitions for that; yet none that I recall—not one—which approached so closely to the company of His Majesty and with so murderous an intent, madame."

"Fie!" the marquise exclaimed with a haughty toss of her head. "And who, pray, would credit you, sir? Who would even entertain a report from so base a source as a dwarf? A dwarf, sir, who works at the lowest level of this court, who is charged with shoveling slops and ashes!"

"Madame," I rejoined, "dwarf though I be and slops though I may shovel, yet I am charged with other duties, madame, and I am indeed put to other uses, as well Your Ladyship knows. And thus it is that I am right well familiar with those intimate parts of Your Ladyship's person—and could indeed provide descriptive evidence of the same for corroboration—with those parts, I say, by which I recognized Your Ladyship's presence at that particular Mass and Your Ladyship's most particular service to it."

There was a deathly silence; then:

"Cur," she growled, "filthy, despicable, damnable cur!" And suddenly she rose, reader, and lunged forward toward me; but yet I darted quickly from beyond her grasp, dashing to the other side of the table; whereupon she followed me and thus began to chase me about the room, the two of us dodging in and out among the piles of tables, chairs, and carpeting, and she crying out the whiles in fury what a vile, wretched cur I was for using her thus: until, at last, I seized upon a chance to fly to the door and to slip out through one of the lower swinging panels; for if I were to be called a cur, why then, like a cur I would behave. And I hastened away, the echoes ringing in my ears of her shouts and cries and of her fists pounding upon the door, which, as you know, was locked.

There followed then a day of great anxiety for me: for the deep pleasure of my encounter with the marquise was eventually tempered by the cool return of reason: and I shall borrow an image from the gaming world: I having made the opening service to her, the ball was now landed on her side of the net; and I could do nothing but await her return play in the match. Nor could I imagine, as the long hours wore on throughout the night and then the winter morning, and as I went, most absent-mindedly, about my various chores, what play I myself should next make were she to choose, as certainly was possible, to retire from the field and simply make no volley in return. The strength of my position lay only in that piece of intelligence which I had come upon: if she did not choose to respond, what was I then to do with it? To whom, that is, report the thing? And I determined that it must be to Monsieur de la Reynie that I would report the thing, to that most estimable man and one whom I had come to admire above all other men—save only one. But next: how then was I to find Monsieur de la Reynie? I had no access to that gentleman, and most especially now that we had quit the city. Why then, I decided, I should simply have to wait upon him when next he came out to Versailles, as indeed he was most like to do; but yet then I could not imagine how I might persuade the distinguished gentleman even to grant me a hearing, for he was seriously preoccupied with the pressures of his office. Moreover, I then recalled, Monsieur de la Reynie was himself in less than excellent graces at the court, his office having lately suffered at the hands of the La Voisins and his information discredited. But then, if not he, who? Must I approach Monsieur Colbert? And the mere thought of addressing myself to that old lion put me entirely out of appetite for lunch. Later that afternoon, I stumbled, in my ruminations, upon the odds that the marquise, a woman of no few means, might not retaliate against me with some unexpected and devastating return of her own. Might I now be facing exile or imprisonment? Physical pain? The agency of Alpha, Ley, Agla, Beelzebub, Ahriman, Abaddon, and Belial? Was in fact my very life in danger of being snuffed out? For who would take amiss a missing dwarf? And one missing from within my ladyship's own personal company? No, no: it had been harebrained of me to begin the match, unthinking, impulsive, with never a plan to follow through, with never a proper strategy in mind! And to have confronted herself, the Marquise de Montespan, Athénaïs, Françoise de la Rochechouart-Mortemart—nay, the very boldness, baldness, the reckless, rash temerity of such a scheme—surely it spelled my utter and imminent downfall, however short that fall would be!

Thus, by the time that Mlle des Œillets did indeed come seeking me that evening and to conduct me once again to the marquise, I had sunk into such a ruinous state of confusion and fear—my chin unshaved, my clothes in disarray—that mademoiselle spent several minutes trying to restore me to some more proper order. For even the realization that the marquise had, it seemed, elected to return my opening shot was, by now, but the coldest of comforts.

"Whatever did you say to her last night?" mademoiselle asked as she fought with my cowlick. "Or do? Such a vile temper the creature's been in all day, I thought she would quite snap my head off!"

And so, as yet again I entered that furniture-laden room and yet again approached the figure of the marquise, my heart indeed was thumping yet again and this time out of all-too-human-fear. She was not seated, her ladyship, but was standing, one hand resting firmly upon the table, herself facing the window and the dark, cold night outside. She did not turn to see me but she knew that I was there.

"Sign this," she said, with scant ceremony.

It was then that I saw that beneath her fingertips there lay on the table a sheet of paper and with some writing upon it; and there was an ink-stand nearby.

"Madame, I fear that I cannot," I replied, my voice reasonably steady, somewhat to my own surprise.

"What! You cannot? I will be the judge, if you please, of what you can and cannot do. You will sign the thing."

"Madame," I replied, "I have not the gift of either reading or writing."

There was a lengthy pause.

"Then, sir, you shall mark it with an $X$," said she. "And pray you do so this instant."

I was torn, reader, between an impulse to do exactly as she bade me, and forthwith, so that our interview might end with all due speed; and a nagging curiosity, which I believe you will grant was not unnatural, to

know what it was that I should be *X*-ing. For as hateful as that moment
was, yet how much more hateful would it in retrospect become were it
to turn out that it was an order for my immediate banishment which lay
beneath her fingertips or even a warrant for my own death!

"Madame," quoth I with a courage I did not know I possessed, "it
would much oblige me to know what document it is."

"Audacity!" she exclaimed, as though to herself. "It is but a simple
contract, sir," she went on, now speaking to me and with some impatience in her voice, "a simple statement that you will not speak again of,
nor make any reference whatsoever, veiled or otherwise, to the matter
addressed—with great disrespect, I might add—by yourself to me last
evening." She did not continue into the matter of what penalty there
would be if I should break the contract; yet I doubted not that she would
be able to devise one.

There was a pause.

"Madame," I said, "I flatter myself to believe that I made my intentions
clear in our previous interview, when I sought Your Ladyship's support
of my petition to his Majesty." And I continued: "My keen interest in the
matter has not waned, nor would it preclude my *X*-ing that particular
contract, were I to receive an assurance of Your Ladyship's participation
on my behalf. A contract, after all, madame, has, at least theoretically,
some benefit for both signatories."

It was at that moment as though another being inhabited my frame,
reader, though there was scarcely room in it for myself; and as though
that other being had now spoken through me to her ladyship; for in my
most extravagant dreams, I would never have conceived myself capable
of such forwardness.

"Fie, fie!" exclaimed the marquise and turning to face me for the first
time. "Damn you, then you shall have it! I shall do it! Why, what an
utterly preposterous issue even to be speaking to you about! Fie on it,
fie! But I shall do it, I shall speak with His Majesty; but I do not assure
you of any favorable outcome, and I shall in no way press the matter upon
Him, for there are certainly other, more urgent issues and many of them
which are demanding of His Majesty's attention at present. There now,"
she concluded, "be quick about it, there is a pen, make your *X*, and I pray
you, let us have done with the thing."

I approached the table, reached up to the inkwell, and took up the quill; it was the very first time in my life that I had ever held a pen, but not, as you know who have come thus far with me, if indeed you have, the last. I dipped the point into the well of black ink, then moved it to just above the page.

And then I paused.

"Madame," the voice within me said, "shall I know when it is that you will solicit His Majesty upon the matter?"

A thick drop of ink fell from the pen down upon the paper.

"Why, you are a very mule!" cried the marquise. "And a right insolent one at that! I am appointed to see His Majesty tomorrow evening, if you must needs know, and see! See what a vile mess you are making! It is intolerable! You will have ink stains all about the room! Wretched creature!"

Slowly I fashioned a large $X$ upon the paper.

"Now go, go, begone!" she cried and, seizing the pen from my hand, she cuffed my ear. "And mark me, dwarf: I shall play no more games with you; do not provoke me further, or you will learn of what mettle my anger is composed. And so: now off with you!"

Whereupon I withdrew from the chamber. And straight away I hastened, with many leapings and skippings and prancings about, all the way over to the other side of the palace and out to the kitchen, where I found a basin of water in which I washed my unwashed face and hands and dampened down my rumpled hair; then I ran all the way back to the north side and up into my rookery, where I combed my hair and my cowlick and mowed a while upon my chin with my razor—and right glad I was that it was no longer the marquise's gift which I was using but that of the sweet Mlle des Œillets, what though it were of inferior manufacture?—and I put upon me a fresh, clean neckerchief. My utter astonishment that the marquise should have thus acquiesced to my request was quite thoroughly overwhelmed by joy and a sense of triumph and a rapturous expectation of all the glorious things that were to come! And with a buoyant heart, I hastened to my evening chores.

# 18

THOUGH—JOYFULLY—I HAD SECURED the Marquise de Montespan's
agreement that she would speak for me to my lord King Louis, yet upon
reflection I began to have creeping doubts as to how effective an emissary
to my lord King Louis she would be. For consider, reader: the Duchesse
de Fontanges, though confined to her apartment until her recovery, was
still very much in my lord's favor, a fact which did not suggest that the
Marquise de Montespan ought expect a return to it for herself any time
soon; that shifting of my lord's affections had even resulted in a shifting
of the marquise's furniture from out of her apartment; additionally, the
fact that she knew when it was, as by a scheduled appointment, that she
was next to be in my lord's company, bespoke of the current lack of
commerce between them. And what is more, Mme de Montespan had
made quite clear her own indifference to the cause of my legitimization—nay, her actual disdain for it: why should she vigorously pursue a
course she did not espouse in such uncertain waters?

I therefore grew doubtful of any favorable outcome of my plan and,
once more, quite discouraged. Even so, I decided upon a precautionary
tactic: in order to assure myself that my $X$ would not go utterly disre-
garded, I resolved, though with misgivings, to take up once again my role
of eavesdropper and to listen in at the meeting that was to take place
between the two of them.

The displacement of her furnishings into her drawing room, sign of
disfavor though it was for her, now fell as a boon to me, for I found that
I could make use of a loosely rolled Aubusson tapestry (a hunting scene

thought to depict François I and his courtiers), which had been tossed on the floor not far from the chimney place, and into which I could burrow, reader, somewhat in the manner of a mole (which term I mean in no ironic or disrespectful way). And it was there that I stowed myself that evening; by adjusting the Aubusson, I found that I could see, through a row of dangling fringework, out into the room: it was a partial view, but yet better than from beneath a card table. Which reminded me that time spent in the Aubusson that evening would be time spent not without risk; for my clients, I knew, would be busy running up massive debts and clutching about underneath the tables in frantic search of my assistance; and as well, my women clients would be much in want; and later I would most certainly suffer blows and insults from all of them, male and female. But yet there are circumstances in which we choose to endure such trials for the sake of more pressing concerns, as indeed mine that evening were.

Shortly before ten o'clock, the marquise entered the room, followed by a maid, who placed a chocolate service upon the table in front of the fireplace along with a pitcher of iced water flavored with orange blossom extract, for that was a singular favorite of my lord King Louis's, both summer and winter. Then, as I heard the hour strike from a clock on the mantel, I heard as well a cry from without of "Gentlemen! The King!" and the sound of approaching footsteps; and His Majesty, I could tell although I could not see, now came through the doorway: there was always a hush which settled upon a room, even one that was already still, whenever His Majesty entered.

"My lord," I heard the marquise say in a respectful manner.

"Madame," came back the forthright reply. "You are well, we trust." This last was less a query as to her ladyship's health than a kind of instruction to it, for my lord had little patience with illness or poor health of any kind.

There was a silence once more as His Majesty moved to sit in one of two chairs which had been placed near the fire; and through the fringe, I caught a glimpse of my most divine lord; once again of His extraordinary bearing and grace, of His high and noble brow, of His commanding gaze, and most especially of His magnificent nose; surely in His splendor no man might even approach Him, nor no God excel.

The marquise, in turn, sat; the servant girl poured a glass of orange

water for Him and a cup of chocolate for her and then withdrew. The
silence continued for yet several moments more, until at length the
marquise spoke:

"My lord," said she, "I am grateful to you for granting me this visit; and
indeed I am quite well, sir, in reply to your greeting, quite well indeed;
but except for one matter to which I would crave your attention."

"Madame?" spoke His Majesty.

"I pray you, sir, if you would look about you, sir, you will see that
my drawing room has become quite burdened with furnishings of one
sort and another, all of them from other nearby rooms; rooms which
were previously at my disposal, sir, but which I have resigned myself
to surrendering." She paused. "My lord, to use me thus is not to use
me well."

"Yes, yes," replied the king. "Those rooms were required, you understand, for other purposes; and you will allow that there are—"

"Sir," the marquise interrupted, "indeed I do not 'understand' nor will
I indeed 'allow.' It is intolerable, sir, intolerable, I say, that I should be
thus—" and she sought for the word "—'shunted' about. Where it is that
I stand in your affections, my lord, I can no longer determine, alas; but
I would most respectfully request, and do feel entitled to respectfully
do so, sir, that my private chambers not be used, sir, as some—how shall
I say?—as some warehouse, simply because that trollop doesn't like the
upholstery!"

"Yes, yes, we know," came my lord's now somewhat wearied response.
"The matter—"

"Look at it! You have but to look at it!" cried the marquise, the which
His Majesty then did, half rising in His chair and quickly surveying the
crowded room; for not even He would appear to have had much other
choice.

"Yes, yes, we shall have it all removed," He said with a wave of His
hand, and He sat back down.

"The baggage!" persisted the marquise, now fully engaged in the skir-
mish. "Why, the girl cannot even carry a child to term, it seems, the
feeble brat."

"My dear, my dear, kindly do not go on. The matter will be—"

"I am not 'going on,' as you say."

"But you are. The matter is—"

"I deny it! I am merely stating the facts, my lord, which are as——"

"Madame!" It was now my lord's turn to interrupt. "You are working yourself up into a state over absolutely nothing. I am quite——"

"Nothing? Over nothing, say you?"

"Over nothing, I say, yes, and I do say it," He answered firmly. "If truth be known, I am thoroughly vexed with the duchess myself, if you will listen for one moment and not go about leaping to conclusions. I am entirely vexed with her myself, I say, for she has turned quite unbearably sickly over this ridiculous miscarriage of hers and does nothing but complain all the day long and lie about in her bed, wheedling and whining; and I have no patience with such childishness, none whatsoever, not any more I haven't. No: the girl must be packed off to a convent, and right soon. And so I pray you, do not waste your breath upon the matter." A lengthy silence followed this statement. "And pray, madame, let me say," He continued and with a notable change in the tone of His voice, "let me say that I was right well pleased to receive your request to see me; for madame, I shall confess, it had fully been my intention to call upon you this evening."

"My lord." With a note of surprise, yet in a most deferential tone, the marquise acknowledged the sudden shift in His position.

"Indeed I have grown quite weary of these incessant demands and of this infantile self-indulgence; and I have come to realize, my dear Athénaïs"—and here He stretched out His hand toward her—"how very much you are to me; and have always been; for you understand me as no one else has ever done, and it joys my heart and right gladly to see you again and your cheerful face: but it is a face which has grown quite pale, madame, quite winter pale: you have been too long absent from the sun."

Whereupon she placed her hand in His. "Sir, I thank you." And in that simple gesture and in those four most simple words, reader, I sensed once again that rare divinity which, over the years, I had, like my lord Sun King Louis Himself, come to worship.

Now, reader, there then followed between the two of them words of such warmth and so rich an abundance of endearments and blandishments, tears and sighs, dalliances, coquetries, gallantries, and the like as I think modesty demands that once more I let drop the curtain. Were it a scene played by lesser beings, I would be tempted to leave the curtain aloft; but I let it drop, for divinity commands its own privileges. And yet, alas, the scene appeared to have ended on my own blighted expectations; for my petition to His Majesty was going quite by the boards in the midst of their affectionate reconciliation. And yet I beseech you to stay: remain where you are, as I did, however cramped the Aubusson: for there is an epilogue, reader, to the drama of which we have witnessed but the opening act, which epilogue you shall hear, and it is well worth your inconvenience.

"My dear," quoth at length the marquise, and upon this cue we raise the curtain once again and relight the chandelier above the stage. "My dear," said she, "there is indeed another matter, and a bothersome and foolish one it is, but one to which I pray you give some thought; and especially in these parlous and incautious times."

"Athénaïs: you shall name it."

There followed a pause.

"It is the matter, quite frankly, my lord, of my dwarf."

There followed another pause.

"Of your dwarf."

"Of Hugues. The creature is some twenty years of age now, is it not, and for some while has been most utterly fixated upon one particular issue: that, my lord, of his legitimacy."

"How? Of his legitimacy?" My lord's voice seemed quite calm and steady.

"Of his legitimacy, sir," the marquise continued, "and has opportuned me, sir, to intercede for himself with you; to present you a petition— or what is clearly a misguided petition—requesting that you grant him, as he expresses it, 'the legitimization of his person and the establishment of a fair and upright name for himself.'"

I would have been glad, reader, had she not characterized my petition as "clearly misguided"; but yet I held my breath—you may imagine—as I heard my suit, however prejudicially, actually voiced in the presence of my lord King Louis, Fourteenth of that Name.

"Grant him——?" King Louis XIV paused. And still I dared not breathe as I waited for Him to continue, that Godhead into whose divine hands had just been placed my being and the very reason for it. He cleared His celestial throat. "No, no, it is impossible, madame, and surely so; you know it yourself. No, no."

Impossible.

"Pray you, my lord," the marquise pressed forward, "do not dismiss it thus——"

"I shall dismiss it, and I do dismiss it, madame," my lord replied. "What on earth would you have me do? Given his origin? Why no, the thing is preposterous."

Preposterous.

My spirits sank. It was hardly the first time that my fortunes had been so summarily dismissed—indeed, most of my comings and goings, those that were acknowledged at all, were routinely dismissed; but yet in this instance, upon which I had pinned so great a hope, it was cruel, cruel! to hear those words, even from the lips of my lord, whose every utterance I honored and cherished; and my spirits sank.

"My lord," the marquise continued, "I readily understand, sir, and I quite well take your point. And yet—and yet; there is another—and if I may say so, a more delicate—issue—or at least the creature claims, that is to say, that there is another issue which somewhat affects the greater picture."

"Yes?" rejoined the king, and with a note of some impatience now.

"He says, sir—he claims—that he has acquired some dangerous and incriminating evidence, my lord."

There was a silence.

"Evidence?" enquired King Louis. "Incriminating evidence? And to whom is it incriminating, if it is not too much to ask?"

"Why, sir——" The marquise faltered slightly but quickly regained her composure. "Why, sir, he would not specify; but he claims that it is dangerous to a person of some note, to a person of station about the court; and that the matter, if divulged, would be most seriously damaging to the entire stability and conduct of the state."

Now, reader: you know right well yourself that I never said anything of the kind! Tosh!

"Tosh!" cried King Louis. "And tosh again! It is all too common a claim; why, everyone these days is producing evidence of this and evidence of that and completely incontrovertible proofs of such-and-such-and-such. It is all become nonsense! No: let the child produce his evidence, if evidence he has."

"He refuses, and quite stubbornly, sir——"

"Enough, I will hear no more of it! The entire matter is absolutely impossible."

Absolutely impossible.

And after a brief pause:

"What's more," He continued, "it is very blackmail that the child should assert himself thus." And His voice took on a tone of great vexation. "And I am astounded that you should even speak on his behalf under the circumstances. Blackmail, I say it is, madame, pure and simple blackmail, and quite wretchedly handled at that. He 'claims,' does he? No: you shall not answer to his 'claims,' no, I forbid it."

There was another pause.

"And yet, my lord," offered the marquise, "the creature is very sly; I do not doubt but that—"

"Madame, the matter is closed."

"My lord, with all respect—"

"Closed, I say!" His Majesty's voice rose. "Pray do not put me further out of humor."

"He states—" the marquise began. But:

"No!" His Majesty said firmly. "Let us hear no more of this rubbish!"

"My lord." The marquise finally acceded, for she feared, and rightly so, His anger.

There was an unpleasant silence.

"If then, madame, there is nothing further upon your mind," said my lord with ill-disguised irritation, "we shall take our present leave of you." He rose; and He thrust His chin forward and His nose upward in the proud manner which He commanded. "And bid you a most excellent evening."

Whereupon He took her hand and kissed it and with no further ado withdrew from the drawing room; and as He made His way back to His own apartments, distant shouts throughout the hallways accompanied His passage:

"Gentlemen! The King! Gentlemen! The King! Gentlemen! The King!"

"Fie! Fie! Fie!" shouted in turn the marquise, thinking herself now unattended. "Vile, detestable toad! I shall furnish some reward for the troubles he has put me to, that dwarf! Beshrew him! Fie!" And she ranted to herself a while longer in like manner and with similar threats and exclamations, for her reprieve from exile had been all too brief, and she

saw no help for it; but at length she too retired from the room. Whereupon, despite the keenness of my disappointment, I leapt up from my
parterre location and hastened back to the gaming rooms; and just in
time, too, to deliver the Comte de Vendeuvre from such sweeping financial devastation that but for me his excellent chateau southeast of Caen
would have been on the auction block the following morning.

I did not sleep that night, reader, but sat, once again wide awake up
inside my rookery, or paced about, if one may be said to "pace" in so limited an area. By this point in my life, my ears had become so attuned
to every nuance, to every innuendo in those discourses to which I lent
them—to every subtlety which, previously, I had quite let slip—that I
found myself rehearsing that evening's conversation in some close detail:
and I came to weigh most carefully the words with which my lord had
characterized my earnest petition, to wit, two "impossibles," one of which
was absolute, against one "preposterous." It being my lord's opinion that
it would be preposterous to grant me legitimization, that opinion must
be accepted as beyond dispute, I reasoned, for who shall question the
opinion of a God? But yet, "impossible," reader? "Impossible?" And that
"impossible"—nay, that pair of "impossibles," and most especially the
absolute one of the two "impossibles," gave me pause: for what shall be
impossible to my divine lord—what even absolutely so—to His omnipotence, save the commission of sin and of evil? And was I then to understand that a simple act declaring that I, Hugues, though dwarf, was a legal
human being—was I to understand that such an act would be a sin? some
instance of ungodly evil and hence impossible to perform? No, I could
not think it so. And once again I confronted, but now from the other
side of the coin, the thickets of that theological conundrum, that of the
all-powerful but sinless deity; and I could make no more sense of it than
ever before. "You know it yourself, madame," my lord had said in passing; what, pray, did the marquise know? Was it the very solution to
the conundrum that she was blessed withal? and which had so entirely
eluded me?

Yet a second observation by my lord now captured my hungry attention: ". . . given his origin: what on earth would you have me do, given
his origin?" He had asked rhetorically. Was there something in that phrase
that I was overlooking, or of which I was ignorant? And I began to cull
back through my life to see if I could not happen upon anything more

of my origin than I had customarily come to accept: my birth (though I cannot say in all honesty that I recall the event), my birthplace (St. Germain-en-Laye), my condition (dwarf), the length of my nose (note-worthy), the monastery of St. Sauveur (bleak), the kitchen floor of the monastery (filthy), the curs thereabouts (vicious), the other children thereabouts with whom I did not play (malicious), the cook (slatternly), the labor of removing ashes (debilitating), and the early morning manip-ulations of my parts by Brother Dagobert (stimulating): nothing, how-ever, satisfied my mounting curiosity vis-à-vis those words of my lord's, "given his origin." And thus, with no hope of settling the first matter— I mean the ever-baffling conundrum of the divine and its capacities—I resolved, as those early morning hours crept once again toward dawn, to pursue the second issue, that of my origin, and to seek out, in my quest to become a satisfactory human being, indeed exactly who it was that I was: and what it was about the thing that presented such a stumbling block to my request; in short, reader, to unearth whence it was indeed that I had come.

Yet how might I go about that search? My lord King Louis, who, being omniscient, was clearly aware of my origin, as apparently was the Mar-quise de Montespan herself, I felt, of course, no freedom to approach. Who else would be aware of my whereabouts at birth some twenty years since? Any eyewitness to that harrowing moment in my history was un-known to me; and so I must rely upon an informed but more remote source. It was possible that if my lord knew, why then His brother might, Monsieur, Duc d'Orléans, being exceedingly well informed upon a num-ber of issues, many quite trivial; and yet on second thought, it was doubt-ful that even he could be bothered with such an extremely trivial matter as my birth; moreover, the gentleman was so much given to waggishness and to sport and to larking about, that I doubted not but that I would be the object of derision at his hands and come away still uninformed. Then I recalled that Her Majesty the Queen had once voiced an opinion as to the year of my birth; and yet I could not countenance approaching that lady; for given her dour and splenetic disposition, to say nothing of the danger she always posed as a collector of dwarves, I had had virtually no contact with her since our interview and certainly wished for none. Fur-ther afield, I doubted seriously that Brother Dagobert of the monastery of St. Sauveur, if he yet breathed, would know, or the miserable cook at that place; yet it was conceivable that the Abbé Hilaire Guibourg, the learnèd vicar, would know, but I had no access to him, not, that is, until I should be called back to his service; moreover, I was not altogether convinced that I could endure a face-to-face encounter with him, given the state of his teeth. And thus, reader, at length I was obliged, though fighting it all the way, let me assure you, obliged, I say, to concede what I had suspected from the start of my study of the problem but only in the very back of my mind, to wit: that the one person who was likely to know what I needed now myself to know was Mme Françoise Scarron.

"I am under some constraint," that lady had said to me when first we met on page 29, "to accept you into this house and to provide you bed and board"; and then she had gone on to speak of "other children here, who will be superior to you." Such statements were no guarantee that Mme Scarron held the key to the puzzle; yet it was not inconceivable that that "constraint" could have some bearing on the matter; and that in asserting the other children to be superior, she would be somewhat informed as to my inferior nature, which might be to say, of my origin.

And to be honest, reader, what was more, I could think of no one else.

It had been some while since our paths had crossed, I having my own regimen of chores and she being still very much taken up with tending my lord's offspring. I had observed that it was her habit to escort the children for vigorous walks about the garden, even in the dead of winter; each afternoon, the troop of them would be marched down the new staircase in the south wing, now usable though still under construction, and out onto the south parterre. And I resolved to watch for them there on the staircase whenever I could seize a spare moment and to approach Scarron in order to request an interview. Several days went by before our comings and goings converged; but upon that occasion she quite ignored my greeting although it could not have been more courteous, for I bowed to her with great deference and condescension; but she passed me by without so much as a sniff in my direction. So that I was obliged to spend several days more, dashing over to the south wing in the afternoons, through the crowds and then through the thicket of scaffoldings and riggings, and onto the stairs in the hopes of meeting her again. At length my efforts were rewarded; and approaching her, I bowed (again) most obsequiously and then bowed to the company of attendant children behind her, and I spoke.

"Madame," said I, "with all due respect to Your Ladyship, I should be most deeply indebted to Your Ladyship for the favor of but five minutes of Your Ladyship's time."

Whereupon, to my astonishment, I heard my words repeated, and parroted in a high-pitched voice mocking my own: "Madame, with all due respect, madame, to Your Ladyship, madame, I should be, madame, most deeply indebted, madame, to Your Ladyship, madame——" At which point the speaker could no longer go on but burst into gales of laughter. Looking about me, I spotted Louis-Auguste, the Duc du Maine, two steps to the rear of his governess and quite doubled over with hilarity; and this was a rare display of the young duke's humor as he was given more often to blubbering; and now the other children (except for Louis-Alexandre, who, at the age of two, was unversed in the arts of derision, but the child would learn), began shrieking along with the duke at his sport.

"Silence!" commanded Scarron, at which, immediately, the children attempted to stifle their mirth; but they were not altogether successful. "What do you want, Hugues?" she continued, now speaking to me, and the sound of my name produced yet another wave of laughter. "Why are you hounding me?"

"Madame, if I may be so bold, I request but an instant of your private time upon a matter of some moment to myself."

Behind the stout figure of Mme Scarron and out of the corner of my eye, I saw the young duke silently mouthing my words and in a most exaggerated and preposterous manner; and the others, their hands over their mouths, began snickering again despite themselves.

"Bother! Well, if there is nothing for it," said she, "tomorrow evening. A quarter to ten." And she swept on down the stairs. "Be punctual, I shan't wait."

The children in turn followed her down. Now, reader, you may wish to censure me for what next I did, and then you must do so, but I could not help myself, nor, I trust, could you have done, if you have but a smidgen of humanity in your veins: for just as the Duc du Maine was passing by me, I quickly stuck out my tongue at him; and so taken aback was he by the violence of the gesture and as well, I believe, by the sheer length of my instrument, that he faltered and stumbled; for with his club foot, his leg brace, and the disparity in the lengths of his limbs, he was not a sure-footed lad; and he fell; and then he rolled down the rest of the flight of stairs all the way to the bottom, where his iron brace went crashing into a segment of timber scaffolding, which in turn fell upon the duke. And as I went racing headlong back up the stairs and around the first corner that I came to—for I had not touched him, reader, I had not set finger upon the child! no, nor even the tip of my tongue—I heard screams and prolonged wails and howls and bellows from down below.

(You will recall perhaps that I had whimsically fancied, when first I saw the infant duke and by virtue of his stumpy left foot, that he and I were remotely kindred souls; and you know as well that there had been some commerce between us. But I decided that day, hastening away from the scene, that the creature would never be kin of mine: no, nor no friend neither.)

Thus, when I went for my appointment the following evening with Mme Scarron, I was not certain but that my gesture to the duke might not mar my reception by her; but although she was in no way friendly (which I would not have expected in any case), she did not seem more than usually put out; and I believe that as her theory of rearing children incorporated a healthy amount of physical pain, she may well have felt that the young duke had indeed deserved to fall down the stairs, though not for making mock of me (she would not have found that reprehensible) but simply on general disciplinary principles appropriate for a ten-year-old. For whatever reason, she made no reference to the incident when I presented myself in her drawing room, but bade me speak up, for her time was precious, there being a devotional service at ten.

"Madame," I began. "I need never remind you that it was Your Ladyship who took me in at the tender age of eight, under your most gracious protection; and for some years thence maintained me with the care, attention, and warmth such as only a mother bears towards her child." I had thought that a touch of flattery would not be misplaced with the lady.

"Get on with it," she snapped.

"Fondly recalling which," I continued, "it would be my—I hope not misguided—assumption that Your Ladyship may chance to possess some information as to my origins."

Settling her face squarely upon both of her chins, Mme Scarron stared at me fixedly with her piercing eyes.

"Your origins," she repeated slowly.

"Yes, madame. Where, if I may make so bold to enquire of you, am I from? Whose offspring, madame, am I?"

There was a pause.

"That," said she, "is none of your business. Why do you ask?"

I had anticipated that question.

"Madame, it is but a natural human desire to wish to know one's lineage."

She snorted. "But," she replied, "what has put the business into your head just now? You have never known where you come from, what is your present interest?"

I had not planned to delve into the issue but saw nothing for it.

"The matter is relevant, madame, only insofar as it may bear upon a certain—ah—petition which at present I have in mind." I did not care to elaborate further. There was a brief silence.

"Petition?" she asked. "And for what, if I may enquire, are your proposing to petition?"

"Madame," I replied, but not willingly, "I am taking the liberty of seeking letters patent which may grant me legitimization and establish for myself a fair and upright name."

Scarron looked down her nose at me; this was not a protracted exercise, given the length of that feature. "Legitimization, is it?" said she. "Effrontery." At that moment, I would swear that her second chin gave unmistakable signs of developing a third. "Everybody in the world, it seems, is expecting to be made legitimate these days, it is preposterous. And just how, sir, do you propose to go about this so-called legitimization?"

I had not wished our conversation to veer thus off course, for those were murky waters; and yet I could find no way of avoiding an answer.

"Madame, in the only way that I can conceive as fit: my lord His Majesty King Louis is the only authority, I firmly believe, empowered to render such a reversal of one's original circumstances, and I shall make bold to present my appeal to Him."

Reader: you must have detected that I was not being utterly candid with the lady; for my appeal had already been made to His Majesty; and yet if she were going to press her enquiries, as now seemed likely, I saw no virtue in having to admit that my lord had already found my petition impossible to fulfill and preposterous: this information would not advance my cause with her, I did not think likely.

"Why, sir, you are most forward," she replied. "And exactly how is it that you propose to present your appeal to His Majesty? You have not the wit to write the thing; and you will surely never gain a personal audience with Him. What is your scheme, dwarf?"

Alas, this again was not the object of my interview!

"Why, madame, I have—that is—" I stumbled, "the Marquise de Montespan has graciously consented to intercede for me. But if you please, my present concern, madame, is—"

"That one," sneered Scarron. "Why, she is hardly in a position, I do not think, to present requests of her own these days; why should she bother with one of yours?"

"Your Ladyship, I—this is, this is not—Madame, I have come—"

"What? What?" she demanded. "Speak up, sir, I have no patience with stutterers. Answer the question."

This entire effort, I could see now, was quite hopeless; and yet I knew not how to extricate myself.

"I was able, madame," I replied, "to persuade the marquise. And she consented."

"To persuade the marquise? Why, I vow," said she, "you must indeed be most persuasive, monsieur, for she is not much easily persuaded upon trivial matters. And I should be most interested to learn the means by which you have succeeded in such 'persuasion.'"

"Madame, I cannot say."

"Beg pardon, did I hear you? You cannot say, sir?"

"It is somewhat privileged, madame."

"Is it somewhat so indeed? I think, sir," and she spoke quite slowly, "that I myself should like to be somewhat privileged, sir: I bid you: spit it out."

"It was—that is, how shall I say?—there was a certain matter, madame, of which I had learned." Reader: the moment—the very instant—that the word slipped from out of my mouth, I knew I should much regret it: a certain "matter."

"A certain matter?" she repeated. "A 'matter'? Ah, I see: a 'matter' indeed." Suddenly and to my great surprise, she rose, strode to the door of the drawing room, withdrew from her bosom a key, and locked the door. She replaced the key, turned, came back to her chair, and sat. "Now let us hear of this 'matter.' 'Matters,' sir, are sources of great interest to us. Indeed 'matters' are very much part of our business. Speak."

"Madame," I replied, hoping that the shaking in my knees was not evident and fearing that the shaking in my voice must surely have been, "madame, I may not—I must not say."

There was a pause.

"See here," said Mme Scarron, heaving her bosoms upward, "at the age of eight, as you yourself have duly noted, sir, you were placed into my charge. That charge has not expired, sir, pray do not think so, however much you may have forged a life beyond its boundaries. It is my prerogative simply to renew the charge and to reclaim you if need there be and quite to dispose of you as I see fit. And, sir, I shall not hesitate to do so, sir; and when I do so, sir, I will send you packing, sir, and out into exile; and not into the sunny meadows of Normandy, sir, no; but out to the West Indies, sir, for I am right well connected there; and you will find, sir, that the natives of the West Indies are not well disposed toward arrogant, insolent dwarves, sir, nor to any dwarves, for that matter, I would surely hope; for those climes, sir, are where dwell the anthropophagi, which is to say, the cannibals, sir; and these are beings taller than any man and more ferocious than any bear. Kindly, therefore, do not play puerile games with me."

Reader, now indeed I trembled; for I had seen pictures of the anthropophagi in my own picture book and knew that what she said was true; and I have since studied the matter in other, more learnèd texts, and it is true; and if you should go to Martinique or Guadaloupe or any of the Antilles or St. Barthélemy, beware, for you will see them for yourself. Standing there, before Mme Scarron, I felt my heart pounding at the thought of impending exile out into the new world among the anthropophagi; and large, hot tears streamed down both my cheeks, and I could not stop them; and I began to fear, moreover, that I might have an accident in my breeches. Suddenly she reached out and seized me by both ears. "Speak!" she commanded; and then she administered a wrenching twist.

"Madame!" I cried, "hold! I pray you leave off!"

"Speak, villain!" she insisted; but she did not release me from her powerful grip. "Speak!"

"Madame! It is only that I happened to learn that she had—that is, the marquise had—taken part, or that is, that she had simply been present, at a certain Mass."

There was a pause.

"A Mass? A Mass?" she repeated. "And pray, what of it if she went to a Mass? Does not everyone go to a Mass? What was the nature of this particular Mass, sir, if it is not too much to enquire?"

"It was of no particular nature, if it please you, madame."

"It does not please me. What was this Mass all about, creature?"

"Madame: it was said, madame, simply for the intention of causing a— a—an effect upon a person."

"Which is to say?"

"An effect, madame." At which I felt her grip on my ears to tighten. "An injury, if you will."

Mme Scarron leaned forward still further so that her face quite confronted my own; and still she did not release my ears.

"Sir, I will indeed," she whispered. "Be so good, monsieur, as to describe that injury to me, sir, and most explicitly, I pray you. And be quick about it!"

"An injury, madame; that is to say, madame, an injurious—ah—a miscarriage."

"Oho! A miscarriage, say you?" And her voice rose and fell like a giant wave. She drew still closer to my face. "And pray, sir, if it is not an inconvenience to you to reply, a miscarriage on the part of whom?" And she began a steady twisting of my ears.

I protest! What choice was there?

"Of the Duchesse de Fontanges!" I blurted out. "And her demise."

"Fontanges," she repeated very quietly. "And her demise. Do you say so indeed?" At that, reader, she let go of me and leaned most gently back into her chair. Quickly my hands flew to my ears and I pressed them tightly against my head; and I quelled a sudden and almost overwhelming need to bepiss myself, I quelled it; and through a shimmering wall of tears, tears of great fear of the anthropophagi, I will not deny it to you, and of sheer pain about the ears, and of the recollection of earlier, similar pain inflicted by Scarron—through all this, I saw a thin smile curl up the corners of her mouth; the third chin reappeared unequivocally; and slowly she closed her eyes in what seemed to be a kind of exotic physical pleasure.

Instinctively I raced to the door and tried to escape, forgetting that it was locked, and I rattled the handle vigorously but quite in vain.

"Are you going out and about somewhere, Monsieur Hugues?" I heard from the other side of the room.

"Madame, I pray you, unlock the door, and I shall take my most respectful leave of you at once, madame."

There was a silence.

"No, sir, I think not so, sir. I do not believe that our business, sir, has as yet been concluded." I turned to face her. "For what you have told me is of a criminal matter, and a matter of some considerable import to the state, sir, and it is a matter for the police authorities; and you are responsible, sir, as by your confession you have now forced me to become as well, we are responsible, I say, to report this matter and in full detail. And that report," she concluded, "will be made, Monsieur Hugues, in person—and I shall be witness to this myself—in person, sir, it will be made, I say, by you in person, to His Royal Highness the King."

# 19

FOR A LINGERING MOMENT, our eyes were locked in a fearsome tug of
wills, the outcome of which could hardly have been in doubt; yet during
that brief confrontation, an hundred thoughts swirled through my brains,
the chiefest being a sense of self-recrimination at having now unmasked,
as it were, the Marquise de Montespan. And to have unmasked her before
Mme Scarron of all people, whose rivalry with the marquise was now
surely poised on the brink of a gloriously satisfying resolution, only increased my sense of guilt. It mattered not that I could reason and wrangle
with myself this way and that and argue, and with complete justification,
that the marquise had hardly kept up her end of our bargain, for she had
not: certainly not in the manner in which she had spoken for me to
my lord, referring to my petition as "misguided" and to myself as "sly,"
no! None of those considerations produced any mitigation of the fact that
I had indeed betrayed her and moreover, to make matters worse, to her
stubborn adversary.

From a strategic standpoint, of course, I had just squandered, unwillingly but recklessly, that valuable intelligence about the marquise; and if
I were now to report it as well to my lord King Louis—as was Scarron's
announced intent—the loss would be total, with nothing whatever to
show for it. It is quite possible that this latter realization contributed to
the remorse which I have described to you, I confess it.

I have since then, by the way, entirely overcome that remorse and
have come to regret that I could not have been even more destructive to
the Marquise de Montespan's good name, in whatever manner available;

but of that more later; we do what we can with what we are given to go on.

With these admissions made to you, reader, I shall close the scene in Scarron's drawing room, just as it happened that evening, and continue my narrative.

Having issued her pronouncement upon my obligations to the state, the justice system, and to the royal throne of France, madame stood up, crossed once again to the door and unlocked it; then, seizing a handful of my hair, she propelled me through the door, across several passages, and directly into the king's guardroom. There, what had been a disorderly cluster of military men—some playing cards, others lolling on the floor, others idly milling about—all leapt to their feet and quickly stepped aside to clear a path; and seven or eight snarling dogs also cringed back out of her way.

Through the guardroom we swept and, unannounced, into the chamber beyond. There, we came upon a huge assembly of courtiers, all of them standing quietly, and all facing towards the opposite end of the room. Without a moment's hesitation, Scarron steered me directly into this crowd, which jumped and jostled aside for us; whereupon we quickly found ourselves out in the vast middle of the space.

To our left was a group of musicians, plying their divers instruments in a lively concert; to our right, a tall bank of windows, many of them wide open despite the wintry weather. But in the distance, reader, at the farthest end of the hall, was an imposing and most majestic sight to behold: for there I saw, seated at an enormous table where they were finishing off a large supper—and they were flanked by a bustling squadron of footmen, butlers, and serving men—I saw, I say, the most immediate members of the royal family of the Kingdom of France: the queen, Marie-Thérèse, who was devouring a massive plateful of food; the grand dauphin, Louis (Monseigneur), eating heartily himself and well on his way to becoming the bulging heap that his mother was; Philippe, Duc d'Orléans (Monsieur), my lord's brother, at the moment vigorously cleaning underneath his fingernails with a meat knife; the Duchesse de Fontanges, not a true member of the family but not yet entirely cast away from grace, though she did not appear to be eating or in fact doing anything more than sulking to herself; and lastly, at the head of the table, Himself: my magnificent lord, the King, His Majesty, Fourteenth of the Name of Louis.

Reader, I have recalled the details of this setting for you entirely in retrospect; but yet my very strongest recollection of that moment was of utter panic: voices and sounds reached my ears as though from afar, for my head was thoroughly crammed with panic; panic ruled my very limbs, convulsed them, and there was no controlling them; in panic the hairs stood up on the back of my neck, and I felt a cold sweat breaking out all over me; and the utmost bottom of my stomach was full and leaden with a deep-seated, wrenching terror.

As we strode forward—it is the only word for Mme Scarron's gait and since I kept up with her, being clutched still by a tuft of hair, I conclude that I too must have stridden—as we strode on, I say, beyond the middle of the chamber, our unexpected and abrupt appearance all at once caught the eye of my lord King Louis; and perhaps of others, I cannot tell, but I saw only my lord's majestic gaze upon us.

"Madame?" He cried out as we sailed toward the table, and He half rose in place, for my lord was always full of courtesy even in the face of an impropriety.

"Oh? Buzz, buzz, buzz! What have we here?" said Monsieur, sensing, by our unceremonious arrival at the family's private gathering, the possibility of a crisis; and he tossed aside the meat knife.

Three or four dogs leapt up and bared their teeth as we neared the table; but His Majesty clapped His hands but once and the curs crept off to the side.

"Your Majesty," spoke Mme Scarron when at length we stood before them all, curtseying briskly to my lord, her action jogging loose my own presence of mind so that I bowed as deeply as I could and so remained for some while. "Your Majesty," she continued, "I beg His Majesty's pardon for my intrusion upon His privacy, and indeed upon Her Majesty's privacy and upon that of my lords; but there is a matter and a weighty matter it is, which I bring to you, and which, I vow will be acknowledged, craves Your Majesty's most immediate attention."

The queen belched.

"La, la!" quoth Monsieur. "To judge by the looks of what you bring with you, it is a most pygmy-like matter indeed!" Whereupon he tossed a napkin at my bowed head; but it landed on the floor, for Monsieur was not well practiced in the outdoor sports, however deft he was at the indoor ones, and his eyesight was somewhat wanting. Yet recalling it, I think it was a cruel thing to have done, to have thrown the napkin at me, even if he missed. From where I was standing, my head still lowered, I caught now, in the shadows behind the figure of the queen, a glimpse of one of her dwarf pets, Alonso, his pudgy hands across his mouth, laughing silently at my discomfort.

"Tut, sir," said Scarron sternly, "tut! and His Majesty will best be the judge of that, sir."

"Tut, tut, tut, madame," replied Monsieur mockingly, "and tut, tut, tut once more!" At which the dauphin snickered, but barely enough to be heard.

Although still inclined forward, I caught a glimpse of the Duchesse de Fontanges's face exactly opposite me: her eyes were red and quite puffy, and her blond curls hung limply about her ears.

"My lord," continued Mme Scarron, "will you be gracious enough to hear of this matter, sir?"

The dauphin belched.

"Pray, speak," said the king.

"My lord," said she, "and shall I speak before this company, sir? It is a matter which——"

Whereat His Majesty signaled almost imperceptibly to a chamberlain, who himself signaled almost imperceptibly to all the rest of the room; and I saw the servants quickly withdraw from out of the place; instantly the music ceased, and I heard the crowds in back of me, along with the musicians, recede; and I heard the tall double doors thundering shut behind them, and even the dogs retreated into the shadows of the far corners of the hall.

Whereupon Monsieur kicked off his left shoe, revealing a foot clad in a dark silken stocking. "Good riddance!" he exclaimed as the shoe, with a high red heel and a bow of stiff purple satin, sailed through the air and landed on its side, not far, as it happened, from a fresh dog turd.

"Now, madame?" said my lord King Louis with a smile.

"My lord," replied Mme Scarron, "with all respect for the present company, shall I yet speak? For, my lord, it is a matter of some delicacy which——"

"You may speak," His Majesty replied.

"Do pray speak, madame," said Monsieur in a most quizzical tone. "We are all indeed itching to hear what fresh gossip you bring us. Are we not, nephew? Ha, ha, ha!" And he laughed at the solemn dauphin and right mockingly, for the dauphin, I believe, was slow and had no gift for the arts of gossiping.

"This dwarf, Your Majesty," Scarron continued and ignoring Monsieur, "one Hugues by name and well known hereabouts as a member of the Marquise de Montespan's household, has relayed to me a piece of information regarding the marquise which is not idle gossip, I can assure you, sir, but highly consequential. And he will repeat to you what he said to me; whereupon Your Majesty will do as He sees fit; yet I should myself advise that the dwarf be rigorously questioned."

Again she grabbed my hair and pulled me up from my obeisance so that I was now directly facing the entire company. "Speak!" said she.

I swallowed hard.

"With your leave, my lord," I began.

"Say on."

But I could not say on.

"Speak!" said Mme Scarron, and she gave my hair a tug.

An immense candelabra which stood in the middle of the table cast a bright glow upon their various faces; and the jewels sparkled, the rings on their fingers, the queen's necklace, brooch and tiara, a single golden earring which Monsieur wore, His Majesty's diamond buttons; and the thick, lacquered curls in the wigs which framed their faces glittered; and the queen's false teeth, which lay upon the table, for she could not eat with them, shone in the candlelight; and the drips of sweat upon all their foreheads and cheeks and noses and the grease upon their fingers glistened, for it was warm in the chamber despite the open windows, and they had consumed a tureenful of hot fish soup and three bottles of mulled burgundy.

"Speak, I say!"

"Your Majesty," I began again, for had I not been given my wretched cue? And in that divine presence, what hesitation or reluctance dared I show to say my text? Nay, what choice had I? I had none; and all the room had fallen silent and all fourteen eyes stared down upon me. "Your Majesty—" But yet I could not go on, like an actor frighted on the stage; and I looked about in terror, wishing that His Majesty's hounds would suddenly pounce upon me and tear me limb from limb.

"Ha!" said Monsieur. "Out with it, Monsieur Hugues, out with it! Or, ha ha ha! has the cat got your tongue, sir?"

There was a pause.

"How come he doesn't say anything?" asked the dauphin, his eyelids drooping. "Is he dumb?" And then, "How come you don't say anything, Hugues?" he asked me.

Everyone waited.

"*Miren,* these is all rubbish, madame," said the queen. "That dwarf isn't of no uses." Clearly she felt an unrivaled expertise on the subject of dwarves. Monsieur whooped at her observation and likely as much at her wretched grammar, and began slapping his hands upon the table; and presently the dauphin joined in the laughter, though perhaps not knowing why; and the queen emitted several other noises. And in the increasing merriment of that moment, Alonso, peering out again from behind the queen's chair, now allowed himself to burst into quite vocal and open mirth.

"Speak!" cried Scarron, and she began boxing my ears and right vigorously. "Speak, you devil!"

"Hold," said my lord King Louis, and instantly calm and order were restored to the room. "Monsieur Hugues," continued He in a most quiet, soothing tone, "I bid you, sir, speak; you need not fear, sir."

Reader, earlier I have described my lord's voice as being like that of a cello, and so it was at that sweet moment; and the music which it produced was celestial, for it sounded to my abused ears like nothing so much as the voice of a gentle father addressing and encouraging His son. And I found then that I was indeed able to speak and to address Him in return, and so I said to Him the following:

"Your Most Gracious Majesty: I have the honor to serve as acolyte to the Abbé Hilaire Guibourg, formerly sacristan of St. Marcel's at St. Denis. My lord, customarily, Father Guibourg's devotions are offered late at night, my lord, and in what might be considered a somewhat unorthodox fashion; for, sir, the liturgy is said in reverse, the Mass is spoken backwards." I took a slight pause, and during it I heard Monsieur begin actually to mew, though gently and to himself, but to mew: for he saw now that a thing was on the way and no idle chitter-chat. "My lord," I continued, "eight days ago, eight nights ago, Father Guibourg's Mass was offered with the express intention of provoking a miscarriage on the part of the Duchesse de Fontanges, a prodigious loss of blood, and the duchess's subsequent demise; present, my most gracious lord, at the

Mass and a participant in it, sir, for it was upon her unclad hummock, sir, that the Mass was said, was the Marquise de Montespan."

Everyone's jaw dropped open in astonishment at my words; and as for the duchess, she had gasped at the mention of her name, and now tears burst out of her eyes and coursed down her cheeks, and she choked and sobbed aloud.

"Quiet!" said my lord King Louis; whereupon she smothered her face and her sobs in a linen napkin.

Now a frigid silence fell upon the room.

The only perceptible motion was the delicate flickering of the flames on the candelabra.

At length my lord the king, Fourteenth of the Name of Louis, rose slowly to His full height. Whereupon the four others at the table also rose and slowly, though none to my lord's height. He stood, His fingers resting on the table; I dared not look away, and yet the sight of Him did indeed awe me; for I saw a great darkness sweep across my lord's heroic face, and the perfectly curved nostrils at the base of His godlike nose quivered; His brows were furrowed, and His deep eyes shot a most piercing gaze down into my own. In that frozen moment, all that I could hear was a low, slathering panting noise coming from the direction of Monsieur.

"Monsieur Hugues," said my lord King Louis quietly but firmly, "you are to come with me, sir."

Reader, at that moment I thought, in all honesty, that I was most like to suffer an accident inside my breeches; and yet I controlled an almost irresistible impulse to make a puddle on the floor; I mastered it and suppressed and did squelch it! with all the manfulness in my power. And though I knew not where it was that I should be going with Him, and though I trembled indeed to go with Him wherever He should lead me, yet I knew that resistance was inconceivable, and that follow Him I would—helpless, worshipful, and most thoroughly struck by awe— were He to lead me into the fires of hell.

Thereupon, I made a second deep obeisance to my lord King Louis; and the two of us, unaccompanied—but think of it!—left the others still standing at the table, all of whom bowed or curtseyed as we withdrew, including Mme Scarron, for whom—at such a triumphant moment— that physical act of humility cannot have been costly; but for Alonso, who made a lewd gesture at me. My lord preceded me by several paces, as was meet, I nearly running to keep up with His immense strides.

"Gentlemen! The King!" shouted the guards in the adjoining second antechamber, as both doors swung open wide and His Majesty proceeded across the room, not acknowledging the bows and curtsies of the dinner servants, who were awaiting further instructions there, nor heeding their murmurs of "Your Majesty"; and "Gentlemen! The King!" shouted yet other guards as I followed Him into the adjacent chamber, where many of the courtiers had regrouped, who also bowed, curtsied, and murmured; and "Gentlemen! The King!" resounded as we swept through the length of the west wing of the palace past scattered groups of courtiers, all of whom bowed, curtsied, and murmured, "Your Majesty"; and from there into the northern wing. "Gentlemen! The King!" rang out as doors flew open as though by themselves, and we marched through a series of several more chambers, including the council chamber, where, from my aerie, I had spied down upon my lord's conference with Monsieur de la Reynie; but there was no time to look up and seek out the plastering that had been laid over my peephole, nor time even to glance quickly upwards, for my lord was in no humor to tarry; and I was growing quite out of breath with the chase He was leading me; yet I kept up, though breaking out into something of a light sweat, as I waddled—alas, it is the word—as I waddled in His mighty wake.

"Gentlemen! The King!"

Presently—bolting past a throng of military officers, who snapped to most respectful attention and lustily cried out, "Your Majesty!"—we reached the Marquise de Montespan's apartment, which, to my horror, it seemed, was my lord's destination; and we entered immediately into her drawing room: suddenly, everything about us was silent and empty: no one was present; and where only lately there had been a bewildering clutter of tables and chairs, carpets and pictures, desks and *torchères*, commodes and an Aubusson tapestry, there now was nothing. The room had been stripped entirely bare, and even the fireplace screen was gone behind which I had overheard Monsieur Pussort's report to the marquise; that same fireplace stood bare as well; so that not only was the room unoccupied, it was cold.

Then there appeared Mlle des Œillets, as though on cue, but arriving from the opposite direction.

"Yes?" said my lord King Louis to her, not once breaking His stride.

"Madame has retired for the night, Your Majesty," replied mademoiselle with a most respectful curtsey.

To which report the king made no reply, but continued His passage across the room where He burst into the chamber beyond, which was, reader, the marquise's bedchamber. You can imagine my reluctance to proceed into my lady's boudoir, for up to that time my personal attentions to her ladyship had been strictly limited to those which could be administered from beneath tables; and to speak quite bluntly, I had never been inside her ladyship's bedroom for all the occasions on which I had been inside her ladyship. But yet as I had been ordered by my lord His Majesty to accompany Him, I dared not hesitate one jot; nor did I, but followed Him forthwith into the chamber.

The marquise was sitting up in her bed, wearing a flimsy cotton nightgown; her hair was an utter jungle of pins and clamps and dangling bits of string and paper; her face had been scrubbed clean of the various rouges and pigments of one sort or another which, each morning, her maid was wont to apply; and she was covered over by a light quilt, which she instantly pulled up across her bosom.

"My lord!" she cried as the king marched into the room; and I was uncertain as to whether her words were an exclamation or a greeting, and yet I think it more likely the former, for there was a look of great alarm in her unpainted eyes. At the sight of me behind His Majesty, she leapt from the bed and began frantically searching about for some garment with which to cover herself; and not finding any at hand, called out "Des Œillets! Des Œillets! My robe!" But as Mlle des Œillets failed to reappear, the marquise tugged at the quilt until she loosened it from the bed and wrapped it about her person.

"We shall stand upon no ceremony, madame," said my lord, "for here is a matter of great urgency which we bring to you, which we would have you respond to and right directly. Monsieur Hugues," He continued, turning now to me for I had stayed well to the rear of my lord, stationing myself at a respectable distance though not so far that it might seem I had left off following Him, "Monsieur Hugues has brought the matter to our notice; and it is our intention that he repeat to you and in our presence what he has reported." He gestured to me. "Monsieur Hugues."

At that, the alarm upon the marquise's face greatly increased.

Reader: my lord having used the word "repeat" and I respecting and honoring Him more than any man on earth or any god in heaven, I therefore chose to reiterate word for word what I had said before:

"Your Most Gracious Majesty: I have the honor to serve as acolyte to the Abbé Hilaire Guibourg, formerly sacristan of St. Marcel's at St. Denis. My lord, customarily, Father Guibourg's devotions are offered late at night, my lord, and in what might be considered a somewhat unorthodox fashion; for, sir, the liturgy is said in reverse, the Mass is spoken backwards. My lord, eight days ago, eight nights ago, Father Guibourg's Mass was offered with the express intention of provoking a miscarriage on the part of the Duchesse de Fontanges, a prodigious loss of blood, and the duchess's subsequent demise; present, my most gracious lord, at the Mass and a participant in it, sir, for it was upon her unclad hummock, sir, that the Mass was said, was the Marquise de Montespan."

I spoke my text in a full, clear voice and believe that my second delivery improved much upon the first. For just as an actor, by constant vocal repetitions of his speeches, betters his elocution, diction, and declamation, I found that to be my own experience. And as I reached this new command of my performance, I was able at the same time to better command my sense of the audience, to wit, that of the marquise, who, standing at the side of her bed and quite encased in the quilting, grew more and more agitated at certain salient words occurring in my recitation: "Guibourg," "backwards," "eight nights ago"—that is to say, as the details of my account became more and more specific, the marquise's countenance became more and more highly fraught; until I spoke the word "miscarriage," at which she started quite audibly; and likewise, I observed, "demise" and "unclad hummock" afforded the lady no degree of comfort.

When I reached the final word, which was "Montespan," I felt it appropriate to bow once again, the which I did; even before I could rise from that position, I heard the marquise speak:

"The liar! It is an unvarnished lie, my lord!" And I must say that given the extent of her alarm, she spoke with a control which surprised me, and her voice was deep and steady.

"A liar?" queried my lord. "Why should the creature lie? What incentive has he? Moreover, madame, the duchess—"

"He does! He is a very liar!" The marquise spat out the words and would have continued but that my lord continued Himself:

"Moreover," said He and with some emphasis this time, "the duchess did in fact suffer a miscarriage, which has been a source of great annoyance to us; the plain fact is there."

The marquise gathered her wrap up more closely about her shoulders.

"The dwarf is telling these wretched tales, my lord," said she, "out of sheer revenge! Out of a malicious revenge because I did not secure for him your consent, sir, that he be legitimized! It is for that, sir, and purely and simply for that, that he stoops to accuse me and falsely thus to treat me. But yet, nay, sir, he is already so low that he has indeed no need to 'stoop'! For he is himself composed of the very dung through which now he crawls."

Patiently my lord waited for the marquise to spew forth her rage; and His firm voice displayed little emotion when next He spoke:

"This, then, is that incriminating evidence with which he threatened you, is it not? It was this very piece of information with which he sought to blackmail you, madame; is that not so?"

"Rubbish! Rubbish, my lord!" she exclaimed. "The wretch has now quite changed his story—it was upon someone else he had the evidence, upon another party altogether! And involving quite another scheme! You see what ghastly lies the creature tells!"

There followed a long silence.

"Madame," said my lord King Louis, "what possibly can you mean? When last we spoke upon this matter, madame, you stated that Monsieur Hugues had adamantly refused to name the accused party—or indeed to recite the scheme. What can you mean now?"

"No, no, I—that is, my lord, he—" The marquise fumbled about for words. "I meant, my lord, precisely as you say, sir, quite so, he did—"

"Here are liars and liars," said my lord, shaking His head. "Liars, madame. It is gone quite mad, the world, quite mad; and yet, madame, we had not thought that you, madame—never you, madame—would yourself have engaged in the reckless madness of these times. No, surely we had not thought it."

"My lord!" cried the marquise. "Do not believe him! It is not, sir, as I am charged. Indeed, you are right, sir, the world is gone mad, but it is I, sir, who am a victim of that madness!"

Yet it was as though my lord had not heard her.

"Indeed we ought not be surprised: for see, how many worthy—nay, how many unimpeachable persons have there not been about us who—"

"But, sir!" she cried. "Hear me out, my lord, I beseech you! I am a victim, sir! And not only of this false and most slanderous report, most viciously slanderous, indeed, sir, but of cold-blooded plots that have threatened my very life." And now the marquise had regained some of her wonted composure. "And well you do know it, sir; well, sir, you do know that Mme de St. Estève was found guilty of a malicious plot to poison me, sir. For the woman long wished to gain your affections, my lord, and yet found that I was there, sir, in your favor, standing in her path. Thus she sought to clear me from her path, sir, and by heinous means, most heinous means indeed."

"Just so, madame," rejoined my lord, for He was not now to be deflected, "and just so have you lately found the Duchesse de Fontanges, though but a silly child, positioned in *your* pathway, madame; and just so have you sought the means, and heinous ones at that, to clear that path once more."

"My lord!" cried the marquise. "It is a calumnious charge, my lord!" And several pins flew out from her hair and landed here and there onto the floor, so great was the lady's agitation.

"I am grown weary, madame," the king continued, "most weary indeed of these vile jealousies and cruel plots and quarrels—and from every corner! From you, madame, from the duchess, yes indeed, and from everyone! And I will have no more of it! These endless maneuvers, this wrangling, these tiresome schemes—no, no! No more of them!" Now His voice was risen in anger, and it was a fearsome thing to behold, reader, the Sun King in anger, for a God in anger is a fearsome, fearsome thing.

"But these are deceptions, sir! Tricks! To mislead you, sir—" the marquise began, but my lord now cut her off again.

"Hugues!" He called. "Say again, sir, upon what exact night it was that you witnessed that most despicable sight."

I wondered if I ought once more to bow, but thought the better of it.

"Your Gracious Majesty," quoth I forthrightly, "it was exactly upon the night, sir, preceding the day of our latest return to Versailles." I paused, not certain whether to add yet one more fact; and then determined that I would. "Which was also, sir, the very same day of the duchess's mishap."

"Alas," said my lord, "the dwarf does not lie, madame." He turned back to face her. "You, madame, did that deed."

Whereupon, reader: the marquise pulled herself up to her full height though she was wearing no shoes, and with undisguised rage and yet with a momentous exertion of control, delivered herself of the following address; and I pray you, heedful reader, we are now come to it, so that you will do well to attend especially closely to what next she spoke, and I urge that you do so:

"Why, man, you simple man! You credit that dwarf only because of who he is. If he were not indeed your own son, sir, you would have dismissed him forthwith for the monster that he is. But because it is your son, sir, you credit him, because it is your firstborn son, sir—that squat runt your queen supplied you with and which, for his runtishness, you later put out to pasture, telling all the world—preposterous lie!—when the child was only one that he had suddenly died of the smallpox—why, man, I say, because it is your very flesh and blood, you credit the creature." She paused and inhaled a deep breath. "And there, my most gracious and my most illustrious lord, is at last an end to it."

Lo, reader, lo.

Lo. Her words struck like a sudden bolt of lightening.

How could I believe my ears? But yet what I had heard I had heard.

Lo. Suddenly the hairs on the nape of my neck stiffened.

A quick chill flew up my spine.

My blood ran cold; my face burst into a fiery purple blush.

"Your own son. Your firstborn son."

And lo, then, reader, I did indeed bepiss myself in my breeches.

Helpless, I turned my gaze back to my lord. That divinity—that father!—was now staring down at me; and upon His proud face was an expression of stern gravity.

The room was deathly silent.

A moment passed. I lowered my eyes. My lord turned to face the marquise.

"In these most private matters of the House of France, what you have done is both desperate and intolerable," King Louis XIV now said, speaking in a steady, even tone; but I saw that His left fist was tightly clenched, the knuckles sharp and white. "You have recklessly and wantonly abused my confidence, Madame de Mortemart."

"Sir," replied the marquise after a brief pause, "it seems that I am no longer privileged to enjoy that confidence, which in the past you bestowed so generously upon me."

My lord continued to fix her with His gaze; His nose inclined slightly upward.

"That," He rejoined, "—and you know it, madame—is neither here nor there."

Whereupon He turned, walked to the door, opened it, and strode back through the empty drawing room and out into the antechamber.

"Gentlemen! The King!"

I could hear His Majesty speaking quietly to the guard, and then the guard's footsteps as he sprinted away. My lord stopped where He was.

I waited there on the now-sodden carpet. Adding to the wetness all about my lower regions, I began to feel the clamminess of rolling, drenching sweat. I dared not look up at the marquise. I stared fixedly ahead. I do not know what the marquise did. I stood there in great misery.

And yet for a single and most intense moment, and despite what she had just revealed, the enormity of which I had not even begun to grasp, for that single moment, I say, reader, alone in the room with the marquise though not facing her, I felt a palpable bond between the wretched woman and myself, the icy communion of two human beings both found guilty of laying bare that which had been inviolable, both caught red-handed in acts of outright betrayal.

Two towering officers dashed into the bedchamber.

"Madame," they muttered to the marquise in great confusion. Whereupon they strode over to me, and picking me up and carrying me between themselves, they swept me back out through the drawing room, into the antechamber (and I leaving something of a trail, I must confess), past my lord His Divine Majesty the King, Fourteenth of the Name of Louis, down the hall, down the stairs, and into the lower guardroom, where they thrust me into a large straw hamper, which they secured and loaded into a coach.

The horses set off; and they galloped for miles and miles through the cold February night, all the way, I later was to learn, back into the city of Paris and across it and quite through it, until, leaving it behind, they arrived at length at the Prison of Vincennes, a distance beyond the city walls in the east, into the hands of whose governor I was, without ado, delivered.

# 20

I SAY "WITHOUT ADO" BUT SHOULD NOTE, for the sake of accuracy, that the prison governor was quite aggravated to be awakened in the dead of a February night for the arrival of a prisoner and of a dwarf prisoner at that, which seemed to him not at all worth the bother; though the fact that I took up less room than the average prisoner had its advantages, for the gaol being quite overcrowded at the time, Governor Ferronay's grumblings would surely have been commensurately louder, longer, and more intense had I been taller, weightier, and more full grown. However such a matter may be measured, grumble indeed the governor did as he led me down into the basement and thence into a still lower chamber, where he said I might take up residence next to an elaborate array of pumps; pumps which I learned later were used to control the level of the water in the moat which surrounded the building and to drain water from out of the basement itself, which was somewhat given to springing leaks.

There was nothing that I could do in fact to "take up residence" except perhaps to lie down and try, though in vain, to sleep during that tumultuous night; for I had none of my possessions with me—my brush, my razor, my picture book—those items which customarily I would arrange in whatever nook I had chosen to inhabit, laying thereby a sort of rudimentary claim to the place. And I fretted that I would not be able to attend properly to brushing my hair nor to keeping my chin smooth; nor could I while away a tedious hour or two studying pictures of the West Indian anthropophagi and other like frightening curiosities which were shown in my book.

It was right cold and damp, reader, that first night in Vincennes Prison; and although later I would abandon the basement in favor of a nest far up in the highest level of the uppermost story of the dungeon (or "keep" as it is sometimes called), yet that first night was spent below; and it was very much filled with the fear of those strange and dark surroundings; and with the sounds of armies of rats with whom, it seemed, I was to share those lodgings and who were diligent all night long galloping around on various errands which apparently they had; and with the cold of that infernal tomb and a gnawing hunger in my belly, for I had not taken supper that night. Yet quite and most utterly beyond all those many discomforts, as you may well imagine, I was overcome with a mounting sense of awe at what I had heard the marquise blurt out to my lord King Louis but two hours previous.

"If he were not indeed your own son, sir . . . your firstborn son . . . your very flesh and blood."

My mind had been racing with thoughts of this astounding revelation throughout the lengthy journey to Vincennes Prison; now, alone in the rumbling darkness, I set about to look back, with as much care and system as my teeming brain could muster, through those parts of my life that would square with it, as though testing the truth of what the marquise had said by fitting the pieces of a puzzle together, one by one, in the hopes of arriving at a conclusive picture of the whole.

"If he were not your own son, sir, . . . which, for his runtishness, you later put out to pasture."

Thus it was—or thus I presume it, reader—that my earliest days—or rather, those past the age of one, when encroaching dwarfishness must at last have made known its hateful presence, were it by the bow of my legs, the height of my forehead, a certain depression in the bridge of my otherwise excellent nose, or merely my curious reluctance to grow—that my earliest days, I say, had been spent at the monastery of St. Sauveur at Louveciennes, along with those other abandoned children, if not indeed in their company. Yet I had later been removed to the house at Vaugirard: "I am under some constraint," Mme Scarron had said to me on that occasion, "to take you into this house"; that "constraint" was surely a direction from my lord King Louis, who, at the time establishing a proper home for His first produced offspring by the Marquise de Montespan (Louis-Auguste, the Duc du Maine) and later for those others of His by her, must have been stirred by some hitherto unperceived paternal impulse to establish for His very firstborn by anyone a minimum of the same. Yet He declined to make recognition of me in any other manner; and thus amid sculleries and ash piles, surrounded by a mocking society, and under the sway of the vile-tempered mistress of Vaugirard had spent his youth the unacknowledged heir to the throne of France.

Thus as well that presentiment which I had experienced when first in the company of the infant Duc du Maine of some unspoken kinship with him; for indeed, alas, he was my half brother; and he is to this day; and his legitimacy, remarkable as it is, merely an imitation of my own! And surely these facts must have given Scarron no small degree of ironic satisfaction in arranging for my visible participation in the ceremony marking the young duke's deliverance from bastardy.

Moreover: 1661 is indeed the year of my birth, if ever there were any doubt: for it was in the previous year that my lord took to wife Marie-Thérèse, Infanta of Spain, that belching, gluttonous, farting, odorous, and unutterably stupid creature which was my mother—think of it, reader, my own dear mama!—and the following year in which she brought forth their firstborn, myself, into this world; and thus it was that she had been of an opinion at the Duc du Maine's birthday celebration, you will recall, as to my age. So too had she sought to incorporate me into her house-hold—not, as I had thought, in the capacity of a pet dwarf, but in the unacknowledged capacity of a son. And would that different capacity, acknowledged or not, have made residence with mother any more toler-able? No, I did not in all honesty believe it, neither with mother nor with her brood; and thus it was most fortunate that I had successfully resisted her proposal. Fortunate as well that over the years I had never entered into her service at the gaming tables; and fortunate—oh, most fortunate of all!—that I had not extended my other, more delicate nether services to Marie-Thérèse, Infanta of Spain, Royal Queen of France, and mother.

My thoughts spun back yet again to the Duc du Maine's seventh birth-day celebration and to the curious interest which my lord King Louis had taken in me upon that same occasion, for in publicly examining a dwarf who was part of His mistress's entourage, my lord, I now understood, was in fact privately examining His own offspring! And those warm feel-ings which I had intuitively experienced, those of a child for its father, had indeed been true and genuine! Thus I formed two widely divergent views of my mother and father: and I, having no practice as an offspring, did not know if such a divergence of feelings were normal or even proper. But yet, putting that puzzlement aside, I did rejoice in the thought that indeed offspring I now authentically and incontrovertibly was!

Now next: and I do not believe that I was guilty of fabrication here: but recall that it was on the day following du Maine's birthday that I was made the gift of a razor; and though it had been delivered as though from the Marquise de Montespan, yet might it not quite as well, following His interrogation of me, have been my lord's own kindness to His son? But for the sake of discretion, it was credited to the marquise. For what gift would be more appropriate or more loving for a father to make to His son as he enters upon manhood than a fine razor for reaping his chin? No woman would make that gift to a youth: she would send him a silken handkerchief or an edifying book or perhaps a riding crop or a snuffbox, but never so personal yet so bracing and so gallant a gift as a fine razor for reaping his chin! And thereupon, alone in the darkness of Vincennes Prison, I fell to weeping at the recollection that I had so cruelly and unfeelingly thrown that same razor, that most excellent of gifts from my own father, out deep into the Seine—vilest of rivers!—where now and forever more it lay rusting and useless, uncared for and unloved!

Despite my resolve to proceed with care in these matters, my mind was fairly reeling, as one realization swiftly followed another and not in any particular order; and there were yet others to come! And I scarcely knew where next to turn my thoughts, so rapidly now were they racing through my brains!

I now realized that not only had I mistakenly ascribed an act of generosity—the gift of a razor—to Mme de Montespan, but later, in my concern that she was capable of some deadly reprisal against me for my act of blackmail (I shall be blunt and label it), I had failed to understand that had she undertaken any lethal action against the king's own offspring, unacknowledged though he was, she would have only brought down havoc upon her own already precarious head.

And not unrelated to that circumstance:

You will recall an incident which I have reported to you, along with my own puzzlement about it at the time, to wit, the occasion on which Mlle des Œillets, as directed by the marquise it now seems, had cut my hand with a second razor and then sopped up the blood in her napkin, that same napkin appearing later, as I told you, upon the altar at Mass; and my blood mingled with that of the sacrificial infant. In praying to Alpha, Ley, Agla, Beelzebub, Ahriman, Abaddon, and Belial, Father Guibourg had invoked their help, you will recall, "by this babe's blood" (which would be the blood of the sacrificed infant) and next, reader, "by that of the House of France"!

Now whether it were the offering of the royal blood of the House of France or rather the presence of the Marquise de Montespan upon the altar which was the more efficacious, I know not; but I do know this: that what had been sought before and had not been granted, to wit, a miscarriage by the Duchesse de Fontanges, was now indeed achieved and right soon, in fact upon the very next morning. You have witnessed the scene. I shall leave this theological question entirely in your hands, reader, to sort through as best you may; it is not crucial to the greater picture, yet neither is it to be lightly dismissed.

Yet with all due modesty, I vow that it was exactly by virtue of my consanguinity with the House of France that His Majesty had chosen to incarcerate me at this time; for were it to be discovered, and I shall speak quite bluntly and quite to the point, that it was I who was the true and most legitimate heir to the royal throne of France, the social, political, judicial, administrative, financial, military, diplomatic, and international ramifications would be immeasurable. And so you would have sent me packing yourself if some nineteen years previous you had elected to reverse the order of things and proclaim the second born now to be the earliest born and legal inheritor of the throne, the firstborn having joined the ranks of the angels through the offices of the smallpox: then most mischievous would be the return of the firstborn to the stage; and posing a grave threat to the state were it discovered that the bulbous creature known as "dauphin" was no longer dauphin and that the future monarch of France was but three feet tall. The nation was later to wage war over the issue of the inheritance of the Spanish throne; how might it react, irrespective of justice and righteousness and honor, if the inheritance of its own throne were to be contested? Alas, my lord King Louis would find Himself opposed by all the enemies of the nation arrayed against Him, both within and without the realm, who would seize upon the opportunity to do what manner of mischief they could to the Kingdom of France, to the House of Bourbon, and to His Majesty Himself.

And thus, reader, it was for the security of the state that I had been denied not only my rightful position as a legitimate son of that royal House and as the first successor to His Royal Highness Fourteenth of the Name of Louis, but was now denied as well my own, albeit small, personal freedom. And all because I had been born a runt.

Yet I could not resolve a nagging paradox: those political issues aside, on the face of it I call it an instance of rank injustice, not only to me personally but to the rightful order of things. And yet, it was my lord King Louis Himself who had perpetrated it. And though some while ago I had fairly well resigned myself to the understanding that Athénaïs, Marquise de Montespan, was not in fact, as I had long believed, divine, yet my lord King Louis was, and is, and will continue to be; and fittingly, He enjoys those divine rights as bestowed by Him to whom He must one day Himself give answer, the Divine Almighty. And as God can do no evil, nor can my lord King Louis: it is the conundrum of old, reader, we have been over this already; and I had—and have—over the years, as you know, come to hold with those who state that the divine cannot in fact commit ill. Thus, my lord's repudiation of me at the tender age of one as well as my present incarceration must therefore be all to the good: but in the cold cellars of Vincennes Prison, it was a difficult good to perceive.

No: I could not resolve it.

Not then. Not now.

No.

And since I could not, I pressed on forward; and I did find comfort in one regard: if, as was the case, I was the legitimate heir to the royal throne of France, there could be no doubt, no uncertainty nor ambiguity, no gnawing skepticism nor niggling reservation that clearly I was a proper and legitimate person in my own right and having now no need of any royal act asserting that legitimacy; no, I was and had always been already there; and that moreover, I was thereby entirely and thoroughly a member of humankind: no creature less than human might have stood in line—no matter that that line, unknown to my fellow men, had been rendered now a theoretical line—to succeed the most illustrious human being of us all, He whose radiant humanity had attained divinity. I did find comfort in that.

And the final revelation and, to my way of thinking, the most crowning revelation of that long, dark night in Vincennes Prison was, fittingly, of a most palpably human bond between my lord King Louis and myself. The sterner of my critics will wish to dismiss it, saying, tosh, it is but an instance of pure coincidence, a random throw of the dice! and, not being unique to the subject at hand, must therefore not be admitted into evidence. And yet I say that those critics are wrong; and if you be amongst them, reader, then you and I must take issue with one another, and how we shall resolve the matter I cannot tell. Yet it is no small matter, but rather, indeed, one of some size; for the question of size is exactly the matter itself, and more specifically a matter of length, a term which earlier in my text I have labeled inappropriate to my person: yet with two exceptions; and one being, to wit, except insofar as it addresses the length of my nose. For my nose is lengthy, and you do know that already; and likewise, as you do also know, is the nose of my lord His Majesty, Fourteenth of the Name of Louis, being similarly of a most estimable length: and this, I claim, bespeaks of His paternity to me—nay, it loudly proclaims it!—more than all else, this kindred length transcends more mundane concerns as birth date, blood, childhood history, or the politics of the state; and though many another excellent and well-endowed man of France may surely be possessed of a lengthy nozzle, yet it is my particular length of nose, reader, above all, and I say it with all candor and with no trace of hubris, it is the exact and prodigious length of my nose which bears witness to my consanguinity with the House of Bourbon and thence to my link with the previous House of Valois and with the yet previous Capetian monarchs, the Carolingians and the Merovingians; and which corroborates my direct lineage to such admirable figures as Their Majesties Henri IV, Henri II, François I, Louis IX (who became St. Louis), and Hugues Capet; and indeed to Charlemagne and thence to Clovis, founder of the kingdom, whose instant conversion to faith in our Lord Jesus took place at the Battle of Tolbac in 496 A D; for he had solemnly vowed to become a Christian if Jesus our Lord (not then His) would agree to effect a rout among the enemy forces; Jesus providing, Clovis abiding, there followed the celebrated baptism at Reims, which marks the inauguration of the entity of France.

Thus, having fit those divers pieces of the puzzle now quite undeniably into place, the true heir to the royal throne of France spent the rest of the night, exhausted but sleepless, in the dripping darkness of Vincennes Prison, shivering with cold and apprehension, filled with awe at the events of late, and listening to legions of rats thundering back and forth in all directions, and not much distant from His own royal head.

One small blessing there was: that I found myself that night in Vincennes Prison and not in Bastille Prison or in some other in the town; for I knew full well that the inmates at Vincennes were of an unquestion-ably higher caliber than those elsewhere, most of them aristocratic—like myself—albeit not royal, whether poisoners, murderers, adulterers, or abortionists, their presence in Vincennes adding no inconsiderable cachet to the institution. And I think—nay, I know it as a member of the royal family—that my humiliation in lodging in a basement would have been quite complete and almost unbearable had it been the basement of some lesser gaol.

And now I shall describe the Vincennes Prison to you.

It is a most imposing building, of military aspect, constructed by Philippe VI, John the Good, and Charles V, who completed it in 1370, and it was intended as a royal residence and fortress; but ever since the beginning of the sixteenth century, it has been used instead as a prison. Its chiefest feature is its extreme height, for it consists of some five full stories and rises a vertiginous 170 feet into the air. Only the towers of Notre Dame Cathedral surpass it, they being at 226 feet the tallest structures in all of France and I would venture to say throughout all of Christendom. (From a more global outlook, I cannot say what towers the other peoples of the world may have erected: I speak, for instance, of the Chinese people or the Russian or even of the dreaded anthropophagi, who yet are not truly people; or of the Indians, the swarthy moham-metans, or the negroes; yet I think the negroes will not have raised any tall towers.) These five stories of Vincennes stand surrounded by an en-closure of low service buildings, themselves surrounded by a moat, its waters controlled, as I have mentioned, by pumps and divers locks; and at the time that water was most uncommonly foul, for the moat served as a gigantic slop basin, all manner of ordures and rotting muck being thrown down into it from the windows of every one of the five floors, producing a stinking and most feculent soup at the base of the prison; which is a point of some irony that such a noble edifice should rise aloft from out of the midst of a sewer.

Inside, a thick central column supports all of the five stories, with ad-joining spiral stairs between them located in the south wall; and at each

of the four corners rises a turret the full height of the building; a pro-
jection on the northwest angle contains latrines on every level, which
drain down into the moat. The turrets and the five interconnecting floors
served at the time as the prison residences.

Yet I would not have you think that there existed a series of enclosed
cells such as you might find at other, inferior gaols; no, not a bit of it.
The prisoners at Vincennes, many of whom you will recognize as former
clients of mine—and a fine surprise it was to find so many of them reassembled together!—were allowed to devise for themselves whatever
living spaces they could, and by the judicious use of screens and various
tall pieces of furniture—secretaries, cupboards, armoires, and the like,
and even long tables which had been stood up on end, and lengths of
drapery and other fabrics suspended from hooks and nails—they were
able to form a series of partitions such as afforded them a semblance of
private quarters. These they furnished most elaborately, for they were
permitted to take whatever furniture they cared to into the prison; and
thus, surrounded by thick stone walls of a military caste, had sprung up
entire suites of salons and drawing rooms, dining rooms and bedcham-
bers, all of a thoroughly makeshift nature and fairly much crammed into
whatever areas were available, space being at a great premium. In certain
instances these furnishings even reflected a degree of taste; but nine times
out of ten, taste gave way to a rabid competition amongst the inmates
as to who could amass the greatest quantity of stuff within his allotted
confines.

A strict order of rank was observed; so that princes and dukes, outranking all others, had laid claim to the most advantageous story, which
was the third, for its ceilings are the highest and its windows the widest;
and they had allowed the Maréchal de Luxembourg a corner of that floor
in light of his extraordinary service to the entire nation; the fact that that
gentleman's mistress, the Princesse de Tingry, was also situated there
conveniently allowed him to continue his service to at least one piece of
the nation. Next, on the second floor, were marquises and counts, including the Comtesse de Pommeret, much to my surprise, for I had not
thought her clever enough to have become a criminal element, and I
must allow that I have misjudged the lady; yet some of the lesser counts
had been obliged to settle for accommodation one floor below, the second having become severely overcrowded: for in a rare exception to the

ranking, Mme de St. Estève, a commoner, who had been found guilty of an attempted crime impressively but one step removed from regicide, her poisonous designs upon the Marquise de Montespan I mean, had been allowed to seize, as by some divine right, a vast amount of territory on the floor, indeed the entire western third of it; and thus, less celebrated counts and countesses, authors of less spectacular misdeeds, were demoted to the first; moreover, Mme de St. Estève maintained her large pack of hunting dogs, and the entire second floor felt their impact, for she claimed that there were far too many stairs to climb and far too many dogs for her servants to take them outside more than once every few days. Thus, there were disadvantages to the second floor despite its relatively high-ranking position; but yet the Marquis de Feuquières having installed a laboratory there, equipped with several large, wood-burning furnaces and some time before the arrival of Mme de St. Estève, refused to budge an inch and was obliged to spend as much time whipping the dogs away from his crucibles and ovens (for dogs are much attracted to the odor of arsenic when it is being processed) as he did in the production of chemicals. I myself avoided the floor as much as possible, for the dogs were constantly hungry; though for all that, they produced an uncommon amount of foulness.

On the first story were found, as I have said, minor counts and others of the lesser nobility, viscounts, barons, and the like, few of whom were of any interest. But there also dwelt there the majority of the clergy, and a goodly number there was, the highest in rank being His Eminence, Emile Cardinal LeMoine, that clerical prince into whose crotch I had run upon one occasion (if you have forgot the incident it is not important), and who, it was discovered, had been flagrantly manufacturing not a few of the confessions reported to General de la Reynie from the stalls at Notre Dame. Across the floor from the cardinal was a certain Father Davot, who daily climbed the stairs to the topmost floor and from the southeast windows preached thunderous sermons upon the sin of sloth out to the snowbound fields beyond and down to the purulent moat below; Father Davot, I learned, had been nearly as persevering at celebrating late night devotions as Father Guibourg himself; and indeed I suspected Father Davot of eyeing me on more than one occasion for there were no young lads and certainly no other dwarves about the place who might have served him as acolytes.

The two uppermost of the floors being the least accessible and of
meaner proportions, were given over to the commoners; many of them
of some position in society, there was much wrangling amongst them
about precedence and rank, for they had no clear titles by which they
might be classified. Here I came across such persons as Mlle La Voisin (on
the fifth floor, though most resentful of that inferior lodging, for she said
and with some justification that she had shouldered the burden of naming names ever since her poor mother had been executed; yet because
many of the names she had named were now in the prison themselves,
an active movement grew up to consign mademoiselle to an even inferior dwelling, some proposing the basement, and one or two the bottom
of the moat; thus Mlle La Voisin was in no better humor than when last
I had encountered her); Monsieur Romani (on the fourth, that gentleman having, I remind you, undertaken efforts against the Duchesse de
Fontanges); Mlle Louise-Adélaïde Marsy (fifth floor, for she had sought
only to poison her father for his money; and the vileness of her temper
would have consigned her to the worser floor if the banality of her crime
had not); a couple named de Lessac (fifth, despite the bold donation they
had made of their firstborn child to Beelzebub and Belial). But see here:
I shall not go on cataloguing the entire population of the place, for there
were a great many of them and you will grow weary, reader, despite your
present interest, and I would thus quite defeat my own purposes, which
have been merely to provide you with an overall view of the living
arrangements at Vincennes in those days.

Now I myself (I have made allusion to this), having explored about the
place in the first few weeks whenever I had a spare moment (for the governor assigned chores to me, primarily those of manning the pumps)—
I myself, I say, discovered in my wanderings a small protuberance above
the topmost floor, the purpose of which was to serve as a lookout, there
being an opening that gave upon the fields to the west; unless it were
designed for hurling stones and other heavy objects down upon an enemy
below; though it were difficult to hurl stones of any considerable size, the
opening being small and the protuberance itself exceedingly cramped.
Yet I came upon traces of lead gutter pipe up there which might well
have served for pouring down oil upon an enemy. Whatever medieval
purpose this place had had, it was now unused, its existence unknown
in all likelihood; and it was there that I took up my next residence, the

governor either not noticing the change or uncaring about it, for his hands were quite full, as more and more newly arriving convicts kept crowding into all five layers of the towering prison below me.

The opening in that aerie, being as high and as exposed as it was to the elements, was quite drafty; but I was able to pile a collection of boards in front of it on windy days. Opposite the opening was a stone ledge, where now I stored a shard of glass which I had found on the second floor and which I had taken to using as a razor, though it left much to be desired, along with a well-worn scrub brush from the kitchen which I made serve for attending to my hair. And I slept on my ledge despite the extraordinary height, the single window in the place being too narrow for even me to slip through, as was not the case in the lower stories; for I had taken to avoiding the larger windows throughout the prison, as I did not wish to fall out of one of them, down below into the stagnant swill of the moat.

It will come as no surprise to you that with all the furnishings gathered into Vincennes Prison by its wealthy though now-ruined inhabitants, there was an abundance of gaming tables and a right ample supply of playing cards; and you have recognized the names of many of the inmates as being leading gamesters of old. What, therefore, could be more natural but that, life within the prison walls having become somewhat of a microcosm of life beyond them, the old habits should re-emerge; and the long winter evenings became devoted once again to rounds of *reversi* and *vingt-et-un*. Matters were complicated by the lack of funds among the players, but there were china teacups that would serve as currency and brooches and fire screens and indeed entire suites of furniture; and soon these objects and many others, in the transaction of debts, began shifting with astonishing frequency from one apartment to the next, though the tendency was for them to remain on the same floor where they had begun. That is because the caste system prevailed, for the most part, in all the gaming activity. But there were two exceptions: a certain commerce took up between the fourth and fifth floors, where the commoners resided; and as well, between the second and third floors, where the population being smaller, there was occasional need for the princes and dukes to consent to join the marquises and counts to form full complements of players; and they did so, if begrudgingly. But it was required that the marquises and counts should go upstairs to the third floor for these encounters, the princes and dukes refusing to set foot anywhere that Mme de St. Estève's hounds might well have previously set other matter.

Whereupon I decided that, imprisoned as I was, whether wrongfully or not, there was nothing for it but to take up service once again to my old clients; and I enlisted new as well. And thus I spent my evenings running up and down the stairs from level to level to level to level to level (five of them), keeping my wits about me as best I could; for this was more complex than any gaming I had assisted at before, and it required a most agile memory and rapidity of calculation and the need to keep each set of games discrete unto its own level: for if I should confuse the plays of a second-floor marquis with those of a third-floor duke or of a first-floor count with a fifth-floor ironmonger and muddle them, it would not do: it would be a catastrophe not only for the game but for the prevailing social order.

And as once again I took up my duties in the games being played upon the tables, so too did I re-establish those sports beneath the tables such as benefited my female clients; and they were right grateful; and I was much in demand, which only increased my industry during the evenings at Vincennes.

And it was while I was dashing from one level to the next one evening that I was suddenly struck with the thought that even in adverse circumstances, God's design is indeed truly wonderful: for unwittingly but as though guided by His hand, I had taken up residence in a roost far, far above all five of those levels where now I labored; and though that had always been my custom, yet it was more meet at present than ever that I should be lodged aloft, on my ledge, at the very summit of those layers of mankind. For whether those layers of mankind were aware of it or not, I was in fact, by birth, the most superior being then resident at Vincennes: for in my veins there ran the blood of kings, reader; and I say it with all due modesty but yet in all due honesty: surely I shared that aspect of my lord the king of France, Fourteenth of the Name of Louis, which rendered Him the most glorious being in all the realm: His Son, I was, like Him, divine.

And my ledge the seat of divinity.

(Was I then sinless? and incapable of error? Reader, I could not categorically say it in all honesty. I knew that I had been guilty of haste on occasion and thence of running into others in the halls and throwing them off balance. I had tormented Louis-Auguste for a period of time years before but had more than made up for it, I firmly believe, by conveying to the lad who his true mother was, the knowledge of one's true parentage being a matter of no small concern, as this entire chronicle attests; and later, I had stuck my tongue out at him on the staircase and frighted him, which I think was sinful, but then so had he done to me years earlier and on a most public occasion. Yet when I had looked up the skirts of Mme Douge, Marquise d'Œu, I was only five years old or six at most and not responsible; but I had had impure thoughts since that time, I confess it; I had occasionally eaten meat on Friday, if suet is anyone's idea of meat, but I truly think that if God would ever try a piece of it Himself, He would not include it in His ban, there being no pleasure to be derived from it; I had performed servile tasks on Sundays, but reader, you know yourself, sewerage does not cease because it is the Lord's Day, and therefore that may not be accounted against me; I had had no father or mother to dishonor up to this point; I had eavesdropped extensively, though in a stretch, that might be chalked up as a reasonable business expense; I had never been unkind to animals though I had struck dogs on more than one occasion, but always in self-defense; yet I had betrayed the Marquise de Montespan—I had, do not protest it!—and though I was now actively paying for that sin, yet sin it had been. What then was I to make of such a very mixed tally?

At length I took refuge in the greater wisdom of the Fathers of the Church, who, you will recall, refuse to hold accountable the very young— up to seven years—because having not the powers of reason, they can have no concept of sin or the lack thereof; and applying that formula to my own case, I resolved that not having known all those years of my divinity, having even been expressly deprived of that knowledge, I could not be held liable to behave in an altogether divine manner. And yet, like the youth who, on his seventh birthday, attains consciousness of his wretched estate, I must now acknowledge my own estate, that is, my elevated and most sublime estate, and in future never sin more.)

Late at night, when I retired to my ledge, I often fancied what that future held. From what I knew, I could expect to be in Vincennes Prison the rest of my life, for there were several most ancient and doddering inmates who had been there for decades and did not expect ever to leave.

At the death of my lord the king, Fourteenth of the Name of Louis, I would grieve as for the death of God, but within the prison walls; at that moment, my own reign within those walls would begin: "Le roi est mort, vive le roi" is the saying. My reign would in no way be as my lord's had been, He Himself being most free and open, walking daily amongst His subjects, conquering His enemies at the front, receiving delegates from all the corners of the world at His royal palaces; no, mine would be a silent reign, continuing within the walls, most unheralded, quite hidden from view, and utterly private: a mystic reign, if I may so call it, the ineffable reign of Hugues II. Alas, mine would also be the final genuine reign of the House of Bourbon, if the truth were known, for as the acknowledged successor to my lord King Louis XIV, the dauphin would perforce be a false successor, and as there would be no true heir from out of my loins through whom a correction might be made in the next generation (the truth having been exposed by this chronicle), the entire Bourbon succession would have swerved permanently off course in a warped and essentially, if I may thus express it, bastardized lineage stretching forever into the future.

Yet for all that, my own reign would, in its own way, be glorious, reader; for I would be munificent, of a noble bearing, liberal and forgiving, patriarchal and just; I would be proud, serene, eloquent, gracious, and majestical; yet in wrath I would be most terrible. I would forever display a great respect for all my subjects, and although evenhanded in all ways, yet I would be most especially kind to my shorter subjects. I think that I would not keep hunting dogs. Nor would I keep mistresses; and my government would be quite contained. I should not be encumbered with any of the elaborate trappings of monarchy; but in like manner to my lord King Louis, His Royal Highness (the irony!) Hugues II, myself, was and would ever be possessed of a long and most regal nose.

I even gave some less fanciful thought to declaring the truth of the matter to the other prisoners at Vincennes, nobility and commoners alike, so that when the fateful day should arrive, they at least, if only within the confines of the prison, might recognize my proper reign and so become dutiful and loyal subjects; but then, I decided that with no evidence to support my claim, they would think it utterly harebrained and would very likely kick me down five flights of stairs. Thus, there hatched inside my mind, though in the very back of it for the moment, an idea that one day I should learn, I knew in no way how, to read and write, with which skills I might then set down the truth of all these matters, with corroborations and substantive proofs, whether it were merely for the reading populace of the Vincennes Prison or indeed, as began to seem of even greater value, for a broader general public outside. In which latter case, whatever might follow from that revelation would, in the natural course of time, follow.

I do not believe that it was sinful that I should have had such thoughts, and they were most private. They were not harmful; though upon occasion, reader, they made me weep somewhat.

One evening in March, as I was racing from some service performed on the fifth floor for Madame Gramont in a round of *vingt-et-un,* to furnish Mme de St. Estève with an ace of clubs which, according to my calculations, she would then be needing if she did not wish to lose her Louis XIII settee—as I was racing, I say, around a corner and toward the staircase—and I have told you of the dangers of racing around corners—I ran most headlong into a gentleman's crotch; as usual, alas, I quite felled its owner and like him, went sprawling myself. Despite the pressures of time, as soon as I had recovered myself, I hastened to the aid of my victim and discovered, to my complete amazement, that it was none other than the Archbishop of Lisieux, this being the third occasion, may I remind you, that I had thus encountered that cleric's nether region.

"Villain!" he shouted as he floundered quite helplessly on the floor. And he continued to call out various epithets at me during the somewhat lengthy process of hoisting him back up onto his feet, the which was executed by three strapping workmen using a system of pulleys and winches.

The archbishop, it turned out, had himself had considerable illicit commerce with the toxicologist Abbé Lesage, whose hearings he had haunted with such glee; and he had secured Lesage's silence by a threat of excommunication, for it seems that Lesage, though a cleric himself, yet had a pious streak and cared for the health of his soul; until, that is, the man broke down from the pressure of the interrogations and the humiliation of the archbishop's constant mocking laughter during them and proclaimed for all the court to hear that the mass of chortling flesh in bishop's garb was himself a trafficker in aphrodisiacs, chiefest among them the Spanish fly, which he had ordered served up to the Sisters of

Charity in the convent adjoining the Cathedral of Lisieux. Having arrived at Vincennes Prison only that afternoon (though I had not known of it), the archbishop, it seems, had been engaged in supervising the installation of a large confessional stall, large enough to accommodate a confessor and three penitents simultaneously, onto the topmost floor of the prison (for he held that penance might be performed by climbing the five flights of stairs to go to confession if the climber were in the proper frame of mind; and this would save everyone time); and the machine was then just halfway up the staircase leading to that upper level.

"Vile Hugues," at length quoth the cleric, fixing me with his stare though only from the thin slits of his eyes, "most execrable creature! And after all that I have done for you over the years! Thrice now you have been my downfall, dwarf, and thrice, thrice! miserable being, you have caused an upset in my bowel calculations! For yes, you wretch, I have once again bes———t myself, and you are the instrument of it! And after my considerable expense at being transferred here from Bastille Prison, these are the thanks I have for my pains! Fie! And to think of all I have done for you! Blackguard! Did I not warn you? Did I not put you on notice, lo, these many years ago, that if ever again you toppled me over I would pull out all your hair, twist your arms, thrash you senseless, and kick you down the stairs? That was my very caution to you, villain! Monstrous cur! And has it then gone unheeded? But now you shall see, sir, that I am a man of my word!"

Whereupon he seized me by a thick tuft of hair, twisted my ears, thrashed me, though not senseless as he had promised to do, for he was not a vigorous man for all his girth, and because the staircase was entirely blocked for the moment by the immense bulk of the confessional stall, he dragged me over to the nearest window and threw me out.

Now reader, the archbishop having defenestrated me with a certain *élan,* I did not fall directly downward as would have been the case had I been merely dropped from out of the window; but rather, I pursued (quite involuntarily) a trajectory more nearly the line of the hypotenuse of a right triangle, the vertical member of which being the height of the Vincennes Prison itself up to the fifth floor and the horizontal being the distance from a point somewhere deep in the basement and one located, alas, in the exact middle of the moat; and the hypotenuse—and myself along with it—was to join it there. Thus I dove, and as it happened,

upside down, that sloping distance (the square of whose length, Pyth-
agorus asserts, is the sum of the squares of the other two sides), from the
fifth story to the fourth story and thence to all the others, gazing out, for
visibility was excellent that evening under a full, bright moon, gazing
out, I say, across the flat, snowbound fields which lay beyond, even as I
was in the process of approaching their own level; until, the lowest story
of all now swiftly rising past me, my hypotenuse took me past the level
of the fields by several feet and subsequently headfirst into the fecal gruel
that all the while had lain in wait below.

First, my head plunged into the gruel, followed by my shoulders,
chest, belly, buttocks, ———, thighs, knees, calves, ankles, feet, and toes;
and when at length that plunge deep into muck slackened and then
ended, indeed by virtue of the muck itself, exactly at the closure of the
presumed triangle, I began to rise slowly back up through it, and did
rise through it, and thence partially back into the air, now right side
up, where I bobbed about for some moments upon the heavily coated
surface of the soup.

The moonlight being as bright as it was, I was able, unfortunately, to
perceive quite clearly the full extent of my situation: after recovering
from the surprise of finding myself, the unrecognized heir to the throne
of France, in the middle of a moat, and in the middle of that particular
moat, and a most vile moat it was, I began to realize how utterly and
comprehensively miserable my present circumstances were. Yet once I
had done so and had accepted the situation, at least partially, there was
nothing for it but to set about to swim back toward the tower; and I was
obliged to swim from the south moat around into the east moat in order
to find access to the shore. It was my first experience of swimming and
yet not dangerous, I do not think, for the waters being as thick and as
charged with matter as they were, I am certain that I could not have sunk
to any extent into them. At length, as I was approaching the entrance
tower, I fell to searching my brains as to indeed what exactly it was that
the archbishop had done for me over the years; for I did not wish to
appear ungrateful to any man; but yet I could think of little.

Presently I reached the base of the entrance where there hung a heavy
iron chain down into the moat, the which I scrambled up and gained the
roadway back into the prison yard itself. As I stood there catching my
breath, shivering in the cold, dripping with the reeking bilgewater, and

quite drenched in scum and other matter, I suddenly realized that had I
had the wits to swim in the opposite direction, that is to say to the opposite shore, I should now be a free man. As I was pondering whether to
dive back into those muck-infested waters and make my way across,
uncertain that freedom would indeed be worth a second swim, I heard,
all at once, a heavy grinding, clanking noise; and looking up, I saw that
the wooden drawbridge which leads from the prison across the moat and
onto the stone bridge beyond was being lowered; and presently, just as
it touched upon the shore, I heard the sharp clatter of horse's hooves
striking the surface of the outer road and then of the bridge; and suddenly before me I saw the figure of Emil Vergeyck himself, upon his steed
and driving it forward with his usual dispatch.

"Monsieur Emil!" I cried, for I was right happy—indeed overjoyed—
to see the man once more. "Monsieur Emil! Over here, sir!"

Vergeyck reined the horse to a halt.

"Is it Monsieur Hugues then?" he enquired, for in my present condition, even in the full moonlight, it was doubtless not easy to know for a
certainty who I was; yet I think he could identify me by my stature, there
being no little children in the prison. "You are the very man I have come
in search of," he continued. "Pray, sir, make haste!" And he leapt down
from his horse and approached me, carrying a canvas sack. "Faugh, faugh,
and pew! Oh, Monsieur Hugues!" cried he when he neared me. "You do
stink, sir, I cannot help but say it, faugh! You do stink indeed and stink
right godawful damnably too!"

With that, he flung the sack over my head, swept me up inside it, and
threw me onto the back of the horse. Then cursing and spitting and roaring at the animal, he galloped off once more.

Though I could not tell where we were going, yet I had no reason
to doubt that we were headed for the cathedral, as was our wont; and in
spite of my wet clothing and the stench which quickly filled the canvas
sack and the chill of the wind, I was right happy to be riding there once
more, slung upon the back of Emil's horse, while his master cursed and
raged as of yore. When we had reached our destination and I had made
my way out of the sack (for Emil was loath to handle it again), to my joy
I discovered that we were indeed at Notre Dame and at the small rear
door of the cathedral which leads down into the catacombs and which I

knew so well! Entering, we descended as we had so many times before, into the lower passages. I knew that neither La Voisin, mother or child, would be there to attend to me; instead, an unknown youth (and a most sullen youth it was, with one eye badly crossed and several black front teeth, I happened to note) took charge of me and led me down into the lower chapel; yet he held his nose the whiles and refused to touch even my sleeve to guide me, saying only, "This way!" or "That way!" or "Down those steps, stinking pig!" and like expressions. I chose not to tell him that I could have found my way by myself and a great deal more easily than he, we having taken a wrong turn at one point; for I felt no impulse to be in any manner helpful to so boorish and disrespectful a villain.

"Sit there," the villain commanded, pointing to a low wooden stool nearby to the altar; whereupon he turned and disappeared into the clouds of incense that filled the tiny sanctuary, though not before I stuck out my tongue at his receding back and fairly waggled it at him.

Whereupon I looked about me, recalling that first occasion I had been ushered into this very chapel and at such an hour in the night some twelve years previous; as then, the altar now was draped in black and the crucifix above; upon it six candles, made of black wax, sputtered and smoked (for the quality of black wax is poor, and the savings are hardly worth the extra aggravation; yet in this case, black wax candles are canonically correct, as I understand it); once again, at the foot of the altar was another source of smoke, the censer, which had been recently diddled with, for it was belching out fragrance in great rolling billows.

One thing there was which was absent, reader: the hamper next to the altar containing whatever hapless babe was to be offered that night to the powers of darkness; and where it ought to have been, there was only a tin basin.

Yet at the time I did not question the matter, being so gratified to be once more in my belovèd sanctuary. At length, however, as I sat there in the stone vault, my teeth began to chatter and my limbs to shiver quite uncontrollably; my clothes were still soaked quite through and through, my shoes two muggy swamps, my hair matted down upon my head and most out of order, my skin grown clammy with the wet. Nor could I take issue with the verdict of Emil Vergeyck or the lout of an acolyte, for vilely stink I did indeed, and most entirely from head to toe; which is yet not a great distance; but the quality and power of the reek more than made up for it. Even so, I was able to relieve myself somewhat, first by deeply inhaling the incense, which served to muffle my own aroma; and next I dared to rise and approach the smoking censer and to warm my hands at it; and these comforts, coupled with my happiness at being once again in that familiar place, which seemed then, after all that I had been through, like nothing so much as a second home, greatly eased my vexatious condition.

But had I not labored under such a mixture of pleasing sensations and welcomed recollections, had I been wiser, reader, had I indeed been wiser, I would have allowed neither the stench and the cold and the wet nor those few comforts which I found nor the pleasure at being in well-known surroundings once again to distract me from questioning the absence, next to the altar, of any hamper.

I would not have omitted to note, and with greater care than I did and with great trepidation, the absence of the hamper.

*"Aspairges may!"* Suddenly from within the smoke-filled background there emerged a loud wail, followed by the appearance of the Abbé Hilaire Guibourg. I rose. Almost instantly the abbé's breath quite dispelled the fragrance of incense and even my own quite foul stench; and yet I cannot state to you that that misfortune was without its compensations, for it heightened my sense of being restored to familiar ground and to my service not only to the abbé himself but to Holy Mother Church.

Father Guibourg's vision had clearly deteriorated even more since I had last served him though he was still wearing only one hard-boiled egg; but he stumbled at the first step leading up to the altar. Whereupon I bounded forth and guided him securely up onto the stone platform, and not missing a beat at my cue for the *sicut erat* and continuing on with the *et salutaray tuum,* the *et clamor mayus,* and the others. And I have told you earlier, much much earlier, of the comfort and companionship which those Latin words furnished me; and so it was again on this occasion. And I vowed to myself there at the foot of the altar that when I should have learned how to read and write, I would find out what the words meant. (And yet I have not done so, as I have preferred instead a study of our native French tongue; and I believe as well that on second thought I somewhat feared the loss of the mysterious power of those Latin words if ever I were to know what it was they were all about.)

After the opening prayers, Father Guibourg sat at the side of the altar, and we both awaited the arrival of the females, who presently appeared, the one assisting the second to mount upon the altar, as was the custom, and adjusting her garments above her waist. I did not recognize the assistant; but I thought that I saw, but yet I cannot confirm it, but I had the brief impression of a scaly tail from beneath the hem of her robe; which might indeed have been so, for as she withdrew from the place, her buttocks appeared to be quite ill-shaped, though her garment obscured much.

Nor could I see the female parts, my stool being too low to the ground; and I dared not stand; but it is really of little matter; no, it is in fact of no matter; it is of no matter whatsoever, reader, let us not for the sake of some prurient curiosity dwell upon it; for what I am now to relate to you will overwhelm all that has gone before, including such details as the nature of the female parts, whosoever's they were.

Now, careful reader, now slowly rose the ancient priest, and slowly did he approach me where I sat upon the stool, I, at that moment, only wishing to avoid his breath. Now with one hand he seized a hunk of my hair, and he lifted me to stand, then pulled me forward, up toward the altar; it had not been his custom thus to maneuver me, for I knew right well where I should go, when to stand, at what point to kneel, to move this way and that. Yet I followed Father Guibourg willingly. But now, once arrived at the altar, with his free hand he withdrew from within his vestments an instrument; and the instrument was a razor; and he slipped it open. At the sight of which, instinctively I began to resist him; but the man was right vigorous despite his crooked spine and his advanced years, and he wrestled me downward onto the floor, next to the metal basin; and now suddenly, out from the shadows emerged the youth with the crossed eye, and he threw himself upon me to hold me down in place. At that, the abbé released my hair and forced open my mouth, as one does a horse's or other animal's to observe the state of its health; and now he reached inside and clamped his callused fingers around the girth of my tongue; the which he then did pull from out of my mouth as far as it was possible to pull it, and quite far; whereupon, though I let forth a most bloodcurdling shriek, he did, with five or six downward hacking stabs, sunder that tongue down to its very root; and did fling the thing into the basin. Blood gushed from my mouth and nostrils. And now the priest struck off the lid to the censer, which stood, still smoking, nearby, pulled from it a long coal, at one end of which was a hotly glowing ember, and, plunging it deep into my mouth and with the exertion of some force, he stamped it, hissing and steaming, down onto the blood-spouting stump of my tongue.

# 21

THOUGHT I:

If there is indeed a God in heaven, why will He not in this moment grant me the boon of blessèd death? Or if not of death at least of sweet unconsciousness? Why? But likely there is no God; or else He refuses to do it for some divine perversity; or else the forces of darkness are at present stronger and they have prevailed, as surely as they did in 1631 when the Italian volcano erupted, killing eighteen thousand people: for where was God's infinite goodness then, His vaunted mercy to mankind? And how can we justify such evil in the world if God is indeed all-good as we believe Him to be? Hark, reader, it is part of the old conundrum; and if you shall say that the scalding annihilation of my tongue compares but ill with the scalding annihilation of eighteen thousand people, Italians or not, submerged in a flow of boiling lava, why I say, fie! to your nice distinctions and fie again! and I pray you may never know such searing pain as cries out for oblivion or the favor of consciousness lost!

But neither death nor consciousness lost was to be; I was blessed with neither; no; but instead lay crumpled on the floor in a stinking, sodden, bloody heap, my eyes swollen shut with violence, all sensation obliterated save that of scorching, choking pain: the pain of my hacked flesh, the second pain of it cooked and charred. And yet blood did seep out in places through the grilled stump, it bubbled up into my cheeks and filled them; and then leaked through my helpless, bloated lips to pour out down over the stone; and eventually I felt the wounded stump itself, deep inside my neck, begin to swell and to crowd forward, like the head of some dull, thick serpent which had lain coiled inside my belly, poking its way upward through my constricted throat and thrusting into my mouth.

It seemed an eternity that I lay there on the stone floor, a hideous bundle of pain, unaware of anything that went on about me, which was the Mass being celebrated by Father Guibourg; yet at length, despite the shock which clogged my brain, I did begin to perceive certain sounds, words, but all as though from a great distance; yet one phrase did at last come clearly through:

"*Introibo ad altare dayi.*" Which is, as you know, at the conclusion of the Mass.

Without thinking, instinctively, reader, I was moved to respond, "*Ad dayum qui laytificat yuventutem mayum.*"

But yet I could not respond, for I had nothing with which to respond: I had a mouth and two lips, to be sure, and the larynx box still left within my throat; but I had no longer any tongue, but only the bloated root of one, upon which to place those words. And it was a pity, for they were words of great comfort, and of a most warm familiarity to me, as you know, words which had become my companions, and which are still so, if only in my mind, to this present day; but yet I could speak none of them, despite my urgent need.

*Ad dayum qui laytificat yuventutem mayum quia tu es dayus fortitudo maya quaray may repulisti et quaray tristis inchedo dum affligit may inimicus et introibo ad altare dayi ad dayum qui laytificat yuventutem mayum spera in dayo quoniam adhuc confitaybor illi salutaray vultus mayi et dayus mayus sicut erat in princhipio et nunc et sempair et in saycula sayculorum amen.*

*Amen.*

Now, I pray you, agree to fly forward with me over the next several hours and through the jumbled maze of sounds and sensations which I experienced; for my mind then being unable to register, in any coherent fashion, what was happening to my person beyond the outrage which it had suffered, little is clear to me at present of those several hours. Yet here is what I do know: that I was removed from the catacombs of Notre Dame, though by whom I know not; and that I was transported, again in a kind of hamper, which protected me but little from the cold morning air, some distance away, the distance being, I know now, that from Notre Dame to the Palace of Versailles; that once arrived, there was much shouting and badgering and cursing as the hamper was lifted and jostled from hand to hand; then left standing alone for some hours; then hoisted once more by other hands, or so it seemed, with more grumbling and oaths, and carried up a flight of stairs; presently all grew quite silent, but yet the porters still hastened forward until after a series of turns and other maneuvers, they arrived amidst what I sensed must have been a large assemblage of people; and the people were quite taken aback by the porters' arrival, for I heard gasps and cries and murmurs of surprise; whereupon the porters stopped, set down the hamper, opened the lid and rolled me out upon the floor; and I landed face downward.

A cry went up.

"What! See here!" I remember voices calling out: "No! Monstrous!"

And numerous exclamations of astonishment.

And then a female cried out, "What is it!" and another shrieked and (I believe) swooned, for there was some ado and commotion and shouts for smelling salts.

And then there was silence.

Summoning all my strength, I managed, inch by inch, to push myself over onto my side; and although my eyes were still swollen, I was able to force them open a crack. Instantly they were almost blinded by a disorderly profusion of oriental ostentation, a cluster of thick, voluminous, and elaborately woven robes worn by giant moguls with curling black beards; of extravagant, iridescent colors, of betassled cushions, of deep Persian carpets, of dazzling jewels, of fringed umbrellas, of half-naked, glimmering Ethiopes, of massive turbans and glittering scimitars, of carved chests and of goblets, of giant fans made of peacock feathers, of monkeys on golden chains, of swarthy skins and of pointed, damask slippers—a garish trumpery which stood before me, out from which a score or more of dark eyes stared in stunned disbelief down at the foul bundle which had been cast at their gaudily shod feet.

Why, I cannot say, but presently, reader, I rolled over onto my back; and there, far above me, through a labyrinth of shimmering crystal, and streaking across the ceiling, was an image of the God of War, Mars Himself: He was most ill clad—nay, nearly naked, and truly an embarrassment— aloft in the painted heavens, bristling with arms, charging in His chariot through banks of clouds, most ferocious of expression, and accompanied by a baffling array of the four seasons, the seven seas, a menagerie of voracious beasts, and of what other chaos of heavenly host following in His warlike wake had been depicted there, all of them clearly intent on mischief; and although I dimly recognized this tumultuous vision, yet I could not then recall from what particular heavens it issued.

Once again, and again with much effort, I rolled myself over, this time upon my other side; and there I beheld yet a third vision, and a most serene vision, this, for all here was harmony and order: upon a magnificent dais, at the summit of five carpeted stairs and positioned before a silver throne, surrounded on His right by the Grand Dauphin (Monseigneur) and on His left by Philippe, Duc d'Orléans (Monsieur), and on both sides by the princes of the blood in descending order, and then by other members of the court, according to rank; and clad, Himself, in a black velvet suit studded with diamonds; I beheld, I say, His Royal Majesty, the Sun King Apollo, Fourteenth of the Name of Louis; who, though, as ever, in stately command, His noble chin as ever held high, was staring down upon the sight of me, upon the stinking, bloody, maimed, and broken heap of me, in disbelief. And likewise, I, His wretched heir, so abjectly overthrown before Him, so vile and so disgraced at the feet of my lord His Majesty, reader, could scarcely credit any of my own senses.

The silence throughout that company was utter.

No one spoke.

And scarcely did any appear to breathe.

At length, I began to try to rise to my feet; for no one dare do aught but stand or bow when in the presence of my lord King Louis XIV; but yet once unsteadily on my feet, as I was attempting to offer my lord a deep bow of respect and obeisance, my balance being faulty, I fell once again, most ingloriously, and again, flat upon my back, where I lay like some miserable, helpless beetle in the throes of death.

My lord spoke not a word; but His noble brow was deeply furrowed and His celestial eyes flashed with ill-concealed rage. For my part, I could not hold back the thick, hot tears which now flew up into my eyes at the sight of my own father and at the evident distress which my appearance was now inflicting upon Him in the midst of so public an array; and the tears streamed down across my sooty temples and along the edge of the length of my nose and into my blood-stained mouth; but I could not taste the salt of them.

I adored my father.

And I longed for Him.

But yet had I been able to address Him at that moment, I should never have dared, so abject was my state.

Presently, my lord, Fourteenth of the Name of Louis, with an angry wave of His hand, summoned that I should be removed. At which signal, two strapping blue boys leapt forth, for it was they who had been my recent porters; and they tossed me back into the hamper, closed it, and hastened away with it out of the chamber, myself wrenched away from the glowing, sun-filled vision before me and plunged once again into darkness.

Once outside the throne room, the blue boys, who, like all their fellows, were right full of sparkish pranks and mischief, hauled the hamper across to the new staircase in the south wing and threw it down the stairs; and they went about their way. The hamper fell in amongst some scaffolding, but it did not break open, being a well-crafted hamper; and thus I lay there until that afternoon, when two masons discovered me and released me, laughing right heartily at my appearance and my plight.

At which point, I began to work my way back up the stairs, setting forth upon a long journey across the palace to return to my aerie in the north wing; but I could move only with great difficulty, for my limbs were stiff and my eyesight impaired by the swelling; and I hugged the walls as I crept forward so that if I stumbled, I might fall against them and not go crashing onto the open floor for all the world to see, and so that as well, I might conceal myself, behind furniture or in alcoves, from the packs of dogs (for I was not up to wrestling with any of them that day) and from the crowds of people milling about; for I did not wish another human being to see me nor to stare at me nor to speak to me nor to point his finger at me nor to topple me over onto the floor with the end of his walking stick nor to laugh at me nor to make sport. At length, late that evening, I did reach my aerie, the final climb up into it being a most painful effort, as you may imagine. Once there, I looked at my hairbrush and at my cake of soap and at my picture book, still in place after all this while; and then at my razor: but this last was a most frightening sight to me and I dared not open the blade or even to touch the thing. Then I threw myself upon my pile of straw, and comforting myself somewhat with the words of the *confiteor dayi omni,* I fell, at last, into a heavy slumber.

Reader, I awoke after how many hours of sleep I know not; but it was some time in the following morning; the unwelcome lump of flesh at the back of my mouth instantly recalled to me my much altered state; but I dared not look at it in a glass but was only glad that the staggering pain had now been reduced to a staggering ache.

Yet a second ache, a terrible gnawing in my belly, reminded me that I had not eaten for some considerable while; and thus, I resolved to go all the way back downstairs and out to the kitchen, for I had no choice unless it were to starve. This journey was the easier, descent being so, and because I had rested; yet the emptiness in my belly was debilitating. I decided to take an outside route in order to avoid the public, which were always so numerous at Versailles; and so I went down the king's staircase in the north wing and out into the Marble Courtyard: I fought my way through high drifts of snow, past the south wing, and over to the kitchen door, where I waited until someone happened by and opened it, the latch, as always, being too high for me to reach. As I stood there shivering, I scooped up a handful of snow and with great care slipped it into my mouth, and the sharp chill seemed to deaden sensation some-what. Once inside the kitchen, I approached cook and made to beg of her some scrap of food; yet no sound but a kind of sighing moan could I pro-duce, no words could I form, nor no sense utter; she growing curious about my new circumstances, wished to examine inside my mouth, but I would not have it; and I was reduced to pointing to this and to that and to making primitive gestures of one sort or another, until at length I was able to indicate my need for something to eat; whereupon she poured me out some chicken stock into a basin; but I could not consume any of the suet or biscuits which she also set forth for me. The heat of the liquid burned in my throat, though once past the thick obstruction, served me well enough in the belly. But as I stood there struggling to spoon it down, I realized that pointing and making primitive gestures, as I had just done to cook, would be my only means of communication from now on; which harrowing thought caused me to go and sit on the floor in the corner, for I felt somewhat faint; and lost. And yet the warm broth soon did me good, reader, and in part revived my belly and my body, if not my spirits.

It was to that body, if I may speak of it to you, that now my attention turned: for it had reached a state of thorough foulness as I think not the most loathsome beggar would have tolerated. Having brought my cake of soap down with me, I went out to where the privies stand along the south side of the palace, where there stands also a pump; knocking off the icicles that had formed on the spout and then taking off all my clothes, despite the wretched, biting cold and my own sense of modesty, I began the task of washing myself. A stableboy who was passing by fell to laughing at the sight of my naked bum, but when I turned to shake my fist at him (in better days, I would have stuck my tongue out at him), and he saw the length of my ———, he then fell silent and scurried off. After I had scrubbed my person and its parts, I scrubbed all of my clothes, ridding them of the vile remains of the Vincennes moat and of bloodstains and soot; but there were some holes which had been burned in my kerchief. I put the clothing back on, soaking wet though it was, for I could not go about naked, however clammy the circumstances.

Whence I crept once again the long distance back up into my nook; I brushed my hair; but could not smooth down the cowlick; and I decided to let it be. I had a needle and a lengthy piece of thread, yet I did not care to repair the holes in my kerchief; and I let them be as well. I pondered whether or not to shave my chin, for by then there had appeared several tendrils of growth; but yet I dared not open the blade of the razor, so vivid still was the memory of that other razor upon my person; and I let my chin be.

Reader, having attended to those matters of food, drink, and personal cleanliness, I now put them aside, vital as they are, for it was meet at that point that I address a greater matter, and you will have already anticipated me; I mean the matter of my persecutor: she who had done this cruelty to me—for was that "she" in any doubt? Nay, surely, Françoise Athénaïs de Mortemart, Marquise de Montespan, it was who had commanded the deed, for who else might have? Or to what end? Nay, it was she, reader, I say, and the time had come that I should seek her out. She: who had ordered the eradication of my tongue, of voice, of speech, of all proper communication such as did not mimic the language of apes; she who had had me flung down before the court, before my kin, before my royal father, a wad of humiliation, a befouled wretch, a mere thing! Why she, I say, who had stripped me of every scrap of dignity and reduced me to the shrinking, shirking shadow of the less than human, she, reader, that woman, I would now seek her out!

For reader, we are curious beasts. We may know and know a thing; and know it deep within our souls; and know it though it break our very hearts; yet still must we prove that thing. Still in the vastness of our human perversity, we long to hear it from the woman we had loved, from the goddess whom we had adored, we must needs hear her speak the words we hate as much as now we hate the lips that speak them: "I did the deed."

Yes, I would seek her out.

I would seek her out, though in what manner I should address her I knew not; yet I was certain that she would instantly seize upon the meaning of my visitation, no explanation on my part being needed, and confront the matter head on. I would seek her out whatever risks I ran in doing so; for was it not clear that the woman was entirely ruthless? And so much so that she herself had risked the wrath of my lord King Louis by causing irreversible destruction to His firstborn son? Nay, but I would seek her out; the time indeed had come to seek her out.

And set about to do it I did that very day; and in the following manner:

Again making my surreptitious way through the passages so as to avoid encounters, human or canine, I came at length to the marquise's apartment. As I paused to study whether I should scratch upon the door and wait, or not wait but scratch upon the door and enter, or neither scratch nor wait but enter unannounced; as I was contemplating these options, I say, I began to detect a most unlikely sound coming from within: it was the unmistakable murmurish sound of prayer. I had never known the Marquise de Montespan to espouse prayer or to recommend it to anyone or to sponsor it or to encourage it in any way, let alone to indulge in the business of it herself; and thus I was somewhat mystified; and so I decided that my best course in those most uncertain waters was not to scratch nor to wait nor to enter unannounced but to slip silently in through one of the hinged dog panels in order to spy what I could spy; the which I did.

The drawing room was entirely unlike any of its former selves: neither the charmingly furnished salon of old nor the crowded warehouse of later days nor the empty wasteland which I had seen most recently: an entirely new set of furnishings had been installed, heavy and quite somber, with thick draperies at the windows and dark carpeting here and there about the floor; and on the walls hung paintings of the Fathers of the Church and of saints and of the Holy Family. Before me, and with their backs to me, knelt some ten or a dozen women, clad in sober colors; but yet I could not recognize any of them from the view; and they were reciting together their beads; and they were being led in that pious exercise by a woman who knelt in front of them and who was facing them; and thus she was also facing me; and I her. And in a moment our eyes locked together: mine and those of Mme Françoise Scarron.

Now the recitation was just in the middle of one of the fifty-three *avays* which form that extended litany: "Blessèd art thou amongst women——"

"Filthy devil!" cried Mme Scarron the moment she beheld me; whereupon all the women twisted about on their knees to see what particular Antichrist had come to spoil their devotions. "What do you want in here?" she demanded. And when I made her no reply, she rose and strode through the assembly and over to me and seized me by the collar: "What are you up to now?" she cried, and the unmistakable aroma of leeks now reached my nose. "And how is it you come to be here——I thought you had been packed off to prison, sir, and a right suitable place for you, too. You have then been set free?" But I made her no response. "Speak, dwarf, why are you silent!" she commanded and began boxing me about the ears. "Oh, I see!" she said at length. "You dare not say it, but have come looking for your diabolical mistress; is it so? And are you up to more of your devilment with that witch? Ha, sir! Seek her not here, for she no longer resides in this apartment, and we who do will tolerate no satanic mischief here, sir. Be off, I say, this instant! Fiendish dwarf: go look for your hag in hell!"

Reader, I was right glad to be off, and I beat a hasty retreat through the same panel by which I had entered, and hearing, as I did so, madame's return to her devotions: "——and blessèd is the fruit of thy womb, Jesus."

And I slipped undetected back upstairs into my rookery.

Clearly, in that brief encounter, I had chanced upon an entirely new development: Mme Scarron had occupied, and right thoroughly so, to judge by the complete change in the décor, the former quarters of the Marquise de Montespan, quarters second in luxury only to His Majesty's; and thus Scarron had successfully completed her rout of her longtime adversary, wherever it was that she herself now stood in my lord's favor. The marquise, on the other hand, could no longer have been situated anywhere near my lord's favor; and although her displacement should come as no great surprise to either you or me, reader, given my lord's encounter with her in her bedchamber, which you will recall, yet even so, her present and conclusive banishment was surely of much greater moment than those periodic exiles which she had suffered of old: it was an event of historic proportions.

My mission to seek out the lady had now become more difficult, for I had no idea where even to start. If she had withdrawn from the Palace of Versailles, my hopes were dashed, for I had no horse to take me about to seek her; if she were still within the palace, my chances were improved, yet a laborious search would face me ahead, Versailles being the gigantic place that it is. Scarron had bade me seek out my lady in hell, a prospect only a bit more daunting than seeking her out in the palace (and one I rejected out of hand). Nor could I even ask anyone where she was, for I could not utter her name.

I resolved nevertheless to seek her out at Mass in the Royal Chapel the following morning, though how I might confront her during the holy office on so delicate and personal an issue as the removal of my tongue never crossed my purposed mind. As it turned out, the matter was moot, for she was not there; or at least not visible from the hiding place which I had chosen inside a confessional. At an even greater risk to myself, I next sought her out at the gaming tables; I say "risk," for the marquise had been wont to play in the presence of my lord Himself and of members of the royal family, and I had not leave to enter unescorted into that inner sanctum. Thus I devised to lower myself on a rope secured to some exterior scaffolding, head first, no more than the distance needed to allow me to peer through the uppermost window pane and into the king's game room. It was dark outside and brightly lit within, so that the risk of detection was slight; but yet I had no sooner abandoned hope of seeing the marquise there, for she did not appear for upwards of two hours, than the rope came quite undone and I fell some twenty feet, my head striking the paving below; which incident served somewhat to dampen my resolve. It had become increasingly apparent to me that seeking out the marquise in a public setting was entirely useless anyway. Thwarted thus, I saw nothing for it: I should have to wait and watch and keep my ear to the ground. (I was obliged also to seek out a plaster for my broken head, but could find none; and I wrapped my kerchief around it and bound it tightly.)

During those several comings and goings, I had time to reflect upon many things, reader; and I came eventually to understand how it was that my lord King Louis had not acknowledged me the day on which I had been flung at His feet; for in the humiliation imposed upon Him and His court by so public a gesture, He deliberately chose not to, nor indeed ought He to have acknowledged me: not with the Grand Sophy of Persia and all his entourage as witness—for I had learned that he it was I had seen that morning in the Throne Room, in all the oriental pomp and display of his eastern court, on a state visit to present himself to the royal court of France—not, I say, with the Grand Sophy of Persia witness; not with the royal family, legitimate and legitimated, witness; nor the entire royal court witness; nor indeed in fact the entire nation witness, for news travels most swiftly in this realm. No: He might have done nothing but that which in His wisdom He did do, no, not without great risk: and I speak not of risk to Himself, for my lord had faced many a risk throughout His most heroic lifetime, and He feared no man nor no thing neither in regard to His own person; nay, but risk indeed to the fortunes of the state, the which every great leader must put before all else, the which every father of His people must protect even as He would protect His own child, and for the which every divinity on this earth must answer in heaven to no less a divinity than God the Almighty Father Himself.

And since forgiveness partakes of divinity—His divinity and my own— I forgave Him and right gladly and with all my heart.

With the matter of the marquise's whereabouts held for the moment in abeyance, I took up another pressing matter, to wit, my status as a resident of the palace myself. And I confess that I had no idea what it was. For was it not possible that I might now be held to be an escaped convict? Even though in all fairness I could not have been accused of executing that escape myself. Still, a fugitive is a fugitive, and for all I knew, Monsieur de la Reynie's excellent men might well have been combing the countryside in search of me, cursing, and fiercely too, that their prey, being small, was so elusive; and although it was unlikely that they would think to search out a renegade within the very halls of Versailles, yet word moves quickly, as you know, reader. And thus I decided that I must maintain an entirely inconspicuous presence.

On the other hand, after several days mewed up inside my snuggery with only an occasional stealthy foray down for food and drink, I was able to persuade myself that I must, however surreptitiously, take up once again some industry down below if I did not wish to go mad from solitude; this was a choice which you will find typical of the thinking of many a fugitive, for they say that the miscreant, unwisely, will not stay safely put in hiding but feels a compulsion to return to the scene of the crime. Yet not having committed any crime that I could think of, unless the accident of my very birth were a crime—oh, harsh justice! to accuse the helpless babe merely of sliding out; what else, pray, might the creature do?—having, I say, committed no crime, I knew of no scene to which I might now, unwisely, return; unless it were to St. Germain-en-Laye, where I was born, for by tradition it is the birthplace of kings. Yet I had neither means to travel the distance to St. Germain nor no desire: the royal court being presently at Versailles, the older palace would be quite closed up, I knew, and deserted, and a cold and mournful place it is when so. No: I would stay on at Versailles, in the hope that Monsieur de la Reynie would not extend his operations there (a foolish hope perhaps for, as you know, many a resident of the Vincennes gaol had held fine sway at Versailles); and I would begin to explore, though with great prudence and great circumspection, what employment I might next put my hand to.

Thus it was that very quietly I stole downstairs the following morning to what had been my accustomed daily post outside the door to the royal bedchamber. From practice I was able to avoid the crowds of spectators; and I slipped behind at Italian settee of the *cinquecento* and waited; and then watched in some surprise as I saw the Marquis d'Effiat—of all people!—much bedecked in ribbons and lace trimmings as was his wont and holding a handkerchief up to his nose, receive from the hands of the Marquis de Lamballe the vessel containing the morning's royal defecation. So it was this most elegant gentleman who now held my former post! Intrigued, I shadowed the Marquis d'Effiat as he sauntered away out of the crowded antechamber; and sometimes he strutted along and occasionally minced and skipped his way downstairs and out to the privies, all the while maintaining a great distance between his feet so as not to step on his shoe ribbons, and as well a distance between the vessel and his nose.

From behind a large tub I watched as he set about to cleanse the vessel, and it was obvious that the task was most distasteful to the fastidious marquis and that he did it quite poorly; yet it was also borne in upon

me more clearly than ever before just how privileged a position I had
held as the bearer and cleaner of that vessel: for as you know, all such
chores which are performed at Versailles by members of the nobility are
designated as formal offices, for which the nobles pay most handsome
sums; thus, my sudden absence at that chore had produced the creation
of an entirely new office for which the Marquis d'Effiat had apparently
outbid all others, he being a man of substance, if not in his particular person, in his holdings.

Seeing his unhappy efforts at cleansing the vessel, I felt a strong
impulse to offer my assistance, for I was well practiced in the work; yet
I recalled the marquis's tendency to sudden anger and did not wish to
provoke it by implying, with my offer, that he was insufficient to the task.
And yet on the other hand, my lord King Louis's vessel was not receiving at all the attention required and might therefore give offense. And
so, having weighed these matters, I decided, out of a compelling sense
of duty, to seize, as it were, the day; and I stepped forth from behind
the tub and approached the marquis. But the instant he saw me and
before I could begin gesturing my offer of aid, he interrupted his task
and spoke:

"Monsieur Hugues is it, then!" quoth he. "La, sir! And you have been
the subject of some enquiry hereabouts! And they will be right glad that
I have found you out again." And seeing the kerchief bound around my
forehead: "And have you split your skull, sir? But where in the world,
pray tell, have you kept yourself this while?"

Now reader, I could only assume that "they" were Monsieur de la
Reynie's excellent men and that I faced an imminent return to Vincennes
gaol; but the marquis, noting the expression of dismay which must have
appeared on my face, spoke once more:

"Come, come, you shall not be afraid, dwarf; but tell: where have you
been?" When again I said nothing in reply: "What is it?" he demanded.
"Have you lost your voice, wretch?" And in the face of my continuing
silence, he returned to his chore. "Bother this vessel!" he said as though
to himself. "It is a vile thing!"

Reader, I was shocked to hear him speak thus about the royal vessel;
and at the same time even more emboldened to take matters into my
own hands; the which I did; and silently I lifted it from him and proceeded to wash it out myself, hastening to the shed where I kept my

supply of wood ashes, salt, sand, tallow, lye soap, rosin, bone marrow, and pumice. As he watched my expert attentions to the vessel—with its curious blue decorations—the Marquis d'Effiat began prancing about with great delight, clapping his hands together and whistling tunes and exclaiming such things as "Lovely, lovely!" and "It is an excellent dwarf!" and "La, la, la, la, la!"

After he had returned the vessel to the royal chamber, to which, at his bidding, I had accompanied him, he scampered away, with myself still in tow, to the apartment of Philippe, Duc d'Orléans, my lord King Louis's brother, of whom I have spoken any number of times before, it is the effete gentleman known as "Monsieur." The Marquis d'Effiat being one of Monsieur's closest intimates, he did not request the footman to announce him to the duke, but burst directly into the bedchamber, crying aloud:

"See, see, see! Ha ha, look, sweetheart! Look what a delicious thing I have brought you!"

By that hour, the morning was well along on its way; and yet there, at a table near a fireplace, sat the figure of Monsieur, still in the process of taking his breakfast. And I say the "figure" of Monsieur; but yet it was indeed Monsieur himself: but I could scarcely recognize the gentleman, for he had no wig upon his head, and what hair he was naturally possessed of fell in stringy, skimpy ringlets about his ears; furthermore, his face appeared quite pale and blank, and I realized that he had not yet applied those rouges, mascaras, powders, and other such colorings as was his wont to wear. He had on a white silken nightgown with a great profusion of lace about the throat and cuffs, and over it a winter dressing robe; yet even in this state of *déshabille,* there were necklaces and bracelets and rings about his person, along with two dangling gold earrings; and despite the distance at which I was standing from him, I quickly detected a sweet, almost overpowering fragrance of perfume. Yet for all his elegance, it appeared that his fingers were greasy and somewhat caked with scraps of breakfast food, and he wiped them from time to time on his dressing gown.

That person over there is my uncle, I suddenly thought to myself.

My uncle did not look back in my direction but threw a thick loaf of bread at the marquis and roared, "Didi, you rotten, ——ing whore! I am having my goddamn breakfast! I tell you, I do not wish—"

"Why, pooh pooh! What a grump she is today!" cried the marquis, now fluttering all about the breakfast table and tossing a hard-boiled egg into his mouth.

"Fie! I have told you a thousand times, Didi," said Monsieur and quite vehemently, "do not! I say, do *not* bring your wanton traffic in here when I am having my breakfast!"

At which the marquis let forth a tinkling laugh. "'Wanton traffic!' Ha ha, 'traffic' indeed! Why, I would not be caught dead! No, no: but only look over there, lover, and see what 'traffic' it is! Look: it is the famous lost dwarf!"

Whereupon Monsieur picked up a small spyglass from off the table, turned toward me and applied the glass to his right eye, for as I have told you, he was somewhat myopic.

"I found the creature out at the privies," the marquis chattered on. "It has cracked open its head, it seems; and God alone knows what else it has been up to; and yet—"

"Monsieur Hugues!" the duke exclaimed. "Aha!" And setting down the spyglass: "Come forward, sir; where have you been this while?"

Reader, I did as my uncle bade me and approached the table; and I bowed to him a most respectful bow.

"Well?" insisted Monsieur. "What have you to say for yourself?"

"The creature quite adamantly refuses to speak," said the marquis, "and believe me, I myself asked it the very same thing, and over and over again too, I shall tell you; but yet the stubborn mule that it is—"

"Babble, babble, babble!" said Monsieur. "Hold your tongue, Didi, I say!" At which command the marquis snorted and shook his curls and appeared to be quite vexed. "Monsieur Hugues," continued the duke, turning his pallid face back to me and speaking now in a gentle tone of voice: "We have wondered, sir, what became of you since your—" and he paused a moment, "—your most unusual return to court the other day. Where, sir, have you kept yourself?"

But I could not think of how to go about replying.

"Seeking out his mistress, I'll warrant, for employment," chimed in the marquis. "Ha, ha, ha! and he will have some keen seeking to do to locate that lady, ha, ha, ha! And yet I vow," he continued with a leer at me, "she is in great need of Monsieur Hugues's services just now!"

"Is it so, sir?" said Monsieur to me. "Have you been seeking the marquise?"

To which, reader, I nodded my head most vigorously; for surely my uncle, who was privy to every intrigue about the court and moreover, took much delight in furthering them and expanding upon them, must have known where the lady was now situated; and this was just the opportunity for which I had set my marks.

"Ha, ha!" Monsieur joined in the marquis's mirth. "Why, then, sir, indeed! You must seek her out down below, sir; for your mistress has recently suffered something of a slip from out of her state of grace!"

"A slip! A slip!" now cried the marquis and fairly clapping his hands in glee. "Why, nay, *il mio innamorato*" (an Italian term meaning "my belovèd"; and the marquis rolled the *R* in a most lascivious manner), "I vow his mistress has suffered a right swift kick in the seat of her drawers from out of her state of grace; and she did not land quite upon her feet, I can tell you," he said now to me, "but rather, sir, upon her increasingly well-insulated tail!"

At which wit, the two gentlemen fell to roaring at the marquise; and I could not tell, reader, if it were at her ill fortune or her tail.

"And yet I know not," said Monsieur at length, wiping his eyes with his sleeve. "Most likely we ought now to be weeping, Didi, and not laughing so; for see what a creature it is my brother has set in her place!"

"Oh, a vile creature it is!" said the marquis. "A vile, contemptible creature that Scarron, indeed and indeed: a pious, sermonizing, sanctimonious, jesuitical, unctuous, moralizing, judgmental, righteous, fanatical, dogmatic, pietistical, priest-ridden, ill-humored, stern, sober, sour—"

"Hold!" cried Monsieur, laughing once again. "Enough!"

"—stolid, ponderous, cheerless, funereal, down-in-the mouth, mumpish, bilious, splenetic, dour, fusty, dowdy, antediluvian, hide-bound, querulous, captious, finicky, ill-tempered, petulant, peevish, crabbèd, obstinate, tenacious, mule-headed, sullen, willful, caustic, fretful, testy, waspish, shrewish, quarrelsome, contentious, cantankerous, churlish, fractious—"

"Nay, Didi, leave off!" shouted Monsieur, and yet he was laughing harder than ever before and holding his sides.

"—censorious, carping, disdainful, imperious, intolerant, devious, hypocritical, tyrannical, vindictive, opinionated, insinuating, conniving, bigoted, scheming, prudish, priggish, prim, puritanical, smug, snobbish, straight-laced, peremptory, stiff-necked, narrow-minded, jaundiced—"

Whereupon Monsieur threw another loaf of bread at the marquis's head, who, dodging it right prettily, fell into a heap upon the floor and rolled about, helpless with glee at his dazzling performance.

When the two gentlemen had at length somewhat recovered themselves, Monsieur turned again to me:

"He exaggerates, Monsieur Hugues, but only to an extent," said he, still chuckling. "Yet to the point: if you would now seek your present mistress, she has been installed below in the Baths Apartment, and you will find her down there."

"A naughty lady, your present mistress, Monsieur Hugues," said the marquis. "For it is hinted, yet I do not know, yet it is rumored about that your mistress had been right busy in certain—how shall I say?—late-night devotions." The marquis approached me and now stooped down to place his rouged and powdered face up close to mine; and he stared into my eyes with a mocking expression in his own; and he lowered his voice when next he said: "Devotions which were considered somewhat irregular, sir, and which therefore displeased." He paused. "And what do you yourself know of that matter, sir? What? Nothing? Nothing, you say? Take care, Monsieur Hugues: for I vow, the flames will make quick work of it with one so short."

Reader, he quite startled me, pressing so closely up to my face and staring so; and uttering such menacing words; and I stood frozen upon the spot.

"Leave off, Didi," said my uncle; at which the marquis laughed and began hopping about the room. "Say, now, Monsieur Hugues," my uncle continued, "what is your design? Truly, can you not speak to us, sir?"

At which I might simply have shaken my head in reply; but yet I did not like to.

"Come, come," he persisted, "you must not be frighted. Pay that fool no heed. No one seeks to harm you." Whereupon he beckoned me to approach yet nearer; and now he spoke in a whisper so that the marquis should not hear. "Come then, cousin," said he, "the king will not send you back to prison, nor burn you at the stake: it is His intention that you stay on now at court; you may come and go about without fear."

Oh, but his words were of comfort to me, reader! as I believe you must understand, for they quite delivered me from my fears of being a fugitive from the law; but what was more, and much more, he had called me "cousin." And so grateful was I to him at that moment, that I made him a second deep, respectful, and most reverent bow.

"But yet, why do you still not speak?" insisted Monsieur. Then suddenly an idea appeared to flash across his mind. "Come closer, Monsieur Hugues, pray," said he. And I did so, all the way up to where he sat, wreathed in perfume and lace and clusters of jewelry. Whereupon with his somewhat greasy fingers, he gently opened my mouth; and he peered inside.

"Ah!" he cried, much horrified by the sight, and "Ah!" again as he leapt from his chair in dismay. "Ah!" he cried a third time. "His tongue! Why, who—? No, it is monstrous, too, too monstrous! The creature's tongue has been cut right from out of his mouth!"

At which news, the Marquis d'Effiat let forth a high and piercing shriek; and but a moment later, across the room, the draperies which hung in front of my uncle's bed suddenly burst open; and through them appeared the head of a youth, and a right pretty fellow it was, reader, and his face was quite delicately painted with rouges and powders; the youth looked about the room and then over at me; and thereupon he let out a loud whoop of hilarity at the thought that my tongue had been cut right from out of my mouth, and he withdrew behind the drapery once more; at which there followed whoops from several other young fellows who were, it seems, stored away there behind the drapery with him.

Now despite the brutality which was the object of everyone's attention, the Marquis d'Effiat had clearly seen the pretty fellow as well as I had, brief though the boy's appearance had been; and then he had heard the gleeful whoops from within the bed; and I watched as his face turned bright crimson with rage and as his arms and legs began to quiver in great agitation. Whereat he sprinted across the room with a loud cry, reached into the bed, and pulled out first one fellow, then a second and a third and a fourth and a fifth; and all of the fellows were well painted and right pretty, and all of them were as well right naked, and not a few of them, and I blush to tell it to you, reader, displayed advanced states of turgidity; and they began bounding about the room looking for whatever they might wrap themselves in and squealing and bawling and crying out; and I recognized three of them as blue boys; and when he had pulled out a sixth and a seventh, the marquis screamed:

"You bitch, you bitch! You ——ing, ——ing bitch!" And he began throwing hard-boiled eggs at Monsieur and bread and plates and a fish and then all the breakfast things from off the table. At which Monsieur began to chase him and to strike at him with the spyglass, shouting I know not what exclamations, for by then there was utter pandemonium throughout the chamber; and although I had not been given leave to be excused, I nevertheless took leave, reader, and bolted from the chamber and in great haste.

But despite the haste of my retreat, there was now in my hurried step a kind of quiet ebullience: for attend: Monsieur had called me "cousin." Now it is true, that to do so he had lowered his voice so that no one else in the room should hear; but yet he had called me "cousin." And it is also true that a cousin is more distant than a nephew, and that the term may be used (loosely) to apply to a second cousin (even more distant) or to a third, or indeed to cousins several times removed; yet still, he had called me "cousin." Himself a somewhat foolish figure, the Duc d'Orléans, with his mincing ways and his powders and fits of temperament and ribbons and his bevies of naked, pretty youths, and people laughed at him, I knew, behind his back, and they made mock of him: and yet, reader, the man had called me "cousin."

And as I was darting through the second antechamber, having first made certain that there was no one in it, suddenly a foxhound appeared; and when he approached me, baring his teeth and snarling and then snapping at my ——, I struck him such a hard blow with my bare fist and so smartly across the muzzle that the fiend crept away, yelping and whining; for by then, reader, I was feeling somewhat reckless.

# 22

Reader, at this point I think it useful to inform you of my thoughts about the publication of this text. It is a thing which I shall seek to do either within a few years, though not before the passing of my lord King Louis; or some while later, let us say ten to fifteen years from now. Yet it will be an issue of controversy, and I cannot tell: for I conceive that forces well beyond my control may not license the circulation of this, my own history, so incendiary it will be considered; and thus it is quite possible that you are the only person to learn of my fate and of the fate of the House of Bourbon. In which case, I am led to enquire, who then are you, reader? And how do you come by this text? Are you the printer? For if any man shall print the words of another, I think that first he must surely read them, if only to set them into type. Is that who you are? If so, you a daring man indeed, for it is most likely that the printer of this chronicle will be implicated along with the author. Or are you some eager member of the literary set who, sprinting but two steps ahead of the censor, has seized up the latest unlicensed text with the aim of being more au courant than all the others at my lady's next salon? Or are you perhaps a member of His Majesty's government, and might you even be the regent himself, whether the Duc de Chartres or someone else, we do not know at present, who, by the very nature of your position, will not tolerate what here you read of the House of Bourbon nor the continuing presence of its author, for it thoroughly spells the end of your office and of your charge: and thus it is quite possible that after our toiling together throughout these many pages, you will at the last become my executioner. But yet whoever you are, whatever your estimation of this work and however you pursue it, I must, on a somewhat metaphysical level, yet be grateful to you; for it is your very act of reading that commutes to these words any meaningful existence at all; for the act of writing is but halfway there, and if no eye receive what is written, the thing may be said not ever to have happened. The tree falling in a creatureless, earless forest crashes down without a sound. Thus I am beholden to you for giving birth to this my testament, even as you may be giving orders to put its creator to death.

(One last note: if you are in fact not an officer of His Majesty's government, you would be wise to be circumspect about your knowledge of this work. Whatever the condition of the forests, walls do indeed have ears. Caution.)

Continuing.

Monsieur's assurance that I was now at liberty to come and go about the palace did not embolden me at first to do so; for despite his close ties to my lord King Louis and his recent kindness to me, yet still I was less than certain of Monsieur's strict reliability, for he was somewhat of a flighty gentleman, as you have seen. Yet his words did passably well relieve me of the fear that I might be considered an actual fugitive from the law; and I did resolve to try and return to certain daily chores. But I was shy of meeting all people, all men and all women alike, as you have witnessed, being no longer able to reply when addressed by another human being, a singular loss, reader, speech being one of the chiefest attributes of humankind; and still feeling a fiery reddening across my face every time I recalled the shame of my disfigurement and the bitter humiliation which I had endured the morning of my return to Versailles, I eschewed the company of others; and unable still to bring myself to open my razor and reap about on my chin and jaw, and being thus most ill-groomed about the face, I did not care to be seen by any persons and certainly not by any of fashion and most certainly not by any of the ladies; and so I continued to go about in a guarded manner; and I sought out untrafficked paths as frequently as possible, offtimes journeying outside and around the corners of the massive building to avoid the throngs of people, for I could easily endure the cold. The presence of scaffolding throughout much of the palace was a distinct boon and often afforded me a well-concealed indoor route, for I found that I could make my way amongst the thickets of posts and buttresses and beneath low-standing platforms; and thus could move about unnoticed.

And yet there were times, and many of them, when, scruffy of chin, I would be creeping behind a scaffold beam or dashing through snowdrifts close up to the building or dodging from alcove to alcove in some public gallery within, that I felt, by this ignoble conduct, how greatly I was betraying my own royal lineage and the more than twelve hundred glorious years of the French monarchy, extending back even beyond Clovis to Pharamond and Clodion, who were kings of the Franks (I did not know these names at the time but have discovered them since in books; but at the time I did know that my lord King Louis had had a father, that father a father, that father's father a father, and so on back I knew not how many noble generations, which in fact number sixty-six rearwards from my lord). Betraying my lineage, I say: for what king or kingdom's rightful heir would scurry around through scaffolding and snowdrifts, when he ought to comport himself with bearing and with royalty of presence—were it indeed but three feet's worth of those commanding traits. But it was the ignominy of my condition and of the circumstances of my unhappy life which had led to this betrayal, and I will not conceal from you the deep bitterness which all these things have engendered in my heart.

Armed with the information that Monsieur had provided me as to the marquise's whereabouts, I went that very evening around nine thirty, when customarily she was at some leisure, down to the ground floor of the palace, thence through the chambers there until I stood before the door to the Baths Apartment, the suite to which she had recently been removed. I had made my outward appearance as presentable as possible, not from any regard for her, though alas, alas, I had loved her once; no: but rather to reinforce my own sense of dignity. But yet I still had not shaved and could not bring myself to do it even on that occasion, and so my chin was replete with a bristling crop of whiskers; and my kerchief was still wound about my cracked head.

And I still did not know what I should express to her nor any means.

The Baths Apartment, as you have already guessed, was the place where His Majesty bathed; and there was an ordinary drawing room there, as well as the more intimate bathing cabinet. But it has been altered since, reader, and you will not find these rooms today as they then were. Curiously, there were no hinged panels in the doors to this apartment; and I say "curiously" for why should not my lord have entertained the royal hounds in those more private quarters as well as elsewhere throughout the palace? For I believe that there were even certain dogs which slept with Him on nights when He had chosen not to summon other bedding companions; yet He did not admit them to the baths: the dogs, I mean, not the bedding companions; and it may have been a simple matter of hygiene, for as you know, the beasts were given to fouling, and prodigiously, anywhere they put their minds to it. No matter: but thus, without the panels, I had no choice but to scratch upon the door; and I chose as well to scratch and wait rather than to scratch and enter unannounced, given the more personal nature of the apartment itself.

I scratched; and waited; and at length the door was opened and I looked up to see Mlle des Œillets.

"Monsieur Hugues!" she cried. "Where have you kept yourself! I have been trying to find you these many days now, sir; for my lady has more often than once expressed the wish to see you. Come inside then, pray, and I shall tell her that you are here."

She admitted me into the room, then stopped a moment to study me.

"Why, sir," said she, "you are somewhat altered, is it not so? Aha! I see it now: you have split open your head, have you, sir? And you have not shaved off your beard this while! I vow, Monsieur Hugues, you look quite fierce, quite fierce indeed! I shall needs forewarn my mistress."

With that, she withdrew into the rear of the apartment. The room in which I stood was somewhat sparsely supplied with the few pieces of furniture and carpeting to which the marquise apparently had clung during the recent changes in her living arrangements; but as well, there was a goodly number of unpacked crates and baskets about the place, some of them quite large, as though its occupant intended to linger there no more than a week or so. The room was chill, there being no fire in the chimney. The windows in the western wall gave onto the water terrace and out across the Parterre of Latona and along the Royal Avenue all the way to the canal; but on that dark and moonless night, all that was visible were raindrops beating against the panes and streaming downward. The gloominess of the night outside and the unfriendliness of the room within did little to dispel my feelings of apprehension as I waited to confront the creature around whom my willing world had orbited but shortly ago and who was now the object of my eternal hate. I have written "apprehension": but "fear" may, in all honesty, be more nearly the word.

Presently, I heard the rear door open; my heart began to beat faster; and I watched as herself, the Marquise de Montespan, entered into the room. Without a word, without a glance in my direction, nor even any acknowledgment of my presence, she walked, in a most imperious manner, across the room and sat down upon a chair which stood next to a small table.

Reader: I am not mistaken: I saw, whipping briefly out from beneath the marquise's skirts, a long and scaly reptilian tail; but once she had sat, it remained quite hidden beneath the folds of cloth.

The marquise moved more slowly than before, I noticed, but I believe that it was because there was now somewhat more of her to move; and when I say that she sat upon the chair, it would be more accurate in fact to say that she encamped upon the chair, or indeed that she somewhat weighted it down. Be that as it may, her face and hair were quite presentable, as indeed they had not been when last we met; she wore a garment of a somber hue; and a heavy woolen shawl which she held about her shoulders produced the impression of a woman who had become distinctly and undeniably of a certain age.

Presently she turned to me and fixed me with a look of unmistakable loathing and contempt.

"Dwarf," she addressed me coldly, and she let the word somewhat hover in the chill air, "where have you been, dwarf? You have led my woman a fine chase, sir, it is quite intolerable." She paused, but not as though awaiting a reply, which would have been quite futile. "I trust that you do not perceive your present state as one affording you the leisure to come and go about as you please: pray have no such illusions, sir, you still have me to answer to—even if—" she added with a smile, "—answer you cannot make."

Reader, I held her stare with my own most steady one, despite a trembling I felt in my knees.

"When last we met, dwarf," she continued, "you caused me some damage. Clearly you are aware of that; in fact, you quite intended it You caused, I might add, some damage to my carpet as well, but I shall not dwell upon that, it is the act of an incompetent child, of a mewling child—and pitiful. I dismiss it."

I thought it most petty of her to mention the carpet at all (though it shamed me that she did and I turned quite red) when issues of such greater moment were more to the point.

"No small damage, I say, dwarf; and you find me at present in circumstances that are to an extent reduced." She glanced quickly about the sparsely furnished chamber. "Yet, sir," she continued, "do not presume from this evidence that I am now entirely incapacitated: nay, sir, I am quite capable yet, and you ought not forget it." She lowered her voice somewhat. "The fact that the Duchesse de Fontanges was packed off to a convent two weeks ago this Wednesday will, I believe, attest to that. And I speak to you of this particular matter, sir, of Fontanges, for I believe that this particular matter has a most particular ring for us both, does it not? And that the two of us," she paused, "having had a hand, so to speak, in this matter, understand one another on it, do we not? In somewhat the same manner, sir, if I may so express myself, as felons may be said to understand one another's doubtful doings; or as one Judas understands another."

At that, the sudden chill returned to me of that awful moment in her bedchamber when I had sensed—though most unwillingly!—a bond with her, that hideous bond which indeed two traitors must feel between themselves, both doers of treacherous deeds.

"Dwarf," she began again and though with renewed energy yet with no trace of warmth in her voice, "I no longer tolerate well your residence at this court; and were it my choice, you would not now remain here; but it is not my choice, nor ever was. His Majesty has elected that you may stay; but I would have you to understand, sir, that He does so only because you have been rendered harmless, because you are become useless and impotent and of no more danger to anyone or anything. The slanders which you had begun to spread are now quite nipped in the bud, whatever jots of truth they may have once contained; and even the intelligence which inadvertently and most unjustifiably you gained as to your own person and its origins has been likewise quite contained; for you are silent, sir, and silent, sir, you shall remain, and for the rest of your wretched days; silent and quite useless now to yourself or to anyone else."

Once more she paused; and then adjusting the shawl more closely about her shoulders:

"And to me as well, Monsieur Hugues. You are utterly useless now to me: indeed, of what use were you ever to me, pray, but for that lengthy, busy tongue of yours?" Reader, I blushed most fully at the reference to the service furnished her ladyship by the employment of my tongue; but she, for her part, displayed no reticence to speak of it. "Yet," she continued, "I part most willingly with that use, sir, knowing that your days of bustling and blabbing are quite done with as well." She paused; and lowering her voice, she now allowed a note of pleasure to creep into it: "My woman has been searching for you, sir, but to no avail; and now instead, it is you who have sought me out. Nor does that surprise me: for you have done so with the certain expectation, I see, of hearing what I shall now declare to you: indeed, you are as perversely hungry to hear it as I am justifiably pleased to speak it. I rejoice then in my soul to assure you, Monsieur Hugues of the House of Bourbon, that yes, indeed it was most assuredly I who ordered that long and most busy tongue of yours to be slit from out of your throat (and parenthetically, I find no small delight in the irony that it was the Abbé Guibourg who served you up that operation to whom you have in turn rendered such long and invaluable service). Moreover, it was I who arranged for your appearance at court the following morning before the presence of the Persian Sophy and that of His Majesty Our Own Sovereign." She paused. "I am right fond of public occasions, Monsieur Hugues, and was glad for your appearance that day."

There: I had heard it now, all of it, and from the lips that once I had longed for. Again my heart was pounding in my breast; but yet I stood my ground, continuing to face her; and I prayed that she would not hear that heart pounding; and I prayed again that I might yet find some means to express my hatred to her; and I prayed yet as fervently again that I would not have another accident on her carpet.

Next, she withdrew from her bosom a sheet of paper, unfolded it, and held it out for me to see; on the bottom was the crude $X$ which I had fashioned there some months before and the thick inky drips of my careless pen.

"Had you troubled to read this document, sir," she said, "you would have stood warned, as the penalty for blabbing is fully spelled out and in no uncertain terms; and thus you will agree that you have only yourself to blame for what debasement has befallen you." For the first time

during our interview she smiled, and I recalled that gracious smile of
hers of old. "And entirely appropriate it is," she went on, "that you have
come to this abject end: for base you have always been, Monsieur
Hugues—monsieur dwarf—and base you shall now forever remain."

Her words, as harsh as they were, produced quite a contrary effect
within my breast: for I felt no baseness, but instead a kind of warmth
began to suffuse me and a strange, unwonted sense of power. I looked
about the room and saw, not far away, one of the tall packing crates, in
front of which stood a chair. Without a second's thought, I turned and
walked over to the chair; and I climbed up upon it (and at that moment,
and for only that moment, recalling that other chair—her chair—upon
which I had stood the night of our first convergence, of that first and
what I had thought Holy Communion); next I hoisted myself up onto the
back of the chair, and grasping the sides of the packing crate, I inched
my way up it, slowly but steadily (in much the same way that I crawl up
gutter pipes in the conduct of my daily chores); and presently, I reached
the very height of the crate, up onto which I hauled myself. When, now
standing atop the crate, I turned back to face the marquise, I saw that she
had risen from her seat in great puzzlement at my action, and she stood
below me, a look of utter surprise and, to an extent, alarm on her features. Next, I pulled myself up to my full height, thrust forth my chin
as I had so often seen my noble father do, and stared down at the marquise with an expression of serene command. Slowly I placed my right
forefinger upon the bridge of my nose and then, inch by inch, I traced
it downward the entire prodigious length of that organ, down, down,
down to the very tip.

Nay, let me no longer creep about nor dodge nor scurry nor hide,
thought I: no longer betray my royal line, my royal fathers, or deny my
true divinity—nay, my hour has struck!

Below me, I saw madame's face begin to grow quite pale and her
breathing to come in uneven spurts; and she turned back to her table to
steady herself against it, clutching the rim of it with both hands. And I
saw that she dared not look back up at me but averted her eyes from my
stare, as one dare not look up into the resplendent face of the sun.

Cowed now though she was in my royal presence, yet the creature
was tough, and toughened over many years; and more than once she had
dealt with the powerful and come nose-to-nose with divinity, for all

her lack of it; and thus, though she continued to avoid my gaze, I heard her speak yet again, but in a voice that resembled the thick growl of some low brute:

"Monsieur Hugues: you may assert yourself by whatever means are at your disposal, sir, by gesture or by pose or by look; but yet you say nothing, sir, and that is indeed most incongruous." I sensed a certain regathering of her forces. "Are you then," she continued, "too cowardly to speak, sir? Nay, not you, Monsieur Hugues, not so royal a figure of a man as you! It cannot be! But it is for want of a tongue, is it not, that you are dumb, for the simple want of a tongue. And a most burdensome plight it must be for you, I vow. But see, Monsieur Hugues! You shall suffer that lack no longer, sir; for I have wisely saved that tongue, sir, and I shall lend you the ugly thing back again, Monsieur Hugues, and thus you may quite freely speak your mind, sir."

With that, she took up from the table a dainty covered dish, which she held up to me; whereupon slowly she lifted the lid.

There, upon the platter, lay my tongue; or rather, what had once been my most glorious and lengthy tongue: for what I saw now in the dish before me was a puny nub, a blackened, shriveled, leathery nub, a dry and helpless scrap.

Reader, in my madness at being unable to respond to such barbarity and in the hot fury which her mockery had aroused in my breast; in the shock of beholding the pathetic knob of my tongue, and in the outrage which I felt that anyone might so cruelly use another human being; and in my righteous wrath that she should ridicule the most legitimate heir to the royal throne of France, I impulsively did the following: I leapt from my heights down onto the chair and thence back to the floor before her; slowly I opened wide my mouth to her; and I strained, with all the muscles of my neck and throat, to stick my tongue out at the malicious creature; but having none to stick out, for it lay in the dish, I succeeded instead in stretching the stump of it somewhat farther forward up into my mouth and in sticking it at least outwards toward her; and the in-tensity of the effort which I made pulled taut all the bones and flesh and veins of my neck and jaw, and an instant purple heat flamed all across my face, and my nostrils flared, my whiskers bristled, and my lips curled back into a distended snarl, baring the two rows of my teeth at her whom I had once adored as though a goddess; and the exertion on the stump of my tongue now caused the scar to crack open, and blood began gushing out into my mouth and down my lips and chin and even dripping down onto the carpet; and the violence of my gesture, the savagery of it— nay, its utterly inhuman ferocity—startled the woman and alarmed and frighted her so sorely that she grew ashen, and she cried out aloud I know not what brutish utterance; and as her eyes stared wildly at the discharge of vicious hatred before her, her face drained entirely of color, her hands began to tremble, and her bosoms to heave; whereat she toppled and fell down upon the floor, crumpled in a deep swoon. The dish landed on the floor as well and broke to pieces; and my black tongue bounced several times across the bloodied carpet.

Whereupon I saw—indeed, I did see it—I saw that scaly reptile whose tail I had glimpsed earlier, I saw the creature itself now dart forth from the disordered pile of madame's skirts; and flicking out its own long and sticky tongue, in an instant it seized upon *my* tongue and consumed it whole; and the animal disappeared once more.

At that, though the hairs had shot straight out on the back of my neck and though my spine had turned to ice, I gathered myself nevertheless together, turned and strode from the room, even as I heard Mlle des Œillets dashing in from the other direction. But the effort I had made cost me dearly in breath, as a healthy extrusion of hatred will always do; and I stood on the other side of the door gasping in order to regain my wind; I pressed my handkerchief into my mouth to soak up the blood; during which moments I experienced an overwhelming sense of relief and satisfaction and even of exultant fulfillment: the presence of blood in the mouth, reader, is downright invigorating, though it is likely to be more so if it is someone else's than one's own. No matter, beggars are not choosers, and I was refreshed and fortified thereby, and I knew moreover that I should have—nor should desire—no further commerce with the diabolical marquise—most certainly not divine!—and I hoped that at last she might at least be robbed of some several moments of sleep by the recollection of the sight of that naked, straining, bleeding tongue-stump and of the unspeakable loathing which I had bared to her. Unspeakable indeed! No words could have better served me than that mute eruption of hatred.

After I had regained my breath, I hastened back up into my nest; once there I lit a small tallow candle and set it next to my piece of mirror. I sat before the mirror. I opened my lips and stared at my bloodstained teeth; then I opened up my mouth. For the first time since my disfigurement, I peered inside. I looked at the toasted rump which lay far back in the rear. The bleeding had slowed, for the skin had broken open only in two or three places; the earlier thick swelling had much subsided, a thing which I had already known, for swallowing had become somewhat more possible again; and now I perceived that the flesh which had been charred black had begun to restore itself and here and there to grow pinkish; but what struck me the most keenly of all, reader, was the empty, gaping socket which was now my mouth.

I closed my socket.

Slowly I took up my razor and most carefully opened the blade; and applying some soap to my chin, I began to shave it.

# 23

IF YOU WOULD KNOW SOMETHING of what I looked like at the moment that I frighted the Marquise de Montespan into a swoon, reader, you may go to the Palace of Versailles and out into the gardens and to the Fountain of Latona: for the faces of the cruel Lycian peasants who are shown there, rendered in sculpture, and who, by the will of Jupiter, are in the process of being changed into frogs for having beset Latona and her children—their stone mouths flung open wide in silent screams of infuriation—were surely mirrored by my own distorted face that night as I shrieked my rage at the marquise from out of an utterly soundless mouth.

But even though my gesture to the marquise had had of it a most bestial quality, like the frozen cries of those newly created frogs, yet still, within, I knew that unlike them in their metamorphosis, I remained an entire human being. Bereft of human speech, to be sure; and with but the remnants left of human dignity; yet still I knew, within, I was a man. And quite unlike my doomed and froggy counterparts, I now determined to find the way to proclaim that humanity: and ironically I chose to do so by the means of human speech, for I saw no other way as clearly or as surely: but not, obviously, through the spoken word but through the silent, written word: that is, I would now undertake, as I had resolved to do in Vincennes Prison, to study how to read and write; with which knowledge, acquired over how much time I knew not, I would eventually set down my story; that story once read by others and known by them— that of the chiefest events of my life, of my mutilation and disgrace and that of my lineage—I would once again stand tall (the word is apt) and true—nay, royal, not to say divine—amongst my fellow human beings.

Which resolution, as you must know, is the origin of the chronicle that now you read. But resolutions, easily come by, are much less easily carried out; for at the time I could conceive no way whereby I might begin to decipher the inky scratchings on a sheet of paper into human words; and having no words myself thus to use, how might I even convey to another the hope of doing so and the need for help? Moreover, to what other could I appeal? For I had little commerce now with others, and those few with whom I might begin again to associate—I mean the sewerage workers and the cooks, the scullery boys—were as illiterate as I.

Yet, it seems, it was to be: for by a most fortuitous happenstance, as will occur when one is least expecting it and in some most unlikely quarter, I stumbled into the means to pursue my resolve and forthwith seized upon the opportunity. I say "unlikely quarter": for it was out among the privies that I received my first and only lesson in the art of reading and from, of all people, the Marquis d'Effiat.

In the weeks following my return to Versailles, I had taken up the habit of meeting the marquis out at the privies each morning, where I relieved him of the chore of scrubbing out the royal vessel; he clung to the office of bearing the vessel, which he had purchased at a goodly price; but was glad to relinquish the actual cleaning work to me.

Now there figured, as I have told you, on the side of the royal vessel and again within it at the very bottom, a certain device which had been wrought in blue pigment and baked into the chinaware at its manufacture and which from time to time had attracted my attention; and it was thus:

The lines varied somewhat in thickness along their lengths according to their curves, and from the two uppermost loops there hung a series of delicately fashioned leaves. I have rendered the design as well as I might and only simply, but it was of a much more pleasing and leafy aspect than what you see here.

I had often wondered if the device had any significance, for I had seen the very same two lines on a shield being held aloft by two sculptured *putti* in a niche adjacent to the queen's new staircase and as well on many of the window blinds; or if instead it were, as I assumed was the case of much of the ornament at Versailles, simply a decoration, albeit derived from floral patterns; and one morning, as I was putting the final flourish on the surface of the vessel, it occurred to me to ask the Marquis d'Effiat for some explanation; for, thought I, this gentleman is much informed on matters of decoration. Thus I first pointed to the device and then gestured enquiringly to the marquis.

"You are asking me what that is, Monsieur Hugues?" said he. "Why, look you, sir, it is the symbol of His Majesty in the form of an *L*. Or rather, I should say in the form of two *L*s, for observe, pray: one is set forward and the other backward. Can you not tell?"

Once again I studied the device but failed to understand; reader, need I confess to you that at the time I did not know what an *L* was? And so once more I gestured my confusion.

"See here," said the marquis, "observe, Monsieur Hugues, the thing is not so complex: here is the proper *L*." And he traced one of the two leafy lines with his painted fingernail. "And here the reverse of it."

Yet still, reader, I could not understand; I knew of no flower or tree or bush or shrub or weed which was called an *L*; nor could I fathom why one spray of leaves might be judged proper and the other reversed. And I stood once again studying the matter in an obvious state of puzzlement.

"Do you not know what an *L* is then, Monsieur Hugues? Is that the matter?" said the marquis; and when I nodded my head vigorously, "Ha ha ha!" cried he. "Why think of it! not to know what an *L* is!" And he shook his head in wonderment, so that a light mist of powder floated out into the morning air. "Why, sir, any schoolboy will tell you what an *L* is. An *L*, sir, is a letter of the alphabet; and it is the twelfth, if I am not much mistaken. *L*." And on the ground before him with the point of his walking stick he traced two connected strokes, one upright, the other horizontal: thus:

L

"And can you not imagine, sir, what name would begin with the letter *L*?"

Reader, when he asked me what name began with *L*, I could only assume, judging from the personal use to which the royal vessel was put, that it must be that of my lord: Louis. And yet lacking speech, I knew not how to signify this to the marquis, for I did not like to pretend some imitation of His Majesty as might be disrespectful. Presently however, I thought to run the tip of my finger down the length of my nose, as I had done on another occasion; for although the marquis knew nothing of my lineage, yet surely he would recognize that most distinctive feature which I held in common with my lord, as had been noted, I remind you, by the Duc d'Orléans.

"Why, so it is, Monsieur Hugues!" cried the marquis, and he clapped his hands together and skipped about. "Louis! It is Louis, most assuredly! *L* begins the name of Louis. An apt scholar, the dwarf is, and who would have thought so much?" And once again he clapped his hands together. "And now, Monsieur Hugues, pray let me have the pot back, sir—but hark, now: d'ye hear? I said, 'Let me have it.' And there is yet another word beginning with *L*: 'let.' 'Louis' and 'let,' both are *L* words, sir, they are both most worthy *L* words!" And seizing the vessel from my hands, he concluded: "And you shall take the rest of it from there for your-self!" And he sprinted away, back toward the palace, with the double-*L*-emblazoned chamber pot.

*L,* thought I and studied the marks he had made in the earth; so that is what writing is, I realized, it is the pictures of sounds; and each letter the picture of one such particular sound, in this case *L* for "Louis" and *L* for "let." And what a remarkable thing it is, I mused, which I have come upon: two words, both beginning with the same letter, *L,* though one be a simple everyday word such as we scarcely even hear at all, for we use it an hundred times a day, as in "let me see" or "let down the sluice" or "let go of me"; whilst the other word is the name of the most illus-trious monarch in all of Europe and of the world for that matter, my lord His Majesty, Fourteenth of the Name of Louis, beginning with the mag-nificent letter *L*!

And so it was by the purest happenstance that my introduction to the world of letters presented itself and that my resolve to learn to read at last took flight!

Continuing: I fell to pondering if there were other such words which began with the letter *L,* and if so, how many there might be and where I should be able to locate them.

"Letter."

Why, the very word "letter" itself, thought I, the very subject of my musing, must also begin with *L,* for the opening sound of it corresponds exactly to the opening sound of "let." "Letter" and "let." And I began to feel accomplished and indeed somewhat lettered myself that I should now possess three *L* words, as the marquis had called them.

But yet, hold, how might that be? For the opening sound of "let" and "letter" was indeed not the same as the opening sound of "Louis," "Louis" and the other two being similar yet somehow quite different; and I began listening to the trio of them inside my head, trying to recall how my lips and tongue, in the days when I had a tongue, must have moved to form the words aloud. Which led me eventually to the conclusion, after several hours, that *L* must be the picture of only the very front tip of each of those three words and not the full sound of them at all, nor even half, but only the "luh" of them being rendered by *L*; as would likely be the case in the word "La Voisin"; and in "latrine" and "Lisieux"; and in "lion." But then, what a vast quantity of letters must there be, thought I, if each be restricted to expressing so small an amount of sound within a word; why, there must needs be thousands of letters to indicate all the sounds which we make whilst merely talking about the weather. And it was not that I was given to wasting time talking about the weather, that is, when talk I could; but I simply point out my thought that some trifling chatter must require legions of letters, to say nothing of the accumulated knowledge of mankind in the arts, in governance, and in the sciences; and having mastered up to then only one letter and that imperfectly, for I did not know all the *L* words which were, I quickly realized the enormity of the task to which I had set myself. But daunting as the thought was, it did not deflect me from my resolve.

Late that night, up in my rookery, I took up my picture book, opened it, and began looking at the figures printed at the bottom of each page, figures heretofore of no use to me, for there was no sense I could make of them; yet now it was clear that these were sets of letters forming words; and there being one set to each page, and every set different, as I noted by a hasty skimming of the entire book, there was a chance, it seemed to me, that these might be words identifying the creatures illustrated above them, the book depicting some twenty-six animals and beasts, one to a page.

And thus it was, reader, that as I turned from one well-thumbed page to the next, I suddenly recalled that one of the creatures shown was a lion. Quickly I skipped ahead to the very center of the volume, where from long habit I knew that I would find him. And there he stood, the king of beasts, a proud mane framing his noble head, and he held a frightened, wriggling bear cub clenched in his dripping jaws. And there below him, at the base of his page, was a short, four-lettered word—and the first of the four letters in the word was clearly, decisively, and most unmistakably, with one upright stroke and another horizontal, the letter *L*!

LION!

"Lion": a word different from "Louis," "letter," or "let" but yet which shares with all three of them that undeniable *L* sound at its beginning!

With great haste I leafed through the volume to see if there were not any other words which began with *L*: but there was none; and then I recalled that indeed there were no lice in the book (as many as there were about the palace) nor no lampreys or loons; yet even so, in my search, I did come upon several *L*s but in the middle of words, as beneath the picture of the basilisk and that of the mollusk, the latter even possessing two; and an *L* at the end of jackal.

Quickly I turned back to the lion to study what letters there were in the middle and end of his word and found: *I, O,* and *N*. And I copied each of them out, along with the initial *L,* in the light layer of lint which lay along the lower ledge of the louver. ("Louver": another *L* word, I was sure of it!)

And if *L* was as steady in its behavior as it had proved to be from "Louis" through "lion," why might not these other, newer letters be so too, I reasoned; and I set out to hear each one in my mind as they would sound aloud in the word "lion":

*I* as in the words "eye" and "I."

*O* as in no single word, but it seemed a kind of gruntish sound as one would make when coughing lightly into a handkerchief or in the midst of some physical exertion.

*N*, a sound which settled somewhat up inside the nose and in fact quite likely the very sound which began that word itself: "nose."

But there were no "eyes" or "Is" depicted separately in the book, whereby I might verify my findings, nor no gruntish sounds nor no noses neither.

Next I searched through to find any words beginning with the letter *I*; and I did find one, and it was beneath a picture of what appeared to be an Indian, who was attired in animal skins and feathers; and yet I would not call him an "Eyen-dian"; and I was disappointed.

Even so, thought I, as I listened to "Indian" in my mind, there must be at least one *N* in that word as at the end of "lion" and more likely two, given the nosy sound which it made; and yet I could find in none of the letters beneath that picture anything resembling the *N* at the end of "lion"; and I questioned how genuine an Indian this Indian was. Now the very word "end"—as in the "end of 'lion'"—must begin with an *N*, thought I; and so I hastened to the last page of the book to find if there were not a word beginning in *N* to mark the conclusion; and although I found a word with an *N* inside it, the word was "FINIS" and it did not begin with *N*, and so I quite put it aside. Whereupon I recalled there being an animal depicted which must certainly begin with an *N*, and I turned to find him: and beneath the picture was printed the three-letter word "GNU." There, indeed, was an *N*; yet before it stood something else, blocking it, it seemed, in a way that was not detectable when the word was spoken, or at least by no speaker of the word "GNU" I had ever known. Fie! thought I, I shall be plagued by this troublesome *N* and for the rest of my days! And promptly and categorically I renounced it.

Thus with *I* and *N* quite lost to me, I returned to the lion to see what I might make of the only other letter of his which I had not explored, that somewhat indeterminate "uh" sound; and yet I feared that it might be even more elusive than the others. Whence I set out to find an animal whose printed name began with that circular *O*; and at length I did find one and which was labeled thus: "ORANGUTAN." The creature resembled a monkey to me, reader, or perhaps a baboon, neither of which seemed in any way indeterminate in its opening sound; and thus I faced failure once again. Yet a thing caught my eye as I lingered a moment with the ape, which was a combination of letters in the middle of his name, to wit, NGU. And I had seen that combination or something like it elsewhere and not long since; and so I began to go through the book once more and came, once more, upon that excellent creature, the gnu.

But although the two combinations of letters, GNU and NGU, were similar, yet they rendered up none of their mystery to me, with but one exception, which was the final letter in "GNU": *U*. And if I was correct that this creature was indeed a gnu, whatever verbal complexities there might be in starting his name, the end of it seemed quite unequivocal, the letter *U* producing, as luck would have it, reader, the very same sound which followed the *L* in my lord's own name, to wit, Louis. This was an excellent discovery, I thought; and in the lint I carefully wrote LU, which must, I reckoned, be the correct writing for his name, lacking only the final letter to round it off!

So heartened was I by this advancement that I flew through the book in search of a creature whose name contained the final sound in my lord's name, and eventually arrived at the picture of a flea (for fleas were most recognizable to me, reader, and to anyone living at the court, quite as well known as lice thereabouts, my lord's hounds being somewhat ridden with both; nor was either creature in any way averse to human company, to which I myself can attest, though I do not like to own it; and though I wash religiously every fortnight, whatever the weather, and with soap, yet still they do plague me; and I have often seen them creeping or leaping about upon persons of quality and rank). To return: beneath that creature's picture was printed the word "THRIPS"; after some careful reflection, I decided that the final sound in "flea" must be allotted roughly one-third of the entire word, that is, two of its six letters, and thus, immediately after LU, I copied out upon my dusty tablet the PS from "THRIPS"; and then I stood back to study the fruits of my effort:

L U P S

—which was, I thought proudly, the written name of my lord, His Divine Majesty, Fourteenth of the Name of Lups.

Now let me burden you no further with the agonizing details of my trials and errors and blunders amongst those hieroglyphics; for you have now witnessed that my progress in learning the alphabet was but slow and most laborious and full of dangerous crossings and wrongful turns and hateful dead ends; and yet eventually, from those two lines which the Marquis d'Effiat had traced out upon the ground, the one upright and the other horizontal, I did at length achieve a grasp of all twenty-six letters, and it was entirely with the use of my picture book, which, as you have surmised, was a child's book of the ABCs; and here I shall list you the beasts depicted in that childish volume:

| | |
|---|---|
| Anthropophagi | Newt |
| Basilisk | Orangutan |
| Cur | Priest |
| Dunghill Cock | Quahog |
| Estritche | Roach |
| Flounder | Succubus |
| Gnu | Thrips |
| Hyena | Uraeus |
| Iroquois | Vermin |
| Jackal | Weasel |
| Kite | Xiphosuran |
| Lion | Yak |
| Mollusk | Zoophyte |

Thus you now see that the Indian was in fact an Iroquois, which is a tribe of Indian; and that the baboon was an orangutan, the flea a simple thrips; but yet the lion was indeed a lion, the gnu a gnu.

It was a considerable while before I mastered the spelling of my own name, a matter of some understandable importance to me, that short sound, which is somewhat of an exclamation; and I wrote it variously UG and EWG and OOG and UEG and EWEG; yet was not much content; and it was not until many years later, as I was studying the works of a certain Hugues Fiesque of Montbéliard, a man who had, it seems, invented a kind of hempen windlass to be used in hauling up vats and tubs onto higher levels, that I realized that he and I must bear the same name; and I was able to inscribe the letters "HUGUES" in the front of my alphabet book.

My studies were conducted in secret, for I was certain that they would be sternly frowned upon; and I picked up odd scraps of paper on which to practice; and quills which had been too long used and discarded, so that the letters which I drew were quite thick and given to blotting, and lacking, I fear, in all delicacy; and ink which I pilfered from the accountants' office. My texts were various: a ledger borrowed from those same accountants which recorded several years' worth of purchases of plaster, putty, and related supplies from a manufactory in St. Quentin-en-Yvelines; Fénelon's *Education of a Girl* (1687); a copy of the Treaty of

Douvres (1670) and one of the Revocation of the Edict of Nantes (1685); and a bundle of letters which I found, written to a certain Madame Hyacinthe Brunelle or Burnelle, for the hand is poor, from a duke who never identifies himself by name and who lived somewhere near Metz, in which letters he describes to that lady, and in most elaborate and enthusiastic detail, various physical exertions which he wished to undertake with her amiable assistance, and there were several curious illustrations; nor shall I tell you where I found these letters.

I trust that I have now made it clear to you, reader, the lengths to which I went—nay, was driven!—to achieve the practices of reading and writing and the quantity of time consumed in doing so, to say nothing of the time and effort required to write down this account. Time is truly the culprit here: for only now am I ready to bring the account to a close, a fact which you have perceived, there being but few pages left; which, having read through, you may go on about your way, and I thank you for your pains and hope that you are enlightened; or if not enlightened, then at the very least, informed.

Yet time, I say, is the culprit: for when I shall have finished the final page, still more time will be needed for me to gather all the text together and to order it: those stacks of pages which I have been storing down in the hollow spaces throughout this system of eaves; I must order them and then bind them together; and then I must send them to the printer's shop so that copies may be made and those copies dispersed to the reading public. And yet I shall not do so before my lord's death, that were a heinous thing to do, and I respect Him too greatly to do it. And though He be much advanced in years, yet I shall not presume to speculate upon His final hour. But when it comes, reader, that fearful moment, then—then at last will the world be given to learn of this history.

Yet here is the thing; and here is why I say that time is truly the culprit: and here is the chiefest source of my great vexation as I now, at last, bring this chronicle to a close: for mark:

The Marquise de Montespan died some seven years ago last Friday.

I was most put out to learn of her death, for it had been my original and primary design that she should read these words to her utmost shame and that others around her would learn of her villainy and that she then suffer repudiation and exile even more bleak than ever she had in the last twenty-six years of her life; for she spent them far from the warmth and radiance of my lord's countenance, as was meet, for He had quite forsworn her. But yet in the name of justice I would have had her endure yet more humiliation, and to be exposed yet further for her false appearances of divinity. But alas, she outwitted me and she died well before I was even halfway into this account, and though there had been rumors enough of her decline, yet it were impossible for me to advance my efforts in time. Thus, still revered by some, though only as a former royal mistress, she went to her grave; and where she went beyond that I know not; but I know where she ought to have gone. Yet in all likelihood, she was well shriven at the end, for her purse was enough supplied and there would be no need for her to suffer eternal hellfire and damnation; not, that is, except for the feeble cries for justice and retribution, which, alas, all too often prevail neither in this life nor in the next. And thus in drawing this account to a close, I must content myself that it will serve at least to besmirch her name for future generations if not, alas, for her own.

But throughout these past seven years, my resolve to complete and publish this account in the greater name of truth, as I told you at the beginning, has not faltered or waned. And indeed I continue to be resolved to publish it although there be strong enough reason not to: for when it is known in the public what I have privately confided to these pages, remains there any question but that my life will be instantly and most perilously in danger? For not a jot do I trust the Duc de Chartres, a conniving man who—but more of him later. Thus my determination to publish may be said to be somewhat mitigated by the sheer instinct for survival; but not, I hasten to add, deterred.

And yet, survival for what purpose, pray? Survival to what end? Reader, I am now quite advanced in years, fifty-four of them in fact; and although my health has in part benefited from an active life, I mean my chores in the drainage system primarily and the long distances which I must travel by foot each day between my aerie (in the north) and the sewerage bowels of the palace (in the south), to say nothing of the lengthy climb to reach the aerie itself; yet any dwarf of fifty-odd years will tell you that the body parts, being confined within limited quarters, do not wear well, that over the years there develop pressures and stresses, strains and the shifting of divers loads and weights, all wear and tear peculiar to dwarves and such as our organs will accommodate but ill; and I believe that my bowels have been weighed down upon and burdened by the size of my liver; and that my kidneys have collapsed somewhat downward to the detriment of the urinary track; and that my spleen has been steadily crushed by incursions of a number of other interior organs and parts; and yet I know not. I am not well. I am tired and my spirits are broken. I am not well.

My lord King Louis has reached the astonishing age of seventy-six, if proof of His divinity were ever needed, and has now most recently and most swiftly outlived three dauphins: three presumed dauphins, I should say, for my lord has not outlived me. The first dauphin, Louis, the bulbous dauphin, my younger brother, died of the smallpox three years ago at the age of fifty; his issue, the second dauphin, my nephew Louis, a harsh person, died of measles two years ago at the age of thirty; the third dauphin, Louis, son of the second dauphin and of Marie Adélaïde of Savoy (who was a grandchild from the union of Monsieur [d. 1701] and Henrietta of England, she who had died of chicory poisoning in 1670), the third dauphin, Louis, I say, of no personality whatsoever, though he were a grandnephew of mine, died of fevers a mere two years ago at the age of five, and his mother had already died in that same year; the fourth and present dauphin, Louis, brother to the third dauphin and hence of the same parentage, is presently but four years old; and there is, I understand, much wrangling afoot currently about the regency, a regency being presumed; though if my lord King Louis XIV lasts another nine years, Louis the fourth dauphin will have reached the year of royal majority—thirteen—and a regent would be uncalled for; yet the chances are slim; and in all likelihood, the office will go to Philippe II d'Orléans, Duc de Chartres, whom I have cited and who is Monsieur's son and, as it turns out, the husband of the youngest daughter of the Marquise de Montespan, to wit, Françoise-Marie, legitimated 1681; yet the gentleman is conniving and moreover much debauched. It is rumored that my lord King Louis in fact favors Louis-Auguste, the Duc du Maine, to become regent in preference to the Duc de Chartres; yet despite his legitimization, the Duc du Maine is not thought of by others as fit for the position, being, as he is (a matter which ought to have no bearing whatsoever upon his eligibility), a former bastard and walking as he does with a limp (an uncontested drawback). These matters are subtle and complex, reader. The issue would not have arisen to begin with had the truth been proclaimed and acknowledged which now you read; for I myself should have replaced all four dauphins well before the death of any one of them as the true and legitimate heir to my dearest father's throne.

But it is of no matter now, this business of succession, or of no great matter. My lord may outlive me and so I pray that He do, I pray daily for my lord's longevity. And I should gladly embrace death whilst yet He breathes, reader, for else it will grate and rankle with me, it will very much vex me to witness that four-year-old child proclaimed monarch of the realm and of all the citizenry of France, whilst I, aloft in my rookery, should be left with only these mountains of paper about me for loyal subjects; nay, but indeed I may not even say "loyal," for these subjects will soon be my undoing. And moreover, the child is right delicate and frail, much given to illnesses; and on the occasions that I have seen him, I have taken satisfactory note that the creature's nose, being some three generations removed from my lord's and only one less from my own, displays no excellence of length whatsoever. And indeed, reader, is not my own person taller than that of any four-year-old child? And as for knowledge and education: if I have neither the Latin nor the ancient Greek, am I not possessed of our own excellent vernacular, speak it though I cannot? Yet I understand it well, and have I not now even mastered the reading and writing of it as no four-year-old child may assert; and would that not serve for the business of monarchy? And should I then, but for a defect in my growth, be stripped of my inheritance?

And yet, reader: and yet; it was my lord King Louis's choice those years and years ago: shall I yet again question His divine decision? No, I shall not. And at present I am grown too old, reader, and I am not well; and I have no child, reader; and to whom then should the throne pass upon my own death? No, no, it is no matter; it is no matter now.

Let us proceed.

Of my employment: the cesspool where I labor is not far from the privies but still farther to the south, and was designed primarily for the reception of slops from the numerous *chaises percées* which are distributed throughout the vast palace; and yet as the palace building has grown in size, it has grown as well in population, and the number of *chaises percées* doubled and then tripled, and the quantity of matter deposited in them by the burgeoning population has increased proportionately; to complicate the issue, Versailles being itself something of a cesspool to begin with, as I have told you, as marshy and fennish as it is and as constantly rank and fetid, the liquid drainage from the several tanks is at best a slow affair; and thus the watery content remains at a high level and impedes the normal clearance of the solid; it strikes me as not unlike the moat at Vincennes, of which I also have some intimate knowledge. My chiefest task is to keep clear certain major conduits between the several vats, for which task I am excellently well suited because of the shortness of my stature: a normal-sized man could not have stood upright in the conduits.

But the work loads increased as the inhabitants increased, until my task has become a full-time one; and it is not necessary that you learn any more of the somewhat excremental details of my daily routines than that they involve a considerable degree of scraping and bailing and shoveling; but I shall not burden you.

Given these heavy daytime exertions, it is as well, I dare swear, though not for my economy, that my evening activities amongst the gamesters at cards have sharply declined, as more and more of my clients were carted off to the prisons or exiled for hatching designs, successful or not, upon their husbands, wives, lovers, rivals, confessors, and the like, they having turned out to be an ingeniously poisonous segment of the society, a surprising development in light of their abysmal performances at card playing; until eventually, my gambling clients quite dried up. Relative to which, but within a more delicate sphere, the altered state of my tongue abruptly ended any further opportunities to provide my female clientele with those additional services from beneath the card tables which had some years previously grown quite rapidly, you will recall, into a most thriving concern; and hence, my female clientele may be said to have quite dried up as well.

Of several persons: following a two-month journey with my lord to the eastern front in the summer of 1683, the queen returned to Versailles in a state of ill health, and shortly thereafter a rumor declared that she had developed, along with an abscess under her arm, raging fevers which no amount of bleeding or the administration of emetics succeeded in lowering. The fact that the doctors and surgeons quarreled bitterly amongst themselves as to the proper treatment for her and that she was carted about in a device somewhat resembling a wheelbarrow from her apartment to the chapel to hear Mass, thence down to the Baths Apartments for long soakings in iced water, and out into the gardens for fresh air (though not a few of the medical experts were diametrically opposed to fresh air), none of this can have much benefited the lady in her sorry decline, I do not think, though medical expert I am none.

As it chanced, our paths crossed one scorching July afternoon as she was returning from the tubs, and we sighted upon one another from afar. With a murmur she gave order for the three blue boys pushing the wheelbarrow to halt. Groping from beneath the thick blankets which wrapped her around and gripping the side of the contraption she was lying in, she raised herself slightly in order to get a better look at me where I stood in the hallway. Our eyes met; or so I imagined that they did, for her face had grown so thoroughly and hideously puffy, whether from the fevers or the waters I cannot say, that I could see little more than two thin lines where her eyes were. She stared thus at me for some moments, and I in horror at her; until I recovered my wits and made a low and most respectful bow to Her Royal Highness of France; but when at length I righted myself, she was still staring. Then, very feebly, she lifted her free hand vaguely in my direction and waved. I could not speak to the lady, I dared do nothing more than make a second, brief bow to her; and thus, although I did not know it at the time, I bade my mother farewell. Exhausted by her efforts, she slumped back into the blanket cocoon, and the blue boys resumed their procession. She died that very evening; and to this day I regret most bitterly that I had not had the presence of mind to wave back to the lady in response.

Of her death, "This is the first time she ever gave me any trouble," my lord King Louis was heard generously to say; He was weeping copiously at the time. Her entourage of dwarves did not appear at her funeral obsequies, although they may well have been the only people who had exhibited any degree of loyalty to the woman during her lifetime; yet neither did they appear overly grieved at her passing, for they were seen romping about in the gardens the following day and throwing things; and in a matter of weeks no one had any idea of where they had got to.

Louis-Auguste, the Duc du Maine, was married to Anne-Louise-Bénédicte de Bourbon Condé in 1692, was subsequently named governor of Languedoc, and in 1694 was advanced in rank to a position immediately below that of the princes of the blood; but these strokes of excellent fortune were much offset by his abysmal performance at the military front in Flanders and on the Rhine, a performance which so enraged his father—King Louis—that He broke a walking stick across a footman's shoulders; and thus du Maine's ultimate repute in court circles was seen to be but slight, as you will witness later.

In the year 1701, Monsieur, my uncle, died at the age of sixty-one; and I pray daily for that gentleman and for the repose of his immortal soul. And though he had quarreled with my lord the very afternoon of his death, yet such was his impetuous nature and it may not be held against him. And I believe that my Lord Jesus will look with favor upon his petition to enter into the Kingdom of Heaven and that Monsieur will make a most entertaining addition to the heavenly host.

The Marquis d'Effiat, persevering in his office of bearer of the royal vessel despite the sensitivity of his nostrils, continued to meet me each morning out at the privies. The quantity of powder used by that gentleman upon his face increased in direct proportion to the advancing number of his years, and there was frequently a light, white mist hovering about him as the powder dusted off into the air. He offered me no further instructions in reading nor could he have known of my pursuit of it, for I was unable to tell him so. Yet despite his propensity to temper tantrums, he was never unkind to me and would occasionally bring me scraps from my uncle's breakfast table as long as that gentleman lived; and once he gave me a brass earring which he said he had of a young Arab; but I did not like to put it on. The marquis would idle the time with me as I went about the chore of washing out the vessel and would sing scraps of songs or whistle; yet one day he sat off to the side and wept.

I saw no more of Emil Vergeyck, there being no occasion to do so, there being no further trips called for to the catacombs of Notre Dame; for eventually, in a formal police hearing, the Abbé Hilaire Guibourg, former sacristan of the Church of St. Marcel at St. Denis, Vicar at Issy and later at Vanves, publicly corroborated my own report of the Marquise de Montespan's role in the Mass directed against Fontanges, whereupon the cleric was quickly shunted off to the town of Vesoul in the Franche-Comté and told never to return to the Paris area under pain of execution; and all police hearings were abruptly closed down in their entirety with Lieutenant General de la Reynie reassigned to supervision of "muck, street lights, and whores"; and the judicial body appointed especially to these matters was disbanded and terminated and all records were destroyed; for clearly, reader, it would not do for the mother of any of my lord's children, no matter what her personal standing with my lord, to be publicly exposed as a participant in such doings, it could only result in mischief for the state. Similarly, the man known as Lesage was banished, but I do not know where. Thus all my somewhat tenuous ties to Emil Vergeyck were broken, and I have never learned what befell him; yet I wish him well, for in his own rough-hewn way, he had shown me certain kindnesses and I believe had himself led a somewhat unhappy existence.

I have sometimes mused upon the fact that those who, like myself, had testified against the marquise, had not been deprived, like myself, of their ability to utter further unacceptable reports; and I have drawn one of two conclusions: either (1) that my lord's justice, though swift, was essentially more merciful than the marquise's, which attests to its appropriate share of divinity; or (2) that there could be found no one willing to confront at close enough range the Abbé Guibourg's breath to be able to execute the removal of his tongue. But pray do not think ill of me, reader, if I confess that, the abbé's betrayal of his devoted acolyte being only several degrees less perfidious than the betrayal by the marquise, upon more than one occasion I have indulged myself in fancies about the removal of his tongue, as executed by some of the sturdy workmen such as one sees about the palace; or at other times by Emil Vergeyck himself, who was a giant of a man; and the business is always extremely bloody, violent, and quite prolonged.

Now you have already witnessed a kind of prologue to my next account; for you have observed that some years before her death, the Marquise de Montespan having been removed to the ground floor of the palace, Mme Scarron had installed herself in that lady's former apartment. Indeed Scarron had become herself a marquise, that of Maintenon, and thus the owner of an excellent estate on the river Eure. Yet even so, it came as something of a surprise, reader, not to say something of a shock and as a matter of personal annoyance to me, I will confess it, ungenerous as the sentiment may be, when she began to supplant both the Marquise de Montespan and the Duchesse de Fontanges in my lord King Louis's social attentions, and then in certain expressions of gallantry by Him, and thence in His amorous affections. (And it has even been rumored, from 1684 onward, that my lord secretly married Scarron

following the death of the queen the year before; but this is not confirmed.) You will protest, and accurately enough, that the Marquise de
Montespan, along with having grown plump, had quite tarnished her
good name in my lord's estimation by her machinations against the
Duchesse de Fontanges; and that the duchess had been foolish enough to
miscarry and then to turn quite sickly, failing to recognize my lord's
complete intolerance for anything smacking of ill health (she went into a
convent, that of Port-Royal in Paris, if I am not mistaken, the following
year and died some three months later); and that Mme Scarron had simply seized upon an opportunity which presented itself. Yet I draw your
careful attention to certain other points: that the Marquise de Montespan, when younger, had been the most exquisite creature in all of my
lord's kingdom, possessed of grace, wit, and matchless beauty, qualities
which I had taken even for divine; and that the duchess, a most comely
creature as well, though slow-witted and petulant, displayed two of the
most bewitching breasts in all of my lord's kingdom; but that Scarron
was never more and certainly no less than a sturdy, squarely built, and
double-chinned member of the kingdom who smelt of leeks and whose
qualities the Marquis d'Effiat had exaggerated but slightly in his enumer-
ation of them to Monsieur. Moreover, madame's sober preoccupation
with matters religious, though of questionable depth in my personal view
for I had endured some less than Christian treatment at the woman's
hands, would not seem entirely compatible with my lord's more liberal
and more gracious outlook and style. And thus it was that many were
caught quite off guard by the meteoric rise of that lady's fortunes in the
early 1680s; and many more were quite put out by it, though they could
say nothing, and most vexed by the more somber atmosphere which
began to prevail at the court; and still others, who earlier had enjoyed
some prominence in the spirited society of Versailles, now fell into utter
disfavor; the gamblers foundered and the gossips hurried underground;
but the clerics thrived; and by design my own comings and goings about
the place became yet more inconspicuous, for I did not care to encounter
Scarron or any of her pious women.

But yet I would not have you think that the palace has turned into a
gloomy cloister; for there continue to be entertainments here and visits by foreign delegations and the bustle of social life and of changing

fashion; the Hall of Mirrors was opened in 1685 and the new Trianon in the nearby forest in 1688; and as late at 1701, my lord inaugurated the elaborate rituals known as *petits levers* and *grands levers*, *grands couchers* and *petits couchers*. And although I have never witnessed these rites, I am told that they are most impressive. Alas, however, they were of no benefit to the fortunes of the Marquis d'Effiat, for the administration of the royal vessel and its contents was altered by the new routine and thenceforth conducted in an altogether different manner, and one which I have never discovered; and thus the marquis lost that dear office of his, and I my own lengthy service in the matter; and I believe that that loss may have quite broken the marquis's already dispirited heart, for Monsieur having died in that same year, 1701, the marquis followed in the succeeding winter.

In the latter years of His own life, my lord King Louis spends more and more time away from the great chateau which He created at Versailles in favor of residence at the Trianon; that smaller palace being dedicated to burgeoning springtime (its workmen replace the flowers in the gardens every night with fresh ones, even late into the autumn) and with numerous images of children and of childhood figuring into much of its décor, my lord passes His advancing age in verdant, youthful surroundings. But His royal presence in the lofty halls of the older and grander palace is secured in part by a magnificent portrait of Him, that one painted by Monsieur Rigaud in 1701; and anyone passing where it hangs in the public reception hall is bidden to bow to it with deep respect as though to the mighty Sovereign Himself.

Now I think this is an end to it, and it is likely the moment that I should offer, reader, figuratively, my own bow, and I should not be displeased for yours in return. And I hope that I may say and that you will agree that I have succeeded well enough in mastering the written tongue, having now no other sort; and that I have told you and whosoever like you may choose to read these pages, all the truth of my life; and now I close, for I am not well today, and I have done all which I set out to do. And you, patient reader, and the rest of the world must make of it what you will; and if there be those, as I know there will be, who will wish to persecute me for what I publish, who would banish me from the realm, or who would even end my life, why then, so it must be, and let them get on with it.

But yet I have here set down my testament most willy-nilly; and so it shall stand. And I defy you, Philippe II d'Orléans, Duc de Chartres—most illegitimate and usurping regent that you are, sir!—I openly defy you to do your worst!

## FINIS

(This word ending the picture book, thus it shall also end mine own.)

# Epilogue

MY LORD AND DEAR FATHER KING LOUIS died two weeks ago on September 1, 1715, a little after eight o'clock in the morning, at the age of seventy-seven; and I weep for Him yet.

One year before His death, and almost to the day, my lord had written out His will with respect to the regency; and the will was sealed and locked away, the contents of it remaining unknown. But what rumor had surmised of those contents was found to be correct: it stipulated that Philippe II d'Orléans, Duc de Chartres, should serve, not as regent but only as head of the regency council, and that despite his military blunders, Louis-Auguste, Duc du Maine, should in fact become the regent. And it was widely held that my lord had set those orders down at the urging of Mme Scarron, who much espoused du Maine's cause, for she had been, you will recall, his governess; and this was so. And yet it was learned later that my lord understood full well that after He died and in despite of His will, there would likely be much ado about the regency and that the Parlement might well overturn His wishes, dismissing the apathetic du Maine in favor of the wily Chartres; but yet He had submitted to Scarron's badgering in order to gain peace and quiet, for she was right adept at badgering, and He was growing old.

Seven days before His death, on the feast of St. Louis (Louis IX, 1214–1270), my lord King Louis XIV, who was in great suffering from gangrene in His leg, received the viaticum and the last rites of the Church, administered by Armand-Gaston-Maximilien, Cardinal de Rohan, who was, as it so happened, the son of the Princesse de Soubise (she who

335

had suffered the loss of a tooth) and in all likelihood of my lord King Louis Himself. Musicians played stately tunes throughout the solemn ceremony.

Six days before His death, He admitted the five-year-old dauphin Louis to His bedchamber in order to impart to the child His final exhortation; and He received other members of the family and of the court, all of them weeping, or appearing to weep, most prodigiously and full-throatedly at His decline; and He bade them farewell and then asked them please to be quiet, because He was not feeling well.

Five days before His death, He summoned the now thirty-five-year-old Duc du Maine to His side, who was then seen hobbling into the bedchamber for the audience; and it was conjectured by all those who stood pressed up against the other side of the door, that my lord was informing the duke of His intentions for the regency and advising him how he might best go about to skewer his rival in the matter.

Four days before His death, a team of doctors, including Guy-Crescent Fagon, His chief physician since 1693, along with certain newly arrived experts, administered a bleeding to Him and primarily of His gangrenous leg, and then prescribed Him an elixir concocted from the body of an animal, which He took.

Three days before His death, Mme Scarron, concluding that the end must then surely be in sight, left Versailles Palace and moved lock, stock, and barrel out to her apartment at St. Cyr.

Two days before His death, He slept fitfully, then rallied somewhat and ate a biscuit.

The day before His death, He slept off and on.

And then He died.

The crowds—courtiers and public—who for days had kept vigil throughout the vast halls of the palace and downstairs out in the courtyards and across the Place d'Armes and even in the mournful gardens, now gave way to their exhaustion and grief and slowly drifted off.

In no time, His Majesty's will was opened and read; and at once there began a series of wranglings and deceptions and backstairs chicanery such as my lord, in His wisdom, had most fully anticipated, all to do with the administration of the succession and of the rivalries for the office of regent and for an hundred other issues, great and small, in the transfer of the power of the throne of France. And presently, Philippe II d'Orléans,

Duc de Chartres, prevailed, as everyone knew that he would, and he sent du Maine packing.

But it was one evening during those rebellious first days of Louis XV's reign, as I was close at work in my rookery on certain corrections which I was making in chapter five or six, I forget which, that I had paused a moment to look out of my louver and down to the moonlit gardens below; much neglected they had become, reader, since the death of my lord, the roots fetid with algae, the flowers rank, the trees untended and wild. Suddenly I heard my name being called from down below within. When I went downstairs, I found two blue boys awaiting me in the passage near the king's staircase; and they laughed to see me, and at my diminished stature and advanced age and at my bald pate (for I have lost all my hair and my cowlick with it) and at my wrinkles and the gaps in my teeth and my painful struggles to move, for I am afflicted with rheumatism in the hips, and I have not the means for the treatment; I have not told you of this before, but it is no matter.

One of the impudent fellows handed me a small packet, wrapped in paper, sealed, and tied with a string.

"Here, Monsieur Hugues," quoth he, "here is a present to you, sir; it is from the king. Or rather," he continued, now smirking to his companion, "the old bugger which was the king but ha, ha, ha! is right dead now, he is, is he not?—as dead as any doorpost!" And they both fell to laughing again. "What say you to that, Monsieur Hugues?" And this last, challenging remark provoked them to even greater merriment, for they knew right well that I could say nothing. So put out was I by their insolence, not only to myself, but to the memory of my lord, that I spat at them and shook my fist and made them rude gestures. But they only laughed the more. And I felt, as I labored back up to my nook, how utterly disordered the world had now grown, how vicious and chaotic, how most entirely out of joint.

Once more above, I studied the packet: within was an object somewhat the size of a pen, or so it seemed; three seals held the wrapping shut, and they were indeed none other than the seals of my lord King Louis XIV Himself, and they were unmistakably so. On the other side of the packet I read the words "Monsieur Hugues."

Whereupon with great care I undid the string and pried open each royal seal; then I folded back the ends of the paper and slowly unrolled the packet.

Within lay a razor, its smooth handle made of glistening mother-of-pearl, the blade of which could be folded back down into the handle when it was not in use; and at the tip of that handle there had been set in purest gold the intricate double *Ls* of my lord's name.

Ah, reader! What a gift was there! A razor; the third such as I had received in my lifetime, but far, far surpassing the previous two: a glittering gem of a razor and one which His own barber had used upon my lord; for although it was in a most excellent condition, yet it was not new minted; and it had been left to me by the hand of His Most Royal and Divine Majesty my lord, Fourteenth of the Name of Louis, Sovereign of France, upon the occasion of His death.

Left to me by the hand of my earthly father upon the occasion of his death.

Ah, what might I think? And throughout all that night, I sat studying the razor and pondering it; and I do ponder it still, to this day, and I have never dared to use it, confining myself to that simpler one from the hand of des Œillets.

Might this gift be, I wondered, a most private and final acknowledgment by my lord of His firstborn son?

Or, instead, might it be a signal that I was to understand and accept without resistance the precise extent of my inheritance: no palaces, no armies, nor no government or wealth, no throne, nor kingship neither: but rather, simply, a razor with which to shave my chin?

Or on the other hand: did it quietly invite me to embrace at last the choice which my lord Louis Himself, Fourteenth of that Name, had made some half a century previous, on or about my first birthday, and thereby silently to validate the succession of the fourth dauphin, Louis, now become His Majesty, Fifteenth of that Name? Was the gift of the razor, that is, an invitation to me to finish off what the Abbé Guibourg had merely begun some thirty years previous and slit my throat?

END

# Editor's Note

Monsieur Hugues died on February 3, 1716, from a fall down the flight of back stairs which lead up into the eaves in the north wing of the Palace of Versailles. The site of his interment is unknown.

His papers were not discovered until 1726, when renovations were undertaken throughout the roofing of the north wing and the eaves rebuilt. The manuscript was first published by A. Berthelot, Paris, 1779.

His picture book is in the collection of the Archives Nationales, Paris.